Felix the Red

STEFAN FRANCIS KELLEHER

Fulton Books, Inc.
Meadville, PA

Published by Fulton Books 2021

ISBN 978-1-63710-064-6 (paperback)
ISBN 978-1-63710-065-3 (digital)

Printed in the United States of America

For Skylar

Africa

Our story begins with a ship sailing into harbor.

It is the first vessel of its kind to ever reach these shores, and the excitement it stirs in the surrounding jungle is nearly frenzied with anticipation. To the sailors onboard, however, all appears calm. What their eyes can not detect are the thousand different life-forms hidden from view behind a thick curtain of vines and trees, creatures who excitedly spread the news of the fabulous "bird" that had suddenly alighted in the warm waters off the shore, its towering sails billowing like a pair of giant white wings against the blue African sky, and who creep ever closer to the shoreline now in order to further investigate the strange new arrival.

Word of the ship is like a lightning strike, spreading like a wild-fire through the untold number of creature communities that thrive largely hidden in the dense and twisted maze of jungle greenery. Before long, a thousand eyes gaze in stunned silence and a thousand animal hearts race with excitement as the sailors lower their boats from the side of the ship and begin to row ashore. To the men row-ing, however, unaware that they are being watched, they are the only species that exist on the planet at this moment.

Naturally, their mission tells them otherwise and reminds them that the jungle is fairly teeming with a whole host of exotic and mythical creatures, some of which they have been sent here to capture for their emperor, Caesar Augustus. Indeed, not a few sail-ors, mostly the youngest among them, had nervously lain awake the previous night, with the ocean rolling beneath them, imagining the fearsome beasts of popular legend that they might encounter on this day: saber-toothed cats capable of tearing them limb from limb, pterodactyl birds ready to sweep them off the ground and carry them aloft to their mountain aeries, snakes as long as the hull of a ship that could mesmerize a man into submission with their hypnotic eyes and swallow his entire body whole.

Always these fears of predation, of consumption, came to them at night, borne of the blood knowledge humans instinctively possess that Man shares the earth with a vast number of populations, some of whom might look upon them as nothing more than a convenient snack. Courage returns only with the dawn, when the sun burns away their darkest fears and allows them to imagine—as the sailors are imaging even now while pulling their boats up onto the virgin sands of this new world they had discovered—that they are *cibum catenam summo*, "top of the food chain."

This kind of courage, based as it is on a false premise, requires a certain amount of willful ignorance to live by. And so it is that the sailors allow their nighttime fears to be dissolved in the startling sunlight overhead as they inch their way cautiously across the burning hot beach toward the tree line ahead. They are no longer mere sailors now that the sun has unburdened them of their fears.

They have become hunters.

*****

He was one of the creatures they were hunting, though he could hardly conceive of such a notion when Dakari, the chattering gray parrot, first brought the news of the ship to him and his brothers as they wrestled together in a circular clearing carved out of the jungle underbrush.

"Have you seen? Have you seen?" the annoying bird called down to them as they rolled about and tussled in the sand.

At first, they ignored him and continued with their play since Dakari was always screeching about something and hardly ever kept quiet. All the creatures who lived in this part of the jungle knew him to be a tiresome nag and frequently ignored him, just as the brothers were choosing to do so now. But Dakari was possessed by a fever of excitement, even more so than usual, and would not be shut out.

"It is a great winged thing, but it does not fly! Rather, it creeps across the skin of the water and was born from the place where the ocean meets the sky!"

Pollux unclamped his teeth from the scruff of his brother's neck and lifted his head to tell the bird to go away and leave them to their fun. The momentary lapse in hostilities was just what his brother needed to twist free of him, however, and to scramble to freedom. A second later, he joined the others, all younger and smaller than their eldest sibling, and dived with them through the leaves, taunting him to give chase.

Pollux, though powerful and agile, was nonetheless exhausted by the relentlessness of his brothers' combined assault. And so he let their teasing words fade before him as he directed his full temper at Dakari.

"You are the stupidest creature of the jungle!" he called up to him, his pride still smarting from his brother's escape. "Far and wide, it is agreed that Dakari does not have a single wise thought in his head!"

"But it is true!" the bird fired back, ignoring Pollux's insults. "A great winged thing that creeps across the water! Never before seen! Magnificent! You must come and look!"

And with that, Dakari lifted himself from the high branch he had been perched upon and flew off in the direction of the beach.

Pollux shook his head in disgust and turned back toward his home. His mother, no doubt, would be waiting with chores for him to do as the oldest and most able. She always had chores for him to do, a fact that made him weary in the contemplation of it, even as he took his first steps in that direction. Why was it that his brothers got to frolic and play all day long while he, Pollux, was constantly made to labor on their behalf? It hardly seemed fair. But he knew with utmost certainty that it was useless to argue the point with his mother, for she would only give him that much more work to do for daring to question her in her wisdom.

Perhaps, though, he would be sent out hunting with his father and the other grown males, something he deeply enjoyed doing and which hardly seemed like a chore at all. Pollux admired nearly everything about his father and took great satisfaction in the way that all the other creatures of their kind looked up to him and thought of him as their undisputed leader. Hunting beside him as his firstborn son, Pollux would sometimes experience such a rush of pride that it would make the blood flow warm in his chest.

The only thing he disliked about being the offspring of such a noble creature, a thought that sometimes kept him awake at night, was that he himself would never be judged half as noble or good as his father was. It panicked him to think that having a father as virtuous and revered as his own would merely give others opportunity to measure how far short the son had fallen from the forebear. And it was this fear of eventually being exposed—as the son being a mere echo of the father—that sometimes caused him to act out with seemingly inexplicable violence toward his brothers, a condition that caused them to band together and to unite in mutual antipathy toward him.

Pollux never once broke stride toward home as these lapidary thoughts occurred to him, for they were the same ones that nearly always descended upon him unbidden whenever he was alone. They hardly registered as thoughts at all; they were as natural to him as breathing. No, it was something else entirely—the ground beneath his feet—that stopped him in his tracks just as he was about to dive back into the dense undergrowth that encircled the clearing.

At first, he felt the sands shifting with the approach of something large and fast-moving. Next, he observed how the low branches before him began to tremble, as though the trees they were attached to were being shaken from their roots. And lastly, faster than he could even gather the thought to somehow hide himself, the curtain of jungle off to his left suddenly burst forth, delivering two leopards, a he and a she, into the circular clearing along with him.

Though Pollux's heart froze in instinctual terror at the sudden sight of the fearsome cats, the leopards paid him little mind as they raced across the sand and crashed back through the stand of greenery on the opposite side. An instant later, the leopards were followed into the clearing by a long unbroken line of creatures moving equally as fast to keep pace. There were the zebras, the lions, the chimpanzees, the addaxes, bonobos, mountain gorillas, the gazelles, and the striped hyenas. Each traversed the circle two by two with great haste, just as the leopards before them had done.

It was only when the last of these, the great gray elephants, had performed their similar transit and disappeared into the trees beyond that the earth ceased its trembling and an eerie silence fell upon the scene once more till eventually the only sound Pollux could hear was the sound of his own blood coursing in his ears. He had witnessed stampedes before in his lifetime but never one such as this. In the past, charges like these had been sparked by a single group of creatures fleeing in a panic from another. But here the creatures were intertwined, former enemies now united in a coordinated procession, and together they did not seem so much to be fleeing *from* something as *toward* it.

What could it be that compelled such mass hysteria that it made them disregard long-established enmities? Could this be the great winged thing that Dakari had trumpeted from the top of the trees? Had the foolish bird finally proclaimed some news worth proclaiming? And though he knew that he was needed back at home—that his mother would be waiting with his chores or his father would be waiting to begin the hunt—he also knew that he needed to see the mysterious new wonder that had arrived in their waters, a thing that had captured the imagination of the entire jungle.

When he arrived at the shore, the animals were gathered three rows deep behind the tree line, staring out at the water, each camouflaged in their fashion so as to seem not there at all, which is the unique gift of all jungle creatures. The strange truce between them continued to hold as they stood side by side stock-still and took in the wonderment unfolding before them. So thickly packed were they and so unmoving that Pollux had to dart between the legs of some of the larger animals just to make it to the front, where he, too, could witness the miracle that had been delivered unto them.

Dakari was right; the great winged thing was magnificent. Its wings, in fact, were so enormous and widespread that they seemed to embrace most of the visible sky, beating in a slow, even rhythm with the soft breeze coming in from the water. It lay stretched out on its long back, staring up into the cloudless dome, making little or no effort to stay afloat but somehow managing not to sink beneath the waves. Most remarkable of all is that it had recently given birth to a liter of peculiar men, who had apparently been delivered from its belly in buoyant half shells that had carried them to shore.

Pollux had seen men before, and he had considered them nothing more than yet another species that occupied the jungle along with him, though he instinctually knew that they were dangerous and that he should steer clear of their kind. The men who had been birthed from the winged thing, however, were different from the ones he had seen before while lingering on the outskirts of their encampments. These were not like the ones whose coloring resembled that of his own coat, with their earthy brown and dark sable skins. These strange new arrivals were without any color at all; they were bleached as white as bone. They smelled differently than the darker ones, too, a fact delivered to him on the breeze, and they draped themselves in strange and unfamiliar hides.

These colorless men seemed far less capable of any real violence than the previous ones that he had encountered, with their pointed sticks that he had seen them use to spear smaller creatures like himself. He knew that the dark ones, like his own kind, ate the flesh of the creatures they managed to capture with their weapons, and Pollux knew to be wary of them, lest he ended up one day on the end of one of their sharp sticks. But these? These colorless ones? What harm could they possibly do? They were like newborn pups in the world, seemingly unaware and defenseless against the many dangers that he took for granted. Any one of the creatures standing at his back, he knew, could make a quick meal of them the instant they stepped foot into the jungle. Yet these colorless men still stumbled forward blindly, inching ever closer to their own doom.

Perhaps it was pity for how vulnerable they appeared to him, how unaware of the dangers they were moving toward, that caused him to set foot out onto the sand—the first creature of the jungle to reveal himself to their eyes. Perhaps it was this, although the thought that preceded his decision to do so was less a thought and more a memory.

In the memory, he was his younger self once more out on his first hunt and struggling to keep up with the others as they raced to track down a family of ground squirrels who had foolishly tried to pass through their territory. Falling behind, he had come across an isolated pygmy mouse barely concealed beneath the brush on the side of the path. Somehow the creature's two hind legs had been crushed, perhaps beneath the feet of the others who had trampled upon him, unaware that they had done so in their hunger for larger game, and it was panting in pain, unable to move, as it stared up at him from the ground unblinkingly.

His hunger directed him immediately to eat the injured mouse. But as he was moving to do so, he became aware of another watching him from the path up ahead. It was his father, staring down at him from the top of a small rise, communicating to him in the way they did, not through sound or word but through a silent kinesis of thought.

"Even in the midst of the hunt, there is room for mercy."

The idea whispered itself into his brain as his father continued to look down from on top of the rise, waiting for him to interpret its meaning. And while he was not able to fully grasp its significance in the moment, with his hunger so great, he saw how pleased his father was when he made the decision to turn away from the mouse and to join him in continuing onward.

How much prouder would his father be now to see him extend the idea of mercy to these strange new foreigners who had come ashore, to see in these vulnerable white ones the same injured mouse he had witnessed out on the path that day? Perhaps after Pollux told his father about it later that night in silent whispers—after the chores had been done, the food eaten, and his family all settled in for sleep—his father would look at him with a pride so great that Pollux could finally put aside his doubts about himself and trust that one day he, too, would be great, as great as his father was.

With these thoughts circling in his head, Pollux advanced across the sand toward the white ones to warn them of the dangers they were inching toward. The white ones stopped and smiled as he moved to narrow the gap between them. They had no pointed sticks, no weapons. They were completely harmless. Despite the thin hides they wore on their backs, they were defenseless, as good as naked in the world, and Pollux felt it was his duty to make them turn back, to show them mercy.

But how would they be able to know what he was trying to express? The darker ones communicated in sounds, he knew, in a language he could not comprehend, not in thought, the way that higher creatures like his own did. Would the white ones be different, or would they need him to speak their language in order to grasp his warning? And if so, how would he ever be able to bridge the divide between them and make his message of mercy known to them?

This thought concerned him even as he stopped and stood within easy arm's reach of the first white one, who towered over him now like a god, seeming far less naked in the world with the sunlight haloing his silhouette from above. Whether the man was defenseless or not, Pollux would make him understand, would make him see, and would bring great pride to his father in doing so. For he was Pollux the Polecat, son of Zeus, and this great act of kindness, witnessed by all out on the beach, would be the true beginning of his rightful ascendance to his father's side.

"See?" he thought as the first white one crouched down on his haunches and held out his hand for him to nose closer. "Mercy needs no language to make itself known. My father was right. And I am Pollux, the son of Zeus."

*****

The mistake, of course, was in thinking that the outstretched hand was not itself a weapon, a weapon more deadly than any sharpened stick borne through the jungle by one of the darker kind. For how much more pain and suffering have been unleashed upon the earth by a single white palm held open in friendship than any spear

12

could ever cause? Be it by stick or palm, however, Man will have his dominion, and in the standoff between *Homo sapiens* and all other species, the only ones who would ever require mercy are those found standing in Man's path.

A short time later, after the first white man had seized him around the neck and lifted him off the ground, Pollux, a North African polecat, *Ictonyx striatus*, found himself imprisoned in the dark belly of the great winged thing along with many others of his kind, who threw themselves against the hard ribs of the beast in a desperate bid to escape even as the ground beneath them rolled and swayed. The white ones had proved themselves far more adept at defending themselves against the creatures of the jungle than Pollux had first imagined.

From the half shells that had carried them ashore, they produced smaller but sharper sticks than the darker ones favored, and they used them to slash and spear their way through the first line of animal observers, sending the others fleeing. Then with the nets they dragged behind them, they gathered up as many of Pollux's kind as they could and brought them out onto the beach to load back into their transports.

Once Pollux, too, had been thrust into a net and roughly slung over the shoulder of the one who had offered him his hand, he observed the other men laughing merrily through the rope mesh around a fire that they had built along the water's edge. His senses racing and confused, he could have no way of knowing why they were doing what they were doing. He only knew that he had been foolish in thinking that they could ever have required mercy to be shown to them by the likes of him.

Being a polecat, Pollux would have been unable to fathom that it was the sixth century AD in human history (for what does time mean to a polecat?) or that a great emperor from across the sea, the Greatest White One of All, had sent these men to round up as many of Pollux's kind as they could find. The emperor had expanded his dominion from Rome recently to take in the Balearic Islands to the west, and he was anxious to use his newly conquered territory as a trading post at the mouth of the Mediterranean. Rabbits, however, were swarming over the islands, spreading their disease (or so it was thought at the time), and the emperor had become determined to eradicate them by importing an army of African polecats to ferret them out and destroy them.

Pollux was entirely incapable of understanding these strange and horrible machinations of Man. He only knew that he was scared now in the belly of the winged thing and that he had thrown his life away the moment he trusted the outstretched hand of the first white one. He also knew that the winged thing was carrying them away across the water and that he would never see his mother or his father again, that he, Pollux the Polecat, son of Zeus, was now enslaved for all eternity to the white ones.

Somewhere in the dark close by, he could make out the familiar yelps of his brothers as they joined in the bedlam of crying and thrashing against their fate, for they, too, had been captured along with him. Perhaps in time this would prove a consolation, that he was not so alone in his grim new reality. Perhaps in time he would gather the courage to comfort them in their despair as an older brother should. He knew that his parents would want this of him, that, however distant he was from him now, his father would somehow look upon him with pride that he had summoned the strength in darkness to do so.

But for now, Pollux could only curl himself into a dark corner against the beast's side and listen to their anguished cries echoing through his mind. Something he had seen back on the beach through the net he was held inside of continued to haunt him and drained away all his desire to help. It was what he had seen when he had looked out upon the white ones gathered around their fire, shoving one another playfully like brothers, the teeth in their mouths as sharp as any spearhead he had ever looked upon.

Suspended above the fire he saw Dakari, pierced through with a stick and turning lifelessly. His beak was open wide to sound one last alarm, one that would never come, and his feathers were consumed in flames.

PART I

England

CHAPTER 1

The year is 1883.

Nearly twelve centuries have passed since Pollux the Polecat was taken from the jungle and forced into the service of Man. Gone is the great emperor Caesar Augustus and his all-consuming dream of a vast Mediterranean empire. Gone, too, are his outposts on the Balearic Islands and the African polecats once brought there to eliminate the indigenous rabbit population. Gone is any outward sign that stories such as these ever actually took place.

Time passes.

Yet fragments of the tale linger on, persist, for time itself can never truly erase what has been. Tiny parts of the past somehow survive into the present, gather up, and reconstitute into an entirely new chapter of the same story. The surviving fragment of Pollux's story, his direct descendant across eons of time, is not even a polecat any longer. He has been made into something else entirely, something strange and new. And yet the blood of his African ancestor still beats inside him as he unknowingly prepares to become the hero of a tale that began a long, long time before he ever existed...

*****

Modern science would quickly identify the cause for Felix's startling appearance as a failure of the adrenal gland brought about by the existence of an impinging tumor. These tumors were a common enough occurrence within his bloodline after hundreds of years of animal husbandry and crossbreeding, although he was unfortunate enough to be the only one in the barn to suffer from the condition in 1883, thus presenting himself as more of an aberration than later statistics would indicate. If only he had known then that there were others just like him elsewhere, he might not have felt so alone, so targeted for ridicule.

A talented and compassionate modern-day veterinarian might even suggest removing the tumor or the adrenal gland altogether through surgery in order to stimulate new hair growth and prevent bacterial or parasitic infection along the surface of the skin. But our story takes place long before such care and consideration were afforded to the likes of our hero, and the alopecia he suffered from birth as a result of his disorder was dismissed by his human handler as little more than further evidence of the mysterious workings of Providence.

Thus, deprived of proper medical treatment, the defect he was cursed to live with did not allow for even a single strand of hair to grow anywhere upon his body or along the thin tail that dragged behind him like a bald whip. He was neither sable colored, like most of the others in the barn, nor black, white, or any other color combination that patterned their thick coats of musky fur once they grew in. Rather, on account of his utter hairlessness, Felix was born a wretched grayish-pink anomaly, his skin so perpetually aggravated by its sheer exposure to the elements that its surface was forever erupting into painful constellations of tiny red sores. He appeared like something buried deep within the body, some shameful organ or muscle that had suddenly become dislodged from its fixed place and violently expelled, causing those who looked upon him to shudder at something recognizable within themselves.

It should be noted that the human heart is just such a reviled muscle. Though romanticized by artists throughout history and made anodyne with a false shape and pleasing coloration, nonetheless, it is, in actuality, a mean-looking pump repugnant to the eye when extracted from its dark cavity and held up to a cold surgical light. Who among us would not prefer to think of our own hearts as bearing more a resemblance to the counterfeit presentation of a hundred million greeting cards than the awful truth of this bloody mess?

Adding to his shocking pigmentation, Felix's eyes had been an unnerving red from the moment he first opened them to the world. If the eyes allow us the ability to see inside another's soul, as poets have long maintained, then Felix's eyes, as shockingly upsetting as they were, gave his persecutors a kind of excuse to mock and deride him as a freak of nature, especially when considered along with his unnatural skin tone.

He was, in truth, a freak of nature, but so were all his brothers and sisters, although they were less obviously so. For Felix was a ferret, *Mustela putorius furo*, domesticated from the European polecat, a creature descended from the generations of children, grandchildren, and great-grandchildren that Pollux and his African brethren had left behind on the (now-)Spanish isles once their part in the tale was concluded.

All three—the African polecat, its European scion, and the modern ferret—belong to the same animal family, the *Mustelidae*. All are mustelids, along with their close cousin the weasel, whose bloodline was first accessed in crossbreeding to dilute that of the polecat. The differences between them are significant, yet each was authored by the hand of Man. For any time Man chooses to subjugate a creature to his will, to tear out what was once wild about its nature and domesticate it, unexpected consequences result, like Felix's tumor, that call into question the wisdom of his desire to do such a thing in the first place.

In the case of the domesticated ferret as a whole, narcolepsy is the most obvious consequence of Man's specious instinct to manipulate and control. Unlike their progenitors in the wild, the domesticated ferret is cursed with a kind of insidious torpor, a listlessness born of Man's invasive experimentation, which requires them to sleep upward of eighteen hours a day. Their daily routine is thus characterized by a six-hour burst of high-energy activity surrounded on both sides by an inescapable, darkening slumber.

Put another way, before it is ever born, every ferret has three-quarters of its waking life stolen from it by Man. In Felix's case, the loss was even more significant since the tumor pressing on his gland would no doubt have shortened his overall life expectancy in the end had it been allowed to exact its final toll. As it was, he was forced to live with its side effects and being singled out and branded an aberration. All ferrets suffer from the abnormality of sleep disorder, but only some of them, the ones that look like Felix, are thought to be freaks and punished for their compounded oddity.

"Demon!" they jeered at him, the hobs (boys) that shared the barn along with him, performing their jerky weasel war dance around him from blood memory while pinning him back up against the wall. Meanwhile, the jills (girls) gathered in a tight circle in the hay on the opposite side of the barn, seemingly amused by the hobs' cruelty at Felix's expense.

"How does a demon survive in the heat of summer without a coat to protect him?"

"How does a demon see from behind his red eyes?"

"Look, he's upset! His eyes are tearing!"

"Those aren't tears at all, you stupid hob. The freak's melting in the heat!"

The barn was filled with their laughter, hobs' and jills' alike, at these regularly repeated taunts. Sometimes it seemed that his sole function in their community was to serve as a target for their coordinated cruelty. Already, though, he could sense their energy winding down because he could feel it in himself as well. They were reaching the end of their six-hour stretch of waking life. Dusk could be seen falling across the sky outside through the half-opened barn door, and soon they would all be asleep once more in a great pile of fur, hardly remembering that this was the way they chose to spend the limited time they were given.

Felix would not forget, however. He would wake up sometime after dawn with all the rest and would assume his role as their common enemy. It was not lost on him that some of his persecutors might actually be his brothers and sisters by birth, although he was never fully sure if identifying them as such would temper any of their behavior toward him. Perhaps it would be the same. And yet his thoughts could not help but gravitate toward the idea whenever his back was up against the wall, and he would find himself searching their faces and their dancing, jeering bodies for some reflection of his own image.

In the past, he had made the mistake of approaching a few of them, the ones who bore some resemblance of movement or manner to him, only to be violently rebuffed. Though he was the only ferret in the barn that was completely hairless, the only one whose eyes were pink, there were a few among them whose features betrayed some variation on the theme—a thinning of the coat or pupils a shade slightly less inky black than normal, for instance. It was these, however, the ones most like him, who denied him the loudest whenever he tried to forge some connection, and he eventually gave up on any efforts to establish a common ancestry with them.

The one inescapable commonality between himself and all the other ferrets in the barn that none could deny was the tiny crucifix that each had stamped upon their right ear, a clear sign that they belonged to the same tribe of hunting ferrets. When each was but a kit (a baby), the Breeder would carry them by the scruff of their neck to a fire he had built beside the barn and stamp them with a tiny brand while they lay asleep across his lap. The pain of the hot brand would jolt them back to consciousness but only long enough to take in the stars in the nighttime sky before the worst of it would pass and they would slip off back into sleep. By morning, they belonged to him.

Even this shared physical attribute, though, had been turned to Felix's disadvantage over time. For where the others' cross was largely hidden from the outside world by the fur that had grown over it, visible only by turning the ear inside out, Felix's crucifix stood out grotesquely on his translucent appendage, a gaudy tattoo of ownership that was impossible to hide. As a result, the brand had become yet another target of their shared derision, and many were the times he had heard one of his tormentors single out the cross for particular mockery, even when they themselves carried the same sign of their collective shame on the inside.

Chief among his tormentors was a hob named Scruffer, who was so close in age to his own that he might have been born of the same liter as Felix. Scruffer, too, possessed a peculiarity almost as striking as Felix's alopecia; although his eyes were a dark marble, he was the only albino in the barn, his coat as blindingly white as a field of newly fallen snow. Familiar with being different, it should have been Scruffer who protected him from the others and bonded with him in solidarity against their attacks. The similarities in their circumstances, however, only inspired Scruffer to outstrip the others in aggression, as though drawing attention away from his own humiliating whiteness required him to direct that much more attention upon another more obviously cursed than himself. It was Scruffer, in fact, who had first hit upon the idea of calling him a demon and who made sure the others picked up on the moniker and did not refer to him by any other name.

Why would a creature that might very well have been Felix's own brother treat him so poorly when all he desired to be was welcomed into their fold? The barn was warm and dry and, in most outer regard, a pleasant enough place to live; the Breeder saw to that. But its ceiling was arched and high, too high it seemed to him, and oftentimes Felix felt lost and lonely in the cavernous space, kept apart as he was by the others. How many times had he dreamed of joining with them in their games during the day while the elders were off hunting, of dancing the weasel war dance with them, or huddling at the center of the sleep pile they formed each night?

Always, however, his dreams were dashed by the first light of day as soon as the elders were led out of the barn and the younger ones, left to their own devices, resumed their campaign against him, egged on by Scruffer. Having to bear it each and every day, Felix sometimes wished he were not related to them in any way, that he shared no bloodline with them at all. But, in truth, he also knew that the secret of their shared origins would likely remain shrouded in mystery forever.

And why was it that Felix was unaware of whom his actual siblings might be? Remember that the modern domesticated ferret does not live together as a community or family group might but as a "business," a term first coined by their human overlords to explain the arrangement. Felix grew up in a barn in England along with a hundred other ferrets, but they were not meant to be a family; they were meant to be a "business." Making the distinction between the two things has required that Man separate children from their parents and siblings from one another at an early age in order to shatter any sense that they were ever connected by anything more than enterprise.

First, they took away the ferrets' sense of family, of somehow belonging to themselves. Then they stamped them with a cross. And finally they gave them a whole new vocabulary with which to describe the way they looked at one another—*outsider, demon, freak.* And in this manner, Man got his way.

Felix was not thinking about this, about the systematic oppression of his kind. His oppressors, so far as he understood the concept, were the ones falling to all fours around him now, their dancing energies spent as dusk continued to darken the distant corners of the barn and sleepiness descended upon them from the high beams above like a soft shroud. Only two thoughts filled his mind at that moment. Both occurred to him in the form of a question, and neither had anything specifically to do with systematic oppression. The first question was "Where do I belong?" And the second question was "When will She return?"

In the end, are these not the same two questions that have occurred to every creature that has ever walked the earth?

In Felix's case, the answer to the second question came not a moment after he had asked it of himself. For the bottom half of the heavy barn door was swung open by the hand of the Breeder, and She returned to him from her day out hunting along with the other adult ferrets. He immediately ran to greet her as he always did upon her return, even as She slunk the short distance to their familiar corner at the front of the barn, too tired from her day's exertions to acknowledge Felix's hungry affections with any outward show.

Meanwhile, the other adult ferrets wearily crossed to the rear of the barn, farthest from the door, to curl themselves up into tight balls against the wall there. His former tormentors would move silently toward them over the course of the next few minutes and use them as the foundations for the great pyramid of sleep that they constructed each night before shutting their eyes.

It had been thus for as long as he could remember—that Felix and She slept apart from the others, uninvited to be a part of their collective warmth. For his part, Felix knew the cause of his estrangement from the rest; it was because he was a freak of nature. But what her crime was, he could never be sure. What had She done to merit her nightly excommunication from the business? There was no sign of any disagreement between her and the other adults whenever they returned from their labors at the end of the day. Perhaps her only crime, he sometimes thought, was of being kind to him, of acting like his mother and spending the last bit of energy she had each day shielding him from the wages of his isolation.

He knew the likelihood of She actually being his mother was slim. Her coat was the rich sable color of good soil, the mask around her eyes even richer, and she was thick and muscular where he was thin and scrawny. To look at them, you would think they were of two different species entirely, a comically mismatched pair. But as he wriggled his way into the half circle of her embrace the moment her body curled into the straw and turned to press his back up against her stomach, their familiar sleeping posture, he knew that She was as good as any mother who had ever birthed a child such as him into the world.

He could smell the blood on her even now as the beating of their hearts became as one, their breathing syncopated, and he knew that he would only have a short while to speak with her before She drifted away into unconsciousness entirely. It was always on the days when She was most successful, when the lingering blood smell indicated that she had captured a significant number of her prey, that she was the most tired and had the least amount of patience for his nightly questions. On such nights as these, She had even shoved him from the warmth of her embrace and forced him to sleep on his own when his questions became too tedious for her to contemplate. So he knew he needed to establish a connection and speak to her quickly if he was to achieve his nightly assurances.

With his mind, he searched hers, for any part of it that had not already given itself over to exhaustion and shut itself down already. He worked his way through memories of her day—so much crawling through the darkness, so much blood—until at last he located the tiny part that was still open to conversation and whispered his words inside.

"Why do they hate me so?"

He asked this question tonight as he had a thousand times before while staring at the sleeping pile of ferrets, still faintly visible on the other side of the barn. He knew what the answer would invariably be, but he needed to hear it just the same so that one day he might not only hear it but believe it.

When her answer came back to him, it was as though the whole barn was speaking, every inch of empty space, even though She never once had to open her mouth or raise her voice to be heard. Her deep, rich voice, thick with the mysteries of earth and blood, surrounded him like a dark embrace on all sides, sheltering him as much as her body ever could. For despite his desire to train their will to his own, the one thing Man has never been able to breed out of lesser creatures is their ability to communicate in this manner despite his efforts to silence them.

"They hate you because they're afraid of you."

Felix smiled and pressed his body farther back against hers, pleased by the comforting response and that she was still awake enough to offer it to him. His own biological mother was perhaps buried at the bottom of the pile across the way, but he would not trade She with any other creature at moments such as these. Still, he could feel her slipping into sleep and knew that he would need to ask the rest of his questions quickly if he was ever hoping to keep her from drifting away.

"But why are they afraid of me?"

"They're afraid of you because of what you might become."

"And what might I become?"

The space in her mind to speak to her was growing narrower, closing in on all sides. He nudged her with his snout to keep her awake and saw a flash of temper cross her thoughts, like a bolt of lightning. Still, he was willing to risk her anger to receive the answers he needed.

"What might I become?" he repeated, once he sensed that her temper had passed.

"They're afraid that you might become…"

She held on to the last word in the sentence for maximum effect. And even though he knew what the word would be, for she had repeated it to him a thousand times before, he still felt his pulse quickening in anticipation until she finally let it go for him to hear.

"…yourself."

He smiled a whole body smile at the sound of it, every cell of his being beaming with satisfaction, and nestled himself farther into her embrace. Now, suddenly, it was he who was slipping away, sinking into a warm slumber, even as he fought against the pull of sleep by continuing on with his questions.

"What does that mean?" he asked. "That they're afraid I might become myself?"

Now her voice, when it came to him, was less all around, as it had been before, than inside the tiny space in his thoughts he kept open for her alone. He closed his eyes and allowed the earth and blood tones of her liquid assurance to pour into his mind and drown him in her love.

"No creature can tell what that means, and it's for this reason that they're afraid. For you are completely unique, Felix, my love, and they have done their best to discourage you into thinking that this is a bad thing. But what if it's not? What if the things about you that are unique are the same things that will lead you to greatness? None can say. This is why they try to break you, to have you believe that you're somehow less than they are. It is their own sameness that they truly hate, and so they try to get you to hate the things about yourself that are not like they are because they fear your greatness."

He was way down at the bottom of consciousness now, his thoughts about to slide into dreams. He could still hear his own voice in his head, but the thoughts he was trying to shape and the words he found to express them with to her were distant, disembodied.

"But aren't all creatures great?"

"All are born to be, but most choose to forget."

"But why?"

"Because it's easier to forget than to remember and to find the thing that will lead them to their greatness. Their cruelty toward you is a great gift because it will not allow you to forget that you are not like the others. Your life is meant for greatness. You only need to discover the path that will lead you there."

The space inside his mind was closing over him like the ocean. Soon he would be unable to fight it.

"I wish to be a great hunter," he muttered.

"Then you will be a great hunter," she whispered back, her voice coming from somewhere far away.

"But when?"

"Soon...soon...soon..."

And then he was gone.

*****

There are a million and one misconceptions about the animal kingdom that Man, in his infinite wisdom, holds to and operates by nonetheless. Take, for example, the case of the humble Norwegian lemming, *Lemmus lemmus*. For many centuries, this brightly colored ancestor of the modern-day hamster was thought by men of great scholarship and intellect to drop directly from the sky due to the periodic discovery of large quantities of lemming bodies that would mysteriously wash up along coastlines. Later, once their migratory patterns had become a subject of closer study, these curious creatures were observed to sometimes leap off high cliffs in great numbers, precipitating their own drowning along the shore, thus giving rise to the lemming suicide theory; i.e., that the lemming is a creature with so little regard for its own life that it would leap to its death in an instant, blindly following after another in an unspoken suicide pact.

Even to this day, this myth of the pathologically stupid, pathologically death-loving lemming persists in the popular imagination even after it has been proven to be false. For lemmings, it turns out, periodically need to seek out new habitats once their numbers become too great in a particular area and make their fearless leaps off cliffs and into oceans with the hope of sustaining their population by swimming to foreign shores. Some survive the grueling swim, while others are washed back upon shore. But the lemmings' instinct to make the leap in the first instance comes not from their instinct to die but from their instinct to live.

A similar misconception, more germane to our story perhaps, is the commonly held notion that all animals are color-blind. A vast array of laboratory experiments have been conducted that prove beyond a shadow of scientific doubt that when a dog, for instance, looks upon his master, he sees him only in shades of black and white. And so we imagine that, except for ourselves, there is not a creature alive who has ever had the experience of recognizing red or blue or any of the other colors of the spectrum we have put a name to.

What about when an animal dreams, though? Is there a scientific instrument available to measure what they see once they have closed their eyes to the black and white world? And supposing that there was? What is to say that we truly know how to access the dream world of another creature? Are not some parts of our brains hidden only to ourselves?

Science might argue otherwise. But then again, science once argued that lemmings fell from the sky. Or maybe some unique gift had been conveyed upon Felix by the tumor growing inside him, the way heroes of comic book legend are frequently invested with a superpower at the start of their journeys by some extraordinary catalyzing event, like the bite of a radioactive spider. Perhaps it was solely on account of the fact that his eyes were red.

Whatever the cause, the only thing known for certain is that when Felix fell asleep that night, cradled in the arms of She, his subconscious imagination burst forth with an endless stream of fantastical dreams about what his life would be like in the future once he had become a great hunter and fully and completely himself.

And they were all in color.

CHAPTER 2

As it happened, Felix did not have to wait much longer for his dreams to become a reality, although when they finally did begin to arrive in their actual forms, they were far less brightly colored than the ones he had imagined while cradled in the warmth of She. The dreams he'd had then were painted in the colors of sunlight. The adventure he was about to embark upon in his waking hours could only be described in infinitely darker shades.

Soon after that night, the Breeder swung open the heavy barn door shortly after daybreak in order to rouse the adult ferrets to their daily task, as was his custom. On this particular morning, however, he stepped inside and closed the door behind him before any of them had had a chance to wake themselves and exit. He moved slowly to the center of the barn, his muddy boots crushing the hay beneath his weight, then stood examining the sleeping pile of ferrets up against the wall, scanning his business. The pile had only just begun to stir to life, with the grown ones at the bottom pushing out from under the younger ones on top, who limply slid down the sides of the pyramid, still in the throes of sleep.

The Breeder was a tall, thin man with yellow fur sprouting from the top of his head. His pronounced beak-like nose gave him the appearance of a hungry bird, although his eyes were as pale as a shallow fishpond. According to the grown ones, he hardly ever uttered a sound, although he was unfailingly kind and gentle toward them, as kind and gentle as any ferret had the right to expect a human to be. He had no mate so far as they could tell, no offspring, and seemed somehow wrapped in a cloak of sadness that kept him cut off from the rest of his kind when out in the world.

The Breeder lifted two of the larger jills whom he had peeled off the pile by the scruffs of their necks, and he held them in the air in front of his long nose to examine them. They hung limply there in his grip, still unconscious and completely unaware that they were being held aloft in this fashion. In general, the Breeder seemed to prefer jills over hobs for hunting, given the greater tendency that hobs often demonstrated for falling asleep on the job. Though a few grown males were mixed in among his regulars, most, like She, were female.

One of the lasting mysteries of the barn, in fact, was what became of some of the grown males taken from them while the Breeder and the others were off hunting. Occasionally, the barn door would swing open during the day while they were away, and a second human, this one older and rounder than the Breeder, would enter and begin to roughly gather up as many of the grown males as he could carry. For their part, the ferrets knew to be fearful of this human and did their best to dance and dodge so as not to be taken. Mostly they feared him for his scent, for he smelled overpoweringly of blood, the blood of their own kind.

Despite their best efforts to escape him, however, a half dozen or more grown hobs were invariably snatched up by this crouched and wrinkled figure, who would storm out of the barn, cursing under his breath, the ferrets thrashing helplessly in his grip. Naturally, rumors spread throughout the barn as to what became of the hobs taken by the Smeller of Blood. The more hopeful among them said that they were released back into the wild or taken to another barn close by for the purposes of breeding. Others, though, maintained a far less optimistic outlook, mostly predicated upon the Smeller's scent of death. These others spread horrible stories throughout the barn about what became of the hobs, stories filled with dreadful images of torture and annihilation.

For example, there had once lived among them a large boastful hob named Hector, who strutted about the place as though he were king of all ferrets. The reason for his excessive pride mostly had to do with his extraordinary coat of fur, which was a sleek layer of gray guard hairs over a thick undercoat of white and gave him the appearance of being nearly silver. Hector was inordinately proud of his coat, which he himself announced to be unspeakably beautiful, and the other ferrets mocked him for his vanity while secretly agreeing with his assessment. It was, in fact, a beautiful coat, more beautiful than any of them had ever seen before, and not a few jills electively chose to mate with Hector in full view of the others even after mocking him for his wild self-regard. They could not help themselves, they argued afterward, because the coat was too magnificent to resist.

One of the hypocritical jills who allowed herself to fall under the spell of the magnificent coat was Princess, so named because of the air of spoiled privilege she moved about in, as though the other ferrets of the barn were merely there to serve her needs, including Hector. Despite her insufferable arrogance, Princess was a surprisingly good hunter, all agreed, and was much favored by the Breeder himself, who would sometimes linger with her alone outside the barn at the end of a successful hunt, gently stroking her in his arms with his long fingers. Such clear favoritism only added to her delusions of grandeur and made life in the barn unbearable for the others, who did their best to block her out and avoid her.

There was no blocking her out, however—no avoiding her—the day she returned with the others visibly shaking and, after she collapsed in the hay, sobbing. Gone were her royal airs, her arrogance, her vanity—anything that had led to her having been named Princess in the first place. By then, she was just a frail, weeping jill, and Felix watched in stunned fascination as the other females, including She, gathered around Princess and softly mothered her in a manner that would have been unthinkable the night before.

And then Princess told her story.

While they were returning home from that day's hunt, she reported, she happened to glance out through a crack in the wood on the side of the Breeder's wagon. And there she saw it. It was a human woman parading herself along the sidewalk of the town they passed through each day to get to and from their hunts, and the skin she wore around her hands to keep them warm was made up of the same unspeakably beautiful silver that she, Princess, had once succumbed to.

Hector had only been taken from them several days earlier in the Smeller's latest reaping, and in truth, the ferrets had been savoring the new quiet that had come over the barn in the absence of his constant loud boasting. Princess's story made them all feel guilty for their callousness, even those who would eventually go on to deny any connection between the Hector they knew and the beautiful gloves upon the woman's hands.

"You know Hector," they argued only minutes after Princess had finished reporting what she had seen. "He's off somewhere even now, wooing some silly jill while bragging about his magnificent coat."

Before they had even assembled back into their pile and fallen asleep that night, the business found itself evenly divided between those who thought that this was so, that Hector was just off somewhere being Hector, and those who heard in Princess's tale something darker and more foreboding for all of them. One thing was for certain, however: Princess herself never fully recovered from what she had seen through the crack in the wagon that day. She slept alone that night, apart from the pile, and refused to rouse herself when the Breeder came for them the next morning. This pattern continued on unbrokenly after that, and she neither ate nor drank anything for days while she slept away her waking hours and sank further into the hay. By the end of the week, she was gone.

On the night Princess had told them what she had seen, Felix asked She if she thought it was true that the gloves worn by the woman were, in fact, Hector, once they had lain down together in their familiar spot.

"Who can tell what Man is capable of?" She had whispered in his mind before drifting off to sleep.

Not a few times thereafter, being taunted and teased by the hobs while the adults were away, Felix had found himself hoping that they, too, would soon be reaped from the barn by the Smeller of Blood and meet the same end as Hector had. And he was frequently ashamed later the same night at the satisfaction such thoughts had given him.

Felix was only now stretching his limbs and yawning, having been shoved awake by She's rising, when the Breeder turned, with the jills still dangling from his hands, and saw him as though for the first time.

"Perhaps," the Breeder thought to himself, assessing Felix's physical malformations as he curled himself back up into a ball for a few more hours rest. "Seems like he'd be narrow enough to fit through the tunnels, without all that fur. Probably fast, too, given how skinny he is. And that color? It might even serve as an advantage in driving the rabbits out; they'll think it was a demon coming for them."

It was the chilly morning breeze on this particular early spring day that first brought Felix to full consciousness. He had never been outside the barn before, and the startling change in temperature first came as a shock, stripping away the last of his torpor. When he opened his eyes, he was gliding through the air toward the horse-drawn wagon the Breeder used to transport his hunters. He was the last to be taken from the barn, carried out by the scruff of his neck. The others, including the jills he had first selected, had already been loaded into the back. The Breeder deposited Felix among them, then climbed up at the front of the wagon, and whistled for the horses to start out for that day's assignment.

Felix found it impossible to make sense of what was happening to him or to gain solid footing in the back of the wagon. Every dip and rut in the dirt road they followed most of the way to town would toss him into the air and throw him roughly back into the hard wooden boards that made up its sides. What was more, the floor beneath his feet vibrated so rapidly with the movement that he could hardly see in front of him; all was a blur.

After several minutes of shaking so violently that it made the teeth in the back of his mouth ache, he suddenly remembered that She would be among the blurry patches of dark fur surrounding him on all sides, and he closed his eyes to try to find her with his mind. He finally located her at the front of the wagon bed, pressed against the backboard. He zigzagged his way falteringly through the other jills until he reached her.

"Please tell me what's happening!" he pleaded, lurching into her side.

"It's only the wheels of the wagon bouncing over the road." She chuckled. "You'll soon grow accustomed to it and find your center."

"But am I to be skinned now as Hector was?"

"What would make you ask that?" She gasped.

"Because I'm a hob, and I've been reaped!"

"You were reaped by the Breeder, not by the Smeller of Blood."

"But who's to say that I still won't be skinned?"

"I say."

"But how do you know?"

"Because I'm here with you, am I not? And I wouldn't allow it."

"Then what's going on?"

"You've been selected for the hunt, silly one. Isn't that what you wanted?"

Even in the midst of the chaos, Felix could not help but smile inwardly at the thought that the day had finally arrived, that his dreams were about to leave the realm of sleep and become flesh-and-blood reality. He leaned himself heavily into She's side for stability and tried to acclimate himself to the violent trembling of the wagon, already imagining what the rest of the day might bring. Would his skills as a hunter reveal themselves all at once, from the very start, so that the Breeder would chastise himself for not choosing him to join them earlier? Or would they reveal themselves slowly, in little increments, from one day's hunt to the next until at last the Breeder would come to realize that he had a reliable talent in the hairless runt that he had picked, one he could always count on to get the job done, and sit him up front in the wagon with him on their way home from the hunt, stroking him with his long fingers as he had stroked Princess before him?

Whether they revealed themselves fast or slow, Felix was determined to prove himself a great hunter to the Breeder and to win his favor so that all the other hobs back in the barn could finally see that they were wrong to look down upon him and to tease him all that time. More than anything else, Felix wanted them to feel shame for how they had treated him, and he knew that winning the respect of the Breeder was the surest way to do it.

Shortly after he thought these things, the road beneath their wheels became far less rutted than it had been, and he was able to hear something more than just the crashing sound of the wagon itself. What he heard were voices, the voices of men, laughing and conversing all about him. He looked and saw that the tops of tall buildings towered above them on either side as they continued to move forward, and he knew that they must be passing through the human settlement that he had heard about, called a town. With the ground beneath his feet far more stable, he crept to a small crack in the wood boards on the side of the wagon—perhaps it was the same crack that Princess had looked through to behold what had become of Hector—and peered out upon this new astonishment.

He had never seen so many humans gathered in one place before. It reminded him of the anthill in the barn he sometimes turned his attention to during the days when the others had targeted him and had begun their teasing. Focusing on the ants, on their manic comings and goings up the side of the dirt hill, carrying items to and from the nest in their tireless display of energy, had been his way sometimes of shutting out their jeers, of removing himself to a better place. Now it seemed he had become part of that better place, had joined the ants in their world of flurried activity, and the feeling was thrilling.

Before that morning, he had only ever known the Breeder and the Smeller of Blood. Here, though, were hundreds and hundreds more like them, hobs and jills alike, living on top of one another like ants in a hole. They moved this way and that in front of their marvelous buildings, draped in the most elaborate furs he had ever seen in his entire life. They talked by moving their mouths and making sounds. They laughed and touched.

It was almost too much for his mind to comprehend. What was more, the space between their tall buildings was crowded with other wagons just like the one he was riding in. They would clatter past regularly, blocking his view of the human activity, and causing him to wonder at how many other creatures like himself were taking in this vast spectacle of Man in his element and growing dizzy from the sight of it. When he turned from the crack in the wood to tell her about what he was witnessing, he saw that She was looking directly at him, pleased that he was pleased, and he knew that nothing more needed to be communicated between them.

Shortly after they left town, the road grew rutted once more, and Felix stumbled back across the wagon bed to her side for the remainder of the trip. Some time later, the Breeder whistled for the horses to stop, and he jumped down from his seat at the front. A moment later, he lowered the rear panel and stood chest high to the wagon.

"Ready to go to work, my beauties?" he asked, speaking in his sad voice.

The ferrets moved toward him obediently, a dozen in all. Felix was the last of them, following closely behind She. When the Breeder gathered them up in his arms, not a single one squirmed or thrashed to get away; they knew their business. Felix found himself on top of the bouquet of ferrets held to the Breeder's chest and heard him humming softly to himself as he turned from the wagon and crossed to a nearby ash tree.

The tree was enormous and stood at the top of a small hill of rolling green that stretched down to the largest human dwelling place that Felix had ever seen. It was at least ten times bigger than the barn, maybe more, and was surrounded by stone statues and fountains that spit forth water, even on this chilly morning. A fat red-faced man in a glistening robe was hurrying up the hill toward them as the Breeder approached the ash, doing a poor job of holding his robe closed and showing off his roiling pink nakedness underneath. A skeletal-looking manservant in a dark black suit followed dutifully in his wake, holding aloft a silver tray with two delicate teacups set on top.

"There you are!" huffed Red Face, tugging at his robe. "I was beginning to think you'd never come!"

The Breeder paid this comment little mind as he stopped before a low fence made of barbed wire that had been staked in the ground several feet back from the trunk of the tree, fully encircling the ash. Red Face came up beside him, huffing and puffing from his exertions, as the Breeder scanned the upper branches of the tree for signs of rot.

"Like some tea?" Red Face asked impatiently while reaching back to the tray that his manservant was holding out to him, still trying to draw the Breeder out into conversation.

"No," the Breeder mumbled distractedly while continuing to examine the treetop for any evidence of infestation.

Red Face looked at him quizzically, as though declining an invitation to tea was one of the strangest things he had ever heard. Then he slurped the drink loudly from his own cup before following the direction of the Breeder's gaze.

"Filthy creatures," he said, although the Breeder hardly seemed to be listening. "I see them from my windows, scurrying about like they own the place. This morning, there must've been nine, ten of them standing about in full view like they were leaping lords of the manor."

"They don't seem to have done much damage," the Breeder responded, still not looking at the man standing close beside him.

"Still," Red Face said, slurping his tea a second time, "I want them gone." Then he lowered his eyes and took in the clutch of ferrets the Breeder continued to hold against his chest. Felix was so close to Red Face that he could feel his hot breath on his naked skin.

"Is this them then?" the man asked, indicating toward Felix. "They smell a bit awful, don't they?"

For the first time, the Breeder turned and looked directly at Red Face, clearly reveling in the fat man's ignorance. "That's the point now, isn't it?"

Then he lifted his leg and stepped over the wire fence, gently setting the clutch of ferrets down on the ground. Some of them had fallen asleep in his arms and needed a moment to rouse themselves back to life again. For his part, Felix thrilled to the sensation of the cool grass that grew in the shadow of the tree, and he lowered his snout to drink in its rich greenness. The Breeder continued to explain to Red Face what the point was in his deliberate, taciturn manner.

"Ferrets go into the burrow, tunnel around. Rabbits pick up on the scent, run in the opposite direction. Either they run into another ferret; the job takes care of itself. Or they come up to the surface. In which case, the fence takes care of the rest."

Felix, who had begun propelling himself through the cool grass by his back legs the whole time the Breeder spoke, cared little for the meaning of the words he said. He only knew that he was enjoying surfing through the tall blades—the glorious feeling that the earth itself was stroking his skin—and wished to never return to the crushing confines of the barn again. So lost was he in his ecstatic reverie that he nearly got himself stepped on by the Breeder, who had begun circling the trunk of the tree while examining the root system for entrance points into the rabbit warren it concealed.

"Whatever it takes," Red Face was saying impatiently. "Just get rid of the damn things. They're an abomination."

Suddenly, Felix was being lifted into the air by the scruff of his neck and carried aloft to the far side of the tree. Gazing down, he noticed that the other ferrets were already gone, already off on the hunt, and that he alone had been left to tarry behind, frolicking in the grass. He desperately searched for She with his mind, to ask her what he should do, but she was too far beneath the surface now for his thoughts to reach her. By the time the Breeder crouched down and released him, Felix was sure that he would fail to ever become the hunter he had dreamed of becoming and that the Breeder would see that he had made a mistake in ever having chosen him and sell him off to the Smeller of Blood to be made into a pair of gloves to warm a woman's hands.

Then the Breeder spoke to him softly, his watery blue eyes looking down upon him with something like real tenderness. "Just follow your instinct, little red one. It'll tell you what to do."

Felix had no ability to interpret what the Breeder was saying into anything like meaning for himself. He only knew that at the exact same moment the words were being said, a strange new sensation was moving toward him, coming from the direction of the ash tree. He turned and examined the root system, an elaborate network of crossed tendrils stretched out across the grass. In some places, the roots had actually lifted up off the ground, exposing small hollows at the base of the tree, and it was one of these hollows that seemed to be beckoning to him now in an ancient tongue that he had never heard before but understood entirely well, in a voice that seemed to echo inside his whole body, inside his blood. He knew that She and the others had already entered these hollows and had already allowed the blood voice to draw them into the inner workings of the tree, just as he himself, as though hypnotized, was being drawn into them now.

Before he was aware of crossing the grass, he had entered the hollow and was pushing down a narrow tunnel into the earth. The tunnel was hardly much wider than he was, but he slid easily down through it just the same, his body seemingly able to bend and contract to its changing dimensions.

All was darkness and earthy decay, but Felix had no fear of pushing onward. It was as though his natural tendency toward fearfulness had abandoned him entirely and something else had replaced it, a scent up ahead that pounded in his blood and called him onward. Perhaps it was the instinct that the Breeder had spoken of; he could not be sure. He only knew that he was completely in its grip and unable to resist where it was taking him.

Then he was in a wider space, a space of frenzied activity and the wild clamor of limbs and fur. Felix could not comprehend that he had found his way into the warren of his quarry, that he had come upon his prey. He only knew that, once the tunnel opened up to deliver him there, he was once more in the company of his own kind who had located the spot before him, though the dark remained unrelenting and he could not see their actual forms. He also knew that there were others there with them at the heart of the tree, others who were not like them, whose scent had beckoned to him from outside and brought him here. These others were scrambling to escape, to get away from the army of invaders, even as they filled the space with the scent that brought the invasion upon them.

Colored stars exploded in Felix's mind as he absorbed the pandemonium unfolding around him in the dark, stars of an infinitely deeper variety than the pastel watercolors of his nightly dreaming. He dived forward into the rich colors, unsure exactly of what he was doing but determined to capture one of the stars, to dominate it, and to make it his own. He settled on the brightest star in the galaxy, a bleeding red sun that appeared at the center of the constellation in his mind, and drove toward it through the riot of other colors until it was the only one that remained.

Then he could feel the grip of the earth around his sides and knew that he was back inside a tunnel once more; only this tunnel was not leading him further down into the dark but upward toward the light. He was following the red star back up to the surface, the star that seemed to originate from within his own body and, as such, allowed him no other choice but to follow.

They were one. He was connected to it. And the scent that first came to him from the hollow of the tree, the one that drove him to discover the red star buried deep in the earth, was like a scent that he had been waiting to experience his whole life, a missing signal from outer space that had finally reached his senses and raised him out of darkness.

The next thing he knew, there was sunlight all around him, sunlight so bright that it seared his eyes and stopped him in his tracks. Then at the center of the white field of his vision, the red star appeared once more. It was smaller now, a fraction of its former size, and it was throbbing like the beating of a tiny heart. It widened across the field of his vision, the sound of its beating heart pulsing in his ear, even as the blacks and whites of his waking life returned to swallow up the velvety red.

Then he knew that he was standing once more outside the base of the tree, looking up at what remained of his star. The Queen hung suspended a foot off the ground from the barbed-wire fence, staring down at him with wild, panicked eyes. Blood dripped from the places where the sharp wire tore into her fur, into her flesh, but the rabbit never indicated the pain that she was surely experiencing, only held him in her unblinking gaze.

After a moment, Felix looked away to his right and saw She standing close by. The limp body of a much smaller rabbit than the one he had ferreted—a baby, really—hung from her mouth. She set it down on the grass before turning to behold his crucified catch. When She turned back to him, he could tell that she was beaming with pride. Other ferrets were pushing their way out from the root system now. Upon seeing what hung from the wire, they each did as She had done before them, setting their own smaller catches down onto the grass to focus their admiration on him.

The ferrets, however, were not the only ones filled with admiration at what he had done, as the Breeder came up from the outside of the fence and stood behind the dangling rabbit. He smiled down at him, his blue eyes sparkling.

"You've done it," he whispered as Red Face and his manservant moved up beside him.

"What's the situation?" asked Red Face, not fully sure why the Breeder was so overtaken with emotion.

The Breeder leaned over the fence and pulled the rabbit off its sharp wire teeth by the base of its long ears. "The situation is that we've captured the doe, the primary breeder."

"Isn't that what I paid you to do?" Red Face muttered before reaching to take hold of the second cup of tea from the butler's tray.

"Tis," said the Breeder, holding the bloody carcass of the Queen up in the air to examine it closer, "but usually they're the hardest to catch. Sometimes you never catch them at all, in which case your problem keeps coming back. But now that we've got the queen, we just have to locate the rest and your problems are solved."

"Huh," belched Red Face, simultaneously pleased and unimpressed, as he indicated toward Felix with the drained cup. "Looks like you've got a hell of a hunter there."

"Indeed, I believe I do."

"Ugly as sin, though. Those eyes! They make him appear demonically possessed."

"It's those eyes that just solved your rabbit problem," the Breeder responded without any discernible emotion to his tone.

"True enough," Red Faced sniffed. "What's the cross on the ear meant to symbolize, as if I didn't know?"

"Meant to symbolize nothing," the Breeder answered, examining his own silhouette projected on the surface of the rabbit's startled eyes. "Just that he's mine."

"Glad to hear it," Red Face said, setting the cup back down on the tray. "Wouldn't want to go recommending you to all my friends if I thought you were one of those King James types, always spouting on about how much they love their Jesus and all that sort of nonsense."

"You don't have to worry about me preaching up to your friends," the Breeder smiled, turning his gaze to Felix. "When my mother passed, she took all the faith I had along with her. The only thing I believe in now is this here fella."

"A belief well founded," Red Face grumbled back irritably, making one last failed attempt to pull close his robe. "'All God's creatures'...so forth and so on." Then he turned and made his way back hurriedly across the rolling green toward the house, calling over his shoulder as his manservant hurried after him.

"Expect to hear from me shortly!"

The Breeder hardly seemed to take notice of Red Face's withdrawal as he smiled benevolently down upon Felix. Then he turned his attention to the Queen one last time, hoisting her back into the air. "You spooked the queen out of her nest on the first try," he said, smiling as he closed his left hand in a tight grip around the throat of the doe. "Well done, Little Red."

*****

Felix heard the neck snap on the Queen as the Breeder made a quick twisting motion with his hand just after bestowing upon him the name that he would refer to him by forever after, Little Red, on account of his inflamed skin and the eerie color of his eyes. It was not the sound of breaking bone, though, that would linger in his thoughts for the rest of the day, a day spent clearing out the remains of the rabbit den from the rich man's estate.

He himself would ferret out many more rabbits from beneath the ash tree that day, from the smallest bunnies to the largest bucks, though none would match in size or significance his capturing of the doe on his first attempt. Still, he felt his hunting instincts growing increasingly sharper with each successive trip back down into the burrow. And he knew the Breeder was proud of him by the end of the day when, after gathering up all the bodies in a burlap sack and tossing them into the back with the other ferrets, he placed Felix on the seat in front beside him as they rode back to the barn, grinning proudly at him from time to time and whispering, "My Little Red." And if Felix had not as of yet killed any of his prey with his teeth, preferring instead to drive them up onto the wire fence, he fully believed that he would develop the blood thirst that the others had over time.

No, it was neither his lack of bloodthirst nor the sound of the doe's neck snapping that had lingered with him throughout the day like the residue of an unwanted memory, impinging upon the great satisfaction he otherwise felt at the success he had had in becoming a hunter. Even now, riding up front in the wagon as they approached the town for a second time, resting his head on the Breeder's lap, he could feel it clinging to the edges of his happiness and sought to block it out by closing his eyes.

But the thing that had haunted him throughout the day only haunted him more powerfully as he drifted into inescapable sleep. For in sleep, he was unable to turn away from what he had seen and heard in the moment before the Breeder had snapped the Queen's neck.

In the instant before his quick motion, she had shut her eyes for the first (and last) time, accepting her fate, and had spoken to him, her words permeating his thoughts as clearly as if She had whispered them herself. And it was these words that caused Felix to twitch and squeak beside the Breeder as he sank deeper into restless sleep.

The words the Queen whispered in his thoughts?

"Ever has it been so."

CHAPTER 3

It was remarkable how quickly Felix's fortunes reversed themselves in the barn after that first time he went out hunting and ferreted out the Queen. News of his great accomplishment spread to the others even as he slept—for he never did wake from his troubled sleep that evening and had to be carried in and set down in the hay by the Breeder—and by the time he arose, he had already been transformed into a hero.

Hobs, who had teased him just the day before for his naked hide, were now affectionately referring to him as Felix the Red—repeating the sounds and intonations they had heard the Breeder make when he carried him into the barn—and jockeying to be his friend. What was more, the jills who used to giggle at his daily humiliations, were now casting longing stares at him from across the barn as he became the most celebrated male in their midst.

Naturally, Scruffer, who had, up until that point, been his arch-nemesis, was now the most adamant and vocal of Felix's newfound admirers, taking every opportunity to point out just how close he and the Red were to each other.

"Look how strange my own white coat is!" he would insist to any who would listen. "See how both of us have been singled out by destiny? What further proof do you need that he and I are closely related?"

And while surely it was better to have Scruffer as a friend rather than an enemy, all the adulation he was now experiencing confused Felix at first since as far as he knew, he was still the same ferret that he had always been. His first instinct, in fact, was to resist all their shallow kindnesses and to instead keep reminding himself of all the cruelties they had forced him to endure for so long. But it become impossible for him to keep recalling the hurt that they had caused him when it felt so much better to accept their love, as false as that love might be, and he quickly gave himself over to it entirely.

By the time he had completed his third or fourth hunt, the legend of Felix the Red, Greatest Hunter of Them All, had become enshrined as a standing article of faith to the other ferrets in the barn, who used it as the basis for anointing him their newly appointed leader. No longer was he teased or shunned for the things that had made him different. Now it was these very differences that made him into the legend he had become in their collective imagination, a figure to be admired and emulated. Within a week of hanging the Queen from the wire fence, young hobs could be seen tearing whole tufts of fur off their bodies with their teeth, hoping one day to be as hairless as he was.

He no longer slept with She by the door of the barn at night; he was invited to take his rest at the very heart of their collective sleeping pile. At first, the sensation of being surrounded by so much bodily affection was unnerving to him, causing him to wake throughout the night with the feeling that he was being buried alive, smothered. Presently, however, he was able to adapt to his role as the focal point of their unconscious lives, just as he had adjusted to becoming the focal point of their waking hours.

He dreamed of nothing but the hunt, of chasing down the colorful stars forever turning in the darkness out in front of him and driving them out into the light. When he awoke in the morning from these dreams, it sometimes felt as though the hunt had already begun, and he eagerly waited by the door in anticipation for the Breeder to come and retrieve them for their day's mission. He rode up front with the Breeder both to and from their destination points from that first day onward, the bouncing of the wagon beneath him no longer an obstacle to taking in all the wonders of the world around him—the beauty of the rolling green countryside, the fascinating human bustle of town—all the while being stroked on the top of his head by the Breeder.

For it was plain to all in short order that Felix had not only become the favorite of the young hobs and jills who occupied the barn but of the Breeder himself. And how could it have been otherwise when each day's hunt ended with Felix having amassed the greatest number of kills? The older ferrets, those who had been at it much longer than he had, were more begrudging in their admiration, perhaps, than the younger ones, sometimes resenting the Breeder's obvious partiality toward him that they themselves had never earned. None could begrudge the fact that Felix was a natural born hunter, though, one possessed of a kind of gift that they could only wish to have.

He was not always able to locate the largest doe on his first dive into a burrow, as he had so spectacularly done on that first hunt. Yet in a surprising number of cases, he was able to find her nonetheless and roust her to the surface. He looked for her star, always the reddest one in his field of vision, and once he found it, he would lock onto it with an unrelenting tenacity that seemed somehow second nature to him, a homing pigeon locking onto its beacon. Larger bucks caused him little problem as well, for their superior size and strength ultimately proved a disadvantage to his ferocious speed and agility in the close confines of the underground warrens. In all, there hardly seemed a rabbit of any size or shape that he could not drive from the nest and in surprising numbers.

On some days, the Breeder would be slow to untangle the rabbits from the wire and leave them hanging there for some time, distracted by other matters. On these days, Felix was able to parade along the fence, stepping carefully over the bodies of the rabbits that the others had laid out on the ground, proudly showing off the number of victims he had managed to crucify. Always, they looked down upon him with a kind of horrified awe that a creature so ugly and strange had, in fact, become their executioner.

Their stares never bothered him in the daylight; he took great pleasure in them, knowing the thoughts that went behind them. It was only at night sometimes while sleeping that he would recall the eyes of that first doe he had put up on the fence and the words that she had sent to his mind: "Ever has it been so."

It was then that he would wake in a panic, feeling once more like the others were trying to bury him beneath their weight, and he would struggle to free himself from the crushing pile. Once he managed to escape, he would feel the cold air of the barn closing in upon him and tiptoe across the hay to wriggle his way back once more into She's embrace.

Ever since his elevation, he had less time to spend with her, his comforting mother, than he had in the months before his first hunt. Back then, she had been his everything, his world, but now the expectations of the Breeder and the other ferrets had somehow pulled him away from her and made her feel somehow less necessary to his being. Yet on these nights when the Queen's voice shook him from his sleep, She was always there to welcome him back into her arms, and she whispered nothing to him about his abandonment of her.

Once, recently, while returning from a particularly successful hunt during which he had amassed more than double the number of kills of any of the others, he had eavesdropped from his seat up front as she had defended him against the jealous whisperings of the others in the back.

"Of course, he enjoys the favor of our man," one of the older, bitterer jills among them hissed to the others from the wagon bed. "That's because he imagines him to be a great hunter. But would a great hunter not have killed a dozen or more rabbits with his teeth by now instead of always relying upon the fence to do the job?"

Several of the other jills murmured that they were in agreement with this, and his heart felt like it would sink in shame—until he heard the voice of She speak up to her elder.

"A great hunter doesn't have to use his teeth, not when he has cunning and guile."

"What are cunning and guile in the face of brute strength?" shot back the old jill, fully aware of the affection She bore for him, the role she had played in mothering him from the time he was a newborn hob.

"Cunning and guile are the gifts a true hunter brings to make it an honorable fight."

"And who speaks of honor when talking about the hunt?"

"The true hunter never forgets it!" She snapped back, bringing the old jill's whispered accusations to a sudden end. "For even in the midst of the hunt, there is room for mercy."

He was not sure that the dangling rabbit carcasses looking down at him from the fence thought that this was what he was doing when he chased them there, that he was showing them mercy, but he appreciated her willingness to defend him at all costs against the slings and arrows of the others. And though he was unsure still what words like *cunning* and *guile* even meant or how it was thought he possessed them, he nevertheless knew from that day forth that she would defend him no matter what and would be there for him on his troubled nights despite the fact that they seemed to be drifting apart.

And so the days and weeks passed in this manner, with Felix's rise to fame ever on the ascent, the occasional naysayer needing to be put in their place by She. Soon, however, spring gave over to summer, then summer to fall, and there was less hunting for the ferrets to do, particularly when the first snows of winter began to fall. With little work to occupy them, they would spend days at a time doing nothing more than sleeping in the barn and getting fat, seeing neither hide nor hair of the Breeder, who had begun to busy himself in town with business other than the business of his ferrets.

Living in this manner, Felix, too, had begun to grow fat and lazy, waking in the late afternoon only to roll over and dine on the chopped meat the Breeder would leave behind for them every morning before setting off for town. One particular morning, as he was rising to the scent of the food, he happened to notice a light snow falling outside through the open top half of the door and thought with amazement of the complete transformation that had overtaken him since the last time he had seen it fall. So many changes had occurred in his life since the previous winter that he almost could not believe that such a thing was even true—that he, Felix the Red, the Greatest Hunter of Them All, was once derided as a demon and cast out by the others.

Just as he was remarking to himself at the wonder of so much change, the bottom half of the door swung open, and the Breeder came into the barn, holding something in his gloved hands. It seemed ages since Felix had seen him, and he stood himself up on his hind legs to greet him where he came to a halt at the center of the barn.

"How are you today, Little Red?" the Breeder asked as he stood before him.

The others did not bother to stir. And although Felix could not answer him in any way, could not even wag his tail as a dumb dog might to indicate his pleasure, he hoped somehow to telegraph the thought that he was exceedingly happy to see his old friend again.

"I brought you something," the Breeder said after a moment of quiet. Then he crouched to set the thing he had been carrying in his hands down on the ground. It was a ferret, a delicate jill, who looked up at him through a sand-colored mask, which gave over to a warm sable coat. She was nearly his own age, he could tell, though much skinnier and frailer than he had allowed himself to become, and her fur contained the deep brown lushness of a riverbed.

"Little girl tried to keep her as a pet, but her parents wouldn't allow it. Gave her to me, and now I'm giving her to you."

Felix was aware that he had stopped breathing as the jill stretched her snout up to quickly touch his before scurrying off to a far corner of the barn. Light-headed, Felix looked up to the Breeder, who smiled knowingly before moving back toward the door.

"Think she likes ya. It's time to start making little babies of your own."

Then the Breeder was gone, and Felix stood there dumbfounded, not completely sure what to do next. He looked first at the new jill, who had curled herself up into the shadows, her face turned away from him. He thought next of waking She up from where she slept beside the door, but quickly thought better of it. Suppose she told him to avoid the young female? Then what would he do? And so, with no other creature to turn to, for most were still sleeping, he slowly inched himself across the hay until he stood within a body's length of the dazzling new apparition.

He tried to find an opening in her mind to speak, but her words came to him, sharp, before he was able to find the entry point.

"Go away," she said. "I don't wish to speak to you."

Felix received her words like a blow across the snout and quickly hurried back to where he had lain before the Breeder arrived to deliver her into his life. But he watched in fascination all day as she lay there motionless, even after the others had roused themselves and begun to whisper about the new member in their midst. Several of the young hobs had even dared to approach her, as he himself had done, and were brusquely turned away, just as he had been. Each time they made their approach, however, his heart raced in fear that she might deign to speak to them when she had been so quick to dismiss him. And each time they were sent away, his heart felt the unmistakable rush of relief.

When dusk showed itself in the sky and the pall of sleep began to weigh them down once more, Felix realized that the new jill had not stirred herself even once, not even for food or water. He also realized that if he did not somehow find a way to talk to her before the day was done, not even the ferret's curse of sleep sickness would be enough to allow his mind to rest. And so, summoning the last of his courage, he crept across the hay once more and stood over her.

"I'm Felix," he said nervously, not sure if she was even listening. "I'm the hairless one you met when you were first brought here."

He could feel her actively trying to block him out but pressed on nonetheless, like he was chasing a star on one of his hunts. "I'm known by the others as a great hunter, the greatest who lives in the barn. Ask any of them. I've killed more rabbits than all the rest."

Suddenly, she maneuvered herself around so that she was looking directly up at him through her beautiful mask, the sandy color of which made her black eyes sparkle in their settings, even in the half-light. It was only after she began speaking, after he heard the crack in her voice, that he realized that part of the reason they were sparkling was because they were filled with tears.

"This time yesterday I was curled up comfortably in a little girl's bed, waiting for her to sing me to sleep, in a warm human house that didn't smell of animal droppings and ferrets. Now I'm here. Why do you think it would interest me that you've tasted the most blood?"

"But I haven't tasted *any* blood," Felix answered in his defense. "I have cunning and guile instead."

"The only thing you have is arrogance," she said, turning away from him once more. "Now please go away, and leave me alone, you ugly creature."

Felix felt as if he had been pierced through with razor wire at the sound of her words and been hung up bloody from a fence. He stumbled back across the barn to find She, who had witnessed the whole exchange but offered not a word as she curled around him for sleep.

As he suspected, though, he could not rest.

*****

Some days later, the Breeder had released them from the barn to play outside in the snow. It had fallen overnight and was well past his knees when he shuffled through it the next morning to deliver their feed. It was so deep, as a matter of fact, that any ferret interested in trying to make an escape would have had a hard time getting so far as three yards from the barn before he would be able to lay a hand on it. It was not that there were many ferrets looking to escape from such a place, he knew, when he made such a regular effort to clean and feed them well. So he thought it might be amusing to lean against the wagon outside in the snow and smoke his pipe while watching his prized possessions wrestle and cavort in the white powder.

Most amusing of all was his Little Red, whose hairless torso hardly seemed to shrink from the icy touch of the snow. Rather, the frozen powder seemed to invigorate his playful spirit as he tunneled through it enthusiastically and leaped out into the air. The Breeder wore a rare smile on his face as Felix dived down into the snow in one place, only to resurface somewhere else, his piercing red eyes blinking back at him. While most of the others made only tentative moves to immerse themselves in the mysterious substance, remaining huddled back up against the outside wall of the barn, Felix felt completely liberated in his new environment and moved through it as effortlessly as a dolphin moved through the sea.

He was imagining that he was chasing rabbits through their underground burrows, driving them up toward the light. It had been so long since the Breeder had taken them out to do any actual hunting that Felix had started to think he had forgotten how to pick up on their scent and track them to the fence. Playing in the snow was a happy reminder that his body could still move with elegant speed when he desired it to do so despite the extra fat he had managed to put on as of late and that his tracking instincts were still intact, even if the quarry he was chasing did not exist anywhere else but in his own mind. He even went so far as to imagine that he could see their signal lights up ahead of him when he was down beneath the surface of the snow, the brightly colored stars that taunted him to give chase.

After pursuing the reddest star of the largest doe in his imagination up toward the light, Felix breached the surface of the snow with such speed that he soared a good two feet into the air. The Breeder roared with laughter at the sight and applauded the antics of his best hunter as Felix lay on his back for a moment in order to catch his breath, appearing like a heaving wound on the white skin of the earth.

He closed his eyes and felt the warm sunlight on his face, even though the snow was cold at his back. Then, sensing the presence of another close by, he opened his eyes and turned his head to see the new jill standing neck deep alone in the snow, looking off in the direction of town. Felix rolled over onto his belly and slid across the surface of the snow as the Breeder raised a gentle warning to him.

"Keep her close, Little Red."

Felix came up cautiously alongside the jill, whose ear now bore the cross-shaped insignia of her recent branding, but she would not turn to look at him. He knew in that instant, however, what she was contemplating, and he turned his own gaze off in the direction of the distant snow-covered steeples and rooftops of the human enclave.

"You'd never make it back," he said, finding a place in her mind to speak.

"I could try," she responded, with a great sadness in her voice. "I *should* try."

"But even if you managed to outwit the Breeder," he went on, "her mother and father would only return you to him a second time. Better to stay with us."

Something about what he had just said struck a deep chord with her because he could hear her sobbing in her mind even though her dark eyes remained devoid of tears. "Why did they send me away?" she asked, her voice stripped and broken before him.

"Humans don't care for our scent," he answered, determined to console her.

"But she was my mother."

"She was your owner, not your mother. And what's owned can be disowned. Better to stay here with your own kind."

"Is the one you cling to then *your* own mother?"

"Not my mother, no, but nearly so. And she would never send me away for my scent because it's the same scent that she bears. We're alike in that."

He could hear the desperation in his own voice now, desperation to convince her not to make the attempt, not to go. He suddenly could not imagine his life without her, and he racked his brain for the magic combination of words to telegraph that would permanently put the idea out of her head. Finally, the only thing he could think to say was the most unartful and obvious thing of all, the only thing that was true.

"Please don't leave me."

"But you're a killer," she responded after a long pause to consider his words, "a killer who drinks blood."

"I told you I've never tasted the blood of a live creature."

"The Breeder brings you meat covered in blood," she persisted.

"But all ferrets need meat to survive," he argued hopelessly in his own defense, feeling her close herself to him because of the matter. Then a question occurred to him: "What did the girl who was like your mother bring you to eat when you lived among the humans in town?"

He could feel her hesitating to answer, trying to shape a response. When she did at last relent to speak, her words were as clipped and cold as they had been the first day that she had arrived in the barn.

"She brought me the dried bodies of dead mice that weren't covered in gouts of blood."

Felix considered the answer carefully, as though his whole life now depended upon his understanding of the distinction she was trying to make. Finally, however, the illogic of her argument was too great to get around or ignore, and he found himself quaking with laughter as he turned his face away so that she would not see. The jill was nevertheless aware that he was mocking her and shifted her gaze from town for the first time to glare at him.

"What's so funny about that?" she hissed inside his brain.

"You don't believe that a mouse is meat because someone kills it for you and washes it clean?"

"I believe it's important for every creature to maintain its dignity, to be civilized!"

When he finally had the courage to look back at her, he could see that she was still trying to hold on to her haughty sense of superiority, even though she was aware that he had exposed the hypocrisy that made it possible. And for some inexplicable reason, this struggle to maintain appearances only made her more perfect to him at that moment since it exposed an underlying fragility at the core of her imperious strength.

"Then teach me to be civilized," he whispered to her with his whole heart before he was even aware of the words that he would say.

"Well," she said, gathering her composure, "your first lesson is not to laugh at a female's reasoning when she is attempting to explain something to you."

"Would that be the case," he asked teasingly, feeling the sudden need for levity, "even when her reasoning makes no sense?"

"Especially," she shot back with false indignation, warming to his mockery, "when her reasoning makes no sense!"

Then the jill—whose name, he would later learn after much questioning and pleading, was Kara—suddenly sprang up into the air, as high as he ever had, and pounced down upon him, sinking her teeth into the scruff of his neck. The two began to playfully roll around and roughhouse in the snow. The others standing by the barn, including She, observed their play and knew in an instant what the Breeder knew as well. He shook his head from his vantage point by the wagon before lighting his pipe and bringing it to his lips.

"Babies by spring."

CHAPTER 4

The Breeder was right in his prediction. Kara's first liter arrived one morning in the very first days of spring when the snow from that winter had not even fully melted from the ground. The occasion turned out to be a sad one, however, for both offspring came out of their mother's womb dead.

Felix looked down at their lifeless bodies, curled around one another in the hay, both as pink and naked in the straw as he was. Meanwhile, the one who had carried them rested nearby in the arms of She. Exhausted from her labors, Kara was, as yet, unaware that the two were stillborn. Felix could feel the eyes of She gazing at him, measuring his response, as he looked down at the intertwined bodies of his would-be children. They were so tiny and still that he could not even be certain of what sex they were intended to be. Had he just been deprived of sons? Daughters? One of each?

Already he was imagining the words he would have to say to Kara later on once the truth became known. She would blame herself; that much was certain. Over the three months of their courtship and coupling, it had become a regularly recurring joke between them how ill equipped she was to deal with the hard scrapple realities of life in the barn. And she was sure to interpret this as a sign of her own weakness, that she was somehow not meant for the rigors of childbirth.

When he brought her food in the mornings and before dusk, he always first made sure to lick it clean of any signs of excess blood and placed it deliberately down on the ground in front of her like he was a servant in the world of Man, carrying it to her on a silver tray.

"Your dried mouse, madam," he would tease, even when the meat, in all likelihood, was some remnant of the rabbit he had chased down last hunting season.

"Very civilized," she would tease back, lowering her mouth to the food.

He was aware that some of the other ferrets in the barn, the jills in particular, were resentful of his attentions toward her, but he did not care. It was his great pleasure to treat her like a queen, and the fact that she was aware that he was doing so, that she knew he was spoiling her, and that she participated in the charade along with him only made it that much more satisfying. But now that this awful thing had occurred, now that death had been the end result of all their play, he knew that the others would secretly see it as retribution for the false airs she put on around them, and he was quite sure that she would see it that way too.

When the Breeder came and saw the stillbirths lying in the hay, he picked them up with one easy motion and slipped them into the pocket of his coat, like they were nothing more than the coins Felix had seen him use to purchase goods in town. Then he crouched low to the ground and stroked the top of Felix's head with his large hand.

"It's okay, Little Red," he said softly. "Others will come."

Then he stood and left the barn, just as Kara was awakening from her rest and asking to see the children.

The days that followed were some of the most difficult in Felix's life. He never once left Kara's side throughout her grieving, even when it seemed that she might die of despair. As he predicted, she blamed herself for what had happened to the babies and cursed herself for her weakness. Many were the nights he woke up to the sound of her whispered voice inside his head, wishing that she had never been born or that she had never come to this terrible barn and agreed to be his partner in the first place.

Kara still had not fully recovered from her grief the morning the Breeder arrived to collect his team for the first hunt of the season. And while a part of Felix was anxious at the thought of leaving her for the day, another part was secretly relieved that he now had some excuse to spend a few hours away from the heaviness of her sadness.

It had been so long since he thought of anything but his mate and her sorrow. He was eager to put all thoughts aside, if that were even possible, and give himself over to the blind instinct of the hunt once more.

This time, the job was to ferret a colony of rabbits out from underneath the expansive house of a wealthy local merchant. The house was constructed out of wood, and the merchant had sought to have a wide porch built all along the front and right side of the house so that he could stand out on it at night with his cognac and watch carriages pass along the road, heading to and from town. The rabbits had dug themselves underneath the porch shortly after the house was completed and established a complex warren via a vast system of tunnels that they hollowed out of the soft earth. The wire fence the Breeder had been required to install the night before was, therefore, given the scale of the challenge, much larger than any fence he had ever had to ring around a tree.

Felix could hear the Breeder talking to the Merchant above him as he slipped through a hole that the rabbits had torn in the wood lattice and entered the cool darkness below the porch. He had no idea how he would perform that day, if his hunting skills were still there to access or if they had abandoned him through the long winter. He only knew that he was out of the barn, away from Kara's tears, and curious to find out for himself if he still had the instincts that distinguished him as a great hunter before she came into his life.

The earth beneath his feet was cold, saturated with the waters of the melting snow, and all smelled of moss and damp. While the other ferrets nosed their way down into the ground via the tunnel holes they found at the front of the house, Felix skirted around these carefully and instead tiptoed to the side of the house, with the idea that the rabbits would choose to hide their most precious possessions furthest away from the entry point into their lair. He found precisely one hole dug into the earth when he came around the side of the house, and it was down that tunnel that he immediately slid himself.

Behind him, he could still make out the echo of the Merchant's hearty laugh, and the earth around him was beginning to vibrate with the rustle of underground movement; the rabbits were becoming aware of the ferrets' invasion. Despite this trembling activity, however, Felix himself had become stuck in the tunnel. The cold dirt surrounding him had unexpectedly narrowed and trapped him nearly upside down in its muddy grip.

Normally, when a burrow went dead on him like this, he merely reversed himself in the tunnel and backed up to the surface to try another tack. Even with the earth's hold around him tighter than usual with the added moisture, he knew he had the strength to free himself in just that manner. Something about his dilemma, though, caused him to remain in his unfortunate position for a long min-ute—upside down, buried alive in mud—even as the vibrations caused by all the underground commotion were growing more and more pronounced.

"What had he done with them?" he found himself wondering in that strange moment of suspended animation. "Once the Breeder slipped them into his pocket? Did he bury them outside in the ground like this, the way I've seen him bury others when their life runs out? Or did he just toss them off into the grass for the cats to eat, thinking that they were too small to make the effort? What has become of my children?"

Then another thought occurred to him more surprising than the first as, all around him, the ground was erupting in an earthquake of panic. What if Kara was not the weak one after all? What if the cause of their death was not some fundamental flaw on her part but his? Had it not been little more than a year ago that he was pinned back up against the wall of the barn by the others who were calling him demon, calling him a freak? Maybe they had been right back then. Maybe he *was* a freak. And everything that followed afterward, the radical reversal of his fortunes—maybe it was all just built upon a lie. Was there really any way to transform from what you truly were into something you wished to be?

Maybe they were right about him from the start, and he had only been arrogantly pretending otherwise since. Maybe the only thing he ever was, that he would ever be, was a freak—not Felix the Red, Greatest Hunter of Them All, but Felix the Freak, who had had the foolish audacity to mate with a creature infinitely finer than he could ever be, who had deceived her into thinking that he was something other than he was, a freak whose blood had contaminated hers, brought monsters into the world, brought death…his contaminated blood…his blood…

Overtaken by a kind of rage he had never known before, a rage fueled by the recognition of his true nature, Felix began tearing at the muddy wall that blocked the path in front of him rather than to reverse, as he had planned to do. He could feel the nails of his front paws bend, then break, as he scratched away handfuls of earth, compelling himself forward with a singular idea: "It was my blood that did it…mine…"

Then the wall in front of him that seemed so impassable suddenly gave way, and Felix tumbled end over end into a vast galaxy of stars. For the floor that he had been digging at was also the roof of the rabbits' underground warren, and once the two became one, Felix was deposited directly into the heart of the nest. There were giant stars of every conceivable color exploding all around him as the rabbits fled, and Felix immediately leaped at the boldest and reddest of these, clamping his jaws around its throat.

He could feel the warm liquid surging at the back of his throat and clamped down even harder to deny his repulsion at the infusion of the hot, sticky substance. Then he began to hear the rabbit's own pounding pulse start to reverberate in his inner ear as their heartbeats joined together and began to syncopate. And then a pinpoint of white light at the center of the galaxy widened in his mind's eye until it had eliminated all the other stars and she was hanging there before him once more, the first rabbit he had ever crucified, the Queen. Her body ran with rivers of blood from each of her many wounds as she looked down upon him unblinkingly from her hanging place, just as she had done the morning of his first hunt. Then her voice whispered to him once more from somewhere inside the slowing heartbeat.

"Ever has it been so. A creature seeks to outrun itself by trampling upon another. *(Ever…)* A creature seeks to deny its hate by hating another. *(Ever has it…)* A creature seeks dominion over another because it has no dominion over itself. *(Ever…)* Ever has it been. Ever shall it be. *(Ever…)* And you are forgiven, Felix, my love. *(Ever my love...)* As are all creatures... *(Ever...)* everlastingly... *(Ever...)* forgiven."

Once the Queen disappeared from his inner vision, the rabbit in his jaws hung limp and still. He had done it. He had killed with his teeth, tasted blood for the first time. And for a brief moment, he felt temporarily relieved of the doubts that had plagued him since the morning of the stillbirths, since the Queen herself had blessed and forgiven him for all that was in his nature to be.

Later, when it was all over, Felix could hardly remember the details of the hunt at all. The last thing he could recall with any certainty was carrying the dead rabbit up to the surface—it was another large doe, just as the first had been—and laying its body flat out on the grass before diving back underneath the porch. What followed was the familiar blur of battle only more so as Felix gave himself over to it completely, supercharged by the taste of blood in his mouth and his desire to forget. He would kill nearly a dozen rabbits that day— some with his teeth, others on the fence—but he never once thought again about his two dead children or his own contaminated blood.

When the last of the rabbit bodies had been bagged and tossed into the back of the wagon, Felix and the others were allowed to drowse on the lawn in front of the Merchant's house in a pile, while the men sat up on the porch, enjoying their pipes and cognac. Felix's raw skin was still caked with the blood of the creatures he had killed, but he was too tired from his exertions to clean it off just yet. He lay there contently at the center of a sea of ferrets—smelling of earth and musk and blood—and allowed his thoughts to drift down into nothingness.

When he awoke, he could tell that he had been sleeping for some time. Despite the warm bodies around him, some cooler night air had begun seeping into the pile to reach him where he lay, and he nosed his way through the walls of fur until he could get a sense of where the sun was at in the sky.

When he poked his head out, he could tell that the sky had indeed grown darker, that several hours had been allowed to pass. He could also see that there were three men on the porch now, smoking and drinking: the Breeder, the Merchant, and the Smeller of Blood.

Felix let out a small involuntary yip of surprise as he acknowledged the presence of this unpleasant human standing by the railing and smoking his cigar while staring down at him.

"I'm telling you," the Merchant was saying while pacing behind him, stopping only to clap the Breeder on the back, "that demon's a natural-born killer! I've seen it with my own eyes! You'll be sure to get a pretty penny for him because that one is a *killer!*"

The Breeder was somewhat sunk down in his chair, the long hours of drinking having gotten the better of him, but he roused himself to speak at this. Even as he did, the Smeller of Blood's gaze never once moved off Felix.

"Now nothin's been finally decided," the Breeder slurred. "I'm just allowin' my thoughts out t' breathe. I'm not sayin' that I'm willin' to sell just yet."

"You have to give something to get something, my boy!" the Merchant boomed. "You can't expect to get yourself a wife without giving a little something in return! Besides, they're desperate down there! You're liable to make yourself a fortune in the process!"

"All I'm sayin' ith… I'll think about it," the Breeder slurred and then allowed his head to drop over the back of the chair before closing his eyes.

"He'll think about it." The Merchant sighed, poking the air with his pipe while taking back up his pacing. "Did you hear that? Best opportunity of his life presents itself, and he'll think about it. Well, he better think fast because there's a fortune to be made here for those wise enough to make it. And I'm telling you, I've seen it with my own eyes! That demon's a killer! A natural-born *killer!*"

Though he was uncertain of what their words actually meant, Felix was fairly certain from the way the Smeller of Blood's eyes bore down from the top of the porch that they were talking about him.

And that something in his life was about to change.

CHAPTER 5

Change arrived several months later in the form of a mysterious young woman in a muslin dress with a plain white bonnet tied under her chin. She appeared up the dirt road to the barn one afternoon, riding up front in the wagon alongside the Breeder. Once the Breeder brought the horses to a halt, he immediately leaped down from the seat and began lifting a great many suitcases and boxes out of the bed of the wagon and setting them down on the dry grass at his feet. Meanwhile, the young woman continued to look straight ahead at the scene unfolding before her, the parasol on her shoulder partially obscuring her features in its shade.

There had been a brutally hot stretch of weather in late May of that year, with temperatures regularly soaring so high that the Breeder had already made the decision not to accept any new jobs or to take his little hunters out until matters cooled themselves off a bit. As a result of being trapped in the barn day after day under these conditions, however, the ferrets had made the place almost unbearable to enter with the combined odors of their natural musk and steaming waste. Before setting out for town that morning—and possibly as a way of impressing the visitor he was about to retrieve, who would not have to suffer the smell—the Breeder had arranged for Amos to come over that morning and perform one of his annual cleanings.

Amos had only just turned sixteen but looked even younger than his years. To anyone who had ever seen him work out in the fields, though, he was commonly regarded as one of the hardest working farmhands in the county, besting men two and three times his age. His father owned several hundred acres of winter wheat land just a mile or so west of the Breeder's property; and between October, when the wheat was planted, and the following September, when it was harvested, Amos proved himself an invaluable resource in bringing the crop to market. In the slower months, however, throughout winter and spring, when mostly what there was left to do was to wait on the wheat and watch, Amos's father lent out his services for a small profit to any of his neighbors who might find themselves in need of help.

So it was that the Breeder had arranged with the father to have his son come by that morning in May to rake out all the old hay from the barn and replace it with new after scrubbing down the walls. Amos looked forward to the job each year since he enjoyed the ferrets, even visited them in the high season sometimes just to play on those rare days when there was no other work for him to do. He arrived that morning early, even before the Breeder had set forth to town, and by the time he had returned in the afternoon with the young woman, all the old bedding was gone, replaced by fresh new hay, and the walls of the barn had been so thoroughly scrubbed that there was hardly any lingering vestige of the ferrets' foul stench.

What the young woman saw when she looked down from the wagon, however, gave little evidence of the hours of backbreaking work that had gone into making the place presentable to her. What she saw was a shirtless faun of a boy with golden curls, a woodland nymph straight out of an engraving she had once admired, frolicking on the grass with a dozen or more of the most curious creatures she had ever beheld.

Having finished the job that was left for him to do ahead of schedule (not an unusual occurrence for him), Amos had taken it upon himself to give each one of the ferrets a bath before returning them to the barn. Climbing into the circular pen of chicken wire that the Breeder had constructed for warehousing his business, Amos set down a tall bucket of water he had been carrying, planning on dipping each one of the ferrets inside before scrubbing them clean with a bar of soap.

As with all best-laid plans (of mice, of men, and of ferrets), Amos's started going awry the second the first ferret was dipped into the water. The moment he felt the cold on his skin, Scruffer immediately began scratching at Amos's grip and thrashing about with his legs. His back paw managed to grab hold of the lip of the bucket and topple it, instantly soaking the other ferrets, who had been gathered together around the boy. Now the pen was a riot of soaked and partially soaked ferrets performing their weasel war dance en masse while dodging around Amos's feet, trying to trip the boy, as he gleefully chased and lunged after them.

The Breeder came around the back now to offer his hand to the young woman and to help her down from the wagon. He, too, seemed to have been given a thorough scrubbing as of late, for his hair was damp and neatly combed into place and he seemed altogether cleaner and more presentable in his Sunday clothes than he had appeared in quite some time.

Felix took note of this as the woman moved closer to the makeshift pen. He had been stretched out next to Kara in the heat, his head resting on her side, when the wagon had first pulled up. Scruffer's tipping of the water bucket and the subsequent chaos it incited had stirred him from a dream of stars, just as the Breeder was helping the woman down. All the commotion in the world, though, could not rouse Kara from one of her sleeps once she had sunk to the depths, and she lay there still as death despite all the shouting and movement about her. She spent more and more of her time now in these impregnable states of slumber since the day her offspring were born into the world unalive; it seemed the only way she could cope with the loss despite all of Felix's efforts to raise her spirits.

The young woman released the Breeder's hand and lowered her parasol as she arrived at the perimeter of the pen. Aware now that he was being observed up close, Amos clamped down on the youthful enthusiasm he had allowed to bubble over and straightened himself to address her. It took all the strength of his concentration, however, not to stare at the large violet-colored birthmark emblazoned on her right cheek.

"Are these the ferrets then?" she asked in a voice filled with sadness.

Clearly she was asking this of the Breeder, but he was still too tongue-tied himself to answer her. Instead he looked to Amos and widened his eyes perceptibly in a plea for him to speak on his behalf.

"Yes, ma'am," Amos answered after clearing his throat and internally reminding himself not to stare too directly at the birthmark on her face. It was not that she was unattractive, he argued with himself silently. She was lean and straight, her features mostly ordinary but fine in their way. His mother would say that she was a handsome woman—not pretty, per se, but handsome. But that purple mark taking up nearly half of her face looked, to his eyes, to be drawn in the shape of Africa. How was anyone ever going to look beyond the Dark Continent stitched to her face in order to see the beauty underneath?

The woman smiled at him and bent forward at the waist to get a closer look at the animals. It was a sweet smile, he thought. Still, it was no wonder that her people had packed her up and shipped her off to be married to a strange man in a foreign country, as he had heard his mother describe to some of the local gossips when the subject had come around to the Breeder.

"Can you imagine it?" she squawked, sucking at her teeth and shaking her head. "What kind of woman allows herself to be bought like cattle?"

This kind, he thought, as she reached down into the pen and began to stroke Felix gently on the top of the head with the fingers of her right hand. Felix rose to his feet in response to her gentle touch and leaned himself against the wire of the pen to allow her to continue.

"And what is this one's name without any hair?" she asked, softly cooing. "He is so odd-looking."

Suddenly feeling ashamed of himself and his mother both, Amos leaped over the ferrets crowded around his feet and grabbed Felix by the scruff of the neck, lifting him up as the woman straightened and stepped back from the pen.

"This one, ma'am?" Amos smiled, tossing back his golden curls as he held the ferret out at arm's length. "This one's name is Little Red. Take him, why don't you?"

The Bride turned to her nervous groom, who smiled and nodded his permission. She then reached her hands out tentatively to take Felix from the boy and to gather him in her arms. Felix snuggled himself against the Bride's chest and took in her talcum scent as he heard her softly breathe out his name.

"Little Red."

*****

The cloak of sadness that had once shrouded the Breeder in a kind of preternatural gloom slowly lifted itself over the course of the next few weeks as he and his bride settled into their new life together up in the big house. Whatever initial misgivings he might have had about the arrangement, owing to the unexpected stain upon her face, were gradually worn away by the many things she was willing to do as a wife to make his house a home and to make a man look beyond such things. By the time the heat finally broke in early June and they were back once more taking ferreting assignments, he found himself whistling as he steered the wagon to their destination at the start of the day and whistling all the way home at the end.

The ferrets in the barn, naturally, took note of the Breeder's new disposition and grew concerned. Ferrets, on the whole, are rather change-adverse creatures, and seeing their lord and master transform from his familiar sullen self to something noticeably more ebullient had the opposite effect than the one you might expect. Though they loved him in their way, they worried that his newfound happiness might somehow drive him away from them and lead to their neglect.

"What if he forgets to feed us?" Scruffer would moan at the end of the day as they crawled into their sleep pile, even though the Breeder had never once done so.

"What if he takes to lying in the big house all day with that ugly mate of his?" some of the older jills would then chime in. "He's a male, after all. You know how powerless they are to resist the allure of the female. Suppose she entices him to stay with her all day up in her nest and he stops taking us out to go hunting? Then the men won't give him the golden coins any longer to feed us, and we'll starve. What if that happens?"

Felix sighed wearily at these nightly speculations and tried his best to block out their voices from his mind. It seemed to him they should be happy for the Breeder, that he had found someone to share his loneliness with, even if he had to send for her halfway around the world. Were not all creatures meant to share their lives with a mate, just as he had been in sharing his with Kara?

Then again...

Kara.

He lowered his eyes to where she was curled up sleeping by his side. What had he ever done for her by inviting her to share his loneliness other than to fill her with dead children and leave her in this state of perpetual sleep? Would she ever fully wake up again and come back to him? See what his longing for a mate had done to her? And as Felix lifted himself slowly, restlessly, and made his way across the barn to talk with She, he could not help but think that, knowing what he knew of love, it was not the Breeder who was at risk from the Bride but perhaps the other way around.

She could not sleep either; the idle chatter of the others was too loud. When Felix came upon her in the evening shadow, he found her curled up in the hay but looking up through the opened top half of the barn door, watching as the sun gave way to stars. He sat down beside her and quickly found an easy route to her thoughts.

It had been a while since they had talked at length as mother and son, if indeed that was what they were, not since the morning of the stillbirths, anyway. Back then he had been too ashamed of his own shame to share what he was thinking and feeling with her and sought instead to make his way through the tangle of emotions on his own. But the taste of blood was growing thick in the back of his throat from all the killing he had done since then to try and take his revenge out on a world that would have visited such sadness upon them, and still Kara was not getting any better. He needed to speak to his mother now despite how badly he had treated her as of late, and he was thrilled that she allowed him access to enter as soon as he sought her out.

"They never stop worrying about the Bride," he began, "all their foolish speculations."

"How is she today?" his mother whispered back, and he knew that she was not wasting any time talking about the Bride, that She had cut directly to the reason that he was here: Kara.

"The same." Felix sighed, admitting defeat.

"You mustn't blame yourself for this." Her voice was all around him now in its warm embrace, and he could see the starlight reflected in the dark pools of her eyes. "I see what it has done to you on the hunt. It's changed you. You're thinking that the stain of your unhappiness can somehow be washed away through blood, but it can't be. There's not enough blood in the world to save the ones we love if they will not be saved."

"But I think of Princess," he confessed, his voice wavering like a baby's, "how she willed herself to die after seeing what had become of Hector. And I don't wish for that to happen to Kara."

"Whether it happens or not," She responded, "there's very little you can do to stop it. You are just a single creature in the vast world. These things don't rest entirely upon your back. True, you have proven yourself to be a great hunter, but that alone is no guarantee that you can save her. In the end, you're just one ferret among many."

"But I love her," he whispered, his voice trailing off.

"And see what that love has made of you. Even in the midst of the hunt, there is room for mercy. But your love has robbed you of your mercy."

He knew that She was right, that his love for Kara had somehow changed him for the worse, even if he did not want to admit that it was true. So he sat there for a while in silence, allowing the sleep to grow heavy upon him, and watched as the pinpoints of light grew brighter in her gaze until he felt as though his whole body was being drawn into the depths of her eyes, that he was drifting through the stars that they contained.

"What terrible things creatures will justify in the name of love."

"Surely not the Breeder, though," he whispered, nestling into her side as he might have in older days, even as he continued to drift through the stars. "For he is plainly in love with his new bride, yet he continues to treat us with kindness, even more so than usual."

"Don't be so sure of the Breeder's heart, my love. These things take a while to reveal themselves."

"Now you sound like one of the old jills." He sighed, releasing himself fully to drift and sleep.

"Do I?" She giggled, feeling the spirit go out of him and knowing that she was talking to herself alone now. "Maybe I do," she thought, blinking away the stars as her own eyes grew heavy with sleep. "Maybe I do."

*****

That night, the dream was more vivid than usual, the stars exploding across the canvas of his resting mind with greater force and frequency, in darker shades of color than he had ever imagined before. There was something else different, too, about that night's dreaming in addition to the violent display of color. The dream was now filled with the sound of voices screaming, a chorus of ferrets crying out for mercy, as though the entire business was suddenly being drowned in a shared ocean of sorrow. Felix could feel himself fighting against the dream, trying to resist its speed and volume even as it increased in intensity, and he felt himself tumbling ever deeper into its vortex of despair...

Suddenly he was awake but unsure exactly of where he was. It took him a moment to conclude that the shining white disk glowing above him was, in fact, the full moon. Given the general condition of their sleep sickness, most ferrets might not ever gaze upon the full moon, and it took him a moment to locate an earlier memory of the object—of waking from a dream of being taunted and ridiculed for his differences when he was very young and seeing it hover in the sky through the barn door—to properly place what it was he was seeing.

But he was not in the barn now, not looking out through the open door, as he had been when he was young, a matter that further confounded his sense of knowing where he was. He could feel the cool night breeze on his skin, smell the scent of grass over hay and musk, and finally concluded that he must be outdoors, fully out in the open. But for the life of him, he could not recall how it was he had gotten himself there.

He rolled over from his back and saw behind, to his left, the barn, inside of which lay Kara and She and all the others. He immediately felt a kind of sadness come over him, to be so close and yet so far away from all the things that he loved most. When he turned away to his right to avoid the sensation, he saw looming above him, like a giant, the dark outline of the Breeder, who was silhouetted by the lighted windows of the big house behind him.

So he had been lifted out of the barn and carried outside by the Breeder to rest in the grass at his feet. But why?

"Don't think I won't miss you, Little Red," the Breeder said, raising his pipe to his lips and drawing in the smoke. Once more his voice contained the familiar sadness that it always had before the Bride had arrived to change all that. "I'll miss you very much. But a man has to think of his future. He can't be expected to spend his whole life alone, living on the edge of civilization with a bunch of stinking ferrets. How is that any way to live?"

Because he was speaking with his words and not his thoughts, Felix had no way of knowing what the Breeder was trying to communicate to him. He only knew that he was sad and that he was trying to explain the cause of that sadness. Searching for clues that might help him to somehow interpret his meaning, Felix looked past the Breeder and saw, through the lighted windows, the Bride moving about in the big house, happily preparing their nest for sleep. From this distance, the stain upon her face was hardly visible at all, and by the amber glow of the candlelight that filled the house, she seemed rather beautiful—for a human female.

How was it that the Breeder could still be so sad with such a companion waiting behind for him to join her?

"Everything I earn is spent on caring for you lot," the Breeder went on, exhaling a great cloud of smoke, as Felix watched the Bride turn down the covers of their bed. "How could I ever afford to get myself a wife if I went on like that? And I'm earning twice as much by sending you off than I would be by keeping you here and hunting locally. They're desperate for your kind down there and are willing to pay handsomely for it. A man's got to think about keeping his wife happy, doesn't he? You understand, Little Red, don't you?"

Felix did not understand, was not even aware that he was being asked to understand. In the end, the ways of Man were far too alien for him to make out, and he eventually stopped searching for meaning in the words the Breeder was saying or the movements of the Bride behind him. Instead he rolled once more onto his back and gazed up at the full moon, basking in its glow and the comforting scent of the pipe smoke wafting down upon him as though dropping from the moon itself.

These were the things that he would recall later on about that night once the screaming voices that had awakened him to it had become a living reality; that the Bride was unblemished and beautiful, as seen from a distance through the window; that the Breeder was somehow sad, nonetheless; and that he, Felix, was the only ferret he knew who had gazed upon a full moon twice.

*****

From a full-page advertisement in *The Daily Telegraph*:

Ministers to the Newly Appointed Gov't.
of
New Zealand
(North Island, Wellington)
in joint-cooperation with
Her Majesty's Gov't.
and
The New Zealand Company (founded 1839)

hereby announce the award of £7.52 sterling per/head to any Breeder in the Realm who might supply to the Colony fully trained hunting ferrets for the purposes of combatting the scourge of Invasive Verminous Populations that pose a threat to life, property, and Economy.

Breeders will only be compensated for hearty specimens who manage to survive the journey alive and intact, traveling from London by way of the Suez Route.

CHAPTER 6

It was the smell that first alerted him to the fact that something was not quite right, that indeed something was terribly wrong. He had been dreaming of two moons hanging together side by side in the same dark sky when it came to him and tore him from the pleasant fog of sleep, the dreaded scent of the Smeller of Blood.

When he opened his eyes, he could not at first make out what he was witnessing, given that there was some membrane, some fabric, draped across his snout, complicating his vision. In addition, there were ferrets squirming about him on all sides, just now awakening as he was to their new reality, and their mass confusion only added to his own as he began to claw at the material, trying desperately to peel away the veil so that he might see. And still the odor of the Smeller of Blood permeated the chaos of the scene, surrounding them; so thick was the scent upon him.

Even as he tore away at the obstruction, Felix was able to make out the dark contours of several humans hovering above him on the opposite side of the veil, their backs to the sun. Presently, he was able to identify the silhouettes as those belonging to the Breeder and the Bride. A moment after making this realization, Felix made a second more horrifying one that froze his paws midmotion. He was inside the burlap sack.

He suddenly recognized the familiar crosshatch of the material that he had seen up close a hundred times coming home from the hunt, though always from the outside. Now he and the others were inside, looking out, an alarming new perspective. And they were alive, not dead, as the occupants of the sack before them had always been. Surely a terrible mistake had been made. How could the Breeder and his wife mistake him and the others for rabbits? They were the hunters, not the prey. He would have to claw even harder, tear a hole through the mesh and warn them of their mistake before matters escalated any further.

Try as he might, his claws flashing before him in a blur of desperate activity, Felix was unable to tear a hole in the burlap. His nails were repeatedly caught in the tiny perforations of the fabric, causing him to spend half his energies pulling his paws free before he could go at the sack once more. Meanwhile, the foul stench of carnage only grew more concentrated, more potent, as a third silhouette joined the other two in staring down from above.

"That the last of 'em then?" said the Smeller of Blood, his voice as insinuating as his smell.

"I suppose," answered the Breeder, his own voice retaining the same tone of wistful sadness from the night before. "Please be gentle with them," he added. "They were my life."

"I'll be gentle with 'em," the blood man sighed. "Ain't none of us being paid for deliverin' a bunch of dead ferrets, is we now?"

A moment after the Smeller of Blood's shadow disappeared from view, Felix saw the outline of the Breeder extend itself down toward him as though he were reaching out to grab hold of him. He had realized the error of his ways! His hand was right there, just on the other side of the membrane. Felix could smell the opened palm despite the Smeller's heavy odor. How many times had he been stroked to sleep by that selfsame palm? And now it was reaching down to rescue him. He was saved!

Then the earth shook, and the Breeder's shadow was torn from him, disappeared into the burning sky. Now he was moving, violently crashing up and down with the others, as the air inside the sack grew hot and thin and pandemonium reigned. Ferrets began kicking and clawing at one another, desperate to breathe, as the stains of their own blood began to appear on the inside walls of the burlap canvas.

"Where is he taking us?" their minds screamed, setting off an agonized chorus of panic.

"We're to be skinned alive as Hector was!"

"All for the Bride!"

"So that she might have our skins to keep her hands warm!"

"You should have listened to me! The Bride's to blame!"

Felix fought the urge to add his voice to the chorus and instead forced himself to grow still and concentrate all his thoughts on trying to locate Kara or She amid the mayhem. His clear line of searching was unable to break through the cacophony of voices, however, so he eventually suspended his attempts to reach them for the time being and focused instead on trying to determine where the wagon was taking them.

He had already concluded from the bumps and potholes he knew all too well that they were riding in the back of a wagon, a wagon much like the one the Breeder drove himself, along the rutted dirt road that led from the barn all the way into town. Once the most violent jolts had ceased, replaced by the more regular bouncing of the cobblestoned road, Felix knew that they were passing through the human settlement, continuing on to someplace beyond.

Initially at least, it seemed like good news, for was it not in town that Hector had last been seen in his final form? It hardly seemed plausible that any one human female could require this many hand warmers. Still, he could not help but wonder as to their final destination or why the Breeder had seen fit to bundle them off in such a strange fashion.

Were they headed back to the rolling green estate of Red Face to pursue their enemy a second time through the labyrinthine network of tunnels beneath his ash tree? Or was it, rather, back to the Merchant's house by the side of the road that they were headed in order to do battle once more in the earthy loam hidden beneath his porch? Felix knew that it was foolish to speculate since it could be to these or any of the other hunting sites the Breeder had taken them to in the past, which was almost too many to recall. But in the absence of his ability to make contact with his two most important jills, he kept at it all the same in the hopes of anticipating what might happen next.

After much time had passed in the wagon, more time than he had ever spent traveling before, Felix knew they were headed someplace that they had never previously been, somewhere far beyond the reach of the human settlement. By this point, the early desperation of the ferrets inside the sack along with him had come to a virtual standstill, the heat and lack of oxygen causing the others to lapse into an impotent torpor, as any hope for deliverance had abandoned them. Some even sank into fitful sleep under the circumstances, periodically kicking out at their burlap shroud as demons from their nightmares pressed in upon them.

Felix fought against the temptation that such relief through sleep might bring and used the unexpected calm that had settled over them to attempt to contact his jills once more. Through a dense curtain of susurrating fears and anxieties, he was finally able to locate the mind of She, barely clinging to the edge of consciousness.

"Is that you, Mother?" he asked tentatively, for he had never encountered her this way, at such a low ebb of being.

"It's me," She whispered back after a long delay, her voice so thin that it hardly registered as a thought in his mind.

"Are you here with me?" he pressed on after acknowledging how weak she was.

"I'm with Kara, and we're close by but not in the same sack. The Smeller of Blood has divided us into hobs and jills."

Though he could tell that it was taking all her strength to respond to his queries, he had to go on; he had to know how his mate was faring through this ordeal.

"Kara is sleeping," She answered before he could form the words in his head. "She's sleeping, but she's fine, as fine as she ever was in the barn. Since she had already sacrificed the last of her hope, she had no hope left to lose. She merely sleeps. To look at her, you wouldn't think that anything's changed."

"But what about you, Mother?" he asked after digesting her report of Kara's condition.

"As for me," her voice echoed, fading out, "it's here that I leave you."

"But you can't!" he shouted, the sudden volume of his exclamation causing the ferrets around him to leap in their fevered dreams.

"I must," She whispered back, smiling. "For hope was all that I had to sustain me in my old age, and now that hope is gone."

"But you mustn't give up!" he exhorted, shouting across the divide. "The Breeder would never betray us to our deaths! Wherever the Smeller of Blood is taking us, surely there must be some hope there!"

"Wherever the Smeller of Blood is taking us," She continued, the tone of her voice growing thicker as it seeped into the burlap sack along with him, surrounding him, "I'm sure it is a place I wasn't meant to live to see. I've seen too much already. I can't survive yet another horror visited upon us by mankind. You can because you are young, my love, and because you have cunning and guile. But you'll need my help. And that is why I must go from you."

"You can't leave me just yet," he faltered, even as he gave over to the encompassing embrace of her voice and allowed it to carry him back to the barn, where it was night once more and he could look up from her side and see her looking down at him, the crown of her head haloed in stars.

"I only leave so that I can be with you once more," She whispered enigmatically, her eyes glistening in the starlight with love for him.

"But I don't know where I'm going," he whimpered, his voice sounding weak and frail to him now as he had once more become the tiny outcast he had been before his gifts had been revealed to the others, when She alone had loved him well.

"Wherever it is, I will be with you always. Remember that. But sleep now. For you'll need all your strength for what comes next."

Then She was gone.

And all was darkness.

*****

So little of what we once were is left behind after we are gone. All that remains is a shell, really, the vaguest outline of the costume we wore when the spirit was within us and we had our brief hour walking about on the earth, having our say, loving and hating in equal measure. Be the final remains cloaked in skin or fur hardly makes a difference in the end since they will only ever be what they are—remains. And so little of what remains can ever truly tell the story of who or what it was to which they were once so inextricably attached.

The following day, once the ship had moved out of harbor and disappeared over the horizon line, the children of England would sift along the muddy banks of the Thames, retrieving the many dead bodies of the ferrets that were judged too old or too feeble to make the journey and were therefore tossed into the river to drown. To gather up their strange collection, these children would have to step over the many drunken reprobates of London, who returned nightly to the shores of the river to make their bed. Still, it was an obstacle course well worth running, for even in death, the prospect of possessing an animal as a playmate, any animal, is a powerful inducement to most children.

There were hundreds of bodies washed up on the shore that day, for the Breeder was only one of the many ferret handlers stretched out across the countryside who had shipped their animal cargo off to London on the preordained date for delivery to a land located halfway around the world, that few would ever look upon in his lifetime. With bouquets of dead ferrets gathered in their arms, the children of England would return to their homes in the blackened city and sneak the bodies inside until time and decay made it clear to their parents that there was something amiss hidden beneath their beds. Until such discovery was made, the children would take out the bodies they had found when they were on their own and seek to breathe a sort of second life back into them by the power of their imaginations. Many high-sea adventures were acted out in this manner with the bodies of dead ferrets on the quilted seas of bedrooms across London until the inevitable rot and its attendant odor brought an end to these reanimating scenarios.

Once the grim discovery was made, most human parents responded as you might imagine, given their species' historical antipathy toward death—by casting it out. And so for many days after the ship had sailed, the streets of the city were filled again with a second tide of ferret carcasses.

Most were content to allow the corpses to thus be slowly ground to extinction beneath the wheels of passing carriages, much as the daily spectacle might cause their offspring to despair, as they looked down from their windows and beheld the gradual desiccation of what was once their imaginary playmate. Some, however, the ones thought to be foolishly indulgent in the eyes of their breed, sought to win a pathway to their scions' hearts by collateralizing a perishable negative into a lasting positive. These spoilers would stay up at night, skinning the hide off the bodies and stuffing them with strips of cloth, fashioning the corpses into dolls that would become the envy of the adolescent flock.

And so it was that She, once so magnificently alive, came to be nothing more than an effigy of her former self, a stuffed doll played with for a short while by a human girl child in thick braids and then abandoned upon a high shelf with all the other dollies that had been crafted to win her love. There She stood for years, undisturbed, looking out silently at the world through button eyes until the day, many years later, when the house itself burned down to the ground and she was released.

In all that time, it was never once suspected by her human handlers that at one point in her journey, She had acted as adoptive mother to a hideously naked ferret named Felix, nicknamed Little Red; that she had rescued him from the heartbreak of his loneliness and steered him to become the Greatest Hunter of Them All; that she could speak to him through her thoughts and he to her; or that she knew what great, great love was before she passed because she had felt it for him.

Upon what evidence would such conjectures be made? The evidence of fur and bone? Of blood and entrails? How so when such things as these can be ground into nothingness beneath the wheels of a wagon?

Again, so little of what we truly were is left after we are gone. And yet...

And yet who is to say that all the blood and bone and slippery substance of our physical forms may not, in fact, be little more than the temporal carapace for something eternal lingering inside? And who is to say that it is not this eternal something, more than any feature of our passing forms, that alone tells the true story of who we were, who we are, a thing as lasting as the earthly body is perishable?

They say that if you cut off the leaf of a plant, it sets out a cry that is heard and responded to by the other plants around it; they have proved it in a lab. What are these silent cries, transmitted and received, other than the eternal part of a plant, a part that could never be suspected if we took its essence to be merely stem and leaf? And if such is the case with plants, can we not also surmise that it would be the case with all living creatures? Even ferrets?

What remained of She after her physical being had passed was no more than what could be used to fashion a little girl's stuffed toy. But even as the knife was seaming her down the middle to initiate her new life as a cloth doll, the eternal part inside was awakening to the sound of her Felix, who was crying for her somewhere off in the far distance. (If it can be so for plants, why not for ferrets?) And even as the ship that bore him in its dark hold was steaming south toward the western mouth of the Mediterranean; even as her insides were being lifted out onto a table, the carcass scraped clean; and even as her eyes were being removed from their sockets, her spirit had begun to return to consciousness after a brief lapse, and she was already devising ways to set it free so that it might fly to him and rescue him from his despair. It would take some time to command her new circumstances, she knew, but she also knew, eventually, that they would be together once more.

Who is to say it could not be so?

PART II

Passage

CHAPTER 7

Gone are the canvas sails and elaborate riggings that gave the first ship to arrive into our story the appearance of being an awesome mythical creature capable of great winged flight. For it is now 1884, and for nearly a century's worth of time, James Watt and that whole bunch had done their best to make cloth and rope obsolete with the invention and manufacture of their modern steam engine. It is the steamship now that is primarily used for transporting populations to and fro across the oceans of the earth against their will. And no creature in the world—not even one as foolish as the gray parrot Dakari—would ever make the mistake of confusing the steel-girded, smoke-belching steamship for anything like a bird.

As plainly uncreature-like as the steamship might appear from the outside, however, it did in fact possess a heart, which was the engine of the ship itself, beating from the dark hidden recesses of the vast metal skeleton that surrounded it. Feed it fire, and it was this engine heart that would carry life flow in the form of steam energy to all the other parts of the organism and propel it across the water, all the while *beating, beating, beating,* much as a human heart would beat.

It is important to remember that everything that occurs in this section of the story does so with the drumming of this ceaseless heart *beating, beating, beating* somewhere close by, filling the air with its frightening urgency.

Were it not for the ship's unrelenting heartbeat, the air would no doubt be filled with the yips and cries of the hundreds upon hundreds of panicked mustelids stored within its belly as cargo. As it was, Felix could only hear the terrified sounds they made within the confines of his own mind, where they joined together into a single monumental chorus of animal despair, a chorus so loud it nearly drowned out the noise of the engine.

And why were they in such pain, you ask, that they would fill the air with their cries? To answer this question with any sort of accuracy, perhaps it is best to imagine ourselves there among them, to immerse our senses in what Felix's own senses were immersed in and to, in this manner, get a truer impression of what it was he and the others were made to endure.

Like any living creature, Felix possessed five corporeal senses, the same five that humans possess: sight, smell, taste, touch, and hearing. And while some of his were more or less acute than our own—his sense of smell infinitely more so, his sense of taste somewhat less—they were nonetheless the primary bodily receptors through which he experienced the physical world around him. In time, She would find a way to restore to him the final, most important incorporeal sense, the sixth, but at present, he was being denied this omnipotent guiding force. And so the remaining five were the only ones he had to go by. And since most humans rarely think beyond their bodily senses, the absence of the sixth and greatest should not be any impediment to our understanding of what Felix was going through down there in the cargo hold of the ship christened the *Embeth Tamara*.

We will consider the matter in the order presented above, with "sight" meriting two observations, in order to draw the distinction between the dark and the light halves of Felix's existence aboard the ship. Are you ready? (Oh, if it were only possible to close one's eyes while reading and imagine more fully!)

Sight (part I). All was blackness, not the blackness of a dark room, not the blackness of the sky at midnight, even one without any visible moon or stars. It was not the kind of blackness that would tempt you to say, "I cannot see my hand in front of my face." Rather, it was the kind of blackness that would make you forget you ever had a hand at all or a face to look upon it, one that dissolved and extended any former notion of one's physical self into the bottomlessness of its darkness. Felix was not *in* darkness. He had *become* darkness.

84

Smell. How should the wretched odor of several hundred ferrets crammed together into such close quarters be described? Imagine the cumulative stench that would be achieved by having all those musk glands firing together in one spot. Imagine! Now cover over all that with the foul malodor of all that animal excrement, all that urine, filling up the crates in which they were held and spilling over through the breaks in the slats. Here one might be tempted to imagine that the overpowering stench would not register as such to the creatures themselves. "What is the smell of a skunk to a skunk?" you might argue. But we are talking about orders of magnitude here. Even a skunk would grow sick of his own smell if he had to experience it to the exclusion of all other smells and have it multiplied by an order of several hundreds. The most beautiful fragrance in the world would ultimately grow sickeningly offensive, would it not, if everyone was wearing it at all times and all were crowding in on you at once? And this is no beautiful fragrance we are attempting to describe but a constant onslaught of musk, feces, and piss. Imagine it.

Taste. Twice a day, a loose hung network of electric bulbs would explode to light overhead, shattering the darkness of the ship's belly, as the Bucket Man arrived to feed them. He carried a bucket in each hand by its handle. And although he wore a torn piece of fabric over his nose and mouth to guard against the smell, tying it at the back of his neck, he whistled as he performed his duties, as though there was no other place that he would rather be than there in the company of an army of caged mustelids. From the bucket on his right, the Bucket Man tossed them scraps of fetid meat through the slats in their wooden crates, where it would be stepped on by other ferrets and left to marinate in pools of standing waste. From the bucket on his left, he held up a ladle filled with warm bilge water that he himself was made to collect before spooning it over to them. Besides these two meager offerings, the only other thing that Felix could taste over time was his own blood coagulating at the back of his throat from all the sores that had opened up on the top of his mouth.

Sight (part II). Felix was not only grateful to the Bucket Man for the sustenance he provided, however distasteful or inadequate it might be; he was also grateful for the electric lights that announced his arrival with each visit since they allowed him the opportunity to gain some insight into the manner in which they were being transported. Dozens of rough-hewn wooden crates stacked one on top of the other on either side of the ship; this was how they had been forced to live, with the offal and excrement of one cage raining down upon the one below it. In the shadowy recesses to the back of the ship, Felix had also been able to determine that the hold had been stuffed nearly to bursting with all other manner of supplies being shipped out to the new colony from the motherland: sacks of grain and other dried goods, barrels filled with rum, and towering mountains of silken fabrics.

Touch. Once the Bucket Man had finished tending to them and threw the switch, blackness consumed the hold once more, and Felix was left with only the crush of bodies around him and the putrid overspill coming from above. He was one of twenty in his particular crate (he counted by the light of the Bucket Man), stacked somewhere toward the bottom of the tower they were a part of. None were from the same barn that he was from. None bore the same cross insignia upon their right ear. None would know who the Breeder was if Felix was to mention his name or mention the names of Hector, Princess, Scruffer, She, Kara. His life had been severed from all its meaning, a meaning he could not hope to communicate because they did not share the same names, and he wondered if this was not done somehow on purpose to further loosen his ties to anything he once knew. They were strangers. And yet they were forced to share a space of such terrible intimacy, under such terrible conditions, their bodies and limbs intertwined in the naked shame of their humiliation, twisted into a single broken mass. How different it was to the feeling of being surrounded by the warmth of the others in the sleeping pile back at the barn. Imagine constantly being exposed to the touch of a stranger in the darkness. Imagine constantly having a stranger's body pressed against yours, smothering yours, and not having the freedom to remove yourself from them, as though you were nothing more than a stranger yourself. Would not such an awful, unrelenting touch make you grow to hate the stranger inflicting it upon you, even if you recognized that they were not really a stranger at all but a creature of a like kind? And would not such recognition make you grow to hate yourself as well?

Hearing. Their voices cried, "Why am I here?" Their voices cried, "What did I do?" And finally, saddest of all, their voices cried, "Won't somebody save me?" And gathering all their cries together, joining them each to the other, was the relentless *beating, beating, beating* of the engine that surrounded them on all sides, engulfing their very being and drowning all their senses in a single sea of sorrow. Nothing more.

And here is where we pick up the tale again now that you have attempted to experience with your own senses but a fraction of what our hero was made to endure during his time aboard the *Embeth Tamara,* the very smallest part that could be communicated through words. Open your eyes if you have had them shut (Oh, if it were only possible!) and return with me to the story of Felix, the Greatest Hunter of Them All, which, as you already know, is in no small part a love story...

*****

Though unaware that she had been thrown into the river to drown, Felix could feel that She was nowhere there with him in the darkness, that she was gone. Hadn't she said that she was leaving? And never once had She not made good on her word. The manner in which she left was almost incidental.

What he was not as sure of was the presence of Kara in the hold. In the lightning flashes of the Bucket Man's visits, he would scan the towering crates around him for any sign of her, often missing out on food and drink as the others pushed their way past him for the freshest feed. He never could apprehend her with his eyes, though, and soon enough the Bucket Man would finish with his duties and cast them back into blackness once more.

But was she somewhere there in that dark, close enough to speak to if not to touch? At first, he had done little more than to cry out her name to try to locate her, but he was certain that his voice was not breaking through the cacophony of voices swirling around him. Thus, he trained himself to wait until the veil of narcolepsy descended upon them all, learned to fight against its strong pull so that, in the relative silence that followed the quieting of their voices, with only the engine sound continuing unabated, he might take the opportunity to signal to her by whispering her name over and over until he himself could no longer resist and fell into sleep.

It was hard to determine how much time passed in this manner, but with still no response from his bride, Felix began to lose any real hope of finding her there. He nonetheless continued with the habit of whispering her name into the darkness when the others fell silent, only it was with far less conviction now. It was merely something to do as he turned end over end through the infinitude of silent black, something to remind him that he had once had a life before this passage, a life that had once included her in it. It was a silly exercise to try to maintain something that was already lost, he knew, but he did it anyway, if only for the consolation of hearing the sound of her beautiful name echoing in his own mind, reminding him that such a thing as beauty ever once existed in his life at all.

Who knew how many days they had been at sea, how long he had been in the habit of repeating her name without any real expectation that she would ever answer before she finally did?

"Yes?"

It was there! He had heard it—the "Yes?"—after listlessly repeating her name for the thousandth time. It was her voice, was it not? Or was he just imagining that it was? Was he losing his mind? He tried to stop the slow rolling sensation that he had given himself over to, that he always gave himself over to before sleep, by fixing his feet firmly beneath him for stability. Then he focused every part of his mind on identifying where she was and making her speak to him again.

"Is that you, Kara?"

Out of the featureless gloom, her pale mask appeared above him, the beautiful sand-colored mask that had first captured his attention to her. It hovered in the air for a moment, disembodied, before her eyes opened with great effort and she looked down upon him. And while in ordinary circumstances her eyes were black, the blackest things he had ever seen, here they were incandescent, illuminating the darkness.

"Yes, it's me," she answered, her eyes glittering like stars.

"But why haven't you answered before?" he whined. "I've been calling and calling."

"I was too weak, my love. For a time, I didn't even think that I would make it. But I heard your voice whenever you called. And it was your voice that led me out of the darkness."

"But you're not going to leave me again, are you?" He could hear the desperation in his voice and he was ashamed.

"No," she sighed. "I'm here with you now, and I won't leave you again."

He could tell that she was still so weak, that it was taking all her strength to linger with him now. But he had been without her for so long that he could not resist the urge to keep her with him for a little while longer.

"She's gone," he found himself blurting out before he even knew what it was he was saying.

"I know. She spoke to me before she went."

"And what did she say?"

"She said that the hour for idle despair was passed and that the thing that was most needed now was courage. And I said that I would try to find the courage for both of us, even if I was not born to be as strong as she was."

"But you're strong in your own way," he quickly responded, suddenly wondering for the first time how she had ever managed to live through the death of their own offspring, the two kits she had carried inside her very body, ones who had slept beneath her very heart.

"And we'll see if that's enough," she whispered, her eyes fluttering closed. "But I must rest now and continue to get well for whatever lies ahead."

Her mask had begun to dissolve in the air, and he raised himself up onto his back legs to try to keep her close, to somehow capture her between his two front paws and draw her to him.

"But will you be back?"

"Of course, my love. Soon."

And then she was gone.

There was something more she needed to tell him, something she had purposely left out of that first conversation. It was a thing she had begun to suspect several days before the Smeller of Blood came to reap them, a thing she had only grown in the certainty of with every passing day since. Sensing his joy at having her back in his life, she could not bear the thought of letting him down a second time, though, should things turn out the way they had the first. It was enough for now that they had found one another again amid the horrors of this nightmare they were trapped in. So she would keep the secret of the life she had growing inside her safe until some later date, when she would have even greater cause to believe that their happiness might last.

Unaware of the secret she was keeping, Felix contentedly lowered himself to the floor of the crate and wedged himself between the two skinny bodies on either side of him. And although he did not enjoy the touch of them pressed close against him any more than he ever had, something was changed within him now. Kara had come back to him. And even as the hob to his right began to shake violently with sickness—he would be dead by morning—Felix felt a strange new sensation come over him as he drifted down into the most undisturbed sleep he had experienced since coming onboard.

Hope.

*****

Each day another ferret died. The Bucket Man would arrive for their regular feeding and lift their stiffened bodies out of the crates, dropping them into the bucket along with the meat scraps. And these were just the ones he managed to see through the burning ureic haze and general squalor. Those he did not locate in this manner were left to rot in the muck and mire, while the others stood crowded about, the stench of their festering corpses hardly adding to or subtracting from the overwhelming reek of their imprisonment.

Yet Felix remained unperturbed by the decline in their already-abhorrent circumstances because he had Kara back in his life. Every time their voices met amid the din, which was nearly all the time now, he could see that she herself was growing stronger and stronger, which made all the death and depredation around him seem of little consequence.

He had her back: his love, his purpose.

Storms would sweep up from Africa across the sea, battering the ship nearly to bits till the others would cry out "Armageddon!" and still he could not be moved to despair. He had her back. For two days, the Bucket Man fell ill, and no one came to feed or water them in his absence. As the hunger and thirst gnawed at their insides, the others cried out "We are doomed!" and still it made no difference to him. What were hunger and thirst to him after the devastating loneliness he had known before her return?

He would not be shaken. He would not give up. He would make it to the end of this nightmarish adventure, wherever it was leading them; of this much alone, he was certain.

For he had her back, and that was all the faith he needed.

*****

The Suez Canal was officially opened in November 1869, thus successfully joining the Mediterranean to the Red Sea in a modern engineering feat of wonder. With the opening of the canal, ships from England no longer had to travel all the way down the western coast of Africa and around the Cape of Good Hope to gain access to ports in the east. The convenience of time and money that travel through the canal provided made it an enormously popular route for merchants to move their goods across the water and almost immediately gave rise to its natural consequence—inconvenience. Ships would sometimes sit for days on end, waiting for permission to pass through the strait, weeks even, as a vast network of bureaucracy sprang up to ensnare them in a complex web of graft and corruption and to impede their easy passage.

Caught in the web and languishing off the coast of Egypt while their captain sought their deliverance from an inscrutable cadre of low-ranking government officials, the crewmen of the *Embeth Tamara* took it upon themselves to row ashore and to bring back with them two items that were nowhere listed on the ship's manifest but which were nevertheless an understood part of their contractual obligation to the New Zealand Company. The Bucket Man rode along with them in their tiny skiff, nervously twisting a burlap sack in his hands while mentally preparing himself for the possible struggle ahead with their secret cargo.

Felix, of course, knew nothing of these developments on shore. He only knew that the ship had come to a halt after being tossed violently in the high seas and that, for the first time, the beating of the engine heart had gone silent. Conversation between them thereby rendered exponentially easier, Felix was content to whisper to Kara throughout the relative quiet and otherwise allow the mystery of the ship's interrupted progress to remain just that, a mystery.

Since her mask had reappeared before him that first night, he had become expert at locating her with his thoughts and kept a nearly constant path of communication open between them. Her crate was stacked directly above his at the top of the tower, which explained why he had never been able to locate her by the flash of the Bucket Man's light. But knowing that all he needed to do was ascend to be with her, he concentrated his thoughts on all things above and never failed to reach her. And although he was aware that others might be listening into their conversations, given the crowded vertical arrangement, he disciplined himself not to pay them any mind, to say to her everything he wished to say, regardless of its sensitive nature, after all those days that he had suffered without her in silence.

And what did they talk about? Mostly, they talked about survival; how, once they made it through this ordeal—for they were both quite confident that they would now that they had each other to rely upon—they would strive to make for themselves an even better life than the one they had known back in the barn. A ship could not sail forever, after all, can it? And once they landed, wherever that might be, they would do everything in their power to stay together and to be each other's better partner throughout the challenges that lay ahead for them next.

Kara would frequently interrupt these passionate testimonials of renewed affection between them with apologies for the way she had acted after her liter had died, for the way that she had given into her sadness and turned her back on him. After everything that they had been through since, she was convinced that the words She had uttered to her in her final moments were true—that the hour for idle despair had indeed passed and that she would struggle to find within herself the courage to go on only with him by her side.

Felix was quick to interrupt these regular mea culpas and assure her that no apologies were necessary, even as his body would betray his words and gleefully weasel dance about his crate below on account of her sweet words of reparation toward him. Nearly half the ferrets that had started out with him in the crate were dead and gone by this point, their rigid bodies disposed of before he ever knew their names, so there was a lot more room now to dance about, even if he did find himself bumping into those others who still remained there in the dark. One of the unexpected benefits of being surrounded by all that death was that it allowed him more room to dance.

They had only just finished the latest iteration of this curious call and response, Kara's words of apology triggering Felix's uncontrollable dancing, when the electric lights suddenly snapped on from above, freezing him in midstep. Felix lowered his front paws to the damp bottom of the crate as a powerful new scent wafted through the air in advance of the Bucket Man. It was a scent both foreign and familiar to him simultaneously, and it caused something cold and knotted to roll over in his stomach as it came to dominate all the other competing odors in the space. He could tell by the sudden stirrings of the remaining survivors around him that it struck them the same way it did him, and they moved as a single organism to the front of the crate to get a better whiff through the spaces in the slats of wood.

When the Bucket Man finally appeared, he brought neither food nor water with him as expected; indeed, and despite his namesake, he carried no buckets with him at all. Instead he held a burlap sack at arm's length in each hand, the kind of sack reminiscent of the one Felix and the others had first been carried away in from the barn. Both sacks twisted violently in his grip as sharp claws from inside tore through the mesh and reached for him. The Bucket Man cursed vehemently from behind the cloth covering his mouth at the scratching, spitting demons contained within, sweat pouring from his brow and soaking through his shirt. Finally, standing between the towers of ferret crates on either side, he was able to set the sacks down on the floor of the ship and step back as they continued to fling themselves about on the ground in a mad fury.

Then there was the combined growling sound of the creatures as they tore themselves free of their captivity. And then there was the sound of their claws scratching along the ship's bottom as they scrambled this way and that, desperate to hide themselves somewhere in their new environment. The gloom toward the floor beneath his crate was too thick for Felix to make out their shape or size, however. He only knew that there were at least two of them tearing about and, judging from the sound of their treads, that they were significantly larger than any ferret he had ever encountered before.

After the initial burst of activity upon the creatures arrival, an eerie quiet fell upon the hold, a quiet so deep and powerful that Felix did not even think of trying to obliterate it by reaching out to Kara. Instead he watched as the Bucket Man crept softly back in the direction he had first come from, only to return a moment later with a long wooden pole, at the end of which hung a leather strap fashioned into a noose. After taking one last opportunity to curse the fate that had brought him to such a task, the Bucket Man pointed the strap end of the pole toward the ground and proceeded to bang about the towers of crates, attempting to roust the demons from their hiding places and lasso them with the device. Each of his fumbling efforts to ensnare them in this fashion was met with a new round of spitting and snarling from the unseen devils until at last he managed to slip the noose around one and tighten it with a quick pull on the strap as he lifted it off the ground.

Surprised at his own success, the Bucket Man stumbled with his catch twisting at the end of the pole to a crate directly opposite Felix's own, one that death had emptied of all its occupants over the course of the voyage. Using a foot to push open the door, the Bucket Man turned his back to Felix and carefully inserted his ferocious catch inside before releasing the strap and slamming the door shut behind him. The creature never gave up fighting, however, and continued to scratch and tear at his fingers even as he sought to fix the lock into place, eliciting howls of pain from the Bucket Man.

Though Felix was unable to understand his words, he could see that the Bucket Man's fingers were bleeding badly from the encounter as he turned away from the crate that he had finally managed to secure, still obscuring the contents with his girth. "I don't need this feckin' aggravation," he hissed, throwing down the pole while pulling the cloth from his neck to wrap around his injured hand. Then, stepping to the stack of crates on Felix's side of the ship, his thick midsection pressing up against Felix's own cage, he stood on tiptoe and reached his hands up to where the jills were housed above.

For a moment, Felix's heart froze as he heard the lock being rustled, the door of one of the crates being opened and then shut. He breathed a sigh of relief, though, when the Bucket Man lowered his arms, revealing a bewildered-looking jill being held by the scruff of the neck in his right hand, a jill that was not Kara.

"What is the meaning of this, love?" Kara asked as the Bucket Man turned and carried the jill with him to the back of the ship, somewhere out of sight amid the stacks of supplies. "Where is he taking her?"

Before he could answer—although, in truth, he did not know what to say—Felix discovered that he was staring across the narrow distance between them directly into the eyes of the creature that had been captured and imprisoned there.

"Turn your eyes away!" the creature's voice boomed in his head. "I do not give you permission to look upon me!"

Felix immediately cast his eyes downward as the echoing voice of the creature in his head commanded him to do so. Meanwhile, the others with him in the crate slunk back to the far corners for safety, anxious to put as much distance as possible between themselves and the demon that glared from across the way. Something inside Felix, some blood-deep curiosity at the demon's purpose, kept him riveted to his spot, however, albeit with his eyes cast down in supplication.

Suddenly, a single sharp cry of terror knifed across the field of his thought, causing him to drop his head in response to its shrillness. With his snout nearly touching the urine-soaked ground, he listened as the cry was replaced by a litany of desperate protestations, which were, in turn, replaced by the unmistakable sounds of a fearsome struggle. And then, finally, there was only silence, punctuated by a soft distant whimpering.

Now the entire cargo of ferrets began to whisper and chatter anxiously at once, wondering what had befallen the jill who had been taken from them, and it was all Felix could do to tamp down the noise inside his head as he straightened his neck and opened his eyes. When he did, he saw that the demon had moved out of the shadows but was continuing to glare at him through the slats at the front of the crate. Having finally revealed himself thus, Felix observed for the first time that the creature's undercoat was of a dirty-bronze hue, though he was more strikingly distinguished by the bold pattern of concentric white stripes that ringed his body from head to tail, giving him the air of something wild and untamed. He took up nearly all the available space in the crate, making him three or four times larger than any of the other ferrets in the hold. Despite the difference in size and the dramatic patterning of his coat, there was something oddly familiar about him nonetheless, something Felix instantly knew they held in common, even if he could not place just then what that something was.

The demon's eyes, each twice as big as his own and black as onyx, bore into him from behind a tawny mask that, in shape and coloration, resembled the same one that Kara wore on her face.

"And yet still you look upon me," the creature growled, holding Felix in his gaze.

"I want to know what you are," Felix answered, his voice timorous as he struggled to block out the other voices babbling away in his head.

"But I am you, brother," the demon responded, his tone twisting into a sneer. "Do you not recognize me?"

"In truth, I do recognize you. Have we met somewhere before?"

"Met? You might more accurately say that we have never been apart."

A further piercing shriek from the jill caused him to shut his eyes and bow his head a second time. He could sense Kara's thoughts reaching out to him, trying to find their way through the din of anxious ferret chattering, but when he opened his eyes once more, it was the demon alone who commanded his attention.

"Who are you?" he asked, feeling somewhat more emboldened as his courage began to return.

"I am named Pollux."

"And what form of creature are you?"

"You really do not know?" the one called Pollux chuckled.

"You are not one of our kind."

"Oh, but I am. I am the very *first* of your kind."

Felix's blood froze to the sound of the words he had just heard since they seemed to express the very thing he had somehow known instinctually ever since the demon had joined them aboard the ship. Taking his dumbfounded silence for recognition, Pollux chuckled once more and went on.

"I am Pollux the Polecat, descended from a great line of warriors before me who have roamed this continent for as far back as memory serves. My earliest ancestor, whose namesake I bear, was one of the first of our kind to be torn from African shores and pressed into servitude. You were once as I am now before the first man arrived to abduct our kind and to rob you of your original self. Since that day, he has sought to break your will by causing you to forget your former greatness. He has done this by breeding you with a host of others across the centuries—weasels, stoats—weakening the connection to the original bloodline and changing your nature to one that can better serve Man's needs. He has made you smaller. He has made you weaker. He has made you completely dependent upon him so that you might do his bidding, and he has placed his brand upon you. But make no mistake, little red one, somewhere within that naked abomination of the thing he has forced you to become lurks the knowledge, even still, that you were once a mighty African polecat."

How had he known to call him by his second name, Little Red—the same name the Breeder had once affectionately bestowed upon him? Could this mean that there was some truth to the words he said, that the story he told, one of capture and enslavement, was, in fact, Felix's own story, though he had not ever thought to consider it until this moment?

"And now he seeks to change your nature once more," Pollux continued, his voice easily dominating the chorus of other voices in his head, "by infusing the weakened line with the blood of your original ancestors to strengthen you for the task ahead. This is why we have been brought here, my companion and I—to cast out the weasel and stoat, to change you back to what you once were. For you see, even the mighty polecat can be made to do his bidding. And in the end, we are all just slaves to the will of Man."

As Felix considered Pollux's last words and what they might mean with a dawning dread, the Bucket Man stumbled over several sacks of grain as he pushed his way back from the rear of the ship, the jill dangling by the scruff of her neck once more. "If I knew I was to be made Master of Animal Copulations, I would've listened to my sweet mother and never gone off to sea in the first place!"

The jill seemed to be sleeping or dead now from what Felix could tell before the Bucket Man hoisted her back above his head. He could hear the lock clang and the door of the crate swing open as she was returned to her cage. And then he heard the Bucket Man say, "It's your turn now, beauty." And then it was Kara dangling by the scruff directly in front of him, looking at him with unconcealed terror.

"Save me, love…"

But Felix could not move.

Felix could not think.

Felix could not speak.

While fumbling with the lock on Pollux's cage with his injured right hand, the Bucket Man held Kara close up to the slats with his left as though to provide the hunter with a good scent to go by. Then he quickly stepped back as the door to the crate slowly swung open.

"Now be a good boy," the Bucket Man said, his face twisted in a comic rictus of panic. "Just come easy like your friend, and you'll get a treat. But a swear if you bite me, I'm going to stamp you into dust. Come on now."

The door was fully open now, but Pollux did not immediately leap free of the cage. Instead he lingered at the edge for a moment, staring across at Felix as though he were waiting for him to say something.

"But she is *my* mate" were the only words he could think to communicate, although he wished to say so much more than that.

"Sorry about this, brother," Pollux replied, betraying for the first time something like empathy, something like kindness, "but we all have to play our part in His story."

Then Pollux leaped to the ground, landing with a heavy thud, and streaked past the Bucket Man to the back of the vessel, to where his friend lay in purged and satiated slumber.

"Thatta boy," the Bucket Man sighed with relief. "And here comes your reward." And then he followed after him, swinging Kara by the scruff of her neck.

Felix could feel her trying to reach him still, but he blocked her out. He blocked out the words she called to him when she was begging for him to rescue her. He blocked out her cries of terror, the sounds of her struggle, and her tears as she eventually submitted. He blocked out everything: Kara, Pollux, the ferrets around him. He went to a place so deep inside himself that no thought could reach him—the deepest, darkest place he had ever been—and shut out all the rest.

And that was where he remained, in that place of dark nothingness, even after Kara was returned to her crate and a half dozen other jills were likewise delivered to the back of the ship throughout the ordeal, each for the express purpose of bringing forth a new race of superior killers, all on behalf of the New Zealand Company. It was a night of screams and terror, but Felix heard none of it. He had gone to the place beyond such suffering, to the place of complete silence.

And that was where he would stay for the remainder of the journey. He would not even hear the cry of Pollux the following morning before he and his companion were tossed overboard once the ship had finally received permission to enter the canal and continue on its way.

"Remember who you are, brother!"

And forty-two days after setting out from London, roughly the average gestation period for a ferret, just as the *Embeth Tamara* was making port at Wellington, North Island, New Zealand, it was all he could do not to hear Kara's voice as it struggled to pierce the empty darkness he had gathered around him like a shroud.

"Behold," she whispered, "I give to you a son."

PART III

New Zealand

CHAPTER 8

Leaning out over the rail and breathing in the clean salty air while basking in the afternoon sunlight, it was hard to imagine that he was the same Amos who had set out from London but a fortnight ago. That Amos had discovered soon after the ship slipped the channel and passed into open waters that his body had zero aptitude for maintaining its equilibrium on the rolling seas and spent four entire days below deck in his tiny quarters, vomiting into a bucket that he clung to for precious life. One day bled woozily into the next as he slipped in and out of consciousness over the course of the crisis, there on the floor of his sparse room, while resting his chin heavily on the rusted rim of the bucket. Were it not for the constant rhythm of the ship's engine beating someplace below and rising up to penetrate his unconscious mind, his own heart might well have forgotten how to sustain its internal rhythm, and Amos might well have slipped from this earth during one of his violent swoons, never to awaken again.

As it was, he suddenly and inexplicably found himself relieved of the sickness that had plagued him those first four days of the voyage, and he eagerly mounted the stairs to the deck on the morning of the fifth day, significantly dehydrated but very much alive. There, like a Lazarus risen from the tomb, he beheld for the first time the shoreline of Africa shimmering off the starboard bow of the ship. And though Amos had no way of knowing how or why his body had so abruptly and mysteriously adapted itself to life on the water, he knew from that moment onward that he never wished to return to his cramped quarters below deck again.

The wonders he beheld while the ship made its slow crawl though the Suez seemed purposely designed by a divine hand to make easy description beyond the bounds of possibility—hump-backed camels parading in stately procession on the near shore and men in turbaned headdresses paddling out in their makeshift boats to sell their hand-woven goods to passengers off the side of the ship, their tanned hides covered by all manner of jeweled ornamentation. Even the trees he saw swaying in the desert breeze filled him with a kind of incredulity. How could one who grew up in an environment surrounded by oak and elm ever truly recover from the astonishment of seeing their first palm tree?

And it was almost with a sense of disappointment that he greeted the news from the captain earlier in the morning that the ship was scheduled to dock at Wellington by nightfall. Having earned his sea legs after a difficult birth, Amos was reluctant now to forego them and return to terra firma. He had even considered asking the captain if there was some way he might sign on to be a member of the crew, but he knew that such a request, should it prove possible, would only betray his father's final commandment, which remained folded on a blood-soaked slip of paper in his inside coat pocket. And reminding himself once more of the existence of the slip of paper so close to his heart and how it came to be blood soaked in the first place, Amos closed his eyes there at the rail as the *Union Star* completed the final leg of its journey and allowed the memory of that day to pierce him through as he had a hundred times before.

Neither he nor his mother had heard the shot, though clearly the gun had been fired while the two were in the house not ten yards away, eating their morning meal in silence. Where could the sound have gone to, he wondered countless times thereafter, with the barn. being so close and not a hint of wind or weather on that day? All was quiet, perfectly still, as far as he could recollect. So how could they have missed the blast in a sea of such calm?

Then he was entering the barn to begin his harvesting chores for the day and found his father's body sprawled there in the dirt on its back, the revolver still clutched in his right hand. The blood from the exit wound at the back of his neck had mostly been absorbed into the soil by the time Amos made his discovery, causing the dirt around his head to dampen into a dark corona that lent him an angelic appearance. The only evident sign of blood on his person was a narrow thread of crimson running down the corner of his mouth, flowing from the empty space where his right front tooth used to be. The nose of the revolver must have knocked the tooth loose when it was fired, he was told by authorities later on, although they were never able to recover the tooth itself.

It was there in his pocket now, the missing tooth, along with the note left for him to find on the ground nearby, the one containing his father's last injunction to him, a single line from Genesis, heavily embossed with the spray of his expelled plasma:

SUBDUE THE EARTH.

Had he known that his father was under pressure to make the harvest profitable? Of course, he had known. But then, growing up the son of a wheat farmer in rural England, there hardly ever seemed to be a time in his life when they were not under some kind of pressure to turn a profit. So his father's recent complaints about shrinking margins and the tumbling market hardly seemed much different from what he had always known as a child. Indeed, many were the nights that he would lie awake in bed and listen as his father, having had one too many ports after evening supper, would rail at his mother about how he wished debtors' prisons had not been abolished in the kingdom so that he could voluntarily check himself into one and be done with the whole bloody business.

What Amos had no way of comprehending was that the country was in an ever-deepening agricultural spiral with the opening of the American prairies for cultivation and that, at long last, his father had finally reached the point where he could no longer pull them out of it. His only options were to declare bankruptcy or risk having the farm forcibly taken from them by county officers. How could he bear to live with himself should either scenario come to pass, knowing that he had been the one to lose the land after it had been in his family's name for over two and a half centuries? How could he bear to live with the disgrace of it all and see his wife and child put out and humiliated, cast down into poverty?

Now his mother sat alone, rocking back and forth in her chair before the grimy window in the boarding house flat they could barely manage to afford in town. The only way they did so was by selling off the few items they were allowed to keep after the crown swooped in and took all the rest. The money they made off the sale of a few old nags and their dressings, however, would not hold out forever, and they would eventually be left destitute, just as his father had feared. There was only one way he could think of to save his mother from a life of poverty: win back dominion over the earth as his father's note instructed.

He knew that remaining there in England was impossible for him to do now if they were ever going to survive. As the son of a disgraced man who had killed himself in such a violent fashion, he understood that his father's infamy would mark him like a brand, that he would be considered a harbinger of bad luck by anyone who might take even a moment to consider him for hire. In this part of the world, one deeply in the sway of Christian mysticism, the sins of the father very rarely managed not to fall heavily upon the son. Yet he simply could not abandon his mother there alone—his mother, who seemed to have aged twenty years overnight and had retreated into a kind of stoic isolation since the incident. It was clear that she would be unable to earn a living in the world now in her reduced state, even if the judgment that had fallen on him could not be expected to fall twice as heavily on her (which it could).

With little other option available to him, Amos sought out the one person he knew who might be willing to help, the one man who had always been there for them in the past when times grew hard— the Breeder. He knew from working his property during the off seasons that the Breeder's holdings in the new colony had expanded significantly, so much so that he had been able to afford to build a nursery onto the side of his home with Amos's help shortly after the sale of his hunting ferrets. Perhaps this man who had been so kind to him in the past would see beyond his current ignominy and be able to summon a kindness toward him once more.

In the end, however, it was not the Breeder at all who had arranged his berth aboard the *Union Star*. On the day Amos came around, looking to speak with him, the Breeder was away on business, and he was greeted instead by the Bride, who was eight months pregnant with their first child. Amos had always enjoyed their brief conversations in the past and made it a point to concentrate on the words she said whenever she would speak with him despite the fact that the prominent stain on her face sometimes made it difficult to focus on what she was saying. Seeing how far along she had come since he had worked on the house, how swollen she was with child, released something unexpected in him as well, and by the time she had brought him into the nursery to show him the finishing touches—flowered paper on the walls, lace curtains on the windows—Amos found himself overcome by tears, tears he had denied himself since that morning in the barn, and clutching the side of the new crib at the center of the room to keep from collapsing to the floor in a heap of sobs.

Things moved rapidly thereafter. He had forgotten that she herself, the Bride, was originally from the new colony and had not known until that afternoon that her father remained a figure of some high standing in the New Zealand Company. Once she had helped to calm him and to dry his tears, she immediately set about making the arrangements for him to start over with a clean slate. And by the time the Breeder returned from his business that night, the letter to her father had already been sent, and his journey had officially begun.

Amos was abruptly lifted out of these remembrances by the sound of clanging bells and opened his eyes to a swirl of activity on deck as crewmembers hurried this way and that, preparing to make landfall. Behind him, the sun had finally set upon his old life back in England. Before him, dotted with signal fires and rising out of the ocean like a leviathan, was the dark silhouette of his new life in New Zealand.

*****

The port of Wellington smelled like pig grease as the wagon bounced violently through its muddy streets in the darkness. The buildings he could make out through the gloom from his perch at the front hardly seemed like buildings at all but more like a series of shingled lean-tos listing heavily upon one another to keep from tumbling over. The impression he got was less that of a port city and more a ramshackle outpost that had been built like a house of cards, one that would fall over with the slightest breeze. The few figures he could make out lurking there in the shadows seemed like human phantoms, nodding off against the scattered lampposts in a drunken haze or passed out entirely in the narrow alleyways.

All in all, he was grateful for the fact that he did not have to navigate this landscape of mud and misery on his own in the dark, that the wagon had been waiting for him at the end of the pier the moment he arrived, although he was still not quite sure how he felt about the man who had been sent to retrieve him. Lowering his chin to his chest, Amos could not help but steal sideways glances at the imposing figure holding onto the reigns and steering them away from shore. He was unlike any person he had ever seen before, even the exotics that had rowed out to hawk their wares along the Suez.

This imposing colossus of a man stood well over six and a half feet tall and appeared as wide as a barn door at the shoulders when he took Amos's canvas rucksack from him down at the dock earlier that night. How he was able to determine that Amos was, in fact, the one he had been sent to retrieve and not one of the other passengers to disembark from the ship was a complete mystery. He merely took the bag roughly and tossed it into the back without saying a word before moving around to hoist himself up onto the wagon as Amos was apparently meant to do likewise. It took a moment, though, for him to recover his wits long enough to realize that this was what was expected of him, a moment to overcome the shock that first resulted when he had looked up and beheld the giant's visage revealed by the lamplight. For although he was dressed in traditional English livery, Amos could see that every inch of the inscrutable countenance visible beneath the brim of his stovepipe hat was covered with a vast network of interlocking facial tattoos.

He was a Māori, one of the indigenous peoples to this part of the world that Amos had read about in tales of those who had traveled to these shores before him. He had even seen pictures of them in newspaper accounts and marveled at this custom of decorating their bodies in hieroglyphic scrawl. The pictures he had seen, however, invariably featured these strange aboriginals wrapped in loincloths, staring mutely into the camera's lens while holding a spear at their sides. Never had he beheld one dressed as a proper English driver might be while still sporting the inescapable insignia of his tribal heritage. And it was the collision of these two disparate pictures that produced in his mind the greatest reason for pause until he was able to gather himself—realizing now that the tattooed man was staring down at him and waiting—and climb up into the wagon beside him.

Had the natives taken over control and assumed the place of proper English gentlemen? Would this be the kind of man he would be expected to work for once they arrived at their destination? And if so, what forms of unknown savage tortures would he be forced to endure as their captive?

These were the questions that plagued Amos's thoughts even as the wagon left the listing buildings of the port city behind and rolled into the interior of the island. Once the last of the lamplight had dissolved behind them, the Māori all but disappeared into the blackness that engulfed them on all sides, and Amos instinctually found himself wrapping his arms around his own body to form a protective shield against any possible attack. If the native's hand were to suddenly shoot out of the dark and grab hold of him, as he fully expected it might, he wanted to be able to say to anyone who would ask that he had defended his honor to the best of his ability.

Still the wagon rolled onward. And the longer it did so, the more Amos found himself involuntarily letting go of his protective vigilance and relaxing into the native's company. The tattooed man had still not uttered a sound, but the silence between them grew to feel more familiar than foreign as they rode along since Amos himself was known to be a man of few words back home, one who largely kept his own council. But while their shared dispositions toward quiet made them somewhat brothers-in-arms over the course of the trip, Amos could never fully shake the notion that the Māori's keen eyesight was more animal than human since, like a jungle cat, he seemed perfectly capable of seeing in the dark. While Amos was roughly aware that the rutted path they followed cut through a vast plain of tall grass that shushed in the night wind on either side of the wagon, the path itself was all but invisible to him. How the man with the reigns in his hands managed to keep them from plunging off into an abyss seemed to argue for some supernatural ability, and Amos eventually had to close his eyes and trust in that ability or worry himself to death by anticipating the fall.

Much to his surprise, Amos discovered that he had somehow managed to slip off to sleep in the native's company as they made their slow progress across the sea of whispering grass. The next time he opened his eyes, he found that the wagon had come to a halt and that he was staring at the dark contours of a formidable country estate. There was no light coming from inside the manor, given the late hour. What illumination there was came from the oil lamps held aloft by two women in night dresses who were standing on the front steps of the house to greet him. The Māori had already lifted his rucksack out of the back and was waiting by the side of the wagon for him to retrieve it.

Amos could not resist sneaking one last look at the native's face as he descended, noting how it continued to withhold any legible emotion behind its elaborate mask, before moving toward the spectral women waiting for him with their lamps. One was young and beautiful, her skin the same aboriginal cast as that of his driver's, although her face was blessed free of any visible tattoos. Her nightcap was doing its best to contain an abundance of braided hair hidden beneath it as she stared straight ahead into the darkness, ignoring his presence entirely. The other was as old and grizzled as the first was young and fair and seemed to him more akin to a carrion bird than a withered crone in a nightcap as she lifted her lamp and glared down at him with hawklike intensity.

"It's well past time you arrived."

*****

Surely it was not fate that had brought him here to stand before this glowering wraith at the foot of these steps halfway round the world from anything he had ever known or could identify as vestigial to his former life—or at least not fate as it is meant to be understood in the classic Greek sense of the word. There were no gods conspiring to impose upon him the path that he must follow. And at every step of the way, there had been choices made that could have steered the story in an entirely different direction. His father, for instance, might have sold the farm and opened a dry goods store in town instead of choosing to do what he had done. And Amos might have torn up the note he had hidden away in his pocket and signed onto the *Union Star*, traveling the world as a sailor and seeing its many sights.

Once choice becomes a part of the equation, the idea of predestination starts to lose its hold upon where our stories might lead. And in the absence of the gods, it could fairly be argued that it is up to each one of us to design our own stories, our own fate, just as Amos had done in going to the Breeder that morning and crying before the Bride in the nursery rather than in seeking out some other form of assistance. He had options. This was the path he chose.

So it was less a matter of fate than sheer probability that Amos would unknowingly find himself at that moment, even as he shrank beneath the old crone's critical gaze, standing not thirty yards away from a creature he had once bathed on a warm spring day thousands of miles away from this place and knew by the name of Little Red. Felix's story included the Bride, as did Amos's own. It was only a matter of time and probability before their stories converged, as they do now, the way any one life can join so many other lives together.

For his part, Felix pitched restlessly in the barn nearby, entirely unaware that this unexpected figure from his past had arrived at this late hour to thread their stories together once more and to forge a common destiny. The reason he could not rest comfortably was because his thoughts were haunted by screams at night and he imagined he was being watched by a pair of glowing eyes as he dreamed. It was the same pair of eyes that peered out at him every night, rising up out of the fog of screams and staring directly at him, causing him to whimper and toss in his sleep.

They were the eyes of a polecat.

CHAPTER 9

Since the day Pollux the Polecat, descended from a long line of similarly named polecats before him, had been brought aboard the *Embeth Tamara* by the Bucket Man, it could rightfully be said that Felix had become little more than a ghost in his own story. Given how completely he had retreated inside himself from that day forward, it was all any of the other ferrets could do to remember that he was still alive among them. No longer was he thought of as Felix the Red. He had withdrawn so completely from their company that most had a difficult time recalling that his name was Felix at all, let alone that he had once worn the title of Greatest Hunter of Them All.

He was among them, yes, but he was no longer with them. He was a phantom. A shadow. A ghost.

When the herder Murdough came to get them in the mornings and led them out into the fields, Felix awoke from his tormented sleep as though he was awakening into a fog and trudged after them with his head held low to the ground. He slept apart from the rest once more, hidden away from their collective pile in a dark corner at the far reaches of the barn, and was invariably the last one to exit each day before the herder swung closed the heavy wooden doors on the hobs and jills left behind. Several times, in fact, he had moved so slowly that he had not made it through the doors before they were shut and had to spend the rest of the afternoon listening to the young ones foolish prattle, which had not changed so much since he was their age, slipping in and out of consciousness.

Only Murdough noted his absence on the days when he was left behind and made a note to report to his master on the weary old hairless, who had become a drag on the entire business. "What were they thinkin'," he would mumble bitterly to himself, "sending us a good-for-nothin' like that ugly bastard?"

Otherwise, his absence was hardly noted by the others. What good was he to them, anyway, since all he did during the hunt was find the first opportunity to crawl into the nearest burrow and fall asleep? It was better that he stayed behind than if he came along and blocked them from entering the tunnels and doing their work. As for the young ones, they had learned to look right through him as though he had no actual physical presence in the barn. Were it not for the odor of age and rot that wafted off him as he slept, they would have taken no notice of him at all.

He would hear the others when they came in from the fields, hear the heavy door swinging open to let them back into the barn, but he did his best to block out the chorus of their whispering voices as they arrived. He knew what it was they would be discussing between them since the subject never changed—what had occurred on that day's hunt, how many rabbits had been put up on the fence, how many taken by a bite to the throat. And always they would be animatedly discussing the exploits of the young hob Castor, who invariably put up more kills than all the rest combined. It was Castor now, not Felix, who was being elevated to the level of legend, who was commonly referred to as the Greatest Hunter of Them All by the other ferrets in the business.

Castor's size and strength made him appear more like the wild polecat of their shared ancestry than the puny domesticated ferret they had allowed themselves to become. His coat was blacker and richer than any coat they had ever seen before, and his thick strata of underlying muscle caused it to roll like the surface of a dark sea at midnight on a moonless night. His youth and exuberance poured freely off him in waves, surrounding him in a halo of supercharged vitality, and made him the envy of every hob and jill alike.

It was Castor they could not stop talking about, Castor in all his youth and splendor, the same Castor who had destroyed everything he loved that night on the *Embeth Tamara*. Why would he want to listen to that?

He could tell by the way the young hob looked at him—or, rather, how he looked right through him, as all the others did—that Kara had done her best to conceal whatever connection there might have been between them, which was just as well since, in his own mind, Felix denied that any such bond existed. She had said when they were still aboard the ship that she had given him a son, but those were the last words he had ever allowed her to speak to him, the last words of hers he had ever allowed to penetrate his mind.

This was not his son. This was the unholy offspring of another creature altogether, one sired in violence and bloodshed. This was an abomination, and he would have nothing to do with it.

It took Kara several weeks after they had arrived in their new home to accept the fact that he was resolute in his antipathy toward her and the child she had brought forth. During this time, she begged and pleaded and did everything she could to claw her way back into his affections, but he would not soften to her. Many was the time she had been tempted to reveal to him the secret she had kept from him aboard the ship, that she had been carrying his child before the journey had even begun, but always she resisted the urge to tell him, for she knew he would never accept that the child was his after what had occurred. And could she, with complete certainty, say for sure that it was?

And as her growing child continued to require more and more of her time and energy, Kara eventually began to see that all her petitioning was in vain; it was a luxury she could no longer afford. And remembering the last words that She had communicated to her—that the hour for idle despair had passed and that the thing that was most needed now was courage—she did her best to cast Felix from her heart and resolved to keep the secret of Castor's parentage to herself.

At first, she was not quite sure how she would do this, how she would manage to thwart the child's questions about his father as he grew. But then one night just before sleep, Scruffer located her with his thoughts and confessed all the feelings he had kept from her since she had first entered his life. Only a handful of ferrets from the barn back in England were now a part of their second business in New

Zealand. Many had died during the crossing, and others were separated from them and sent to distant farms once they had arrived in Wellington or released into the wild. She could distinctly remember the surprise she had felt when she first realized that Scruffer was one of the originals who had survived along with her since he had always struck her as being somewhat weak and ineffectual in his silly white coat, a sycophant content to dwell in Felix's shadow.

But now there he was, this stooge she had never considered before as anything other than a bootlicker, pouring out his heart to her in great gusts of emotion and swearing his undying love if she would only accept him as her mate. What was more, he promised that if she did, he would help raise the child as his own and proudly call himself its father. There was hardly any others with the crucifix branded on their ear still left who could remember the events of that night aboard the ship or tell the child otherwise. The only one who might have any inclination to spoil the charade, he argued, was Felix, and they were both aware of his feelings toward the hob by then.

And so she had allowed it to happen, allowed Scruffer to move into her life and to take the place of her Felix, who could no longer even bring himself to look in her direction, let alone speak to her in thought. And each day that passed since, she was more and more certain that she had made the right decision. Scruffer could still be something of a bore, it was true, prattling on at the end of a day's hunt about how many kills he had managed when she knew the number was not nearly half of what he said it was. And they made a comic picture together, father and son, the one so pale and insubstantial, the other so dark and throbbing with physical health.

Scruffer was, at best, a mediocre ferreter, no better than she herself was, but what difference did this make in the larger scheme of things? He was a good and loving father to Castor, encouraging his child's talents and celebrating his great accomplishments along with all the rest while basking in a father's pride. And she could see that the young hob worshipped his father and thirsted for his approval, that his efforts in the fields were largely made to fulfill this longing for parental approbation.

So what if Scruffer was somewhat insecure and liked to inflate himself a little? He had stood by her side and had agreed to take care of the one thing she truly loved, her child, when Felix had all but turned his back on the both of them. He might not ever be a great hunter, but Scruffer had proven himself to be twice the ally, twice the defender as her original mate. And so she allowed herself some time to mourn what once was and might have been, then forced herself to move on, for the sake of Castor.

Felix was aware of the changes in Kara's life as he withdrew further and further from it but only in the way that a ghost was aware of the life it was once a part of. She was there somewhere in the barn along with him—she and Scruffer and the hob—but he could not reach out or break through to her from the realm his spirit was now forced to occupy. Though his heart stubbornly continued to beat, the rest of him had died back on the ocean, including the part that might somehow summon the courage to understand or forgive. Only in sleep was he fully alive, alive with the horror of her cries and the damning eyes of the polecat.

How strange that the one thing that should remain alive in him, despite all his efforts to kill it off, was guilt.

*****

The ornate clock in its gold cabinet ticked loudly on top of the mantel above the fireplace, deepening the silence of the room, as Amos shifted nervously on his feet the following morning, anxiously waiting for the old man in the stiff collar to look up from his papers and to see him standing there. When he finally did speak, his voice came forth in a weary rasp, though he did not deign to look up from the documents he was scrutinizing with squinted eyes.

"And how does she seem to be faring back in Britannia?" the old man queried dispassionately from behind his polished desk. And then added, by way of clarification, "My daughter?"

Amos had to clear his throat before he could summon a response and he could feel the sweat dripping down his back as he shifted uncomfortably in the old man's presence. Meanwhile, the clock on

116

the mantel ticktocked so loudly in the silence following Thackery's questions that Amos felt he had to shout out his answer when the words finally did manage to break free from his lips.

"Very well indeed, sir."

"Indeed," Thackery echoed disdainfully, allowing his eyes to drift from the document in his hand to the gangly young man standing before him in his study, clutching his hat nervously in his hands. Then he slowly laid down the document and pushed up from his chair, sighing heavily as though the act of standing alone required all the strength and patience he could summon before moving out slowly from behind the desk to take a closer look.

"Despite the many improvements made to the colony by the New Zealand Company," he went on, approaching Amos at the center of the room, "the post is still dreadfully slow in arriving. One hardly has a way of knowing *what* is going on elsewhere in the world. I understand, however, that she and her husband are preparing to have a child."

"She well may have had it already, sir," Amos quickly offered. Then he suddenly felt ashamed of what he had said, as though he might have inadvertently pronounced something indelicate or improper.

Thackery loomed directly above him now, staring down the length of his tumescent nose, as Amos lowered his eyes from his waistcoat, whose buttons strained against the pressure of his formidable girth. He was dressed in layers of black and seemed, at this moment, less like a wealthy landowner and more like a prosperous undertaker.

"If she has," he sniffed, "let us hope the child's face is free of the mother's curse."

"I helped build the nursery onto the side of the house," Amos offered in a whisper, although he did not fully understand why. "She was always very kind to me."

The old man seemed somewhat taken aback by the words the boy had chosen, by the sudden flash of guilt they provoked in him, and he turned to settle his emotions for a moment before continuing with their conversation. It was then that he saw his own face reflected back at him from the glass surface of the ornamental gilt clock resting on the mantelpiece. He had had the clock shipped over from Paris the previous Christmas as a gift to himself, and it had become one of the greatest consolations of his life to sit quietly for hours and listen to the steady sound of its ticking. At the moment, however, he could not help but notice that the hands of the clock were running somewhat behind the time.

"You may think it was *un*kind of me to have had her sent away from this place. But this remains a largely backward colony, its people little more than savages, and she would never have been seen as anything more than damaged goods if she had stayed. Arranging to have her sent to a more civilized place was actually the kindest thing a father could have done for such a daughter, to allow her some slim chance at happiness, particularly after the death of her mother."

Having lost himself in thought for a short while, Thackery drew a gold watch connected to a thin chain from the pocket of his waistcoat and compared the time he saw there in his palm with the time shown back from his reflection. Then he moved to the clock on the mantel, opened its glass front, and began to adjust the hands to follow suit.

"My daughter writes that you have some experience with these foul-smelling ferrets," he continued absently, his back turned away while focusing on the time. "The only reason my fellow investors and I saw fit to send for them in the first place was to rid us of these pestilential rabbits that threaten the livestock with plague, but we're hardly seeing the results we had expected. The air is choked with stench, but rabbits continue to abound. If the situation is allowed to continue much further, the entire herd will soon be wiped out and the island overrun with disease, becoming little more than a vast leper colony— while destroying the fortunes of the New Zealand Company in the process, I might add. I, for one, don't intend to allow that to happen, but something must be done to get these bloody ferrets to produce results."

The old man finished bringing time into proper sync and closed the glass front of the clock. Then adjusting the position of a model ship displayed next to it, he turned to face Amos once more.

"That is where you come in. Am I making myself clear?"

"Very much, sir," Amos nodded, thinking for a moment that the tufts of white hair that stood out from either side of the man's head gave him the appearance of being a horned predator.

"Good," Thackery said after a brief moment, stepping back to his desk and taking up a folded letter on top, which he opened and scanned hurriedly. "Now my daughter has explained to me your mother's unfortunate circumstances back in London. Be assured your earnings will be sent directly to her on a regular basis and that, in the meantime, you'll be provided with room and board at no additional expense to you. I trust you've settled into your new quarters?"

"Yes, sir."

"My name is Thackery," the old man said while tossing the letter back onto the desktop, "and I am your master now. And you shall refer to me as such in the future."

"Of course, Master Thackery, sir."

"Very well," Thackery said dismissively, circling back around the desk. "You will answer immediately to the herder, Mr. Murdough, whose presently out in the fields. The man's a hopeless drunk and plainly overwhelmed by the task he's been given, but he's been on the island forever, and the natives fear him. Any further questions?"

As anxious as he was to escape the room, Amos hesitated to bring up the reason he was standing there at all, why he was submitting himself to this interrogation. But his father's tooth bit at him through the fabric of his pocket, and the words written on the note surrounding it flashed across his mind.

SUBDUE THE EARTH.

"About the land shares, Master Thackery?"

Thackery stopped beside his chair and eyed Amos critically across the glistening surface of the desk as though only just now seeing him for the first time.

"Once this business with the ferrets is taken care of," he answered coldly, his eyes unblinking, "and assuming you're successful in ridding us of our vermin situation, we can sit down then and discuss the terms for your purchasing a parcel of land from the company. Only then. Are we clear?"

"Yes, Master Thackery."

"Then that will be all for now," Thackery said, sighing, lowering himself back into his chair, and turning his attention once more to the papers arranged before him.

Amos nodded and turned to leave, overjoyed that the interview was finally at an end. But Thackery suddenly thought of something and called out after him, stopping him in his hasty retreat. "Murdough mentioned something this morning about a hairless monstrosity that needed to be put down. See to that, would you?"

*****

Miss Hollis was waiting directly outside the study with a sharp knife in her hand when Amos exited, as though she had been listening at the door to their conversation and had anticipated what he would need to perform his first task. She was the same old crone who had greeted him out on the steps in her nightdress upon his arrival, who had brusquely introduced herself as head of household before equally as brusquely showing him to his tiny room at the back of the manor. Dressed now in her black linen uniform and lace collar, she appeared even more frightening to him than she had the night before as she handed him the curved instrument without uttering a sound and sailed away down the hall toward the next matter that would require her attention, the crisp hem of her skirts making a distinct hissing sound as they scraped along the surface of the carpet.

Now he was loitering outside the barn, turning the knife over in his hand and wondering what it was he was supposed to do with it. At home, he had only ever been asked to feed and care for the animals, never to take one of their lives as he was being told to do so now. So what end result was he expected to accomplish with the knife? To slash the creature's throat? Skin its hide? The thought of either outcome made him swoon in the noonday heat, and he closed his eyes momentarily against the sudden queasiness he was experiencing in order to recapture his composure. There he saw his father laid out on the ground once more, the thin line of blood running from the side of his mouth, and he snapped his lids open in an instant before reaching out to grab hold of the barn door.

If a blood sacrifice was what was required in order start making sense of his father's death, then a blood sacrifice it would be. And perhaps it was just as well that he was being challenged to perform such a savage act on his first full day in the colony. Had not Thackery already warned him that it was a more savage, backward place than the one he had come from? It was better that he shed his gentility right at the start then and acclimate himself immediately to the brutish ways of his new surroundings if he ever hoped to win the land that was his heart's consolation.

Upon stepping into the cathedral-like half-dark of the barn, he was immediately greeted by the powerful musk odor of a dozen or more ferrets housed together in close confines. And although the ferrets were restricted to a single stall at the very rear of the building— the remaining stalls empty now but otherwise reserved for Thackery's sizable flock of sheep, out grazing the pasture lands at this hour— their potent fragrance overwhelmed all other scents in the place and made it easy for Amos to locate them where they were housed in no time. To most people, he knew, the scent was thought to be so overpoweringly awful that it made them want to run for cover to escape its toxic perfume. To Amos, however, it was a scent that evoked in him vivid memories of a happier time, of playing with the ferrets on the Breeder's property back in England without a care in the world, and he shut his eyes for a moment to breathe in its potent bouquet while following his nose blindly back to the stall. Then, banishing the memories and stealing his resolve for a second time, he opened his eyes to the bloody deed at hand.

Peering over the gate into the stall, Amos beheld a small stack of mustelid bodies at the center, coiled together in their familiar pile of sleep and completely unaware of his purpose. Lifting the latch, he swung open the gate and crept onto the carpet of yellow hay with the knife in his hand, careful not to make any sound that could wake them. He stood over the pyramid and scanned it for a moment but could not detect any hairless form folded within its latticework.

Besides, he reasoned, if the creature he was searching for was sick enough for him to have been sent upon this errand in the first place, then he knew it would likely be set apart from the rest, the way dying animals instinctually know to exile themselves from the pack before they expire. And so he turned away and continued to follow an odorous zephyr of loneliness until it led him to a small hillock of dried grass at the very rear of the stall. Squatting down and gently pushing aside the blanket of hay on top, he discovered a shriveled pink ball curled up into itself beneath the straw.

When he lifted the creature by the scruff of its fleshy neck, it continued to hang limply from his grip, lost in sleep. All Amos could tell by the dim lighting was that it clearly was the "hairless monstrosity" he had been sent to execute, given the way its coat of aggravated flesh stood out against the surrounding darkness like a wound cut into the air itself. Judging by how lightly it hung there from his fingers, hardly measuring as weight at all, he could also tell that the monstrosity was alarmingly frail and malnourished, as near to death as to living. Somehow this thought made it a little easier for him to contemplate what was meant to happen next, that the poor creature was as good as gone anyways, that it would be a mercy kill of sorts, an act of putting it out of its misery.

But he could not allow the notion that he was merely euthanizing the sickly creature to be spoiled by messing up the actual execution. And in the half-light of the barn, he was unsure if he could manage to slip the knife in in just such a way that it would be the least painful for the animal to endure. Suppose he missed killing it outright with the first cut, and it shuddered awake in his hands and looked into the face of its executioner? How much worse would that be than slicing it clean and allowing it to sleep on peacefully into eternity?

After turning the possibility of potentially botching the kill over in his mind, all the while holding the serrated edge of the knife to the ferret's throat, Amos finally decided to carry the creature outside, where he would be able to see better and there dispatch it with maximum efficiency. Stepping back out into the brazen sunlight, however, he was temporarily blinded and needed to shield his eyes with the hand holding the knife until his vision could recover from the shock. Once it did, he discovered just a short distance from the entrance to the barn a severed tree trunk sticking out of the earth, and he moved toward it.

The stump had clearly been used to perform similar sacrifices in the past, judging from the quantity of dried blood baked onto its flat surface and running down along its sides. Perhaps this was where pigs and chickens on the farm were slaughtered in preparation for nightly meals, Amos reasoned as he stretched the naked victim out onto its back across the faded gore and prepared to add its blood to the rest. He knew that he would only have a few moments before the creature, sensing the change in light and temperature, opened its eyes, and he held the blade to its throat for a second time, determining now to slice the head off clean and be done with it.

Just as he was pressing his weight down on the handle and preparing to drag it sideways across the ferret's throat, something unexpected suddenly caught his attention, though, stilling his hand. It was the unmistakable tattoo of a cross glowing out from the translucent pink tissue of the withered creature's ear, the same stamp that the Breeder had used to brand his business back in England. Could this actually be the one they called Little Red, the same one the Breeder had favored for being the finest hunter he possessed?

His questions were answered in the next instant when the ferret, sensing the warmth of the sunlight upon him, fluttered open his lids and stared directly up at Amos from the bloody altar with his fiery red eyes.

*****

For his part, Felix was completely unaware of just how close he had come to death. He only knew that somehow a face from his distant past had been returned to him and that he was being bathed now by the same hands that had bathed him long ago, before the life he once knew had come to an end. The hands held him securely up in the porcelain bowl of warm soapy water as the fingers gently picked away at the various scabs and sores that he had allowed to encyst upon his hide since he had abandoned his own grooming.

Perhaps he had finally willed himself to die, as he had always hoped he would do since losing Kara, and what he was experiencing now was nothing more than a mirage engineered upon his arrival onto the shores of the Land of the Dead. What sweeter way could be devised of welcoming him into the afterlife than to be purified in a warm bath and cleansed of his scars by the same hands that had been so kind to him when he had been young and the world had been filled with so much promise?

Then the boy was feeding him some sort of poultice with the tips of his fingers, gently forcing him to swallow the healing mash. And although he had sworn off food a long time ago in order to hasten his own demise, he saw no reason now not to eat, given that that demise had clearly been achieved. Besides, whatever the potion being placed upon his tongue was made of, it tasted so satisfying and delicious to him that there was no way he could have managed to continue to resist its sweetness, even if he were still alive.

And then he was curled up in a field of soft blankets, sinking down into sleep once more. When he awoke, he promised himself that he would immediately set out to look for She now that they both occupied the same plain of nonexistence. He would seek her out with his mind for the first time since they had been taken away by the Smeller of Death, and they would be reunited again for all eternity. But at the moment, the pull of unconsciousness was too much for him to overcome, and he allowed himself to be pulled further down into the comforting depths of oblivion.

*****

Amos was sure to be back in time to help shepherd the bleating sheep into the barn when Murdough returned with them at the end of the day. The older man hardly seemed to acknowledge his presence at all but merely lingered atop his seat in the wagon at the back of the herd, openly sipping from a flask, as Amos went about directing the wooly flock into their separate stalls and saw to their feeding. When those duties were finished, he hurried out to help unload the army of grown ferrets that were asleep in the back of the wagon, noting how several among them also bore the Breeder's cross upon their ear as he carried them aloft and set them down inside their stall. When the last of them had been placed there, he closed the gate and hurried to Murdough, who was just then slamming shut the rear panel of the wagon he had used to transport his hunters.

"You must be the new boy," Murdough grumbled, sliding the pin through the metal lock in the panel.

"Yes, sir, Mr. Murdough," Amos answered, sweeping the hat from his head. "Master Thackery said I was to report directly to you. My name's Amos."

Murdough straightened and looked at the hand that was being offered for him to shake as though it was a diseased stump. The pock-marked skin hanging from his mottled jowls and stretched across his inflamed noise was of a particularly flamboyant shade of red, as though he had narrowly escaped being boiled alive. And when he peeled off his own hat to sweep his forearm across his damp, grizzled pate, Amos could see that his right eye was dead in the socket, clouded over with an opaque fog of gray.

"Don't rightly care what your name is," Murdough finally snarled, the whiskey thick on his breath. "You're not the first to show up in these parts and you won't be the last. No sense in gettin' to know your name. Just do what you're told for as long as it lasts. Clear?"

"Very much so," Amos responded, accepting the older man's rebuff and lowering his hand.

"You take care of that bald one I told Thackery about?"

"Yes, Mr. Murdough. Earlier today, just after he mentioned it."

"Good," Murdough grumbled even as his one good eye continued to assess him suspiciously like he was some form of invasive insect. "Master Thackery seems to think the way to kill off these bloody plague bunnies is to bring in more of you lot every season," he finally sneered, spitting a wad of tobacco juice onto the dry ground between them. "Well, Master Thackery's wrong. Exactly what I don't need is another child loiterin' about and gettin' in my way. What I need is to be done with these accursed ferrets that ain't worth the coin it takes to feed 'em. I try to tell Master Thackery that, that they ain't no good, but he don't believe me. He's too set in his fancy ways. Because that's how it's done back in merry ole England, and Master Thackery's a proper English gentleman through and through despite what he says to these savages."

At this point in the sermon, Murdough could barely contain his disgust at having to work for such a man as Thackery and emphatically expelled a second gob of tobacco juice into the dirt, this one larger than the first, as though the act of spitting alone could accurately express the emotions he was struggling to express. Then he reached over the panel into the back of the wagon and came up with a creature that had been waiting to be released the whole time. It dangled at the end of his arm by the scruff of its neck, its snout still lined with blood from the day's kills.

"This is the only one of 'em that's any good," the herder growled, "the only one of 'em that's worth a good Goddamn at all."

It was bigger and thicker around than any ferret Amos had ever come across before. What was more, he had never seen a ferret whose coat was as unrelievedly black as this, a pelt the color of spilled ink on a white page. Altogether there was something that seemed more powerful, more ferocious about the specimen than any he had encountered back on the Breeder's farm, even as it continued to blink its round ink-black eyes at him innocently.

"This here's the Black," Murdough concluded, thrusting Castor into Amos's surprised embrace. "See to it you take good care of 'im."

*****

Amos stayed with the ferrets until they had gorged themselves on the buck rabbit he had prepared for them from the day's hunt and had begun to climb atop one another for their nightly rest. When he left the barn, the sun was already setting out over the rolling grasslands that surrounded the estate and he lingered there for a moment, wondering about his mother in her boarding house back in London.

What would she be doing at this very minute as he stood there, thinking about her?

There was an eleven-hour time difference between them, he knew. Eleven hours. Nearly half a day that he was ahead of her. Somehow, in boarding a ship and coming to this place, he had been shot forward in time so that she was probably still asleep in her bed at this hour, not yet awoken to the very same day that he himself was witnessing fade into the past, dissolving into a veil of pink vapor on the horizon.

Thoughts such as these about the way the universe was assembled frequently gave him pause. That the earth was round, that gravity held us in place, that time was a changeable thing depending upon where one stood beneath the sky: how could wonders like these ever cease to astonish, he asked himself, before suddenly remembering the tooth he carried in his pocket and the father who it once belonged to. His father, who was neither sleeping comfortably in his bed nor staring out at a sunset but who was merely gone.

His father, for whom all such wonders had ceased to exist.

Perhaps it was the melancholic state of distraction that this unexpected turn in his thoughts had produced that explained why he had not seen Miss Hollis waiting there outside the door of his room until it was too late. He had no sooner startled at her spectral presence when she stepped from the shadows and opened up her fingers to reveal the knife she held in her right hand, the same knife she had given him that morning to execute Little Red with.

"I see no blood upon the blade."

"Why, no, Miss Hollis," he managed to stammer. "I washed off the blood before returning it to the kitchen."

"I am well aware of how young men clean their instruments." She smiled. "It's very rarely with this degree of dexterity. I also could not help but notice a certain musky odor coming from your room. You will kindly open the door to let me inside."

"I buried the ferret in the fields directly afterward."

"I did not ask where you buried it." She glowered at him, her smile evaporating in an instant as she took a step toward him. "I told you to open this door."

His hand was visibly shaking as he turned the key in the lock and twisted the knob on the door. Her skirts made their familiar hiss as she pushed past him in the doorway and hurried into the room. He remained behind in the hallway, shutting his eyes and awaiting the sound of her recognition, for the audible gasp that would signal that his adventure in New Zealand had come to an end less than a full day from when it had started. But when no such gasp occurred, he opened his eyes to see her standing before him once more, wearing a somewhat puzzled look upon her face.

"It seems I owe you an apology," she uttered, plainly still mystified by what she had, in fact, *not* discovered inside. "I am not in the habit of barging into young men's private rooms. It shan't happen again."

And then she hurried off down the hallway without saying another word, hissing as she went. For a moment, he stood there in dumbfounded amazement, as mystified as Hollis had been by what had transpired. At long last, he summoned the courage to step into the room himself and confront the mystery that had so put her off.

The room was just as he had left it earlier. It was the same small wooden table pushed back against the wall, the same porcelain bowl on top, and the same metal cot beneath the windowsill for sleeping on. Only the thin lace curtains hanging over the glass were billowing in the breeze now, even though he was quite sure that he had left the window shut the last time he was there. And Felix was nowhere to be found.

Amos peered beneath the cot just to make certain, as Hollis surely must have done before him, and then stepped back out into the hallway to absorb the unexpected development. Where had Felix gone? No sooner had he begun to turn the matter over in his mind than he suddenly felt as though he were being watched. He spun on his heels to see the same young Māori girl who had stood silently on the steps in her nightdress just a few short hours before. Stitched into her housemaid's uniform now, her riotous mop of cabled hair reigned back into tight braids against her scalp, she stared at him from the far end of the hallway with the same blank expression she had greeted him with upon his arrival.

Then she placed her index finger across her lips as though instructing him to maintain his silence. And then she was gone.

*****

"Tell me again how well I did today, Father."

It was Castor's voice, rising up to him from his familiar place at the bottom of the pile. Being the largest among them, it had long ago been established that he should serve as the foundational block for their nightly sleep pyramid. Although it would be more accurate to say that it was Castor's thoughts rising up to where he lay buried at the center of the pile, after failing to locate his mother, who hovered somewhere above them both toward the top.

"You heard me tell the young ones earlier how magnificently you performed." Scruffer sighed, twisting his body deeper into the ocean of musky fur surrounding him on all sides. "Now please be still and go back to sleep."

"But I need to hear it one more time," the young hob pleaded, his voice growing more insistent in Scruffer's mind.

"Why do you need to hear it again?" the parent groaned, thirsting for rest.

"Because when I'm actually doing it, when I'm involved in the hunt, I sometimes forget myself entirely and lose all track of who I am. I need you to remind me."

There was a real neediness to Castor's voice now, as though he might suddenly begin to weep. And so Scruffer forced himself to hold on to consciousness for a little while longer, to give his beloved son the reassurances he craved.

"You only forget yourself because you've given over to your instinct."

"Instinct?"

"The voice inside that commands you to hunt, to kill."

"And is it good to have instinct?"

"It is very good. Instinct is the thing that makes you a great hunter, and you are the Greatest Hunter of Them All."

Scruffer could feel Castor's glowing pride warming the pile like a furnace from below.

"Tell me again how well I did today."

"Go to sleep!"

"Please! Just one more time! And then I will go to sleep, I promise!"

Scruffer twitched in hopeless resignation, accepting that there would be no rest for either one of them until he gave in to his demands. And besides, he did so very, very much love his son.

"Very well." He sighed, adjusting his body a second time so that he would be in a more comfortable position for the telling of the tale. "We were nearing the end of the hunt and hardly had anything to show for it. The entire warren had been emptied out, every burrow swept clear of its inhabitants…"

"But there was a hole in the fence!" the hob chimed in excitedly.

"I thought you said you needed me to tell it."

"Please, Father, I'll be still. Go on."

"Yes, there was a hole in the fence," Scruffer continued, "where one of the rabbits had torn through. And by the time the rest of us took notice, they were gone. Every rabbit we had ferreted out from the warren had escaped back into the fields and we were crestfallen. We knew the herder would be back soon and that when he saw what had happened, he would toss us roughly into the back of the wagon, the way he does whenever we fail to please him. And then…"

Here, Scruffer paused for dramatic effect, knowing that Castor would be trembling with anticipation by this point in the story.

"And then what?" he finally asked when it seemed his father would not go on any further.

"And then the ground beneath began to shake."

"Did it really shake, Father, or are you just saying that?"

"I would never lie to you, my son," Scruffer answered. "It palpably shook, like the earth below was splitting in half."

Castor's voice could barely contain his excitement. "And then?"

"And then up you arose from the deepest tunnel," Scruffer beamed, his voice growing thick with pride, "dragging behind you the biggest buck I've ever seen. His body was so big it split the earth as you rose with him, causing the ground to tremble. And when you broke to the surface, a great fountain of blood arced out into the air, and we all celebrated, knowing that, however angry the herder might be, he could never punish us ultimately because you had captured this enormous prize."

"How high did it arc into the air?"

"High."

"And was it the buck we ate tonight for supper?"

"The very same one."

There was a long moment of silence as Castor allowed himself to picture the story his father had just relayed. In the silence, Scruffer grew tired once more and began to drift back toward sleep.

"And is it instinct that prevents me from remembering these things as they are happening?"

"Like I said."

"And are hunting and killing the only things that instinct is good for?"

"We can only be our natures, Castor," Scruffer whispered, his voice drifting toward the void. "A ferret is made to hunt and kill. That is what your instinct is for."

"Then what about Mother?" Castor asked abruptly, pulling Scruffer back from the abyss. "Why does she not take pride in my instinct the way you and the others do?"

"Why do you question your mother's pride?"

"Why was she so sad when we returned to the barn tonight?" Castor pressed, the anger unexpectedly swelling in his voice. "Why didn't she celebrate that I had made the ground shake? And why wouldn't she open her mind to me when I tried to reach her?"

"She was...upset," Scruffer stammered, unsure of how far he was prepared to go to explain Kara's behavior that evening.

"Upset about what?"

"About the one with red eyes who grew sick and had to be disposed of today."

"But who was he to her other than some old wretch who had no instinct at all but to sleep and waste away? Isn't it better that he's gone?"

"He was a friend a long time ago," Scruffer answered, suddenly filled with a degree of fresh sadness that surprised him with its intensity.

"Was he a good friend?"

"No more questions now!" Scruffer snapped at last. "Go to sleep!"

Hearing the impatience in his father's tone and sensing he could push no further, Castor readjusted his position at the bottom of the pile petulantly, causing the whole pyramid to sway violently as he settled onto his side and closed his eyes against the mysteries of a world he could not comprehend. Despite all the emotions roiling inside him, he was able to fall asleep within minutes, which is one of the great consolations of youth. His father, however, was now fully awake and wondering what it was she might be making of all she had just overheard.

Kara, who had been listening the whole time, closed her eyes at the top of the pile in an attempt to prevent Scruffer's thoughts from reaching her. But no matter how hard she tried to erase it, the memory of Felix's face in the snow kept rising up out of the darkness to haunt her. And sleep would not come.

CHAPTER 10

Though he was utterly confused by the radical change in his circumstance, Felix never felt himself afraid or unsure once he had opened his eyes and took in his strange new surroundings. Yes, he was disoriented but disoriented in a good way, like he had finally made it back to a place he had never been before but felt completely at home in nonetheless. Was this, at long last, the afterlife he had been yearning for these many weeks after losing his will to go on? And if so, how should he begin his search for She, who was no doubt lingering close by, anticipating this reunion for as long and as eagerly as he had?

Despite his eagerness to behold She once again, a heavy fatigue continued to weigh upon his body as it had since he returned to consciousness, preventing him as of yet from rolling over onto his feet. Instead he continued to lie upon his back and look up in wonder at the tiny forest of shrunken human heads that dangled from the ceiling above him. Surely, given such an astonishment, She could wait for him a few moments longer, having waited this long already. But the truth was that even if he had wanted to pull himself free from the hypnotic spell of the heads—each twisting slowly at the end of the length of hair from which they were hung, their leathern countenances frozen in every manner of protest at the fate that had befallen them—he probably would not have been able to do so without her help; so profound was their hold upon him.

It was only when a powerfully tall figure opened the door and entered the room that Felix managed to summon the discipline to break free from his reverie and roll over onto his feet. And once the figure had set down his load in the corner of the room and approached him where he stood now shakily on top of a table at the center—the figure's ornately tattooed visage coming into focus before him like an illustrated specter—Felix thought to himself that if this was indeed the shores of the afterlife he had arrived upon, then this towering deity was the perfect spirit guide to carry him across the river.

*****

Amos had to wait for his chance to interrogate the mysterious girl until after his first round of chores had been completed. That morning, those chores had included seeing to the ferrets in their stall, then helping Murdough to herd the sheep out onto the pasture land, where they would be left to graze throughout most of the afternoon. The ferrets themselves had been left behind, with Murdough citing a hole torn in their wire fence during the previous hunt as the reason they could not be put to task that day. In fact, it was Murdough sending him back to the barn to repair this very hole once he had settled the sheep that had finally given him the opportunity he was looking for.

As he suspected, the tear in the fence took only a few minutes to repair. He could tell that Murdough was largely using the break in the wiring as an excuse to lighten his own workload while simultaneously not having to deal with the creatures he so clearly detested. So after twisting the broken strands back together using a pair of tongs he had located in the shearing shed that stood apart from the barn, Amos calculated that he had several hours still left before he was needed back in the fields to bring the sheep in at the end of the day.

Then he set out to find her.

He finally located her in one of the many upstairs bedrooms of the great house, one that he had come upon only after creeping about in rooms where he knew he had no business being in for what seemed to him like an eternity. At every turn, he felt as if he was going to run into Miss Hollis coming along some dark corridor or that Master Thackery was going to throw open a door and catch him there like a thief in the house. And what would he do or say if either of these scenarios came to pass? Try as hard as he might, he could not bring himself to think of a fanciful explanation to explain his presence in the manor at that hour, an inability that only fed into and amplified his fear of being apprehended.

She was down on her hands and knees with her back to him, scrubbing the wooden floor of the room with soap and water, when he dived through the doorway and took hold of her uniform by the shoulder. "What have you done with him?" he hissed, pulling on the fabric and lifting her off the ground.

The girl immediately pulled herself free of his grip as though she had been prepared for this surprise attack, and when she spun around to face him, she was holding her bristled scrubbing brush over her head like a cudgel. There was something terrifyingly wild about the expression she wore on her face, like she would feel no remorse about cracking his skull open with the brush, that immediately caused Amos to throw up his hands in an attempt to protect himself against the blows she appeared determined to rain down upon him.

The girl never softened her expression once or lowered the brush from the air as Amos shrank back from his initial assault. It was only after observing him in his current state of retreat for a moment, cringing back up against the canopied bed and peering out at her like a coward through his fingers, that she grew convinced she was in no real danger and relaxed her pose. Then she stepped quietly to the doorway, looking out into the hall to see that he had not been observed entering, before turning to face him.

Her face seemed only incrementally less ferocious as she moved back toward him across the creaking boards. Amos, nevertheless, gathered the strength to lower his hands from his face as she approached. But he was still incapable of fixing his eyes on anything more than the buckled shoes of her uniform as he opened his mouth to speak.

"I saw the gesture you made to me yesterday," he warbled, after clearing his throat, "and I know that you've taken him somewhere good—for safekeeping, no doubt. And I'm grateful for what you've done, I truly am. I just want to know that he's all right, that he's safe."

These were as many words as any boy her age with his pale complexion had ever uttered to her in her lifetime. And, judging by her past experiences with boys who fit this description, she had no cause to believe that this one cowering before her was truly any different from all the rest. The only pale-faced boys she had ever encountered before were the ones who hung around the docks in Wellington when she rode to the port with her father, the ones who jeered and threw things at her while she waited for him in the wagon to come back with their supplies.

But she found herself thinking at this moment that there was something different about this particular white boy, something kinder and softer, even as her better judgment fought to remind her that they were all the same, that not a one of them was to be trusted. She had not even understood half of what he had only just said to her, given that she was still only beginning to comprehend this strange new language the pale ones had brought with them in their boats from the west. Perhaps he had said nothing sizably different from the cruel taunts they shouted at her in town.

And yet he had chosen not to slaughter the dying creature, had he not? He even went so far as to hide it away in his room for its own protection. Surely none of the dirty boys down at the port with stones in their hands would ever have done something so good on behalf of another creature. And when he finally summoned the courage to lift his chin and look directly at her, she beheld a pair of eyes of such clear and expansive blue they reminded her of nothing more than the vast ceiling of sky that had always hung above and sheltered her since she was a baby.

And her resistance faded.

*****

"Ah-my-ah."

One *my* held between two *ah*s, he thought to himself, hurrying back over the hill to where the sheep were grazing. That was how he would remember her name, a name he had never heard before but wished now never to forget. He only had to say it out loud a hundred times more so that, in the repetition of the sounds, it might be pressed into his memory for all time, something he was only too happy to do.

"Ah-my-ah."

It was Tama (tah-mah), her father, who had first sounded out the name for him; Tama, the same tattooed driver who had delivered him in the wagon from the port in Wellington two nights earlier. And it was Tama, too, whom Amos found nurturing his Felix back to health when the girl opened the door to the weathered old shack that stood at the furthest border of Thackery's property and ushered him inside.

Felix was standing at the edge of the table with his eyes shut, licking some sort of paste off the tip of the Māori's index finger, when Amos first stepped into the small shed. So intent was he on consuming every last particle of the strange concoction that he took no notice of Amos's initial entrance or of his tentative approach when he moved closer to investigate. The potion being offered to him at the end of the long brown finger was far too delicious to allow his attention to be stolen away by anything else, even the familiar face of the boy he knew, and he savored each lick of its mysterious sweetness with complete concentration.

It was sugar, Tama explained in his halting English, that Felix had needed to restore his energy, and so he had created the mash from a mixture of wild berries that grew in the area, blended with an assortment of natural herbs that he kept in a series of glass jars on a shelf by the window. Amos could hardly argue with the Māori's logic as he watched him scoop another small heap of mash out of a tin on the table with his finger, seeing as how Felix appeared to have already put on several ounces of healthy weight in just the brief time since he had bathed him in his room the day before.

"Not just meat," Tama muttered in his deep basso, smiling as the hungry creature continued lapping at his finger. "Animal need sweet, too, to give life."

Once Felix had finished off the entire contents of the tin, he instantly fell asleep without ever once opening his eyes. It was then, as Amos held him across his lap and stroked his skin with the back of his fingers, that Tama came back to the table with a sheet of parchment paper and wrote out his and his daughter's name with a quill pen. Amaia—for that was how the girl's name was spelled, translated into the Latin alphabet from the original Māori—had long since left to return to her duties, leaving him to grow more acquainted with the man whose tattooed visage had once caused him to shudder in fear.

After he had written out and pronounced both names, Tama set aside the paper and quill and stood to prepare a pot of tea for them to share, using the purplish-colored leaves from one of the jars on the shelf. As he heated up the pot on the corner cook stove, Amos took the opportunity to scan the interior while breathing in the unpleasant aroma, doing his best not to focus too much attention on the shrunken heads dangling above him.

He had never spent any time in such a rude dwelling. Besides the cook stove, the table and chairs at the center, and the narrow pallet against the wall covered in a thin layer of straw, there was hardly anything more to remark upon other than the bottles on the wall, the opened window that looked back toward the great house, and the forest of shrunken heads that moved softly in the breeze. And yet for some unknown reason, Amos could not remember ever feeling as comfortable in a home of any sort as he felt in this humble one now.

"Is good you decide no kill this one," Tama said, setting down a steaming cup in front of Amos. As if on cue, Felix yipped and tossed for a moment in Amos's lap before settling back into his regular pattern of sleep.

"His name is Little Red," Amos responded, freeing a hand and reaching out for the cup. "I knew him back in England. It seems like a miracle that we would meet again so far from home."

"No such thing as miracle," Tama responded, sitting in the seat across from him. "It's natural order." He watched as Amos lifted the cup to his lips and sniffed it suspiciously. "You no kill him"—he pointed at Felix—"so I no poison you."

Amos felt a sinking in his stomach as his old fears returned until Tama turned to him and grinned, letting him know that he had only been teasing. Then he relaxed in his chair once more and took a cautious sip from his cup. Surprisingly, the tea tasted rich and sweet, nothing like how it smelled, and he happily took a second sip after overcoming the surprise of the first.

"See?" Tama continued grinning.

Once they had settled into each other's company, Amos listened raptly as Tama told him the tale of how he had come to work on Thackery's land; how his wife, Amaia's mother, had contracted small-pox from the European settlers, along with many other members of their tribe; how he had been left alone to raise an infant child after her long suffering and death; and how he had ultimately decided to cast his lot with the same colonists whose diseased blood had murdered her, by signing up to work for the New Zealand Company. All this he relayed in a hushed, even tone, devoid of any overt feeling. And all the while he was speaking, the shrunken heads of the Māori who had died to make way for European Empire turned slowly above, looking silently down upon them.

And still Felix slept on.

"That is all in the past," he finally concluded, setting down his empty cup. "There is no going back. What I want is that Amaia go forward into the future. And the future is English. I, her father, learn to read a little, yes? Write a little? But still, it is only a little. And with looking like this?" Here, he lifted his powerful hands from the table to touch the sides of his face, drawing attention to his tribal mark-ings. "There is no more future for me other than what is. But this should not be so for Amaia. For her, there should be more."

For the first time in his long oration, Tama broke off speaking and allowed his gaze to drift outside the window. Amos got the sense that there was some powerful emotion that he was wrestling with internally, that he was trying to push down, even as he detected the presence of a tear rising up in the corner of his left eye. And then, swallowing hard and composing himself once more, Tama turned his attention back to the English boy sitting across from him.

"I make with you a deal," he said, his voice recovering its unwavering baritone. "This good animal, he will make good hunter for many years. Master Thackery be very pleased with you for not killing him. But he still weak. He still need to be made well. I make your Little Red well to hunt once more if you teach Amaia English.

That old witch Hollis, she no want her to learn. But *I* want her to learn. *I* want her to learn and leave this place and never come back. You promise to be her teacher, I promise to make your friend well."

It was this deal, which Amos had agreed to in an instant, that had him feeling almost giddy as he hurried past the flock toward the wagon, which was parked beneath the shade of a solitary tree. He had not been able to get her face out of his mind ever since she threatened him with her scrubbing brush, the fearsome beauty of it. And now he was to be her teacher, whatever that meant, while having Little Red restored to him in the bargain? It all seemed too good to be true, and he could not resist letting out one final cry while racing round to the rear of the wagon.

"Ah-my-ah!"

Murdough, who had been passed out since late morning with his hat draped across his face, sat bolt upright at the sound of the Amos's wild cry. For a long moment, he hardly seemed to recognize where he was or the identity of the young man standing in front of him, smiling. Presently, however, the answers to both reemerged through the fog of alcoholic fumes clouding his brain, and he kicked at his new assistant petulantly to drive him back before struggling to heave himself out.

"Must've been a good sleep, Mr. Murdough," Amos observed laughingly, dodging the flying feet. "Time to bring in the herd."

"Y'fix that fence like I told ya'?" Murdough snapped, allowing his legs to dangle off the back of the wagon for a minute while dragging his forearm across his brow to wipe away the sweat.

"Yes sir, Mr. Murdough," Amos teased back while keeping at a safe distance, still in too much of a giddy mood to allow his spirits to be dampened by the old sot. "Just like you said."

Murdough reached back into the bed of the wagon while mumbling at the boy's smart reply and came up with the elixir he had been nursing the whole day. He tossed back his head and drank off the last dregs. Then he threw the empty bottle off into the grass nearby. Dropping to the ground, he shuffled round to slam closed the rear panel and to lock it. When he finished and turned back, Amos was still standing in the same spot, staring at him mockingly.

"Wha' are you lookin' at?" Murdough snarled.

"Nothing, Mr. Murdough," Amos replied innocently. "Only you."

Although he did not have his wits about him enough to know just exactly how he was doing it, Murdough was aware nonetheless that the boy was being insolent, that he was being mocked. If it were up to him, he would fire the lad this instant and be done with him before the situation was allowed to progress any further. Thackery would demand to know why he had suddenly let him go, however, and then what would you say? That the boy was being insolent but he could not quite say how?

No, he would have to wait a little longer till some graver offense was committed. Then he could send him packing, as he had all the others who had come before him. Right now, he would have to suffer his insolence and bide his time. One thing was certain, though—he knew that there was something about this boy that he deeply disliked.

"Jus' watch y'don't get too big for your britches" was all he could manage to come up with at the moment, taking a threatening step toward the boy.

"Oh, I will, Mr. Murdough, sir." Amos grinned, holding his ground as the herder's sour breath assailed him. "You don't have to worry about that. Only, you have to admit, there are some days when a man's britches feel mighty big all on their own."

Peering directly into his dull eyes, Amos could tell that he had won the standoff between them for now. He also knew that he could not afford to push his luck much further or his job as Amaia's English tutor would be over before it had begun.

"I'll gather the sheep."

Amos turned and headed off toward the grazing flock, fully aware that his every step was being scrutinized. Nevertheless, he could not deny himself the final satisfaction of whistling a happy tune as he walked away.

*****

And why had Felix yipped earlier at the table and tossed in his sleep just as Amos and Tama were about to strike their deal?

As it would happen, the two men sitting at the table were not the only ones at that moment striking a deal. For even as he lay asleep across Amos's lap, Felix was chasing a swirl of colored lights down the long dark corridor of his unconscious mind. They were the same lights that used to guide him to his quarry during the hunt, but he had not seen them since he and the others had been boarded upon the ship and sent away. And it was the initial recognition that they had returned to him again that caused him to suddenly stir violently in Amos's lap before settling in to pursue them as he had done before.

It took some effort, but eventually, he located the largest reddest point of light in the constellation and locked on to it exclusively, following it down and down into the darkness until all other colors disappeared from view. The closer he got to overtaking it, the larger it grew until at last it seemed to surround him on all sides, and he was tumbling end over end into the heart of the light. Felix instinctively opened his mouth, expecting that, at any moment, he would feel his jaws clamp down around the throat of his prey.

And that was when the vision of She appeared out of the deepest heart center of the glowing light.

"Mother?" Felix gasped, his jaw growing slack.

"My sweet Felix."

The voice whispered all around him, enfolding him in its warmth, as the endless waves emanating from the center, flowing from her image, carried him gently aloft.

"But you were gone for so long," he heard himself whimper.

"I told you I would return," She admonished softly. "Did you lose faith, my sweet?"

"Never that," he answered disingenuously. "But so much has happened that you weren't here for."

"I was here the whole time, my love."

"Why didn't you come sooner then?" he pressed, his voice becoming more adamant.

Tears began to rise weightlessly from the surface of Felix's eyes as he anticipated her response. They drifted toward her like diamonds, circling around her head.

"Because you wouldn't let me. So long as your heart was closed, there was no way for me to enter. I was waiting by the door, but you wouldn't open it. Until today."

"But how?"

"By opening your heart to others, you opened it to me."

"The boy…" Felix faltered, as though suddenly realizing something important for the first time, "he saved me."

"And the one in the painted mask made you well again. Even a heart as sealed off as your own could no longer go on believing that there was no more goodness left in the world after all they had done for you. And once you allowed that such goodness was possible, you opened the door to me."

Felix felt as though he was being turned inside out by these revelations, like the red had begun to flow inside him with each word she said and take hold of something vital he had buried there deep inside, pulling it out of its hiding place and exposing it to the light of her gaze. He began to convulse in sharp contractions, feeling his whole body seize in pain, and for a moment he experienced a panic that he would not survive the reversal. Until he heard the sound of her shushing him and stopped resisting, surrendered himself completely to the inevitability of her argument, and began to weep.

"But, Mother," he sobbed, hearing once more the sound of the ship's engine and Kara's cries of terror, "there is so much evil in the world."

"Which makes the good we do all the more magnificent. Remember, even in the midst of the hunt, there is room for mercy." The tears he had shed had formed themselves into an unbroken halo around her head as she looked at him with unwavering kindness. "Where is your mercy for Kara?"

"I couldn't save her when she needed me to."

"Maybe not then but what about now? The hunt continues, after all."

"She's found another who's kind to her. Besides, each time I look upon the child, I'm reminded of how I failed. Perhaps I should leave her to love these others and forget about me."

She's black eyes seemed to pierce to his very core as her face began to rise up into the air, growing smaller as it drifted away from him. Meanwhile, Felix began to feel as though he were drifting slowly downward, sinking into the billowing red sea that had carried him aloft thus far.

"If there is one thing I am certain of, my love," she whispered, her voice, too, growing distant as she continued to drift further away, "it's that she needs you now more than ever."

"But wait!" Felix cried, panicked that he was losing her again so soon after finding her. "What should I do? What should I say?"

Then he was clutching at her desperately, trying to hold on to her for as long as he could. But She was moving away from him now at rapid speed, and Felix was spinning further down. Her final words, however, continued to echo in his brain even as he plummeted into the abyss.

"Go to her."

*****

It could hardly be said that Felix's love for Kara came roaring back to life simply because She had come back into his. For despite his mother's inducement to go directly to her, he was still far too weak to return to the barn. Tama had been right when he told Amos that Felix would continue to require his attention in order to be restored to full health.

Indeed, the very next morning after Amos's first visit to the shack, Felix barely awoke from the deep sleep he had fallen into after She's visitation, and his breathing was fast and shallow as a powerful fever fell upon and consumed him. When several days passed in this fashion, with the fever showing no signs of letting up, Tama became nearly convinced that Felix might not make it through, after all.

The fever finally broke on the third day, and Felix emerged from it weakened but very much alive. The aftereffects of the fever set back his overall recovery, however, requiring several additional days of proper care and feeding in order to keep him from slipping back into illness. Tama patiently carried out these healing ministrations while continuing to perform his required livery duties around the farm, frequently racing back to the shack after driving Thackery to or from the port in just enough time to stir up one of his restorative concoctions for the rebounding mustelid.

A powerful bond thus formed between the two over the course of Felix's slow recovery. And many were the nights when Felix found himself anxiously listening for the sound of Tama's footsteps hurrying home to the shack after a long day spent dozing atop his sleeping pallet, staring up at the heads as they swayed and scowled above. His desire for the Māori's return eventually had less to do with any requirement for nourishment on his part and far more to do with his desire for the man's comforting presence. At night, they would lie together in the straw and the aborigine would sing songs in his native tongue so softly and sweetly that Felix could not help but think they were the most beautiful sounds he had ever heard, as he curled up contentedly into Tama's side.

All the while that this was taking place out in the shack, Amos and Amaia were forging their own bond back at the main house. Almost immediately they had started meeting secretly in her tiny servant's quarters off the kitchen to begin their nightly English tutorials. And given that nearly every move Amaia made during the day was performed beneath the watchful eye of Miss Hollis, they frequently had to conduct these lessons at a significantly late hour, once the rest of the house and its headmistress had all gone off to sleep. Amos would lie atop the bedcovers in his room, feeling his heartbeat racing wildly in his chest, and listen for the silence that signaled it was safe for him to creep down the hall to where he knew she would be waiting for him, her own heartbeat racing just as fast.

Yes, they studied letters, the ones he drew out for her on paper stolen from Thackery's study. And, yes, they studied the sounds these letters made when combined together, the sounds they whispered back and forth to each other while sitting close together on the floor, their knees touching, for fear of waking the dreaded Hollis. But mostly they studied their racing heartbeats, each synchronized with the other, so that their lessons in language quickly developed into lessons about something much deeper, something beyond letters and sounds.

We will largely leave the fumblings and flowerings of these clandestine tutorials to the participants themselves. Suffice it to say that time passed in this manner—Felix and Tama developing one language between them and Amos and Amaia developing another—until two whole calendar weeks lay behind them all and Felix was no closer to Kara than he had been the night that She had appeared to him. But just as he was starting to fear that She might appear to him once more to admonish him for losing his purpose, something occurred to finally bring about their long delayed reunion.

It began with the heel of Murdough's heavy boot coming down upon the delicate skull of a young hob and splitting it in half. And while the force of the initial blow had been good enough to terminate the unsuspecting creature's life in an instant, Murdough continued to stomp on it again and again until what had once been its head was now just a bloody pile of pulp at the center of the barn. Meanwhile, the other animals, sheep and ferret alike, fled from the sudden outburst of violence, stampeding themselves back into their designated stalls for fear of being the next to fall beneath the boot of the drunkard's wrath.

Ironically, it had been a fairly productive day out in the field, with the hunters ferreting out over a dozen rabbits from a newly discovered warren and destroying them. The young hob had been found asleep in the mouth of one of the tunnels at the end of the hunt, however, and this fact seemed to enrage Murdough more than the success the animals had had as a whole. He fumed about the lazy creature from his perch atop the wagon the whole ride back to the barn, while Amos walked beside him with his staff, herding the flock before them with the able assistance of an enthusiastic sheepdog named Victoria, named for the current reigning monarch.

Because he himself had decided just that morning that the hob was old enough to join them for its first hunt, Amos came in for a fair amount of Murdough's verbal scorn, with the old sot raining down insults and threatening to report his ineptitude and have him thrown off the farm. Such threats had become part and parcel of his time with Murdough, so Amos hardly paid them any mind. Anyone knew, Thackery included, that young hobs frequently succumbed to the sleep sickness when they were first developing their taste for the hunt. And, besides, his thoughts were already on that night's lesson with Amaia when they planned on using a map she had stolen from the master's study to sound out the names of all the capital cities of the world, each one a destination spot he dreamed of taking her to one day.

In hindsight, he wondered if perhaps it was his indifference to Murdough's invective that had spurred the man to murderous rage. He only knew that he was startled when, carrying the offending hob in his left hand by the scruff of its neck into the barn, the creature was suddenly snatched out of his hand and thrown down onto the hard packed earth. And then all became chaos as the stomping began and the other animals ran for cover. But even in the midst of the chaos, one thought presented itself to him with complete clarity. If he was ever going to make this deranged maniac pay for his crime, he would have to summon Little Red.

*****

Castor had been hanging from Amos's right hand at the time of the mashing and had witnessed the whole incident from above and up close. Looking down from the height of the boy's waist, he saw the blood leap out from the bottom of Murdough's boot, even as he heard the sound of the skull collapsing beneath its weight. It was the same sound made when the herder smashed open the skulls of the rabbits that he and the others managed to ferret out of their nest with his hammer; only this was not a rabbit that he was pulverizing but one of their own. And as he watched what had once been the head of his fellow ferret reduced to pulp with each successive blow, he realized that it could just as well have been him there beneath the herder's boot; that, with the slightest misstep, he, too, might be ground into nothingness.

The fact that he knew the ferret who had been exterminated by name only served to deepen Castor's subsequent sense of panic. His name had been Riker, and they had been born but a few days apart, his mother having been one of the jills, along with Kara, forcibly impregnated aboard the *Embeth Tamara*. Among the younger hobs, he was known to be the one most enamored of Castor's hunting prowess. Oftentimes he would pester him for details about the day's hunt well into the evening after they had returned to the stall, anxious for any bit of information that would reveal how he, too, might one day grow to become a great hunter like his hero, become the hunter they both had been bred to be.

And now after only one chance, he was gone—gone in an instant—simply for committing the one mistake they were all susceptible of making, that of falling asleep. For no amount of polecat blood seemed capable of erasing the flaw that hundreds of years of genetic engineering had built into all their makeups: narcolepsy.

That night, the sleep pyramid veritably shook from its foundations as Castor trembled with a newfound dread that what had happened to Riker might very well happen to him unless he continued to outperform all the rest. He tossed and turned restlessly, formulating new strategies in his mind, new plans of attack, but always these thoughts were interrupted by flashes of the memory of Riker's skull exploding into a bloody mess. It only drove him to panic more and to tremble more as he fought to focus on just one thing—destroying the enemy.

Kara, who had begun to recover from her period of grieving after the death of Felix, tried with all her mental energy to reach out to her son from her place at the top of the pile, sensing his fevered despair. But regardless of how many times she attempted to insinuate her thoughts into his, Castor's mind would not allow him to admit any soothing words, not if he was ever going to survive.

It was kill or be killed; Riker's death had made that clear. And the only way to avoid ending up beneath the herder's boot was to make himself into a killing machine.

This was precisely what he planned on doing.

*****

It was rare that Thackery would abandon his study to join them out in the fields. Rarer still that he would stand among men from outside the farm, men he had paid to have brought out from the port at Wellington just that morning in the back of Tama's wagon. But this was to be no ordinary hunt. As a result, his presence among them in his official capacity seemed to be what was required, given the circumstances. And naturally, given this high position, a speech seemed perfectly in order as well.

"As chief trading officer," he began, "I would like to welcome you all here today and to extend to each and every one of you my deepest gratitude for what you are about to do on behalf of the colony and the New Zealand Company."

The men gathered around him in a circle, listening, seemed unsure as to how to best respond in the pause he allowed after his formal greeting. A few awkwardly attempted to clap their hands together, assuming that this was what the great man before them would have them to do, but the heavy mallets they held in their hands, the ones they had been provided with upon their arrival at the farm, made it difficult to make any appreciable sound of applause. The best they could do was bring the palm of their free hand up against the head of the mallet held in the other, managing only the dull slap of flesh against wood.

The majority barely seemed to be listening at all to the words he was saying and stood there hollow-eyed and silent. Most, he knew, had probably only been rousted from the alleys where they slept a little over an hour before, as he had instructed Tama to do. Most were little more than degenerates and drunkards still not fully recovered from the previous night's debaucheries, but they were men all the same and, as such, were not entirely beyond the reach of salvation. A general must accept the troops he was given, he thought, and any army, no matter how rag-tag, could stand to benefit from a Saint Crispin's-like exhortation.

And so he glanced over the heads of the begrimed assembly to where Miss Hollis and her Māori girl stood with their backs to the darkening sky, hoping for some sort of inspiration, but there was none forthcoming. Tama stood beside them as well, having distributed the last of the mallets, but he, too, seemed incapable of providing any path forward. And so he held to his original plan and pressed on, hoping that a change of heart would soon come over the rabble and settle upon them like a benediction.

"I do not need to tell you, gentlemen," he stammered, shifting nervously atop the empty potato crate that Hollis had brought to serve as a makeshift dais, "that our entire way of life and everything we hope to accomplish in this wilderness is currently under attack by an invasive population that will stop at nothing to destroy what we have built. This is an enemy far more dangerous than the native aboriginals we first encountered, who threatened us merely with their ignorance and who were quickly subdued and brought to the light of reason. This new enemy cannot be brought to the light of reason because it knows not how to reason. It lacks even the primitive reasoning abilities of our darkest-skinned brethren. I speak, of course, of the vermin of the field, who threaten us not only with their animal ignorance but with sickness, disease, and death!"

Thackery could see that his words were doing little to stir the sorry mob, despite his soaring rhetoric. They continued to stare back at him like the somnambulates they were, barely able to keep upright on their feet, let alone to maintain their grips on the mallets in their hands. He would have to trust in the word of his fellow investors and gentlemen farmers, many of whom had employed these very same derelicts in similar enterprise and who assured him that, with the right amount of financial incentive, a man could be made to rise to any challenge, regardless of the lowness of his state.

Besides, the clouds had begun to gather threateningly overhead by this point in his address and Thackery knew that if he did not abbreviate his speech, he stood a good chance of being caught out in the deluge with these foul-smelling mercenaries, something he was determined to avoid at all cost. So it was time to encapsulate his theme and get back inside.

"Just remember the faces of your wives, your children, while you are out there in battle today!" he shouted, just as Murdough and the boy his daughter had sent over from England arrived on the scene in their wagon. "Think of them lying on their deathbeds, dying of plague!"

Their faces betrayed no thought, no feeling. His was an army of stone.

"And if that isn't enough," Thackery surrendered, "remember you're getting paid six pence a hide."

The collective roar that went up from the men was so loud and instantaneous it nearly drowned out the sound of the thunder rumbling overhead as they cheered and shook their mallets in the air. Thackery tried his best to conceal the disgust he felt for their base motives as he stepped down from the potato crate and made his way through the freshly energized throng toward the wagon. When he arrived, Murdough had already gotten down off his seat and was standing before the rear panel.

"For the record, Master Thackery," he said, smiling unctuously while shifting his weight nervously, "I just wanna remind you that I don' think this is such a good idea. Arming all these hooligans, that is, and settin' loose the ferrets without puttin' up a fence first."

"The record is duly noted, Mr. Murdough," Thackery answered, stopping just short of his reprobate employee and looking mad enough to spit. "But may I remind *you* that if you had done your job properly in the first place, such measures would not have become necessary."

"But I only have but one good tracker in the entire bunch!" Murdough protested, abandoning his obsequious grin.

"Isn't it time you stopped blaming a pack of simple-minded beasts for failures of your own doing?" Thackery rejoined sharply. "Why do you suppose I pay you your salary? So that you can stand around, making excuses for why you haven't done what I asked?"

Amos, who had been sitting up front listening to their exchange, hopped down from the wagon at this point, doing his best not to attract any undue attention. There was one person watching him, however, as he undid the canvas sack he had secretly tied earlier to

151

the underside of the wagon—Amaia. And as he came up with the sack, he felt her eyes upon him and turned in her direction.

The breath caught in his throat as it always did whenever he first saw her, and the two exchanged a furtive smile until Miss Hollis appeared out of the corner of his eye and shooed the girl back to her duties in the main house. The officious old woman followed on her heels but not before glowering back at him as though to indicate she was aware that something improper was going on that would soon be exposed. Amos lowered his eyes to the ground abashedly and moved to the rear of the wagon, to where Thackery was putting the last few flourishes onto to his reprimand with venomous intensity.

"Every other property holder on the island swears by this larger-scaled approach and their lands are practically free of the menace by now. Only *my* lands continue to suffer on account of the infestation, thanks to your incompetence, and I simply will not have it be the case any longer. You've run out of time, Mr. Murdough. Now kindly step aside and open that wagon."

Murdough hesitated for a moment longer, telegraphing his contempt, then turned to open the rear panel. "Jus' don' blame ole Murdough if things don' work out the way you'd like," he muttered, unfastening the lock. "Like I told ya, I only have but one good tracker."

"Two," Amos interjected, just as Thackery opened his mouth and was about to lose his composure entirely at Murdough's expense. Both men stopped what they were doing and turned their attention to the young assistant as he reached his hand into a canvas sack at his feet and held up a ferret whose skin was so unnaturally pale and pink, it seemed to glow like a torch against the roiling gray-green of the sky.

"Well, I'll be damned," Murdough exclaimed as the wood slipped from his hand and the back panel of the wagon fell open with a crash.

The ferrets inside had instinctively moved to the rear of the wagon when it had first come to a halt and were standing at the edge in a neat row when the panel dropped open. Thus, they, too, beheld Felix, returned from the dead, mere seconds after the two humans had. The effect of witnessing his resurrection upon them was instantaneous and profound, as they each began to thrash about the wagon in a weasel warrior reel of shock. Some even danced too close to the edge in their lunatic reel and tumbled out onto the ground.

As the business thrashed about in wonderment and Murdough was struck stone still, Thackery took a step toward the boy and reached out his hand to stroke the belly of the ghastly looking creature. Felix blinked his unnerving red eyes at the wealthy capitalist as the old man's veined fingers gently moved across the soft skin of his undercarriage.

"His name is Little Red," Amos began tentatively. "He belonged to your daughter's husband back in England, and he was known to be a great hunter then."

"Little Red," Thackery repeated, as though temporarily mesmerized. "I see. Yes, I think she wrote to me about him long ago. So is this then the same hairless you were told to destroy when you first arrived?"

"The very same one," Amos confessed, trying his best to sound sure of himself. "And I realize that it was wrong not to have done what you'd instructed me to do. I'm truly sorry for my disobedience. But I just felt that with the proper care and treatment, he could be made into a great fighter again. And then you would have *two* good trackers instead of one."

Tama, who had been surreptitiously wending his way through the crowd of men since Amos got down from the wagon, monitoring the scene, came up behind Murdough just as the old inebriate broke from his spell and lurched at his assistant. Grabbing his arms from behind and restraining him, it was all he could do not to accidentally step down on one of the ferrets dancing on the ground around his feet.

"Get your hands off me, savage!" Murdough exclaimed once Tama had pulled him back a safe distance and released him. Then, after spitting a green wad of phlegm at Tama's feet to punctuate his disgust, he turned to his employer, his face florid with rage. "Y'see that there? Treachery! That's wha' that is! Nothin' but treachery!"

"And what," Thackery began, lowering his hand and turning to his incensed herder, "would you have me do about this…treachery?"

A bolt of lightning flashed overhead before Murdough could offer up his answer, causing him to cringe in his shoes. Almost immediately thereafter, there was a long, rumbling roll of thunder; it was clear that the clouds above would not hold out much longer. What was also clear was that the men who had been brought out from Wellington were growing almost uncontrollable in their restlessness to get started and to collect their money. It appeared they were prepared to start using the mallets on each other if the situation by the wagon were not resolved quickly.

"Well?" Thackery prodded.

"Release 'im," Murdough mumbled. Then, clearing his throat, he spoke with greater clarity. "It's the only thing to be done for 'is insubordination. Release 'im."

"I know what I did was insubordinate," Amos interjected, holding Felix out in front of him while stepping toward his employer, "but just look at him. Look at what a terror he could be to those rabbits. And Mr. Murdough was just going to give up on him, get rid of him, just like he got rid of that young hob yesterday when he smashed his skull into the dirt."

Tama let out a low note of disapproval as he began to gather up the ferrets writhing in the dirt, lifting them back into the wagon. Thackery turned back to look squarely into Amos's face, to take the measure of his honesty, then looked to Murdough for some explanation as to what he had just heard.

"Is this true?" he asked. "Did you destroy one of the animals?"

"It was worthless," Murdough snickered uncomfortably. "All he did was sleep."

"From what I've observed," Thackery retorted, "that is all *you* do as well. And the animal's *worth* was not yours to assess. It belonged to me. And as such, it was my property, which you had no right to destroy. You are correct, Mr. Murdough, someone needs to be released, but it is not the boy. It is you. Gather your belongings, and leave my lands immediately."

Murdough glowered at each of the three men united against him now, but it was clear that not a one of them would give an inch. Realizing that he had lost the battle, he allowed a sardonic smile to cross his face as he reached into his coat and produced a small bottle of grain alcohol from the inside pocket. He pulled out the cork, took a long swig, and restoppered the flask before dropping it back into his pocket.

"This ain't over, boy." He grinned, narrowing his eyes at Amos. And then, turning his gaze to Tama, he added, "I'll be seein' you too, savage." And then, buttoning his coat and adjusting the hat on his head, the defeated man turned on his heels and pushed his way through the restless crowd, headed back toward the house.

"Follow him at a distance," Thackery said, watching him go. "Make sure he leaves without incident." Tama obediently sprang into action, pursuing Murdough through the throng, as Thackery turned his attention back to Amos. "That was quite a performance, young man. I hope you know what you're doing."

Amos smiled and lifted Felix to his lips. "Good boy," he whispered in his ear, then lifted him over the side, and released him into the back of the wagon. Taking a small piece of parchment paper from his own inside pocket, he unscrolled it while approaching Thackery to show him what was written there. "I took the liberty of drawing up a map of the fields and made a mark wherever I saw that there was an underground entrance."

The first raindrop fell directly onto one of Amos Xs as Thackery studied the map admiringly, causing the ink to run. He looked up into the clouds overhead, which were promising to open up at any second and release their deluge.

"Don't waste any more time explaining it to me," Thackery said, lowering his eyes and gesturing toward his disorderly corps of hammer wielders. "It's to them you have to explain it."

Thackery turned back to the young man at his side and trained upon him a look of almost fatherly affection. Amos found himself staggered for a moment, overwhelmed by an unexpectedly powerful sense of pride, before he stepped to the wagon and secured the back panel one last time to keep the ferrets in place, now that he was to be in charge of them.

"Back in an instant, little ones." He smiled down at them after locking it in place. "And then we can begin." Then he hurried off to the men with their mallets as Thackery grinned contentedly and trailed behind.

Inside the transport, Felix found himself facing off against the others across the length of the wagon, like a prisoner staring down his firing squad. Now that their wild reel had come to an end, most of the ferrets pressed themselves back against the opposite panel to get as far away from him as they could get, frozen with fear as though they were seeing a ghost.

"It's me, Felix," he offered to them in a whisper as the rain began to beat down on the wagon like a drum. "I've come back."

For a moment, there was nothing but silence and the sound of the driving rain. Then Kara distinguished herself from the business by abandoning the safety of their company at the far side of the wagon and moving toward him. She crossed to the center and stopped, holding him in her gaze. The rainwater had dampened her light-colored mask and darkened it; for an instant, he thought to himself that she had never looked more beautiful. And then she whispered back to him, her voice weary with sadness.

"We thought you were dead," she sighed, sounding almost disappointed that the truth was otherwise. "We thought you were dead."

Castor had crept up to stand beside his mother and was staring at Felix incredulously, like he was a phantom returned from the afterlife to haunt them. Felix could not decide which was worse, Kara's disappointment or Castor's disbelief, and as the downpour soaked his skin, he found himself reaching out to She for guidance.

"What shall I do?" he whispered to her, his voice sounding nervous and frail.

Her answer came back without delay, as though she were standing right there beside him.

"You'll know when the time comes."

*****

156

The rain came teeming down in rippling cataracts that billowed like curtains on the wind by the time the hunt was poised to get underway. It was a rain like none Amos had ever experienced before, tropical in nature and alive at its core, and it had already turned the field upon which the men were spread out into a shallow lake of grass and mud. Blessedly, it was a warm rain despite it being unremitting, leaving him comically drenched to the bone but somehow not chilly in his damp clothes—so very different than anything they had back in England.

The men had been positioned based on the Xs of the map. Along with their heavy mallets, they had each been given a ferret to hold while standing at the entrances to their tunnels, waiting for Amos to give the signal. Judging by the way the animals squirmed uncomfortably in their grip, it was clear that many of them had never held a creature such as this before or imagined that they ever would. Even through the deluge, it was clear that many of them wore disapproving expressions of disgust on their faces as the ferrets twisted and clawed at them to be let go.

From the dryness of the indoors, Thackery watched the events unfolding in the distance through an opening in the lace curtains of his study. Little was he aware that Amaia was standing directly above him at that same moment in his bed chambers, likewise looking out the window, even as she was supposed to be performing her household chores. She could hear Miss Hollis moving about in the kitchen below, preparing food for the men to eat once they were through with their mission, and knew that she would not be caught slacking from her duties.

After distributing the last of the ferrets, Tama hurried back to the wagon, splashing across the flooded earth, and came up beside Amos. Rainwater poured off the rim of his stovepipe hat as he bent at the waist to shout above the din of the monsoon.

"We good to start."

Felix, who had been dangling from Amos's right arm throughout the preparations, monitoring his own quickening heartbeat, suddenly found himself being hoisted up into the air and turned to face the boy who had sailed halfway round the world to save him. Drops of rain fell from the end of his nose and the bottoms of his ears as a gentle smile crossed his face. And his eyes, which were always the color of sky, seemed even more so now as they twinkled with affection behind his damp lashes.

"Show them how it's done, Little Red," he said.

And although the meaning of the words was lost to Felix, his heartbeat calmed perceptively at the sound of their serene tone. Then he was passed to the painted man who had nursed him back to health in the room of shrunken heads and watched as the boy jumped up onto the back of the wagon to address the others in his inscrutable language.

"Be careful not to hit any of the ferrets when they chase them out of the holes," he shouted. "It's only rabbits we're paying for and don't mix up the two. Now are you ready?"

Felix watched as the men knelt to the muddy ground in synchronized fashion, responding en masse to something that the boy had said. Then after the boy had nodded down at the painted one from atop his platform, Felix found himself being led off to a nearby tunnel that had been designated specifically for him. As his healer knelt there and released him, Felix was practically overwhelmed by the intoxicating smell of earth rising up all around him. It was a smell both exotic and familiar—filled with the damp, loamy richness of this particular earth and earth everywhere at the same time—and his first instinct was to curl up in the mud and luxuriate in its heady fragrance.

But just as he was about to relax into the idea, he felt the powerful hand of the painted man nudging him firmly from behind and recalled that he was not here to bask in the glory of the earth, regardless of how rich it was. Then a final few words were shouted from atop the wagon (they were "Release them!"), and Tama stood and backed away, leaving Felix alone at the hollow opening. Immediately he could feel the ground beneath his feet tremble with electric energy as the other ferrets dived into their burrows and scampered down toward their prey. He alone hesitated for a moment before his burrow, suddenly unsure of how to proceed.

Had he been away from it for too long? Could a hunter forget how to hunt if his skills were allowed to fall into disuse? Had he lost his instinct entirely?

These were the questions he asked himself as he slunk through the opening in the ground to avoid Tama's critical gaze. Already the air was filling with the sounds of the enemy's cries as it was being surprised in its underground warren by the invading army. Perhaps if he just lingered here long enough inside the entrance, the job would be taken care of by the others, and he would not have to do a thing.

Just as he had committed to this plan of inactivity, he suddenly found himself propelled forward into the darkness as though racing along a slippery earthen slide. While he had been lost in his deliberations, the soil had become so oversaturated with rainwater that it veritably gave way beneath him, and now he was rocketing down toward the fray with no clear notion of what he could or would do once he got there.

Closing his eyes to the blinding darkness, even as his rate of speed was increasing, he tried his best to concentrate and to locate her face amid all the confusion. Then he watched as the pinpoint of red light that first appeared on the black screen of his mind grew steadily larger until it filled every part of his vision. And then, blossoming out of the deepest red at the heart of his thought, She appeared.

"Mother," he whispered, "I'm lost."

"Remember who you are," She whispered back, "and you can never be lost."

"What if who I am is not who I used to be?" he whimpered.

"You must have faith in yourself, my son," she said, her eyes glowing radiantly. "Follow the light."

Then her image before him began to dissolve as the field of red shrank from around the edges, contracting itself into a concentrated mass. By the time he had arrived at the bottom of the slide and crashed end over end into the warren, it had gathered itself into a tiny red star that hovered in the air above him as he righted himself in the darkness.

There was movement all around, creatures chasing and being chased, and for a brief moment, he became unsure of himself once more, unsure of how to proceed in the chaos. But then he recalled the words that She had said, "Follow the light," and he shut his eyes to the glow of the red star. And there, behind his closed lids, was revealed a galaxy of frantically moving stars, as bright and colorful as any he had ever beheld on any previous hunt.

What had been second nature once before became second nature again as Felix focused on the brightest, reddest star in the galaxy and instinctively gave chase. As he telescoped his mental energies on closing the gap between himself and the fleeing star, he could feel all the fears and doubts he had allowed to accumulate around his thoughts since that terrible night aboard the *Embeth Tamara* lift away and dissolve into dust. There was only one thing that mattered now, just as it had been the only thing that mattered after Kara had given birth to their stillborn kits, the only thing that had saved him: capture the star and extinguish its light.

Who knew how many rabbits Felix drove from their den on the day of that great massacre? So completely consumed was he by the spirit of the hunt that he could hardly keep track himself. He only knew that he could feel the rain upon his face each time he broke surface upon the heels of one of his prey, and then there was the powerful whooshing of air about his snout as the mallet was brought down upon his adversary's skull, pounding it into the muddy earth. And then Felix would dive back into the nearest open hole in pursuit of the next star, little rattled by how close the mallet had come to pounding him into the earth as well.

At the same time, Amos stood beside the wagon with Tama and took in the bloody battle unfolding before them, a battle that he himself was now responsible for, having drawn up the map and positioned his troops in the field. On the face of it, it was a scene of pure bedlam as the human component of his infantry reeled against the slate-gray sky for as far as the eye could see, swinging their mallets through the air with abandon as the rain continued to pour down in torrents. As the hours slipped by and the light faded from behind the clouds, they appeared less and less to be the same corporeal human beings that had been brought in that day from port and more like a brigade composed of silhouetted specters of the men they once were, dark spirits dancing across the surface of a boiling lake, raining down death with each blow of their hammers.

Despite the pandemonium on the surface of things, Amos could tell that the offensive was gradually starting to produce its desired outcome as the decimated corpses of more and more rabbits began to pile up across the battlefield. Largely lost from his vantage point was any sign of his mustelid troops, who flashed too briefly across the inundated theater of war, expertly dodging hammer blows before descending once more into the terra incognita. But if Amos was ever tempted to interrupt the bloody battle in order to ascertain their safety, all he had to do was consult with Tama's serene profile to trust that such intervention was unnecessary, that the campaign was progressing as it was intended to.

Beneath the surface, Felix was starting to sense that the vast warren that underlay a good majority of Thackery's grazing lands was emptying out, that the labyrinthine network of tunnels was beginning to feel less like an active maze and more like a deserted catacomb. When he closed his eyes to concentrate, there were far fewer stars on display, far fewer targets to choose from. The earth no longer vibrated with the explosive energy of the initial raid, and Felix had to search long and hard to find some new quarry visible upon the screen of his internal vision.

Just as he was about to abandon the empty warren, however, a final star appeared out of the blackness; it was as big and red a star as any that had revealed itself to him throughout the hunt. Felix immediately threw himself forward toward its glow, only to be struck by a large moving object that drove him hard sideways into the wall of the cave. For a moment, he was stunned as the object continued to hold him there, pinning him in place, before a voice whispered to him out of the dark.

"This one is mine," it said. "Leave him to me."

Though he was unable to make out any details in the gloom, Felix could tell without even seeing clearly that the voice belonged to Castor. And as his weight drew away from his side, he signaled that he would submit to his will by remaining perfectly still until the younger ferret was satisfied and raced off after the last worthy adversary down a nearby tunnel. Felix took a moment to consider the hostility in Castor's voice and what had transpired between them there beneath the earth, then gathered himself and began to claw back up to the surface via an opposite tunnel.

When he emerged from the hole, he found that the rain had finally let up and that the battle was winding down above just as it had been below. As the storm clouds peeled away to the east, revealing an incongruously beautiful pink sunset to the west, he watched as the men slogged across the muddy field, carrying the shattered corpses of their enemies to the wagon and hurling them into the back, following the orders shouted to them by the blue-eyed boy and the illustrated man who had saved him. By the front wheel of the wagon, he could see that most of the other ferrets had already given into their fatigue and arranged themselves into a sleep pyramid while the men worked around them.

Felix suddenly felt a great weariness come over him as well, a weariness so great that he could not even summon the strength to cross the muddy field and join the others where they lay. Instead he settled himself down upon the damp earth directly outside the mouth of the tunnel from which he had emerged and curled himself up into a ball. And surely that is where he would have stayed until one of the men came to collect him, were it not for the sound of an infinitely smaller creature racing toward him across the vanquished field of battle, a familiar voice that jolted him from his rest.

"He's still down there!"

It was unmistakably Kara's voice and Felix opened his eyes to see her standing over him imploringly. Though much of her features were painted over with mud and gore, he could still read the look of worry on her face as he rose unsteadily to his feet. "Castor!" she went on to explain as he turned to look back down into the abyss from whence he just escaped. "Something's happened! You have to go back and find him!"

Without hesitating, Felix dived back into the tunnel and descended once more into the depths. Scruffer, sensing that something was amiss, abandoned the warm comfort of the business to join his mate at the entrance to the burrow. When he sought her out with his thoughts to ask what she had said to Felix, however, he found that her mind was closed to him and that there was nothing more to do but stand beside her and wait.

Having tallied the final number of rabbits killed on the hunt, Amos signaled for their bodies to be carted away to a distant part of Thackery's fields, where they were to be stacked and burned. The mud-spattered men pushed from behind while Tama drove the horses from his seat above until the wheels eventually pulled free of the earth's wet grip and the wagon was off to make its gruesome deposit. Then the men gathered up their mallets and headed merrily back toward the main house, where Hollis and Amaia were at that moment setting the table in the dining room for their celebratory feast.

With nothing left to do but wait until the wagon returned for them, Amos looked down at the exhausted pile of ferrets and quickly noticed that some were missing. Scanning the muddy field, he noticed two of the missing standing by the opening to a hole and moved closer to investigate. Even before he got to where they were, the fear had begun to dawn on him that perhaps there had been a collapse, that one of the tunnels might have given way on account of the heavy rain, potentially trapping some animals below. His worst fears were confirmed when he arrived at the entrance, only to discover that one of the ferrets buried alive might very well be his own Little Red.

Before the sickening realization could take full hold of him, Felix appeared once more in the mouth of the tunnel, this time moving slowly in reverse. It was nearly impossible at first to identify him, given how much of his body was painted in mud, but it was evident that he was struggling to pull something sizable behind with his teeth. It was only after he had emerged fully into the light, pulling the object free of danger, that what he had managed to do became clear, that not only had he saved himself from a premature burial but that he had also managed to rescue the Black from his underground tomb as well.

Felix relaxed his jaw, releasing Castor to the ministrations of his frantic parents, as he sat back heavily on his haunches to catch his breath. As Kara compulsively licked the mud away from Castor's snout, desperate to create space enough for him to breathe, Felix saw the young hob open his eyes and stare up blankly at her as though waking disoriented from a frightening dream. Scruffer, too, watched from nearby, noting the moment as well when Castor opened his eyes and the great joy it brought to his mother to know that he was alive. Then he turned and fixed Felix with an ambivalent expression that said less about his own gratitude and more about emotions that ran deeper and darker than mere thanks.

"Well done, Little Red" came the words from on high, words that gave him the opportunity to look away from Scruffer's unsettling gaze and into the face of the boy, smiling down at him. "Well done," he repeated, as Felix could no longer hold off the exhaustion he felt but stretched out there and then in the mud, surrendering himself to sleep. The darkness that immediately engulfed him reverberated with She's warm whisper, echoing the boy's praise.

"Well done, my love."

*****

The distant cheers of the mallet wielders' revelries back at the house were carried to him across the dark fields on the back of a gentle breeze. The teeming storm of earlier had given way to a perfectly peaceful twilight, the soft stirrings of air the only remnants that remained of the afternoon gale. Overhead, a quarter moon hung serenely in a cobalt sky, which was only now beginning to fill with stars, as Amos looked to where Tama was seated on the opposite side of the burning pyre, illuminated by the fire's glow.

He was squatted on top of a large rock that pushed up from the earth but his eyes were closed. If it were not for the thin trail of smoke lifting from the bowl of the pipe he held clamped between his teeth, one might conclude that he had fallen asleep in that position. Perhaps he was only thinking and found it easier to do so by closing his eyes and shutting out the interrupting sounds of the crackling flames and the distant celebration. Perhaps he was even thinking the same thought that he, Amos, was thinking now, a thought that had stayed with him and grown in his mind ever since he had pulled one of the shattered corpses off the pile to feed to the ferrets later on before committing the rest to flames. The broken body lay in the grass at his feet, battered to near headlessness but somehow speaking to him nonetheless.

At the same time, he stroked a thoroughly washed and cleaned Felix in his arms as he turned his attention back to the burning tower of bodies. He could not recall what he imagined a burning pile of six hundred and thirty-eight rabbits would look like—which was the number they had destroyed that day, minus the one at his feet—or if he had even imagined it at all. He only knew that, standing before the awful reality of it now, he was filled with a feeling more like sorrow than vindication. Each of the skeletal remains threaded throughout the kindling joined together to form the lattice of an eight-foot pyre, out of which they seemed to be trying to tell him their story now in tongues of flame, a story he had not even thought to consider when he had been intent only on ousting Murdough and winning Thackery's favor.

As though summoned by these ruminations, Thackery appeared out of the darkness at that moment to stand beside him, having walked from the celebration back at the manor house. It was clear he was basking in the glory of the mass kill as he puffed contentedly on his own pipe and stared into the flames.

"A fine job all around, I would say." He sighed with pride, removing the pipe from his mouth. And then, turning to smile at Amos benevolently, he reached out his free hand to stroke Felix gently on the top of his head, as the ferret continued to sleep in Amos's arms.

"I understand this little one saved the day."

"Indeed, Master Thackery," Amos answered timidly, still surprised by his employer's presence. "He pulled the Black from the earth."

"And an excellent hunter from what I've heard," Thackery added, withdrawing his hand. "The men tell me they could hardly keep up with him. It was a wise decision on your part, saving him the way you did. You should be proud of your initiative."

"Yes, Master Thackery."

"Miss Hollis will have all our hides," he called to Tama, lifting his pipe to his lips, "if you don't soon get those drunkards out of her house and back to town."

"Yes, Master Thackery." Tama nodded, opening his eyes and jumping up from the rock. "I bring them back where they came."

"Good luck with that." Thackery chuckled, pulling on his pipe as Tama raced off toward the lighted windows of the house. "Make sure they leave the silverware."

"Yes, Master Thackery."

As Tama's footfalls across the muddy earth faded into darkness, Amos found himself pulling Felix closer to his chest as though he needed to cling to something in the silence that settled upon them. It was a silence so deep it threatened to engulf him entirely, and Amos clung to Felix as one who was shipwrecked might cling to a life raft in high seas. Were it not for the crackling flames and Felix's comforting warmth pressed against him, he would have drowned in it for certain.

"How old are you, boy?" Thackery asked, by way of shattering the silence.

"Why," Amos muttered, having to clear his throat in order to further reply, "I'll be seventeen in a month, Master Thackery."

"Seventeen." Thackery nodded, the pipe clamped between his teeth. "That's hardly a boy any longer. I'd like you to stay on and assume the chief herder's regular responsibilities, tend to the sheep and whatnot, now that we are largely free of these vermin. We'll keep the ferrets around, too, in the event of a reoccurrence."

"But Mr. Murdough—"

"Mr. Murdough is no longer a factor," Thackery interrupted, "I can assure you of that. And I'm aware that I'm asking you to assume greater responsibilities than you might have anticipated, but I believe you can perform them well. I've been impressed so far by what I've seen from you. And should we make it through shearing season without further incident, perhaps we can sit down then and have that conversation about you getting your own bit of land. Maybe even have your mother sent over to join her son, who's making quite a name for himself in the colony. Would you like that?" he asked in summary, turning from the fire.

Reflected flames appeared in both irises as Thackery looked unblinkingly at Amos, waiting for his answer. The effect was to give him the appearance of a man consumed by fires from within as though his eyes were offering a direct glimpse into his combustible soul. Though not especially superstitious, something inside Amos instinctually knew to hesitate in providing his response while pondering the inferno in the older man's eyes.

Still, the offer of both land and his mother's salvation from penury was a proposition far too great to resist, and Amos could feel himself slipping, fire or not. But if he was going to completely seal his fate to Thackery's in a crucible of flame, he felt at least entitled to press upon him the thought that had been plaguing him ever since his selection of the meal rabbit earlier before giving him his final answer.

"If the rabbits carry plague," he began, carefully choosing his words, "then why do we feed them to the ferrets? Aren't we just spreading the disease through different means?"

Thackery, at first seemingly stung by the challenge, allowed a long moment of silence to blossom in its wake. Gradually, however, a wide grin broke out across his face as the flames leaped up in his eyes. "Intelligent as well," he said, sniffing, before turning back to the burning ziggurat. "My daughter certainly knew what she was doing when she delivered you to me."

Though the words were meant to be taken as a complement, the fire in Thackery's eyes hinted at other motives running just below their surface kindness, and the grin on his face all but froze the blood in Amos's veins. Wishing he had kept his questions to himself, Amos began to cling even more desperately to his life raft without being aware he was doing so, inadvertently squeezing Felix up against his torso. Felix eventually became aware of the increased force with which he was being held and reacted to the uncomfortable pressure by twisting his body free of the crushing embrace. Unable to return once more to sleep, he eventually draped himself over the boy's left forearm and opened his eyes to the flames for the first time while the humans continued with their conversation.

Thackery took a long pull from his pipe and exhaled the smoke out the corners of his mouth. For a moment, it seemed as though he was contemplating ignoring the questions entirely, and Amos feared that he might have taken offense at his impertinence to ask them at all and would now withdraw the generous offer he had only just made. Then unexpectedly the old man rocked back on his heels playfully as if amused and let out a hearty chuckle before resuming to speak.

"Were you aware that it takes only seven average-sized rabbits to consume the same quantity of grasslands as any single fully grown sheep?"

"I wasn't aware of the ratio, Master Thackery."

"What you are looking at," Thackery went on, indicating toward the fire with his pipe, "is the reclamation of profits on at least one hundred healthy, wool-producing sheep, assuming your count is correct. Over one hundred sheep will now be able to graze upon the lands provided to them without having to compete against an invasive population for sustenance."

"But weren't they here first," Amos fumbled, "the rabbits?"

"You're referring to semantics, young man," Thackery retorted, "but I'm referring to economics. Who was or wasn't here first is entirely a mandarin argument when looked at through the prism of economics. The hard reality is that the New Zealand Company can never hope to maximize its profits on the wool it exports from the colony if it's constantly made to suffer losses on account of unwanted species. We are here to subdue the earth, my lad, not to break even with it."

It was as though the letter he had been carrying in his pocket had caught fire at that very moment as well. That Thackery was able to quote the very last words his own father had written to him before putting the pistol in his mouth and pulling the trigger? How could such a thing be a coincidence? Surely it was a sign, rather, that he should accept this powerful man's reasoning and follow him despite the unsettled feeling his acquiescence produced in him.

"So the rabbits never did carry plague?" he persisted softly, stroking Felix on his side as he stretched himself out more comfortably along the length of his forearm.

"The science is, as of yet, inconclusive," Thackery responded, sensing the last of the boy's resistance starting to melt away, "but better to err on the side of caution when it comes to these things, don't you think? Besides, most people, like yourself, have a hard time grasping the economic argument of things. They need something they can hold onto, something they can comprehend. Fear is something they can comprehend. So…" He sighed, turning back to Amos, the fires once again leaping up in his eyes. "Do we have an agreement then?"

"Yes," Amos answered after one last moment of hesitation, lowering his own eyes to Felix's glowing body so that he did not have to meet Thackery's fiery gaze when he sealed the compact. "Yes, we do."

At last, the men fell silent, and Felix was able to contemplate the burning tower of bodies free from the sound of their murmuring voices. Naturally he was unaware of the meaning of the words they had exchanged or the nature of the deal that had been struck between them. He would, of course, have no way of anticipating, therefore, how the exchange would dramatically come to shape the events of his life moving forward. He only knew that the sounds they made, while they were making them, had prevented him from focusing clearly on the voice that had been whispering inside his head ever since he had awoken.

At first, he had assumed it was She's voice reaching out to him one last time that day to congratulate him on successfully reinserting himself back into the lives of Kara and her son. But as the human distraction faded away behind him and he was able to concentrate more fully on the message being sent, he gradually came to recognize that it was one he had heard before and that it was not his mother at all transmitting it to him now. Rather the message was emanating from the very heart of the burning pyre before him, a chorus composed of hundreds of voices—all those skeletons, all those bones, all those flames—and all were whispering in unison, "Ever has it been so."

CHAPTER 11

Tama attempted to put aside the ill will he felt toward Miss Hollis by surrendering instead to the pleasures of his pipe as he stood back and watched the dockhands load the last of the supplies she had ordered for the evening's festivities into the back of the wagon. It proved impossible for him to let go of his resentment entirely, however, regardless of the satisfaction that the tobacco provided him. It was the height of shearing season after all, was it not? He should be back on the farm helping Amos with the sheep, not idling about here in port, retrieving her dainties. It was an affront to his powerful sense of personal dignity.

Still, he was well aware that the master put his trust entirely in her to run every aspect of the household, and any order that came from her lips was wise to be understood as an order from his. It was better not to have challenged her on the matter that morning when she sent him forth, he thought, seeing as how it would only ultimately be taken as a challenge to the master himself. And, besides, would not his Amaia be the first to suffer the wrath of the old crone if Thackery had somehow gotten wind of his dissent and seen the wisdom in his argument, seeing as how every feature of her daily life was controlled by the woman's unchecked authority?

No, it was better to have swallowed his foolish pride and to have done as she had instructed without question, regardless of how difficult the offense was to forget. He sometimes thought she made these irrational demands on him deliberately with the goal of provoking him to challenge her, and he knew better than to allow her to do so, to force him to make a mistake, despite how difficult it still proved to be on occasion. There was too much at stake, not the least being his daughter's future beyond the farm, once she was able to go forth and speak for herself in the world. Considered in this light, what a trivial item indeed seemed his honor.

Tama had only just managed to talk himself to this point of philosophical acceptance—a mental exercise he had been required to perform on countless previous occasions—when Weston, the customs inspector, checked off the last of the crates that had been stacked into the back of his wagon and stepped up onto the shaded porch of the general supply store to join him, fanning himself in the heat with the manifest he held in his hand.

Several seasons back, Weston's own daughter had fallen beneath the spell of a powerful fever that had left her stricken in her bed for weeks and close to death. Desperate for a remedy that might cure her and having heard reports of Tama's mysterious potions, the man had humbled himself by making his way out to Thackery's farm and imploring the Māori's assistance. The elixir he was provided with broke the fever instantly and cured the girl seemingly overnight, indebting the customs inspector to him from that point onward and forcing him to at least consider the notion that the savage might be more fully human than he had been taught his whole life to believe.

"I think that's the last of it." He smiled, handing Hollis's list back to Tama. "Looks to be quite a party you're having this year."

"Master Thackery is much pleased with the year that was," Tama replied, clamping his teeth down on his pipe while folding the list back inside his pants pocket.

"Could tell that from the list." Weston laughed, removing his hat and wiping off his brow with the sleeve of his shirt. "Once he kicked that rabbit problem, I guess there was nothing to *keep* it from being a good one. People around here are still talking about that day. They call it the Cleansing or some such thing."

"The Great Cleansing, yes," Tama responded absently, his attention suddenly drawn to a familiar figure shambling down the center of the dirt road. "It was quite a day."

"Whatever they call it," Weston went on in a friendly fashion, unaware that Tama had largely stopped listening, "it's good for the colony—that's for sure. One less thing for folks to have to worry about."

"Yes, Mr. Weston," Tama muttered back, his eyes fixed entirely on Murdough, who had stopped before the store and was glaring directly back at him, "one less thing to worry about."

*****

From the doorway of the shearing shed, it was possible to look directly into the kitchen window of the main house, located a little over two hundred yards away. There, each day at noon since the shearing season had begun, Amaia would appear on the other side of the glass and look back out at him. It was their agreed upon custom to do so and their only real chance to see each other prior to their secret nighttime rendezvous. And Amos had shown up for many of those recently so exhausted from his extra duties fleecing the wool coats off the herd that he could barely keep his eyes open, much less instruct her in his native language.

There was even the night when the two of them, equally tired, had fallen asleep side by side across the top of her bed and were only awakened the next morning when Hollis came rapping on Amaia's door, angrily scolding her to get up and get busy. Blessedly they had remembered to lock the door after he had arrived, but Amos still had to leap out of her bedroom window and race around the back of the house in order to evade the headmistress's fury. He had only just managed to climb back through the (blessedly!) open window of his bedroom when her rapping came upon his own door, insisting that he, too, get on with his duties.

"Yes, Miss Hollis," he had narrowly succeeded in answering before collapsing back across his bedcovers.

Determined to avoid a repeat of that near-disastrous encounter, they had decided that it was not always possible to meet every night as they had done up until that day; that, based upon the level of their exhaustion, they might sometimes have to forgo their regular tutorials, which then only made their noontime audience that much more important. Amos would invent some excuse to the two seasoned farmhands that Thackery had brought on to assist him in the shed and step to the doorway, just in time to watch her appear behind the glass. And when she did, he would signal that he could see her there by reaching up and touching the string of tiny white shells that she had given him to wear around his neck as a gift on his seventeenth birthday.

It had been nearly a month since his birthday in mid-February, the height of the summer season in New Zealand, and nearly two months since the day he had presided over the execution of over six hundred rabbits, a day the locals now referred to as the Great Cleansing. And while he might have been tempted earlier on to share with her what Thackery had confessed to him in front of the fire, that the mass killing was necessary only for financial reasons, he gave up on that idea the moment she lay the shell necklace in the palm of his hand. It was the sweetest gift he had ever received, and he made the decision right there in her room, where she presented it to him the night of his birthday, with the moonlight streaming through the window, that he could not allow anything to diminish his standing in her eyes. He could not afford to lose a person of such kindness, and he somehow intuited that if she were aware that he knew the truth and went along with Thackery's scheme, no matter what the reasoning was, that she would never forgive him. And so he kept the truth to himself and promised that it would be the last thing he ever kept hidden from her.

In other words, he had fallen in love. And like most men who have ever done likewise, he was instinctually aware that if she knew the complete truth about him, she could never love him in return. And so he had buried the truth inside with the vague intention of being a better man moving forward. But at the base of it, he just could not bear the thought of losing her.

And so he lied.

Now in mid-March, with summer quickly coming to an end, he found that he had far too much to do to dwell too much upon the Great Cleansing and the secret it had required him to keep. Thackery had been in earnest in trusting him to assume all of Murdough's former responsibilities, which, at this time in the calendar year, meant primarily to get the herd sheared before the season changed, particularly the ewes, of which there were many. If he failed to get the ewes shorn prior to their lambing, then the newborns would not have enough time to grow in their fleece and would suffer once the cold arrived. And so he would signal to her that he had seen her by touching the necklace, then duck back inside the shed to continue his work.

Ever since his focus had switched from clearing the fields to fleecing sheep, the ferrets had been mostly left to lounge about the barn all day long, having little more to do than to eat and sleep. Once a week or so, Amos would make a great show of setting up the wire fence around some suspicious-looking hole he had located in the ground and releasing the ferrets down into it on the odd chance that some rabbits might have returned to the grazing lands. In the months that had passed since the Great Cleansing, however, not a single one had come back to the fields or been ferreted out of the earth. He kept up the ritual just the same so that Thackery would not get the idea in his head that the ferrets had outlived their usefulness and sell them off or worse. In actual fact, it was Amos himself who would sneak out into the fields at night to dig up the holes with a shovel so as to foment the rationale in his master's mind for keeping them around.

When he was otherwise not making the case for their continued presence on the farm with his duplicitous charade, Amos had largely resorted to amusing himself with their company, just as he had done back in England, looking at them less as a conscripted labor force and more as decommissioned pets. Thus, he would oftentimes engineer situations to have them close at hand strictly because he found them so entertaining and not because they were performing any vital function. Such was the case now in the shearing shed when he had brought a squirming handful of them out with him from the barn that morning for no greater purpose than to frolic about in the soft piles of wooly fleece that piled up on the ground as the men stripped the sheep of their coats.

So it was on this particular noon, six hours before the first guests were due to arrive for Thackery's annual shareholders' banquet, with the entire household thrown into a frenzy in anticipation of the glit-

tering event, that Amos had only the briefest moment to signal to
Amaia in the window, touching his necklace, before she had to race
off and perform the next task that Hollis was no doubt shrieking at
her to take care of. But whatever disappointment he experienced at
their all-too-brief encounter was instantly erased when he turned and
saw the playful mustelids bounding after one another through the
downy clouds of fallen wool. Not only did their antics bring a smile
to his face despite his upset, but he was pleased to note the similar
smiles on the faces of the two men in the shed along with him, both
strong-bodied Māori that Tama had recruited for the assignment.
And while they and Amos were otherwise incapable of sharing any
other language other than the language of hard work, he found it
remarkable that the humor the ferrets brought to them all seemed
to know no speech barrier. He hoisted his shears onto his shoulder
and headed off whistling toward the barn to retrieve the next ewe for
trimming.

Kara had been among the ferrets randomly selected by Amos
to be brought out to the shed that morning. And while she did not
share the same seemingly inexhaustible appetite for hunting games as
the hobs who were chosen along with her, she could not help but be
amused as she sat back and watched the males tracking one another
through the wool, leaping up into the air and pouncing. By chance,
Scruffer had not made the selection but had been left behind in the
barn, giving her the chance to watch Felix and her son interact for
the first time since the first had rescued the second from the earth,
free of her mate's monitoring presence.

Locating Felix's red eyes slipping through the fleece, she watched
from across the shed as he stealthily crept closer to her unsuspecting
Castor, who seemed so big and dark and vulnerable to her in that
field of white. Part of her wanted to call out to him, to warn him
with her thoughts to turn around and to see the danger he was in,
to realize that he was under attack. But a second part so enjoyed
watching this newly revitalized Felix assume his cast-off mantle and
become once more what he had been when they had first met, the
Greatest Hunter of Them All. And it was this part of her divided self

that caused her to remain silent even as Felix locked in on his target and streaked toward the final assault with lightning speed.

They had been inseparable since the day Felix had pulled him from the mud. Castor hung on every word his savior offered and followed him around the barn as though he were a god. At night, while the others were trying to sleep, she could overhear him pestering Felix in thought whispers to answer an endless series of questions, both of a general nature ("What happened to your fur?" "Why are your eyes so red?" "How did you become such a great hunter?") and questions specific to the unusual circumstances under which they had met ("How did you find me after the tunnel collapsed?" "Where did you get the strength to drag me to the surface?"). It was as though the most wondrous thing that had ever occurred to him in his life was the rescuing of it, like he had been waiting since the day he was born for something to lift him out of the darkness and save him.

He had already noted that Felix bore the same mark upon his ear that both Kara and Scruffer had, and she listened one night with bated breath as Felix artfully deflected the "Did you come from the same place as my parents?" question. He hesitated for a moment before whispering back that it had been a sizable business to which they had belonged and that he hardly knew either of them before arriving here. Even around this small bit of minutia, though, Castor's hero worship seemed to know no bounds as he spent the rest of the night decrying the fact that, having been born outside the Breeder's stable, he had been denied the chance to have a brand seared into his own skin like his savior, keeping the entire pile awake until dawn with his complaining.

Little was he aware that his hero worship, like all idolatry of its kind, was built upon a lie.

Scruffer, of course, had been witness to Castor's displays of unalloyed affection for his old rival and burned with a kind of smoldering rage at how easily Felix had managed to insinuate himself back into their lives and to steal away his only son's heart. Kara was aware that it was requiring every last particle of energy on his part not to chastise Castor in front of the others each time the young hob pleaded with Felix to repeat once more the tale of how he had come to rescue him from his subterranean tomb. She knew that if he were not otherwise compelled by the terms of gratitude to hold his tongue, gratitude for having saved their offspring, he would already have unleashed his venom, no doubt in front of the entire business, and openly shamed Felix for being a coward, for abandoning her when she needed him most. She did her best to find him in her thoughts as he smoldered dejectedly under these conditions to assure him that Castor's love would ultimately return to him. But the more she tried, the more he retreated from her to a place where she could not reach him. And gradually she had left off trying altogether, hoping instead that with time Castor would tire of his savior and return to the one who had raised him.

With the one exception of Scruffer, the rest of the ferrets had had little problem welcoming Felix back into the business as their de facto leader. This was partially due to Castor's unequivocal willingness to do so; Castor himself had served in that capacity until Felix's return. In part, too, it was because of the warm memories that the older ones who bore the mark of the cross on their ears continued to cling to regarding their earlier days back on the Breeder's farm, when life in general seemed so much better with Felix in charge. Even the days of his withdrawal from their ranks and his mysterious disappearance, before returning spectacularly resurrected on the day of the Great Cleansing, were ultimately seen as further proof of his indisputable greatness, seeing as how he had come back from the dead to lead them once more to triumph.

The only feelings Kara was unable to interpret regarding Felix's return were her own. On the one side, she could not bring herself to forget how cruel he had been after what had happened to her aboard the ship, much less forgive him for choosing a voluntary death over life with her in this strange new world. On the other side, she could not deny the positive effect his presence seemed to have upon Castor, how glad it made her to see him calmer and more light-hearted, no longer having to carry the burden of being the best hunter in the business.

In truth, though, she knew that, deep down inside, these calculated means of measuring her feelings toward him were largely beside the point and that the sum total of her true affections could not be arrived by any fractional math. The truth was its own answer; it would not be weighed out on a scale of pluses and minuses. And as Felix sprang up out of the fleece to pounce down onto Castor's back, Kara was suddenly transported back to that morning long ago, when he had sprung up out of the snow to capture her heart. And she realized in that moment with a kind of horror that she was still in love with him.

While he had been taken completely by surprise, Castor continued to maintain a significant size and strength advantage over his attacker. And once the initial shock had registered, he was quickly able to roll his thick body onto its back before Felix could take hold with his teeth and repel him with his muscled legs. And it was on account of this powerful thrust that Felix found himself coming to rest at Kara's feet after being hurtled through the air and sliding to a stop.

Kara looked down at him in stunned surprise, having only just come to her unspeakable epiphany. There were so many thoughts racing through her mind as their eyes met, but she knew that if she communicated even one of them, her entire world might come crumbling down in an instant. And so she opted to hold on to every utterance that might have given shape to the way she was feeling and trotted off instead after a moment of awkward silence, leaving him confused by the only question she could not manage to hold back.

"Why did you have to leave me?"

*****

A reader might be forgiven for wondering at this point what exactly the sheep, *Ovis aries*, were making of all this. In a tale about a ferret army sent from England to vanquish the native population of rabbits on their behalf, it might be enlightening to know what they thought of the whole enterprise. Were they grateful to their mustelid brethren for protecting their food supply from the mercenary appropriations of the thieving rabbits? Or were they nagged, perhaps, by lingering feelings of guilt that so much death and destruction had been unleashed solely on their account?

It has already been put forth as a matter of established fact that all species on the earth communicate to one another in a common tongue by means of mental telepathy regardless of how unique or inscrutable the clamor of their external babel might seem—all species, that is, save for the *Homo sapiens*, who, in their ruthless quest to achieve dominion over the rest, sacrificed their ability to listen to and hear the voices of those they trampled upon. So why have we not heard a word from the sheep themselves about all that had transpired, all that they had been witness to thus far? Surely they would have some keen insight into the havoc that proved necessary in order to bring their wool to market, the same wool tumbling so effortlessly from their backs now beneath the sharp blades of the fleecing shears as ferrets dived playfully about in the snowy fluff at their feet.

Alas, while all species might be equal in their ability to communicate (except *Homo sapiens*), not all are equal in their ability to think, and it is a commonly accepted precept throughout most of the animal kingdom that sheep are undeniably the dumbest creatures to walk the face of the planet. If one were disposed to listen in on their thoughts at any given moment, one might find them running along such lines as the following:

> Grass...grass...and...sleep... Sleep...and...sunlight... Such...sunlight...and...

> Noise! Disturbance! Noise! Run! Flee! Afraid! Fear! Help!

> Then...gone...noise...gone...no...fear and...return...to...sunlight...and...grass...

> Such...grass...and...sleep...

It is for this reason that most creatures have simply learned to ignore the sheep and to block out their inane ramblings. In a world where it is difficult merely to survive—let alone to find purpose in one's existence or to find love—who has time to devote to such idiotic mush? The story of Felix continues onward from this point largely without their presence in it anyway, now that they have performed their tiresome but no less pivotal role in it. Why waste any time looking back to them for answers they could not give to questions they could not comprehend?

Rather, we will do as the other animals do and omit any further mention of the inner lives of sheep. Another species is waiting in the wings to be introduced into the narrative, which will drive Felix's saga toward its rightful conclusion. It is a species whose thoughts are infinitely more deserving of our consideration than those of the foolish sheep.

And so we carry on without further delay, leaving it to future historians and ethicists to debate the relative morality of having expended so much blood and treasure on behalf of beasts as stupid as sheep.

*****

The annual shareholders' meeting of the New Zealand Company had always served as little more than an excuse to justify throwing an elaborate party ever since it had come into being. Few trading companies, after all, had rewarded their investors so soon after its incorporation or as handsomely, so the actual facts and figures that spelled out the organization's successes were very rarely called into question or made subject to review. The land had blossomed willingly beneath the nurturing hand of its colonizers, rewarding their care with abundance; that was all investors needed to know to remain convinced that it was divine inspiration that brought them to open up new markets in this savage wilderness. All the rest was simply proof of their well-deserved manna from heaven.

This particular gathering, however, was understood to be even more of a celebratory occasion than in years past, given that it was being held at Thackery's own estate. It was the first year he had offered to host the annual affair, and given his position as chief officer, his willingness to do so was widely interpreted by all those on the guest list to mean that the earnings report this year would be especially good. Needless to say, the anticipated announcement of such positive news had sent a frenzied wave of expectation throughout every corner of New Zealand society since the details of the event were first announced. It seemed that nothing stirred the wealthy to greater heights of revelry quite like the guarantee of further wealth.

In the weeks since the invitations had been sent forth, dressmakers and milliners in Wellington and throughout the island had been kept busy morning, noon, and night catering to the design demands of their elite clientele. Every woman of any stature who was married to or otherwise engaged to a shareholder in the company seized upon the occasion of the gathering to prove her superior sense of style and to demonstrate that she had done her utmost to keep current with fashion trends back in England. And given the doubled importance bestowed upon the event by the choice of venue, it had become that much more important in their minds that they appear in their utmost finery, reflecting glory back on to the men whose arms they would be arriving on.

Guests began to arrive precisely at six and continued to do so for hours thereafter in a steady stream. Once the sun had gone down, it was possible to see the glow from the carriage lamps of those determined to arrive fashionably late dotting the grasslands that surrounded the property, like an incandescent string of pearls stretching all the way back to the port at Wellington. The same army of roustabouts who had been recruited off the docks and brought out to the farm months earlier to pulverize rabbits found themselves once more in high demand as coachmen, chauffeuring their high-ranking clientele to the elegant soiree in all their finery. The job did not require them to be any more sober than they were during their first visit since the horses did most of the work for them.

Just as the dockside rogues had been donned in borrowed liveries to be transformed into something they were not, so, too, had the staff of Thackery's own estate been fitted out in new uniforms in order to play their small role in the social charade. This element of deceit was understood and generally overlooked on both sides so as not to compromise the elegance of the evening. How could Mrs. Rothchester be expected to enjoy the splendor of the occasion, for instance, if she were forced to acknowledge that her coachman was snoring away in a drunken sleep or that the dark-skinned servant offering his hand as she stepped down from the carriage was the same native who hours earlier had exhausted himself shearing sheep, only thinly disguised now in coattails and a powdered wig? Such an acknowledgment would only compel Mrs. Rothchester to question her own part in the deception—her very worthiness, in fact—something that would surely have an adverse effect on her celebratory humor. It was better to play one's part in the masquerade without looking too deeply below the surface, lest one should lose one's faith in the social order as a whole.

In any similar circumstance, Amos would have automatically taken to ridicule such a grotesque performance of privilege, exercising that unique right of youth, which is to mercilessly puncture the pretensions of its elders. On this particular occasion, however, he was thrilled when he returned to his room earlier in the day, his hands numb from handling the shears, only to discover the new set of clothes Thackery had had ordered on his behalf spread out on top of his bedclothes. Whatever fatigue he had been experiencing up until that moment dissolved the second he allowed his fingers to run across the smooth surface of the fine fabrics. And any instinct he might have otherwise indulged to criticize the ostentation of the evening evaporated the instant he beheld the shining silver buttons of his custom tailored coat.

The faith in his ability to pass himself off as a gentleman, a faith that had begun the moment he slipped on the dazzling silver-buttoned coat, began to fade the instant he stepped inside the grand dining hall and beheld the painted mob of well heeled strangers that filled it to the rafters. Seeing them braying loudly at one another's bad jokes while guzzling imported champagne out of fluted glasses, Amos suddenly felt like a boy in short pants who had been set down amid a pack of hungry jackals. Overwhelmed by a violent wave of self-consciousness, he fought the powerful urge to flee their company and retreat back to his room. But just as he had reached his decision to turn and go, his eyes fell upon Amaia, who stood beside the kitchen door on the opposite side of the hall with a bottle of champagne in her hands. And called back to his purpose for being there in the first place, Amos summoned the last of his courage and pushed his way through the crowd to join her at her post.

By the time he had pressed through the throng, Amos was half-convinced that the stowaway he kept hidden beneath his coat must surely be either dead or dying from the crush of people around him. He would have had to have been, given the number of times Amos had been forced to squeeze himself through narrow openings in the unmoving mass of humanity, openings so negligible that it felt as though both the front and back of him were being sheared off in the maneuver. And it was for this reason that he first pulled out his lapels to check inside his coat when he reached the other side of the room in order to ensure that he was not now clutching little more than a ball of ruptured innards to his stomach. Miraculously, the secreted passenger was still alive—dazed but generally unharmed—and Amos smiled down at him before smoothing down his lapels and advancing toward Amaia.

Many was the night of their illicit tutorials when he had seen a smile break out across her face so big and bright at some mistake that he had made, some failed attempt to pronounce a word in Māori before interpolating it into English, that he thought the light of that smile might radiate out of the room and expose them both. Several times he had tried to write about her smile, about its radiance, about the way it crinkled the features of her face into a thousand unexpected patterns, but he was never able to find the right words to accurately describe how revelatory and disarming a smile it was. Now, however, she had retreated behind her servant's mask, a frozen expression that did not allow any feelings to dart out from behind.

He had seen this a hundred times before, how the natives forced to work the farm were divided into two distinct natures. When they were alone together, largely unobserved by their European overlords, they would frequently abandon their maddening reserve and laugh and joke freely among themselves, completely animated by the thrum of life. He had witnessed it just that morning when something that Tama had said to the Māori in the shed with him through the opened doorway as he shuffled to the wagon before heading into town—something derisive about Miss Hollis, no doubt, whom he was perpetually locked in a battle of wills with—caused them to convulse with a childish laughter that was so contagious he found himself joining in along with them, although he was not even aware of what had actually been said. As soon as he chimed in, however, they immediately drew back on their masks of inscrutability, and Amos was left alone smiling in the shed as the others returned to their work as though nothing had happened.

"It's all predicated on a lie," he thought to himself, taking hold of the nearest sheep and cutting away its fleece with the hand shears, the smile left frozen on his face like a sign of rigor mortis. Master, servant, indentured, free—it was all just a lie, one group submitting to the other's abuses while signaling behind its backs. How could any system hope to perpetuate itself into the future, based as it was on such an obvious falsehood, one man profiting off another man's blood and sweat and that other man submitting to his daily humiliations, all the while biding his time while hiding his true face? It seemed a system destined to collapse in upon itself, and he could only hope that there was enough life still left in it for him to benefit personally before it imploded entirely.

As painful as it was to be shut out of the men's company while working in the shed, it was infinitely more painful to watch how Amaia was forced to perform variations on this dance of double identity in her everyday life. Alone at night in her room with him, she was one of the most brilliantly expressive human beings he had ever encountered, even though they hardly spoke the same language. Yet during the day, in her capacity as Hollis's aide-de-camp, she was wooden and remote in her affect, completely closed off to him and the rest of the English-speaking world, to which he reluctantly remained a part.

He knew that her ability to move between these two presentations was a necessary survival tactic on her part, just as it was for her father and the others, a way to stomach the daily indignities foisted upon them while preserving some part of their essential humanity.

And he knew that he should be grateful for the glimmers of that humanity that she was willing to share with him at night and to not risk exposing her to harm after she had so favored him. But on this night, he desperately needed her to be the one and only other human being for him in a room full of jackals, needed her to come out from behind the servant's mask she wore as she stood beside the kitchen door in her uniform, waiting to receive her next command from Miss Hollis, and his need was so great that it made any consideration for her own safety and security seem secondary.

And so he came up alongside her and pulled on his lapels once more, allowing her a glimpse of the stowaway concealed inside his coat. As he hoped would be the case, the mask immediately dissolved away, and her midnight smile broke out across her face as her eyes fell upon Felix, who was staring up at her with his red gaze. Amaia allowed herself to giggle for a second and even raised her hands up as though she was going to reach into his coat and pet the creature, forgetting the bottle in her hand. Then she regained her composure and looked out once more over the thirsty crowd, searching for the first empty glass that needed to be refilled. But he was pleased to see that he had managed to charm her for a brief moment and that the smile had not completely been erased from her lips.

"Why do you do this," she hissed out of the corner of her mouth, surprising him with her anger, "when you know that Miss Hollis will punish me if she should find out?"

"I'm not afraid of that old witch," he sniffed, trying to win her back to him.

"How brave you are when you are not the one who will pay for your foolishness."

"Well, you didn't expect me to face this pack on my own, did you?" he asked, stung by the fact that she had called him foolish. "I needed to bring the cavalry."

"Cavalry?" she whispered, her tone coiling in upon itself as she scanned the room.

"Yes," he said, sighing, assuming that she was confused by his use of the term, "*cavalry*, meaning, 'additional horses.'"

"And is that a horse you have there in your coat?" she asked, her eyes continuing to search the room for any sign of Hollis.

"It's a metaphor," he defended wanly, feeling the moment he had hoped to engineer slipping away into a semantic fog.

"English is a language of many metaphors, is it not?" she inquired, still not deigning to look at him.

"It allows us a greater depth of expression than other languages," he explained, feeling unsure about his argument even as he was making it while looking down at Felix nestled against him. "It gives us the ability to say the same thing but in different ways."

"Yes," she agreed, a smile curling the corner of her lips once more, "this is to the very heart of the English language, is it not? That it allows you to look upon things that are very ugly and call them beautiful and look upon things that are lies and call them the truth."

At the center of the congested room, an empty champagne flute was hoisted up into the air, and Amaia took a step forward to respond. Before she dissolved into the crowd, however, she turned back to him and allowed the mask to slip one last time.

"I am glad you have your metaphors," she said, her smile outshining all the candles burning from the chandelier above combined as she pointed to his coat, "but do keep him safe."

Then she was gone, leaving Amos feeling both exhilarated and deflated at the same time. Was it just a coincidence that she had brought up the subject of lies, given that he himself had been dwelling upon a similar notion that very same morning? Perhaps. Yet sometimes he had the odd sensation that she was reading his mind, that she could see directly through his outer veneer to the thoughts he was struggling with inside, giving them voice. Was this what falling in love felt like, being apprehended in one's own thoughts by the object of one's affections?

Even as he was asking himself these questions, he could feel himself being watched, observed, and he looked up from Felix's quizzical expression to locate her in the crowd. Amaia, though, was concealed among the revelers and was nowhere to be found. Instead he locked onto Tama, who was standing against the wall on the opposite side of the room. Dressed impeccably in his livery and towering above the other guests, he was staring so intently at Amos, so unblinkingly, that it froze him to the spot and caught the breath in his throat.

It was only when Felix began to stir impatiently in his secret burrow, rearranging his position against his torso, that the spell was broken, and Amos managed to look away. While curling himself into a more comfortable pose, Felix's fleshy tail had slipped out of the bottom of Amos's coat and was now dangling between his legs. Realizing this with a gasp, Amos hastily stuffed the offending tail back up into the garment.

When he lifted his eyes again, Tama was gone.

*****

The idea struck him the moment he saw the savage looking down at him. He had only just come from unloading one of the ships and had nearly been eaten alive in the hold by the countless hordes of hungry rats skittering among the crates shipped over from Australia. It was backbreaking work being a stevedore, unloading all the items the colony regularly needed to have imported to sustain itself, but it was the only work he could come by ever since Thackery had relieved him of his farm duties in such a humiliating fashion. He had taken the word of a mere boy over his own, after all his years of hard work and dedication. And then to dismiss him so unceremoniously before the eyes of a grinning savage, casting him down into abject poverty, to have to bend and scrape for his very survival. The rats seemed like just the latest manifestation of his downward slide, one last layer of insult slathered on top of his already boiling sense of injury.

But it was not until he came to a halt in the middle of the road that day and looked once more into the eyes of the same savage who had witnessed his disgrace, staring down at him from the cool shade of the porch outside the general store, that he knew what he had to do. For it was in that same instant that he suddenly came to realize that the rats that had tormented him were nothing less than a blessing in disguise, the necessary means by which to exact his revenge.

Now creeping through the sea of tall grass toward the house he had once been a part of, its lighted windows burning across the dark plain like signal fires, he did not even mind when several of the stowaways he had captured bit at him through the sides of the canvas sack. Let them have their fun one last time at his expense, nipping at his hand and his leg. One last drop of Murdough blood, he thought, was the least he could offer for all that they were about to do for him.

"That's right, y'devils," Murdough hissed as he came out of the grass and scurried behind the nearest wagon, "drink up. I wan' your appetites good and whetted for our guests."

Now that he was close, he could make out the sound of a man's snoring above the general din of the crowd as if one of the hired coachmen were sleeping it off somewhere close by. He hoped that all the sounds of revelry coming from inside would help to drown out whatever noise he made as he crouched low and slipped out from behind the wagon, dragging the canvas sack on the ground beside him. Now all he had to hope for was that his dark silhouette was not somehow spotted as he moved stealthily past the windows at the front and slunk around the corner to the side of the house.

Peering through the window into the larder room, the same window through which Amos hoped to catch a glimpse of his Amaia each day at noon, Murdough could see that although the door to it had been left ajar, opening out into the kitchen, there was nobody currently in it to watch him slide open the frame from the outside. After quietly raising up the window with his free hand, he untied the knot at the top of the canvas bag and raised it even with the sill. Taking hold of the bottom of the squirming sack despite the sharp teeth that immediately sprung out to tear at his fingers, he hoisted it into the air and poured out the living contents into the room.

"Enjoy the party, y'devils," he said, cackling, watching as two dozen of the largest rats he could find instinctively fanned out across the floorboards, heading for the open door. "And give my regards to Master Thackery."

*****

Felix, who had fallen asleep contentedly, awoke with a start to a strange and unfamiliar new scent in the air. It was like nothing he had ever smelled before—sharper, more bitter than any rabbit odor he had ever detected—and it triggered every instinct he possessed to the hunt, firing all his senses at once. He unspooled himself from his comfortable sleep position and began to poke his snout up against the interior fabric of the coat to investigate.

Since his brief conversation with Amaia and the lingering sense of sadness it left him with, Amos had used the occasion of the annual shareholders' banquet to experiment with drinking champagne for the first time. Each time one of the household staff carried past a tray with freshly poured flutes, he was sure to grab one for himself and guzzle the contents down as though it was no more than carbonated water. And while he knew better than to think that it was, having been taught by both his abstemious parents to avoid the evils of drink, he had given himself permission on this night to act against the wisdom of their absent counsel.

When had either of them ever had to decipher the moods of a mysterious aboriginal girl who could twist everything around and use his own words to make him feel small and insecure? He deserved to get a little drunk on free champagne, given as how this was the current circumstance of his life. And besides, he warranted, what had a sober conscience ever done to keep the pistol out of his father's mouth?

The room was already tilted at a forty-five-degree angle when he snatched his latest glass off a floating tray and brought it to his lips. The candles from the chandelier above swirled around him in a gyre of light points, and Amos had the strange sensation that he was drifting backward out into the universe through a galaxy of stars. Amaia appeared before him for a moment, scowling, like an earth he had lost purchase on, before dissolving once more into the vast array of stars that was beginning to circle faster and faster.

"Be that way," he slurred as he leaned back against the wall for support, all but invisible to the other partygoers. "I only meant it as a metaphor."

Amos was too far out into the galaxy to notice when Felix's snout poked itself out from between the silver buttons of his coat. Fortunately, the intoxicated state he found himself in was not unique to him alone, for there was hardly a set of eyes left that were clear-sighted enough to take notice when the rest of the ferret's head emerged through the opening as well. Had there been, the sight of a pair of tiny red eyes scanning the crowded room might have been enough to precipitate a stampede of alarm on its own. As it was, Felix's presence among the human company was, for the moment, completely undetected.

The strange scent that had first aroused him from his sleep had, by this point in the celebration, become nearly overpowering, soaking his mind and his senses. It seemed to permeate the room entirely, practically blotting out the sickly sweet smell of the humans who filled it, but he could not determine as of yet its source or from which direction it came. He only knew that it was compelling him to seek it out, much as the scent of the rabbits in their underground lairs had, and that he was increasingly powerless to resist its beckoning lure.

Meanwhile, Thackery had maneuvered himself to the center of the congested room and was striking the prongs of a fork against the glass of champagne in his hand to draw the crowd's attention to him. It took several strikes to finally silence all the commotion, but eventually, he found himself wreathed by circle upon circle of pink sweaty faces, each turned to him in happy expectation of his words. And to them, Thackery proudly raised his glass in the air after setting down the fork and cleared his throat importantly before speaking.

"Fellow shareholders of the New Zealand Company," he began, continuing after allowing a long pause to bring a hush over the murmuring crowd, "it was only a few short years ago that I, responding to the outcry from our local farmers, came before you as I do tonight to propose having a vast armada of British hunting ferrets shipped over to the colony in order to combat the rapidly multiplying rabbit population, which was siphoning off our profits and exposing us to a myriad of unknown health risks. At the time, you may recall, my plan was met by a healthy dose of skepticism, with some among you speculating that perhaps I had lost my mind and that I should agree to step down from my post. Was I hurt by this furtive campaign of whispers? I'm not too proud to admit that, indeed, there were times when your misgivings wounded my pride to the very quick and kept me up all through the night—I confess it. But your doubts were never without merit, I knew, given the unprecedented ambition of the scheme, and I knew also that the only way I would win back the trust of those who would doubt me was to prove to them that my plan had the greater merit. Over four thousand ferrets and ferret hybrids were imported to us from mother England in order to allow me to make my case. Some of these were delivered to you on your personal farms, others released into the wild. And it is with great pride that I stand before you tonight to announce the near eradication of the native rabbit population on the island as a direct consequence of the ferrets, which has resulted in the fourth consecutive year of record-setting profits since I was duly elected to serve as your chief trading officer!"

The roar this opening announcement provoked from the guests was so spontaneous and spirited it startled Felix and drew his attention off the scent for a moment. Looking right and left from the opening he had made in the coat, he took in the sea of flushed countenances around him, their eyes gleaming with misty satisfaction. And although he was unaware of the meaning of what the humans' leader had just communicated to them, he knew that whatever it was had moved them to a state of feverish well-being, and he marveled at the power that such words had to stir men to frenzy.

"Markets for our wool back in England and Australia have continued to expand exponentially during my tenure," Thackery pressed on, feeling his words being carried aloft by the collective enthusiasm of his listeners, "and trade with the Americas has reached an all-time record-breaking high!"

The cheers that greeted the leader's second announcement were even more ear-splittingly robust than those that greeted the first, and Felix rolled his eyes skyward to absorb the full blow of the sound waves that pounded against him. And there he spotted it at long last, the origin of the mysterious scent that had roused him from sleep in the first place.

It was a creature unlike any he had ever seen before, with a snout more pointed than his but a long flesh-colored tail similar to his own that whipped independently behind as it crept in short hopping leaps. Its body, though more compact, was thicker around than that of the average mustelid, and it was moving now with great speed and dexterity toward the center of the room across a high ceiling beam.

"Can' she see that I'm tryin'?" Amos asked of no one in particular as his chin nodded down against his chest and his eyelids grew heavier with the champagne. As a result of the boy's posture slowly collapsing in upon itself in response to Amaia's sharp words, Felix was forced to inch his long neck out even farther from the protective concealment of the silver-buttoned coat. And while he somehow understood that it would not be wise to be apprehended by the human company overswelling the room, his hunter's instinct would not allow him to lose sight of the strange creature scurrying across the high beam now that that instinct had been activated and given a focal point.

"When you first elected me to serve as your chief officer," Thackery went on, settling into a mode of false modesty, "I made you a promise then that I've endeavored to keep every day since I assumed the position—two promises, to be precise. The first was to make your investment in the New Zealand Company more profitable by increasing production and expanding market outlets. And given the company's record of sustained growth, I think I can fairly say that I have made good upon that promise."

As the fellow attendees cheered and clapped their hands enthusiastically, Felix pushed his way out from beneath the coat and surreptitiously clawed his way down Amos's pant leg as the boy slipped further into drunken oblivion. Once he managed to reach the floor in this fashion, Felix darted smoothly between the legs of the unsuspecting party guests, moving stealthily toward the large window at the front of the house that looked out onto the darkness of the moonless night. What would have been the outcome if any one of the celebrants listening to Thackery's speech at that moment had looked down and noticed the hairless devil flashing his way across the wooden boards through a forest of polished leather feet and silk fabrics? Complete and total pandemonium, no doubt.

As it was, the pandemonium would have to wait a few minutes longer before erupting, as Felix made it to the opposite end of the hall undetected and immediately began to claw his way up the burgundy drapes that framed the window on either side and spilled to the ground in voluptuous folds. He had little trouble hoisting himself to the top, given his long nails and his splendid climbing abilities. The guests, for their part, remained brilliantly unaware of the red-eyed mustelid clawing his way up the column of drapery, so riveted were they to the trumpeting cry of their personal gain.

"The second promise, you may recall," Thackery went on, once the applause had died down, "was to keep the island that we call home safe from the pestilential diseases carried forth by contaminated species, which threatened not only our livelihoods but the very *lives* of those we love."

The hall had fallen into funereal silence, with each person filling it allowing themselves a moment to indulge their most Goya-esque fantasies about what such a world would have come to look like, a landscape overrun with disease and death, as Felix made the leap from the top of the velvet curtain to the wooden beam he had seen the odorous intruder cross earlier. Turning from having refilled the glass of one such guest lost in their baroque imaginings, Amaia alone took note of Felix's leaping form and gasped, though her gasp hardly registered to the hypnotized legion. Spying Amos slouched against a wall nearby, barely able to keep from falling sideways, she winded her way toward him through the narcotized mob, doing her best not to garner any unwanted attention.

The large French-cut glass and ormolu chandelier that hung above the center of the main dining hall was one of Thackery's prized possessions. Having had it shipped from Paris at the time he had accepted his first commission to the colony—when he was still merely one of the company's many functionaries, no less, and hadn't even been elected to his current office—was one of the costliest undertakings of his career, an uncharacteristically extravagant gesture made by an otherwise cautious and frugal man. But even before he set foot onto New Zealand soil, he took it as part of his mission to bring civilization to a backward land, and what could better exemplify the values of Western enlightenment than a glowing decorative chandelier?

It was of little matter to him that gas power was still unavailable to residents of the colony, as it was commonly available elsewhere, and that the chandelier he brought with him continued to achieve its illumination strictly by candlelight like some eighteenth-century relic to progress. Each time the sixty-eight candles that made up its three ever-widening rings were set ablaze, he felt a rush of undiluted pride, as though he alone was responsible for bringing light into the darkness, a modern-day Prometheus. And no amount of grumbling from Miss Hollis at the inconvenience of having to light each wick individually—teetering, as she was that afternoon, atop a shaky ladder—could rob him of the unshakable faith that what he had accomplished in this desolate place stood out as a beacon of light in the vast wilderness of civilization.

The chandelier hung from the underside of the beam across which Felix now scurried, dangling at the end of a long chain of interlocking metal rings. His quarry stood directly above the spot where the metal plate that held the fixture aloft was bolted into place, looking down at the crowd below and seemingly unaware that he was being advanced upon. With so much light to steer by, Felix never had had such an easy time closing in on a prey. He didn't have to close his eyes or locate the reddest star in the darkness. All he had to do was move with speed and hope that the leader's voice coming from below would drown out the sounds of his approach as he closed the distance between them.

"But now," Thackery suddenly boomed to life, providing the perfect cover for Felix's silent steps, "I am happy to report that as a result of the efforts on the part of fighting ferrets dispersed throughout the island, culminating recently in the Great Cleansing, I have also made good on that second promise and that the threat of annihilating disease has all but been swept clean off the face of the colony!"

Felix took advantage of the percussive waves of sound emanating from the thunderous applause coming from below at this announcement to take his few last steps before leaping up into the air. Just as his teeth were about to clamp down around the intruder's neck, however, something in its peripheral vision signaled it to turn in the direction of his attack and open its own jaws wide, revealing a menacing set of razor-sharp teeth at the front of its mouth, just below its snout.

Amaia had only just finished gently slapping Amos on the side of the face, trying her best to rouse him back to consciousness, when the lights began to spin frantically and a terrible shriek rained down from above as though the gods themselves were moved to intervene and curse the assembly. All in attendance gasped and fell silent as their eyes turned heavenward, expecting to look upon the face of their judgment. What they saw there instead were two wild demons doing battle amid the lighted candles of the chandelier, their partially obscured silhouettes biting and slashing at each other with ferocious intensity.

Casting her eyes from the brutal scene above, Mrs. Rothchester was the first in the hall to recognize that the demons overhead were not the only hellish beasts violating the sanctity of their special gathering. Feeling a tickling about her ankles and slowly lifting up the hem of her beautiful new gown, she was the first to recognize that the elegant hall was, in fact, at that very same moment, swarming with giant rats darting and dashing across the parquetted floor in every direction. When she opened her mouth to scream, however, no sound would come forth, but it was not long before some of the other dinner guests, making a similar discovery, helped her in sounding the alarm, raising up a high-pitched screech in the hall as drops of melted candlewax flew from the whirling chandelier like tongues of fire, raining down on the assembly.

It was all Felix could do to hold tight to the gold leaf branches of candelabrum as the centrifugal force of the spinning wheel threated to launch him out into space. Shortly after tumbling from the ceiling beam into its web of metal and flame, he had given up chasing the rat he had first detected around in circles since the only thing his mad pursuit had done was to increase the speed at which the wheel turned. In the resulting blur of candlelight, he had been forced to abandon the hunt in order to save himself from a death by fire or fall, using his long nails to grip and hold tight, sealing his eyes in order to steady his vision.

It was only after the speed of rotation began to slacken somewhat that he felt confidant in opening his eyes once more, having recovered his equilibrium to some degree. The noise of the hysterical guests fleeing the hall by now was nearly deafening as it ricocheted off the ceiling above and curled back down upon him. Despite the chaos below, he was able to search the wax-spattered arms of the fixture and see that his enemy was nowhere to be found. Was it possible he had been flung down upon the guests and crushed beneath their stampeding feet already?

This question had only just occurred to Felix when he heard a threatening chittering sound overhead, tearing its way through the general bedlam. And when he looked up, he saw the rat staring down at him from above, having shimmied halfway up the anchor chain to recover its own ballast. Felix had no sooner registered the disadvantage he was at when the rat released its grip and plunged down upon him. A burning shock radiated throughout the rest of his body as the rat sunk its sharp teeth into the soft meat at the back of his neck and, for a long moment, Felix was paralyzed by the sensation, frozen by the pain, as his adversary had finally gotten the better of him.

If given the time to do so, the rat might have ultimately bled Felix dry since its teeth had made it all the way through the skin, and it was beginning to jerk his head from side to side with the intention of tearing off the sizable patch of flesh it had isolated in the grip of its powerful jaws. Just as Felix, still immobilized, was beginning to feel the odd, dream-like sensation of a significant part of his body breaking free from the rest, his salvation arrived from below in the most unlikely fashion. He himself would not be awake to witness it, though, having lost consciousness from the pain the second before the shot rang out.

Amaia was one of the few humans left to witness the manner by which Felix was rescued from certain death in the clutches of the chandelier. Amos had mostly lost consciousness by that point, and it took all her strength to keep him from falling over by pinning him back up against the wall. And it was for this reason that she had not fled with the others when the tongues of melted wax chased them from the hall and out into the night. And so she was there to watch, looking back over her shoulder, as Mr. Rothchester withdrew his gun and took aim at the demons who had caused Mrs. Rothchester to swoon and faint away into a dead heap at his feet.

Like many wealthy speculators who had purchased large tracks of land in the colony and seen their gamble pay off, Mr. Rothchester liked to imagine himself less a gentlemen in the classic European mold but more as a rugged pioneer who had single-handedly tamed the wilderness and broke it to his will. The pistol he kept in his belt at all times was a critical component of this newly born sense of identity, investing him with a kind of added virility he had never known back in England. The truth, however, was that he had never been given cause to fire the weapon before the night of the shareholders' banquet and that the first shot he took with it spoke more to his privileged upbringing amid the private corridors of Eton than to the more masculinized persona he was trying to carve out for himself in his adopted homeland.

The bullet missed both ferret and rat alike but instead struck the chain holding the chandelier in place, severing it in twain. For days and weeks afterward, as the story was told and retold by all those who had been there that night, it became an article of faith at this point in the telling that it was nothing short of a miracle that Mrs. Rothchester had not been decapitated by the ornate fixture as it came crashing to the ground. Had she been sought out for her own account, Amaia would have provided first-hand confirmation of the miraculous as she watched with horror the outer hoop of the candelabra fall a mere few inches to the right of Mrs. Rothchester's nodding head, leaving her with little more than a smattering of facial burns from the flying hot wax.

Later, Felix's limp body would be recovered from the wreckage, heavily bloodied but still very much of this earth. Few would comment on the equally miraculous nature of his survival from the fall, given that most witnesses to the events that night held him at least partially responsible for precipitating the chaos that nearly cost Mrs. Rothchester her head.

As for his partner in the destructive mayhem, the rat's remains were discovered lying in a bloody mound beneath the heaviest branch of the chandelier. Given the way her carcass had split open upon impact, it soon became clear that she was pregnant, a dam, with no fewer than three kittens inside her at the time of her death. Their lifeless bodies had exploded from the womb and were now sprayed out across the floor in an amniotic arc, tethered to their mother by a twisted umbilical chain. None of the other rats that had stormed the party were ever captured, escaping out of the doors and windows along with the humans and fleeing into the fields under cover of darkness.

Though they had managed to elude capture, the rats were still very much on the minds of the party guests up until the last of their carriages had carried them away before dawn. All through the night, they had berated Thackery for his performance as their host and chief officer, verbally attacking him for prematurely announcing their deliverance from pestilence and plague when clearly there was yet another disease-carrying population that had been visited upon them. Even as Hollis, Tama, and the rest of the household staff spent the long hours of darkness running buckets of water into the house to put out the fires that had spread to the window curtains and that, for a while, threatened to consume the entire manor, they poured out their opprobrium on him for being ignorant of the knowledge that they themselves were already aware of—that the rats inadvertently brought over on ships from Australia had taken over the port and were now as big a threat to their safety and prosperity as the native rabbit population had ever been.

"Perhaps if you weren't ensconced all the way out here in your gilded cage," Mr. Rothchester continued to lecture in this vein, "you'd know what the rest of us have no choice but to acknowledge on a regular basis, that it's the rats that will be the death of us all unless something is done to stop them. The rats!"

At this point in his oration, he shook his head in disgust and climbed up into the back of the carriage to sit beside Mrs. Rothchester, who had only come around in the last hour or so and was now holding a damp cloth to her burned face, compliments of

Miss Hollis. Still somewhat embarrassed by the inaccuracy of his shot, Rothchester had taken on the role of Thackery's chief critic throughout the night to put off any discussion of his marksmanship. It was for this reason that his was the last coach to leave long after the other guests had departed once they had had their say.

As his driver shut the door behind him and climbed up onto his seat to assume the reins, Rothchester took one last opportunity to lay blame for the evening and the risks that remained squarely at the feet of the chief officer. "Given the evidence," he concluded with a sneer, "I only wonder if you're the man to do anything about it."

As smoke from the suppressed fire continued to pour out from the opened windows of the house, Rothchester signaled to his driver, and the carriage pulled away. Hollis and Tama watched from the steps as the coach trailed off after the others, their faces covered with ash and soot from fighting the blaze. Amaia, who had been lingering outside the barn with Amos until the boy had recovered his wits, touched him briefly on the shoulder before moving off to join them there.

His head still pounding from the alcohol, Amos looked down at Felix's unconscious body, which he cradled gently in his hands. The wound at the back of his neck would need to be taken care of since he was still bleeding heavily, but Amaia had managed to tie a cloth napkin around it in the meantime, all the while that he himself had been vomiting his guts out in the tall grass nearby. The guilt for his behavior becoming too much to bear while gazing down upon the injured creature, Amos lifted his eyes to see that Thackery had turned and was staring directly at him now with an expression of almost frightening determination written across his face.

Without uttering a sound, Amos knew full well the message that his master's look was meant to convey.

*****

A Note about Horses

If you were to search the animal kingdom far and wide, you could hardly find a more cynical beast in the entire realm than the common variety workhorse—cynical, that is, in so far as their general opinion of Man is concerned. For the horse, you see, has been there almost from the start of human evolution and has witnessed most of mankind's epochal follies in his desperate attempt to gain dominion over all others. What is more, the horse, unique among creatures, has had to endure the double indignity of not only witnessing these colossal failures but also having to take part in them. Pressed into service almost from the moment humankind stumbled from the darkness of the cave, the horse has had to push, pull, and otherwise carry the lunatic biped aloft across the battlefield of his own raging ego, his trusted beast of burden in the ruining of the earth.

Not surprisingly, when considered in this light, the horse has developed an almost impregnable contempt for the deranged species he has been forced to serve, a contempt that can sometimes be interpreted as a kind of affection. With their spirits crushed beneath Man's boot across the eons of time, the average horse is as fatalistic as any Greek dramatist about the possibilities for change or of breaking free from the cycle that has kept them enslaved almost from the beginning. Rather, they gather their chains about them like a warm blanket and have embraced their fatal outlook as the only thing they can dependably rely upon in a universe empty of any meaning. It is the thing that unites them most, their shared opinion that nothing good will ever be possible so long as mankind is holding the reins, and it comforts them to know that their despair is inescapable, a stain that can never be washed away. As a result, they have grown to love the hand that brandishes the whip even as they recoil from the sting of its lash since he is merely playing his necessary role in keeping the horse's sense of a hopeless cosmos in eternal check.

All this, naturally, has contributed toward making the horse one of the more isolated species among their brethren. While they may complain about their mistreatment on a regular basis—indeed, even while such complaining comes to serve as their daily bread—woe betide any other creature who might presume to register a similar complaint. "What would you know of suffering?" any horse worth his glue is quick to fire back at a creature presumptuous enough to trample upon the exclusive landscape of his grievance. And then, almost as if to maintain some exclusive claim on the source of their despair, that same horse will invariably add, "Leave your bellyaching about Man to me, for no one understands him as I do."

Thus, fatally addicted to its own suffering, the horse has turned his back on its fellow species centuries ago and cast his lot almost entirely with that of mankind. Only the domesticated dog, *Canis lupus familiaris*, could remotely relate to the horse's predicament, having come in out of the wilderness himself to sleep by the fire at the foot of Man's bed. But the dog, it must be admitted, can never fully imagine what it is to be a horse, regardless of the similar pact they have made with their common oppressor since the dog alone enjoys all the positive benefits that this "peculiar institution" has to offer—warmth, shelter, love. While the dog has been invited to sit at the banquet of human prosperity, albeit on the floor, the horse has been banished to the barn, where it can only imagine the soft comforts that its brother-in-shackles enjoys. In short, the dog is the comic iteration of the horse's tragic fate and is hardly taken seriously by any self-respecting equine.

The suffering of *Equus caballus* is theirs alone to fathom and endure. As a result, they have turned their backs on all others, resigned themselves to their fate, and will play little part in the resolution of our tale, despite their unique position to do so. If a fellow creature were ever truly in need, he would know better than to call upon the aid of a horse since he would only be wasting his time.

Horses gave up on life a long time ago.

Still, if there is one thing the horse can be relied upon to provide, it's sarcastic wit. Centuries of enforced servitude have made them dependable satirists, if nothing else.

Therefore, we cannot leave this section of our story without savoring the moment that the two draught horses pulling the Rothchesters' carriage away from Thackery's farm came over a small rise in the grasslands to find Murdough's body lying on the ground, which impeded their progress forward. He had apparently made it that far after unleashing his vermined vengeance on Thackery's house but not before pinching a bottle of port wine through the window of the larder room as one final show of his contempt. Submitting to the effects of the alcohol while toasting his victory beneath the moonless sky, the former chief herdsman had decided at some point in his revelries to lie down in the grass for a few minutes of rest before continuing his journey back to Wellington on foot. There, in the darkness before dawn, he was run over by an earlier carriage that had preceded the Rothchesters' own, which crushed his skull beneath its heavy wooden wheels.

Without even fully appreciating the extent of the irony at play, lacking any knowledge of how Murdough himself had earlier crushed the skull of a young ferret beneath his boot heel, thus precipitating his own downfall, the horse on the left of the Rothchesters' coach nevertheless noted the empty bottle lying in the grass beside the pile of pulp, which was all that remained of the dead man's head. And as the driver leaped down from the top of the carriage to investigate further and as Mrs. Rothchester let out a cry from the back, the horse on the right turned to his partner in misery on the left and whispered in his most sardonic voice, "Someone's gonna have a real headache in the morning."

CHAPTER 12

Their sleeping quarters were little more than two low cots set against the back wall of a cluttered warehouse with a rusted medal pail resting on the floor between them. The cots had been hastily cobbled together from the broken pieces of a smashed wooden pallet and were overlaid with thin canvas mattresses stuffed with dried grass. The pail was there to satisfy all their sundry lavatory needs.

The warehouse itself sat directly across the road from the main loading dock immediately to the right of the general store. Its primary purpose was to serve as a holding facility, a place where imports and exports could be housed temporarily until the persons attached to them could arrange for their transport and delivery. During daylight hours, the tremendous front doors of the vast storeroom were left perpetually ajar, causing the depository to fill with the sounds and smells of the bustling seaport town. At night, however, the doors were shut tight for security purposes, effectively sealing them off inside.

Thackery had said very little to Amos about the disastrous night of the shareholders' banquet. Disappearing into his study shortly after the Rothchesters' carriage set forth, he remained behind closed doors for the rest of the day as the household staff went about the difficult task of surveying the property damage and setting the house aright. A terrible silence clung to the scene as Miss Hollis, stunned at how badly the evening before had turned out, stood as though dazed at the center of the burned out dining hall, dispensing orders but barely able to lift her voice above a whisper.

Amos, along with the two Māori who had been brought in to help with the shearing, joined Amaia and Tama in their efforts to translate and execute her garbled directives—carrying out pieces of the ruined chandelier, sweeping up the shattered glass, removing the scorched drapes, and mopping up the great puddles of water that remained behind once the flames were extinguished. Every few minutes or so, he would leave off what he was doing to dash out the front door and vomit onto the ground outside the disgraced house. When he would stumble back into the hall, both father and daughter would glare at him with ferocious disapproval before turning away and continuing with their labors. Neither would speak a word, leaving him alone to stew in his drunken misery.

On the morning of the second day, after a night of tormented sleep, Hollis came rapping once more upon his door, insisting that he get up and dress quickly. By then, she had recovered much of her coiled menace, and he startled when, opening the door some minutes later, he found her still standing there on the opposite side, waiting, with a cruel gleam in her eyes.

"Master Thackery wishes you to relocate into town." She grinned, the falcon sizing up the field mouse. "Tama will go with you. He is waiting for you outside. You must go at once."

Amos read the letter Thackery had given him on the ride into town while Tama sat silently beside him, steering the wagon. The master had said not a word to him as he passed him the sealed envelope; indeed, it seemed he could hardly look directly at him, darting his eyes away when the boy had sought to make contact. It was for this reason that Amos had originally assumed he was being sacked, that the letter would contain his formal notice of release. So he was surprised to discover upon reading it that Thackery was not letting him go at all or at least not yet. Rather, he was assigning him to a whole new mission, he and his ferret army, which was to destroy the rats of Wellington.

The letter explained how Amos was to take his fighters to the port itself and cut off the flow at its source. The rat that had been crushed beneath the chandelier was found to be not of the native Polynesian variety but a black rat, *Rattus rattus*, a variety more common to European countries before recently making an appearance in their sister colony, Australia. Since the presence of the black rat in their midst now suggested that the creatures were traveling to New Zealand along trade routes from elsewhere, Thackery had determined that the best way to squelch the problem was to eliminate it before it ever got off the boat.

Amos was to work in tandem with the customs inspector, a man named Weston, to make a clean sweep of each ship before it was unloaded and to ferret out any vermin found to be stowing away amid its cargo, employing the aid of two or three of his most trusted hunters. Weston would make the arrangements for his housing while he remained in port and, in turn, he would receive a handsome bonus, courtesy of the New Zealand Company, for all his extra efforts.

"At the risk of stating the obvious," Thackery wrote in his flourishing hand, "the shareholders' faith in my ability to steer this organization into the future has been severely shaken by the events of late, and we must devise a means of restoring that faith before hostile actions are taken against me. It's at moments such as these, I have found in the past, that symbolism plays as great a part as actual deeds in the reclamation of frightened men's hearts and minds."

What the master meant by this last point was that he, Amos, was not only supposed to ferret out the rats from the ships but also to display their bodies by the tail from a giant wooden cross staked in the ground outside the warehouse where he would be staying. It was so that when nervous investors would drive past in their carriages, they might see that definitive action was being taken on a regular basis to vanquish the unwanted intruders.

"Far more than was the case with our rabbit situation," Thackery went on, justifying the need for such a display of carnage, "humankind's apprehension of the rat reaches back to the dawn of recorded time and has a deep and near-intractable hold on his darkest imagination. One need only to consider a catastrophe such as the Black Plague to appreciate just how well founded these ancient fears are. And one can only imagine the devastating effects that such fears would have on our fledgling economy if they were to take hold and be allowed to run rampant among the general population. It is for this reason that we must provide our citizens with unequivocal proof that we have no intention of allowing all that we have rendered from the wilderness to be toppled over into dust by the mere presence of an insidious pest."

The letter concluded with a reminder of the conversation they had had while standing before the burning pyre of rabbits on the night of the Great Cleansing:

> While I had every intention of making good on the promises made to you that evening, events have overtaken us in ways neither could have anticipated, and I will remind you that a job half done is hardly a job done at all. But I give to you my pledge that once this final task is accomplished, we will sit down to negotiate the purchase of your own parcel of land and the terms by which to rescue your mother from her current circumstances. Do this for me, lad, and all this will be yours upon my solemn oath.
>
> Master Thackery

The customs inspector greeted them warmly upon their arrival and guided them through the maze of crates and boxes at the front of the warehouse to the small sleeping area he had carved out for them at the rear. It was clear that Tama and he enjoyed a warm past history and that Weston was prepared to do whatever was in his power to make their stay there in Wellington as comfortable as possible. Cultural attitudes toward the Māori being what they were, however, with the law requiring a clear separation between the races, he was nonetheless forced to apologize for the fact that a space at the back of a warehouse was as good as he could do so far as their housing was concerned.

The prevailing apartheid notwithstanding, Weston invited his guests to partake in a welcoming drink from his hip flask in the dark alley that ran alongside the warehouse once the ferret cage had been settled on the floor and their few belongings tossed on top of the cots. But when Amos stood to join the men for that purpose, after leaving food in the cage for his hunters to find upon awakening, Tama held out his hand to block him, resting his open palm on his chest.

"When I say to you teach her English," he whispered with evident difficulty as Weston made his way back to the front of the warehouse with flask in hand, "I did not mean give her your heart. Stay away from my Amaia."

For a moment afterward, Amos assumed that he had been stabbed through the heart, for the words that Tama had said cut so deeply that it was almost as though he had left a sharp blade in the boy's chest when he removed his hand and turned to join the customs inspector. Adding to Amos's shame and humiliation was the fact that the words that had been uttered clearly caused Tama as much pain to deliver as they had for him to hear, and he sat down heavily on the nearest cot, feeling as though he would never recover from the double wound that they had caused. A second later, he was curled up on his side and facing away toward the wall, wondering why he had ever decided to come to this awful place, where the only things of consequence he had managed to accomplish thus far were to slaughter a defenseless breed of animal based upon a lie and betray the people that he loved most in the process.

Curled up together in a sleeping pile in a corner of the cage at the foot of the cot where he lay were the three ferrets Tama had selected to come with them into port in order to vanquish the new threat posed by the disease carrying rats—Felix, Castor, and Scruffer. The first two had been selected on the basis of their prowess since they had proven themselves to be far and away the two best hunters in all of Thackery's business. The third, Scruffer, had been chosen mostly because of his unique coloring rather than for anything he had ever done to distinguish himself in the field of battle. All three had remained unconscious throughout the entirety of the move from the barn to the warehouse, oblivious to what was taking place around them, and each would awaken in due time to discover just how much the landscape of the field of battle had changed while they were sleeping.

The first to squirm awake and to open his eyes was Felix, although it was many hours after Amos himself had drifted off to sleep and a profound darkness had settled over the warehouse. From the smell of the briny ocean water close by and the sounds of revelers drifting up and down the street at night, he could tell immediately that things were not the same as they had been, and he wriggled his way out from under the two ferrets piled on top of him to see what he might discover about their new circumstances. Allowing a moment for his sight to adjust to the darkness, he could tell right away that Amos had forgotten to secure the lock after leaving their food, so he slipped toward the open door to investigate.

It was just as well that he had shaken off sleep, he thought, inching across the cage, since, in dreams, he had been endlessly frustrated by his inability to track down She in the dark convolutions of his thoughts. Always, it seemed, he could make out the dim echoing of her voice beckoning to him, and he had even detected the faint glow of her red light somewhere up ahead in the inky void. But each time he had tried to surge forward through the black and to close the distance between them, he had only been flung back into further darkness, and when he called out to her for help, to come and rescue him, it was another voice he heard calling back, a voice that was alien to him, a voice that seemed purposely there to confuse the signal to his mother, though he was unable to decipher the message it was trying to impose.

As soon as Felix set his front paw out of the cage, he heard a burst of laughter coming from the opposite side of the nearest wall, rising up above the soft sounds of the boy's snoring. It was unmistakably the sound of Tama's laughter, although, in truth, Felix had never heard the man with the painted mask laugh like this before. It was the sound of the ordinarily disciplined and sober native giving over to drunkenness since he had made the uncharacteristic decision earlier in the evening to take advantage of the customs inspector's generosity and to drown his hurt feelings in the warmth of Weston's cheap whiskey. He would wake up there in the alley the next morning and immediately regret the decision, vowing to never make it again, as all men do. But for now his laughter helped make the darkness seem a little less empty as Felix slipped out of the cage, stumbling, and as the burning sensation at the back of his neck flared up once more, causing him to wince and shudder.

The burning had been with him since the night of the banquet, ever since Amos had lifted his body from the twisted wreckage of the fallen chandelier. It emanated directly from the spot where his adversary had bitten down through the flesh and shot out in all directions like the rays of an angry sun. And while Amos had been diligent initially in cleaning out the wound and caring for it, Felix had been given cause to wonder, each time the sun spot sent out its flares in the days since he had been bitten, if the creature he had done battle with that night hadn't somehow delivered some poison into him that couldn't be detected from the outside and whether the poison even now wasn't coursing through his body, destroying him from within.

It was the reason he had been searching for She in his sleep; he wanted to ask her if the poison he was sure was pulsing through his body, that was being carried in his bloodstream, wasn't somehow killing him or, worse, if he was being transformed into something other than himself because of the contamination, perhaps into something more like the creature itself. But the intruding voice had kept him from receiving the comforts of her consoling answers, blowing her words away like a winter wind before they could reach him, so that he was left now to bear the pain until it passed, with all his fears and apprehensions still upon him.

Normally, the burning sensation would fade after a moment, and Felix would have a few hours of relief before the next episode set in. This time was different, however, in that once the worst of the burning had passed, the pain itself did not fully dissolve but settled into a lesser, though no less present, throb. What was more, the discomfort that lingered and remained had a sound to it now, an audible pulsating reverberation that gradually came to mimic the rhythms of Felix's own beating heart.

Felix opened his eyes to the throbbing sound and scanned the dark towers of wooden crates and boxes that loomed above them imposingly, threatening to topple over and crush them all. As he listened carefully, he was able to detect a second throbbing pulse emanating from somewhere at the top of the highest tower, one that was in perfect syncopation with his own. It seemed to be summoning him, luring him to reconcile his own heartbeat to it, and Felix hesitated but for a moment to look back at the two other ferrets sleeping soundly in their cage before scurrying across the short distance to the bottom crate and beginning his climb.

Digging his sharp nails into the damp wood, Felix was able to lift himself, one box after another, to the top of the ziggurat with great effort. It helped that with each crate he surmounted in this fashion, the burning at the base of his neck grew less acute, gradually allowing him to access the full strength of his powerful legs as he hoisted himself toward the peak. It was though the pain he had had to endure since the banquet was purposely being lessened now by a powerful hand as a reward for heeding the signal and pursuing the source of the second heartbeat.

Still, it required every ounce of strength he had to make it to the top, and by the time he heaved himself over the edge of the last crate, Felix was feeling so spent he could hardly stand. He had to fight the temptation to just lie there as he was, flat on his belly, and give himself over to sleep once again, but the sound of the external heartbeat was so close at hand at this point and so forceful that it would not allow him to give into his need for rest. Lifting his chin from the wood, Felix looked out into the black void at the top of the vaulted ceiling and saw there a sight that surprised every faculty of his being.

It was her, the rat from the chandelier, the Dam, the one who had bitten him before the fall. She was hovering twenty feet above him in the empty air, her body suspended at the center of a glowing orb of blinding white light. Her eyes were closed tight, and her pointed snout was turned upward toward the heavens. Most shockingly, her belly was cleaved in half, as it had been when her corpse was first discovered, and the fetuses of her unborn children dangled from the rope of her swollen umbilical cord, which poured forth from the base of the ghastly wound.

The moment Felix beheld the incredible vision before him, the sound of the pounding heartbeats, which had swelled in volume to a painful intensity, dropped away immediately, plunging them into a silence that was almost as loud as the drumming that had preceded it. Felix felt for a moment as though the quiet might consume him it was so powerfully pervasive, and he had to steady his legs beneath him to keep himself from surrendering to it. As much as he hated to look upon the vision before him—the jagged lips of the wound, the cold stillness of the tethered fetuses—he found he could not look away from it or risk tumbling off the top of the pyramid into the bottomless abyss of quiet.

"Yes," the Dam said at last, her voice moving through the silence like a cold wind howling through dry grass, "it is I, the one you slew. Look upon the consequence of your victory."

Although she was communicating telepathically to him the way his mother always had, without moving her jaws to speak or opening her eyes to look upon him, Felix was unsure if he knew the precise pathway with which to reach her back with his own thoughts. Nevertheless, he understood what she meant by the consequence of his victory, and she in turn seemed to sense his understanding.

"That's right," she went on, "I was there that night in the great house, foraging for my young, the three who had yet to be born. When you slew me, you slew them as well—four rats killed with one stone."

"I'm sorry," Felix whispered in response, still not certain if his thoughts had the power to communicate. "I didn't know."

"Of course, you didn't," the Dam responded, indicating that she was able to hear him. "We very rarely are aware of the consequences of what we do until it's too late."

"I was following my instinct," Felix said, defending himself.

"And is that your only instinct," she shot back, her voice growing more forceful, "the instinct to kill?"

"It's what I was bred to do," he argued, sensing the inadequacy of his defense even as he gave the thought form.

"For this alone you were bred?" the Dam hissed, the surrounding halo of white light increasing in diameter as she went on, "not for finer things, like mercy and forgiveness?"

"It was Man who bred me to kill," he answered, shrinking back from the growing light, "and Man seems little interested in things like mercy and forgiveness."

"It was Man who *trained* you to kill," she countered, the cold wind of her voice reaching down into the deepest recesses of his thoughts, "but surely it was another who *bred* you into this life, who brought you into this world."

"Yes," Felix said, suddenly filled with sadness at thoughts of She. "I was trying to reach her earlier to ask what's becoming of me, but I couldn't reach her in my thoughts. Something kept getting in the way."

"It was I who kept getting in the way," the Dam cackled in her dry, wintery voice. "For now that I am inside of you, I can insinuate myself between your thoughts and those you wish to reach with them."

"The poisoned bite," Felix gasped.

"Yes," she hissed, "the poisoned bite. And now that I am inside of you, I tell you that I will prevent you from ever speaking to your mother again until you do this one thing for me."

"But why would you do such a thing?" Felix challenged, advancing toward the white light while filling with anger at the thought of never speaking to She again. "Animals kill each other to survive. I was only doing what my blood told me to do."

"And is that why you murdered my children?" she suddenly raged, her voice climbing to a piercing shriek as she lowered her head and lifted her eyelids, behind each of which was revealed a burning pyre of flame. "Was it truly a matter of survival that they needed to come to this end? Were you so starved for food that they had to die in order to maintain your survival? Or was it, rather, to protect the needs of your human masters? For whom do you kill?"

Perplexed by her questions, Felix could not bring himself to answer; he merely stood as though hypnotized by the burning flames as they leaped forth from her sockets. He had never stopped to ask himself this question before—"For whom do you kill?"—and he wished that he had She's voice in his head right now, telling him what to think and how to answer.

"I know you wish to speak to her," the fiery rat continued, reading his thoughts, "just as I wish to speak to my own slaughtered pups. But because they were destroyed in my womb before we could establish our connection, I will never be able to do so. I will be tied to them for all eternity and never once be allowed to tell them that I love them. And this gives me certain rights over you, does it not?"

"Yes," Felix whispered, suddenly feeling as if the tower he stood atop of was being shaken from its foundations. "Tell me what you'd have me do so that I can speak to her again."

"Seek out Tiresias," the mother rat commanded, her body dislodging itself from the glowing orb and lowering toward him even as she appeared to grow in size and scope. "He alone will know what to tell you so that my children's deaths should not have been in vain."

Felix found himself fearfully inching backward as the pyramid continued to sway uncertainly beneath his feet and the Dam grew ever closer to him, her features swelling in the air exponentially.

"But who is Tiresias?" he asked, his voice trembling.

"You shall know when you find him."

Her enlarged face was nearly pressed on top of him now, the flames from her eyes singeing his whiskers, as Felix felt his back legs slip over the edge of the crate.

"But where will I find him?" he pleaded as the weight of his hind quarters dangling in the air pulled down upon him, forcing him to desperately cling to the crate with his front paws to keep from falling.

"Seek him out!" she shrieked as the fires from her eyes leaped directly at him, burning the backs of his paws and causing him to release his grip.

Felix plummeted backward from the height of the tower, futilely grasping at the incorporeal air as he spun ever farther down into the darkness. And it was with a great shock that he landed with a jolt, only to discover that he was back once more in his cage, safely buried beneath his sleeping companions.

In the alley outside, the men began to clap their hands and dance a drunken reel as Amos tossed fitfully in his sleep on top of his cot. After considering all that had happened for a minute, Felix moved to adjust his position at the bottom of the pile, convinced that the visitation from the Dam had been nothing more than dream and anxious to return to a more peaceful rest.

That was when he felt the stinging sensation and looked down to discover the angry blisters rising on the backs of his two front paws.

CHAPTER 13

How should I begin making the case for the greater dignity of *Rattus rattus* when so many hearts and minds are predisposed to remain shut to any such case being made in the first place? Perhaps the answer to that question lies in the question itself. Why is it that the common rat, above all other creatures who walk the earth, should be so universally reviled that efforts at his extermination—whether by ferret or toxin, as is the modern practice—are greeted with such indifference, nay, are *celebrated* as acts for the general good? How did such a tiny, seemingly inconsequential creature come to inspire such enmity around the globe that its extinction would be welcomed as a cause for rejoicing?

If not the actual historical source of the global enmity, one has to concede that the Black Death probably went a long way toward solidifying the rat's reputation in the popular imagination as a bringer of disease and death. When fifty million people, up to sixty percent of the European population at the time, contracted the bubonic plague and died painfully as a result of their close proximity to the pathogen carrier, it was a sure bet that the memory of that event would be passed along for generations to come and the rat cast forever after as the chief villain in a million nightmares yet to be dreamed.

Is it not for this reason that its fleshy tail, above all its other anatomical features, should be the focal point for such universal disgust? The mere sight of the tail, so similar in texture to our own hides, serves as a constant reminder of the rat's human connection and that, at one point, we had lived in relative peace with the opportunistic pest, only to be betrayed by him in the end, our lives stolen from us, the flesh of his tail worn like a plume of our defeat.

If not the source of the hatred, the Black Death no doubt sealed the rat's fate in the eyes of mankind worldwide. And yet it is worth noting that at the same time that the rat was sealing its reputation as the devil's messenger who wiped out nearly half the population of Europe, it was enjoying quite a different reputation on the opposite side of the world. For even as the plague was bringing the Middle Ages to the point of collapse in Europe thanks to the pestilential *rattus*, he was being venerated in India for his association to a goddess who brought nothing but life.

The goddess Karni Mata dwelled in the Rajasthan region of India in the fourteenth century and is credited by her believers with the spreading of greenery and new life by raising water in the desert and planting berry bushes to rescue the natural fauna. The story goes that, in her lifetime, the child of a close clansman passed away, and the goddess was petitioned to plead with Yoma, the god of death, that she should be restored to life and returned to the clan. But Karni Mata was late with her petitions; the child had already been reborn into another human form. And so to strike back at the hasty dealer of death, she vowed that all of her tribe's people would be reborn as rats until they could be born back into the familial clan, including the goddess herself.

In summary, ask an Englishman what a rat is, and he will answer that it is the harbinger of disease and death, being the descendant of those who, perhaps, lost their lives to the fleshy-tailed creature. Ask a Rajasthani the same question, however, and you will get from him this answer: "The rat is the very manifestation on Earth of the great goddess Karni Mata, who denied Death his final authority over life."

Is it any wonder then that, at the dawn of the twentieth century, even as the extermination of the rat was assiduously pursued throughout most modern Western cities as a matter of public health, the Maharaja Ganga Singh was building a temple in Deshnoke in honor of Karni Mata? Where, to this day, visitors regularly witness up to twenty thousand rats at a time scurrying about the interior, happily consuming the gifts of food left for them by worshipful

Hindus? Western visitors have been known to cry out in terror upon entering the temple, some even trampling the sacred rats underfoot, yet Hindus remain perfectly calm in the presence of the holy.

Suppose, though, that there was not time enough in the day to persuade you who are not a Rajasthani to see the rat as a Hindu might. Suppose the legacy of the Black Death is so sewn into the strands of your blood memory that you dare not nor care not to stretch your empathetic imagination into another cultural idiom. If that is the case, then all that can be done is to point out that the rats held responsible for the epidemic that swept throughout Europe in the Middle Ages were not themselves the originators of the bacterium that killed all those people all those years ago. That would be the rat flea, *Xenopsylla cheopis*, who preyed upon the rats, infecting them with the microorganism *Yersinia pestis*, from which the rats themselves died after inadvertently passing it along to Man.

So then who was most responsible for killing fifty million Europeans in the fourteenth century, even as Karni Mata was planting her berry bushes and defying Death on the opposite side of the world—the rat or the rat flea? To the author, it seems like a distinction without a difference, a chicken-and-egg conundrum with no satisfying solution.

Besides, if you were to ask the rat flea—poor *Xenopsylla cheopis*—why he did what he did, why he chose to bite the first rat and trigger all the death that followed, he would only say that he, too, was a victim, that he, too, was first bitten by the bacterium *Yersinia pestis* before he ever tasted rat flesh. And what would we do with that information? Unleash a trained business of hunting ferrets upon the microorganism and pin their carcasses to a cross? Impossible. Bacteria are everywhere but are far too small to detect with the naked eye, as are most rat fleas. So we allow ourselves to settle upon *Rattus rattus* as our common enemy and satisfy ourselves with his destruction as the unexecutable bacterium continues to make his mischief however and wherever he chooses.

Granted, we may have reached an unavoidable breaking point, you and I. Perhaps all the argument in the world cannot persuade you to care about the fate of the black rat in nineteenth century New

Zealand the way you (hopefully) cared about the fate of the far more sympathetic rabbit. At this point, as we move toward the climax of our story, I suppose it is even incumbent upon me to consider the sad possibility that you might not have ever even cared about the fate of a hairless ferret named Felix, who was sent there to kill them both. In which case, all hope is lost.

I have to believe, though, that there are some of you out there who care as much about the rat as you do the rabbit, let alone what becomes of our hero, a humble ferret, and it is to you that I dedicate this last section of the tale. It is to you, also, that I offer these words from a popular nursery rhyme, one first published in 1848 in Mrs. Cecil Alexander's *Hymns for Little Children*, to give you strength in the conviction we both share and to seal the bond between us:

> All things bright and beautiful,
> All creatures great and small,
> All things wise and wonderful,
> The Lord God made them all!

*****

The advantage the rat enjoys over the rabbit in the hunt is his sharp front teeth. Any creature involved in tracking him down needs to be mindful of the fact that, once cornered, he might spin his stout body around in a flash and fly at them with his daggerlike incisors. And while the rabbit's hind legs are infinitely more powerful in beating back a foe in one-on-one combat, the teeth of a rat, once they have pierced through the flesh of a predator, are almost impossible to break free from without first relaxing the muscles beneath their relentless grip and relinquishing the chase. The rat alone decides when to release once he's gotten his teeth into you.

All three ferrets had to learn this lesson the hard way and to adjust their tactics accordingly. No longer could they expect to back their quarry up against an earthen wall or drive them out into the light, as had been the case when they were hunting rabbits. Now that the enemy was an army of rats, speed became an even more important element than it had ever been since it was imperative to overtake the rat and pounce on him from above before he could turn and sink his teeth into you. It was for this reason, the absolute requirement for speed, that the three hunters frequently returned to their cage in the warehouse at the end of the day, feeling even more exhausted than they had when they were tracking rabbits down in the field. At the beginning, too, their necks and snouts were oftentimes decorated with bloody scars, souvenirs of the rat's harsh bite. Although as time passed and the ferrets became more knowledgeable about their new adversary, fewer of these scars were on display.

The disadvantage that the rat suffered was obvious: he was contained on a ship. And where a rabbit could duck and dive down an endless maze of tunnels in his underground warren, a rat was more or less imprisoned by his surroundings. There was no place for him to escape to outside the unyielding walls of the cargo hold in which he had stowed away. And while he could use the cargo itself as a shield behind which to hide, employing his own formidable speed to streak from one crate to the next, the truth of the matter was that there was no place left to run once the hunt had begun other than to somehow make it to the upper deck, climb over the railing, and toss himself into the water.

Once Felix and the others learned to adjust their speed to account for their new circumstances, this insurmountable disadvantage of being shipbound was made manifest by the sheer number of dead rats hung by the tail from the cross outside the warehouse at the end of each day. The rat could slash with his incisors at the mustelids pursuing him as much as he liked, but in the end, he could not push back the walls of the prison cell he was trapped within. And if Thackery's plan was to assure his investors that the new threat was being neutralized by displaying evidence of its destruction, the ferrets were, if anything, exceeding his expectations in helping him to do just that.

Within a fortnight of arriving at port, Felix's days fell into a familiar routine. The boy and the painted aborigine would roust them from the warm comfort of their cage and carry them by the scruff of their necks across the rutted road to some pier or another along the dockside, where an incoming ship had only recently arrived, bringing with it supplies for the new colony. Then, after being carried down into the hold, they would be released within the riot of boxes and crates to ferret out their prey. Chaos almost immediately ensued as the rats, getting whiff of the new creature in their midst, instinctually sensed that it was there to hunt them down and automatically began to scatter in a dozen different directions.

The boy and the aborigine would race about in all the commotion, too, listening for the agonized squeal that was always there to signal that yet another rat had been captured. They would arrive as the rat was being pinned to the floor by the jaws of a ferret, thrashing their tails behind them like whips while struggling to break free. Then they would stamp their boots down upon the rat's back, snapping their spines and crushing their organs. Oftentimes, it would require repeated stomping before the rat was destroyed completely, and Felix and the others grew accustomed to holding on until the rat's insides were disgorged through its mouth and nostrils in great heaving sprays of pinks and reds. Then it was on to the next target, while the humans were left to bag up their trophies.

At first, Felix felt confused and out of sorts by the new challenge, lost in the hunt, and he was fully aware that Scruffer and Castor were each producing far more kills than he was. If the two noticed he was lagging behind, however, they gave no indication of it when, back at the warehouse at night, they finished up their evening meal (rat meat, of course) and curled up together in the cage. Their whispered conversations as they waited for sleep to overtake them generally centered on warm reminiscences of the barn and about how much each could not wait to see Kara once more.

Felix struggled to remain silent during these exchanges as father and son expressed their common longing, fearful that his own thoughts on the subject might accidentally intrude into the conversation and turn them against him. Ever since he had rescued the young hob from the tunnel collapse on the day of the Great Cleansing, Castor had been positively adoring of him, near worshipful, and he could not bear to think of his opinion souring if he actually came to know the inner workings of his heart. He wanted the young ferret to think of him only in heroic terms as the savior who had selflessly pulled him from the mud, not as the self-absorbed weakling who, in the despair of his shattered ego, had abandoned his mother to raise him on her own.

He also did not want Scruffer to think that he had any intention of trying to win her back to him now that he had saved Castor and gained back some small part of her admiration. Scruffer had done what he could not; he had loved her in the hour of her greatest need. What was more, he had managed to raise her ill-begotten child as his own, something Felix had also proved incapable of doing. It was for these reasons that Scruffer alone deserved to think of her as his mate and to call her by that name.

Still, it was difficult sometimes to rein in his thoughts once the subject turned to Kara, as determined as he was to keep his true feelings locked up inside. And it was at moments when he could sense himself involuntarily slipping toward the truth that he went searching for She in his mind, as he had always done in the past whenever he needed guidance. Ever since the night the ghost of the pregnant rat from the chandelier had appeared to him in the warehouse, however, he had been unable to reach her, try as he might. And whenever he was tempted to dismiss the Dam's appearance in the air above him as a dream, he would remember the curse she had laid upon him that night, that until he sought out the one called Tiresias, he would be prevented from ever reaching her again.

The apparitional rat hadn't made a second appearance since, nor had he come across any creature who went by the name of Tiresias. And fortunately for Felix, the struggle to locate She in his mind, as fruitless as it had been since that night, was usually enough to exhaust the last amount of energy he had before plummeting into sleep. Either way, he had been successful thus far in keeping Scruffer or Castor from recognizing him as the liar he was.

Felix's ability to find She in his thoughts was not the only thing that had been stripped from him since the visit from the spectral Dam. Something else was gone, too, and it was the loss of this second gift, more than any other change in his circumstances, he knew, that was primarily responsible for his inability to perform as the hunter he once was. From the morning they were brought down into the first ship's hold, the morning after she had appeared to him, it was immediately clear to Felix that he had lost the power to locate his quarry in his mind's eye.

Rather than seeing the heartbeat of the creature he was tracking appear like a throbbing star on the blank screen of his thoughts, as had always the case in the past, he now saw only vague smudges of gray and white where bright colors used to appear, guiding him to his target. Whenever he closed his eyes to concentrate, all that came to him were these indistinct streaks and swirls of nonhue, intersecting and overlapping in unpredictable patterns as though a giant hand was trying to wipe out the chalk lines on a blackboard before their meaning could be deciphered. And each time he struggled to make sense of what had been written there, the pain at the back of his neck would flair up once more and force him to open his eyes.

She was blocking him from seeing the colored stars, the Dam from the chandelier, just as she was preventing him from speaking to She. How could a single bite be so powerful that it would linger in the blood and eventually come to control him? Perhaps it was because she had been filled with her pups at the time she sank her teeth into him so that the single bite, in fact, carried the strength of four. Or perhaps it was because all creatures were vampires to some degree, capable of impregnating their spirits into one another through the blood.

Whatever the explanation, it was clear to Felix from that first morning onward that he would need to rely on his more conventional senses for tracking down his new opponent: sight, smell, sound. With a single bite, he was no longer Felix the Red, Greatest Hunter of Them All. He had lost his supernatural ability and become just like every other ferret. The Dam had seen to that.

"Why isn't he the same hunter I witnessed on the day of the Great Cleansing?" he heard Castor ask Scruffer one night when both had assumed he had fallen off to sleep.

"He's no longer the young ferret he once was," he heard Scruffer whisper back. "Nor am I."

"But still," the hob pressed on, "Mother says he was once the greatest hunter she had ever beheld, back in that faraway place you all once came from."

"She says that, does she?" Scruffer asked in response, a note of irritation creeping into his tone. "When did she say such a thing?"

Castor continued to speculate as though he had not heard Scruffer's question to him or picked up on the mounting irritation in his voice. "No, I believe the reason he's slowed is to give me the chance to become as great a hunter as he once was and to distinguish myself in the eyes of our human handlers. Why else would he have seen fit to save me from the mud if he didn't think I was special in some way?"

The silence that greeted Castor's last question spoke volumes to Felix nonetheless. Imagine having acted as a loving and supportive parent to a child that wasn't even your own, only to hear that child praise the one who had abandoned it over you? Surely that had to sting, which was no doubt the cause of Scruffer's nonresponse.

But as bad as he felt for his old friend in that moment, Felix couldn't also help but feel a certain amount of pride that the hob would think so highly of him that even his flaws would be converted into virtues. Though in truth he was no more Castor's father than was Scruffer, he knew that at one time he could've been if he had only had the strength and the courage to make it so. And to hear the hob speak so highly of him now was, in a way, like getting a second chance to be the exemplar he could and should have been back then.

Apart from the hurt and satisfaction they caused, Castor's words also proved more than prophetic, so far as their mission in Wellington was concerned. For while Felix and Scruffer performed more or less capably, if not exceptionally, Castor never ceased to impress the humans with the stunning number of rats he was able to ferret out of the ships and destroy. Most days, it was all they could do to keep up with him, racing from one squealing victim to the next, barely able to bag up the bodies before the next squeal rang out.

It was safe to say that over half the rats that were captured and hung outside the warehouse at the end of each day for passersby to admire were put there as a result of his efforts alone. And oftentimes at night, his handlers would present him with his own serving of rat meat, which was larger than the portion put aside for the two older ferrets to share by way of showing their admiration. Given that both Felix and Scruffer took pride in the hob, each for his own reason, neither minded the way that he was clearly favored over them.

Throughout the course of that initial fortnight in Wellington, Castor thrived so robustly at the hunt neither father could have suspected that, at night, he remained tortured and driven by a single dream. It was the same dream night after night, one that had been with him for months, although in truth it might be more accurate to say it was more a remembrance than a dream. Whatever name you would call it by, it was always the same. First, he saw the face of the young hob Riker staring at him admiringly, as used to always be the case when they lived together back in the barn. Then, suddenly, the face exploded, shattering into a thousand fragments, just as it did that day beneath Murdough's boot.

Again and again the face shattered, only to reassemble itself before exploding once more in an endless series of ghastly eruptions. And always Castor could hear his own voice in the dream, echoing over the bloody business even as it repeated and repeated, and even as his body twitched and shook in restless unconsciousness.

"Not me," he heard his own voice reverberating, sounding sad and frightened. "Please...please...not me..."

*****

Amos could see Tama staggering toward him out of the corner of his eye but knew better than to turn and look at him. Since their first night in the warehouse, Tama had made it abundantly clear that their friendship had come to an end and that he was no longer invited to speak to him. Despite the fact that they would spend whole days together on the ships with the ferrets, clearing out the rats, their nights were spent in chilly silence, neither uttering a sound despite their close proximity.

As it was, Amos was alone most of the time, anyway, since Tama had fallen into the habit of drinking through the evenings with

Weston and the other men who worked along the docks once their labors were finished for the day. Most nights, he would awaken to the sound of the great doors being pushed back haltingly, then listen as Tama's heavy footsteps threaded their way through the maze of boxes at the front of the warehouse before he made it to their sleeping quarters in the back and collapsed in a heap onto his cot. Miraculously, he was always fresh and ready to go to work the next morning as soon as the sun colored the sky, hardly appearing any worse for the wear.

Still, Amos worried about his old friend, even when he knew that Tama would have resented his concern. It seemed to him that Weston and the others thought of him less as a man of equal value to their own and more like an exotic specimen to be poked at and teased, a curio in a zoo. Many was the night Amos found himself lying on his cot, listening through the wall as the others clapped their hands and stomped their feet in the alley on the other side. He knew that Tama was dancing there at the center of a circle that they had formed, drunkenly performing some sacred dance of his people to the laughter and jeers of the other men.

Why would he make such a mockery of himself for their amusement? Amos often wondered about it, lying there and listening. Whatever became of the proud, noble Māori who had so intimidated him when he had first arrived in this strange new land? Here in port, away from his daughter, away from the land, Tama seemed lost, a man with no roots, clutching at whatever he could to keep from slipping away, like alcohol and the company of men like Weston. Only when they were hunting rats on the ships did he seem anything like the noble warrior he had always seemed to Amos back on Thackery's farm. Then their work would be done, night would fall, and Tama would return to his drunken reeling in the alley once more.

On this particular night, the drinking had started early, for there was still some light left in the sky as Tama shuffled down the middle of the road toward the warehouse. It was to be one of those nights, apparently, when Weston's wife had insisted he come home to her and their children rather than stay out till all hours with his companions. On nights such as these, when Tama found himself abandoned by the others, he would find his way to a shack set some distance back from the water, Amos knew, where they sold cheap grain alcohol by the bottle to some of Wellington's most fallen: thieves, prostitutes, and the other Māori brought to port as cheap laborers, who mostly lived in a tent encampment outside the city limits.

He could hear men and women out for their evening constitutionals on this cool evening tsk at him and curse beneath their breaths as Tama stumbled past them along the road. If the aborigine heard them at all, he gave no sign, dragging his feet through the dirt and stopping periodically to recover his balance before continuing on. He even smiled from time to time at passersby and tipped his stovepipe hat at them as though they were exchanging pleasantries, which only made the angry couples cling closer to one another and shuffle along faster.

Amos was just completing his nightly chore of nailing the day's catch to the cross outside the warehouse as Tama made his fitful approach, standing atop a shaky wooden ladder to complete the task. He was planning to ignore the whole sad spectacle as he had done so a dozen times before, assuming, as had always been the case, that the Māori would stagger inside without uttering a sound and collapse on top of his cot. So he was surprised when, having arrived at the entrance to the warehouse, Tama lingered for a moment instead and then suddenly sat down hard in the dirt at the foot of the ladder.

Amos immediately ceased his hammering as Tama lifted the hat from his head and carefully set it down on the ground beside him. The crucifix Thackery had erected was roughly a dozen feet high, its crossbeam eight or more feet above the earth, and it was from this height that the boy now looked down upon his old friend seated below. He had just driven a nail through the fleshy tail of the last of thirty rats they had ferreted out from the ships that day (an average catch), and their bodies swayed in the evening breeze coming in off the port as Tama let out a faraway sigh and began to speak.

"I always like this story from your holy book about this Jesus fellow and the two thieves hung on the cross with him, how the one thief say to the son of God, 'If you love us, you will forgive us our sins,' while the other say, 'If you love us so much, you will get us down from this here cross!'"

Tama rocked forward in a fit of laughter that shook his whole body, while Amos remained silent from on top of the ladder, observing. When the initial burst of laughter subsided, Tama withdrew a bottle from his inside pocket and took a long swallow, then lowered it from his lips and sighed once more.

"I like this second thief very much," he continued, still chuckling to himself, "the one who say 'If you love us, then get us *down*!'"

The sun was beginning to set out over the water, bathing the scene in an orange glow, as Tama raised the bottle once more and took a second long swig. When he lowered it this time, however, all the humor seemed to have drained from his body as he looked off mournfully at the burning sky, the night air turning cold around him.

"Your missionaries taught us this when they first come here and they always get so angry when we laugh at this man, this thief who say, 'Get us down *now*!' They say we miss the idea of the story but we think we understand the idea fine and we laugh and laugh…"

Tama's words broke off as his eyes narrowed, and he searched the horizon beyond the ships for some antidote for the pain he was experiencing. While the evening breeze continued to stir the bodies of the rats dangling from the crossbeam above him, Amos took the long pause as an opportunity to climb down from the ladder slowly and sit cross-legged next to him in the dirt after gathering his coat around him.

"My wife, too, she get so angry when I laugh. She say, too, I miss the idea. She believe the missionaries when they tell us, 'You are heathens! Your gods are false! You must believe in only one god, our God, because he alone can forgive you of your sins!' She try every day to believe this, to believe as they say, to change. 'It would be good for Amaia, to believe this way, too,' she say. 'To not be a heathen.' She say this till the sickness kill her, the sickness they bring with them. To the last day, she say, 'You miss the idea,' but I think I understand the idea very, very well…"

Tears were now streaming down the side of the Māori's face as he took another drink, yet Amos resisted the urge to speak or to comfort him, so grateful was he that Tama had deigned to speak with him again after weeks of bitter silence.

"I know why you feel what you feel for my Amaia," Tama went on, ignoring his own tears as the last of the sunlight withdrew from the sky and his face grew dark. "I know why you love her because I love her too. Every day I miss her so much. I become this shameful thing, this beast who dances for the amusement of devils. She is the last thing I have left on this earth, and without her, I am no better than this, a beast. So I know what it is like to love my Amaia, but I cannot allow you to give her your sickness—not sickness of the blood, maybe, but…sickness of the mind. It is a sickness you spread, you and your kind, and I cannot allow it to take her from me the way it took her mother. I cannot. Teach her your words, yes, so she can survive in this world that you and your kind have made. But do not love her. Do this for me, friend, please. This humble savage begs you."

Two men sit beneath a cross decorated with the carcasses of dead rats. One, a drunken Māori, lowers his chin to his chest and begins to sob. The other, a pale-faced boy of seventeen, still so new to the ways of the world, shifts awkwardly in his skin but can not think of the words to say. Instead he turns a hammer nervously over in his hands. And in the silence between them, the breeze continues to blow, stirring the bodies above them like wind chimes.

And in this manner, the issue was decided.

*****

Later, Felix woke to the sound of the two men sighing heavily in sleep above his head. There was another sound intermingled with their rhythmic breathing, though a sound that was the actual cause for his stirring. It had reached down into the depths of his dreams like a thin shaft of light and lifted him from the bottom of the ocean floor, back to the surface of consciousness.

It was the sound of a creature crying out for help.

As soon as he opened his eyes amid the sleep pile, he could see that the door to his cage had been left open a second time, just as it had been the night he was visited by the fiery Dam. What was more, the scar at the back of his neck from where he had been bitten burned and throbbed in a way it had not since that night she had first appeared to him.

He pushed his way from beneath Castor's sleeping body and headed for the opening as though summoned, stepping out onto the dry straw scattered about the floor of the humans' sleeping quarters to absorb the odor of their mustelid workers. The cry was nowhere near as voluminous as it was in his sleep, and he had to listen hard so as not to lose it altogether, moving once more toward the tower of shipping crates.

At first, he thought he was meant to climb the tower as he had done the night of his first visitation, but as he approached, he realized that the cry, as thin now as a reed in the wind, was not coming from the summit of the pyramid but rather from someplace outside. Circling round the tower, he slipped along the corridors of looming boxes until he made it to the massive doors at the front of the warehouse. As had become their custom, the men had left the doors somewhat ajar to keep the air circulating throughout the interior while they slept, even on a cold night such as this. And although the space left open was hardly any wider than his torso, Felix easily slipped through the crack and stepped out into the night.

Felix had never ventured outside the warehouse at night before. He was immediately struck by the briny sweetness of the night air and stood still, closing his eyes to enjoy the intoxicating aroma for a moment, as the throbbing at the back of his neck subsided beneath the cool touch of the harbor breeze. When he opened them again, he could see the dark silhouettes of the anchored ships bobbing gently against the shimmering sea while a magnificent full moon, planetary in size, hung low in the sky, casting everything beneath in a silvery light.

Felix's first instinct was to reach out for She—to try to rescue her from the exile she had been cast into so that she might share with him the beauty he was taking in—but something nearer at hand interrupted this thought and drew him back to the immediacy of the scene. It was the cry that had summoned him to be there in the first place.

It came from directly ahead of him, from the upper reaches of the dark cruciform silhouette that was stamped across his view of the harbor. Felix followed the sound to the base of the wooden cross and then began climbing the vertical post until he arrived below the crossbeam. There the odor of death and decay obliterated the sweet smell of saltwater as he pushed his way through a veil of hanging bodies and heaved himself up onto the beam.

It had been hours since Amos had hung the bodies at sunset, and the corpses were in a terrible state of desecration. Seagulls and other scavenger birds had feasted upon them from the moment the two men went inside, and their entrails hung loosely from the openings torn into their hides by ravenous beaks. Most were missing eyes, the soft jelly scraped from the sockets, and some had been robbed of pieces still bigger than that—ears, feet, heads.

As accustomed as he was to scenes of slaughter, having been a hunter his whole life, this was nonetheless a sight almost too appalling to take in all at once, and Felix had to turn his attention to the moon for a moment before closing his eyes to gather his equilibrium once more, lest he swooned and tumbled from the crossbeam to the earth below. Meanwhile, the scent of offal continued to assault his senses as the inverted tails of the crucified vermin stood between him and the infiniteness of the sea like prison bars.

Just as he was prepared to abandon the spot and climb back down from the cross, Felix heard a thin voice drift up to him from directly beneath his feet and snapped his eyes open in surprise. "Whoever's there," it whispered, nearly inaudibly, "have mercy on me. Please help me get down."

Felix dug his nails into the wood he was standing upon and leaned forward between two upright tails so that he could lay his eyes on the creature now speaking to him. At first, its hide was hardly discernible from those that hung around it, but the longer Felix listened, the better he was able to narrow in on the owner of the voice.

"I know I won't survive beyond this night," the voice went on, "but I wish to be among my kind when I expire—not here, to be torn apart by birds and ridiculed by Man. Have mercy on a dying creature."

Felix had at last located the petitioner. He was somewhat older than the rats that hung on either side of him, his coat streaked with gray accents that glittered in the moonlight. Coin-sized wounds were scattered across the glittering coat, exposing ghostly innards that had been pecked and punctured by hungry birds. What was more, it was clear from the empty holes that ran with dark fluid on either side of his pointed snout that the birds had taken his eyes as well.

"Do you know of one called Tiresias?" Felix found himself asking the wounded rat, suddenly remembering what the Dam had said to him that night about finding a rat with that name if he ever hoped to speak with She again.

"Every rat knows of Tiresias," the suspended one answered. "He is our leader."

"If I help you down," Felix proposed after taking a moment to consider the situation, "will you take me to him?"

"If you help me down," the rat answered back, his voice thick with emotion, "I give you my word that I will do as you ask."

Seeing that there was no chance of pulling the nail from the beam into which it was sunk, Felix quickly concluded that if he was to rescue the old rat from the cross, he would have to chew through the tail with his teeth. Not only was the thought of doing so powerfully unappetizing on the face of it, but he also knew that, should he be successful in gnawing through the cartilage, the next risk would come when the injured vermin, once freed, then plummeted to the earth. Could any creature in his wounded condition be expected to survive a fall from such a height?

He would have to trust in his lightning fast reflexes, just as he did instinctually whenever he had been underground, chasing rabbits through their byzantine warrens. Lowering his snout to the place where the nail pierced through the fleshy appendage, he hesitated for just a moment longer before taking his first bite into the rat's tail.

Once he began, Felix tried his best to work quickly and to banish from his thoughts any consideration that might slow him in his progress, such as the matter of taste. Try as he might to rid himself entirely of this consideration, Felix found that he was only partially successful in doing so as he chewed through the thick tissue. And that what was most disturbing was not the presence of any stomach-churning tang to the stuff but the absence of any flavor at all.

For his part, the crucified rat hardly seemed to take notice of what was occurring or had reached the point of suffering where no further pain was registered. And the whole time that Felix tore through his cartilage with his teeth, driving toward the nail, he merely hung there silent and still, not uttering a sound.

Even before making contact with the iron spike, Felix could hear the last sinew of the tail begin to tear on its own and shot his snout down to clamp his sharp teeth into the creature's hindquarters. A second later, the severed tail snapped free, and Felix was immediately pulled forward off the crossbeam by the liberated weight of the rat, now hanging fully suspended between his powerful jaws. Despite the agonizing strain, he was able to lower him safely to the earth below by slowly inching along the vertical post beam while upside down.

As soon as they had arrived at the base of the cross, Felix released the rat from his jaws and rolled over onto the cool dirt of the road to collect his strength once more. Every joint and muscle of his body ached from the strain of what had just occurred, but he knew that they did not have long to rest before the sun came up and his hopes of meeting Tiresias would vanish. And so after only a brief moment, during which he had to fight the almost overwhelming desire to return to sleep, Felix lifted himself off the ground and moved back toward the mutilated rat, who remained just where he had left him in the road, his tail now severed in twain.

"Where is he?" he asked, looking down at the still form.

"Take me to the water."

Clamping his teeth into the flesh at the back of the rat's neck, Felix lifted the creature once more by the scruff and began to drag its nearly lifeless body across the dirt road toward the dock on the opposite side. Little did he know that Castor, who had been stirred from sleep by his leaving, had observed the entire operation through the opening in the warehouse doors and that he was watching even now, trembling with emotion, as Felix disappeared into the darkness at the water's edge.

*****

Slipping in and out of consciousness, the wounded rat's directions to Felix seemed all of a muddle and designed to contradict. One moment he would instruct his carrier to press forward along the harbor, keeping the water to their left, only to reverse himself in the next moment and insist they turn back around, keeping the water to their right. Oftentimes, too, his voice became so faint that Felix could hardly be sure which way he was telling him to turn over the sound of his own tortured breathing, as he dragged the limp creature back and forth across the splintered boards of the dock.

They seemed in general, however, to be headed north along the harbor, to points farthest away from the warehouse and the customs office. Here, only the smallest boats put into shore, ones whose holds were shallow enough so that they could be unloaded without the assistance of a company of stevedores and longshoremen, locally referred to as wharfies. The majority of these vessels had traveled no farther than South Island, carrying with them letters and local goods out of Nelson across Cook Strait. Relegating them to the outer reaches of the port was a means of keeping them out of the way of the larger steamships with their greater cargos since they required neither additional hands to unload their deliveries nor the careful oversight of the customs inspector to record what those deliveries were.

When they reached the point where the lights of Wellington seemed like little more than distant candle flames in the darkness and the boards beneath his paws became increasingly dusted with sand, Felix found he could go no further and released the rat from his jaws before falling over sideways. Every muscle of his body ached from the exertion—he had never had to drag a creature so far, be it rabbit or rat—and he lay there for a moment, utterly collapsed, allowing his lungs to fill with cool air while he stared up into the nighttime sky. Despite the moon's unabated brilliance, it had not been fully successful in erasing the canvas of stars lurking behind it, and Felix took in the distant galaxies turning above his head with a kind of longing.

As his breathing became more regular, he suddenly recalled a night long ago when, back in his original homeland, he had stood beneath another full moon and listened as the Breeder muttered words he could not comprehend while the shadow of the Bride drifted beyond the curtains of the farmhouse behind them. Was this what he was speaking to him about, this strange place he had been sent to? Could the Breeder, in his infinite wisdom, have foreseen all that he would go through to get here, to this moment, halfway around the world? And was he trying to warn him that night about all that would follow and all that lay ahead?

As Felix was pondering these questions, he suddenly heard the wounded rat whisper softly from nearby. "Tiresias is below," he rasped. "I can feel him."

Felix startled at the thought that they might have somehow reached their destination point after all and then twisted over onto his feet to investigate. Moving to the end of the dock, he looked out over the edge to see that a thin slip of beach lay little more than two feet below. The nearest boats were tied up a dozen or more feet in either direction, allowing him enough room to land safely, he reasoned, should he choose to jump.

Looking back at the outline of the one he had rescued from the cross lying behind him, Felix noted his lifeless form and wondered if he had not just heard him whisper his final words. And then, summoning his courage, he turned back toward the water and leaped out into space.

His calculations proved correct, and Felix landed softly onto the powdery sand, with only his tail and hindquarters splashing down into the shallow water. Scurrying quickly farther up onto the beach, he noted how the wooden planks of the dock above formed a low-ceilinged cave with the beach below, the one he now stood upon. Lingering but an instant before the black mouth of the cave, every instinct on high alert, Felix checked back with the full moon one last time before creeping across the threshold.

As soon as he entered the darkness of the cave, his senses were violently assailed by the sad odor of rats in every direction. It was an odor he had become all too familiar with while ferreting on the ships, but here the stench was multiplied to a degree he had never experienced before. There must be hundreds of rats on either side, he thought, swarming in upon him, and he had to fight the urge to strike out at them, to push back against their encroachment. Instead he closed his eyes and continued to press forward, obeying a more powerful instinct that told him that the thing he sought dwelt before him in the further recesses of the cave. Behind his closed lids, however, he could see the combined oily smudge of the rats closing in upon him, closing off his escape, and his entire body became electric with fear as a chorus of threatening squeaks and squeals rose up in the air all around him.

Just when it seemed as though the advancing smudge was poised to overwhelm him or that the walls of sound would come crashing down upon him, all suddenly became silent and still. For a moment, the only sound that Felix could make out was the sound of his own terrified breathing as he scanned the empty darkness of his inner vision for the presence of any other creature nearby. But all had seemingly vanished, and he was alone instead inside the liminal recesses of his mind.

"Speak to me, Tiresias," he whispered, his voice echoing into the chasm. "I've come as the Dam instructed. Now show yourself."

As his words faded away, a red globe of light suddenly appeared upon the black canvas before him and began to expand outward from the center until it occupied every corner of his mind. At first, he thought that it was She returning to him at last since it was the same red light out of which she had emerged in the tunnels underground on the afternoon of the Great Cleansing. But then the red began to shrink from his field of vision as quickly as it had spread, shrinking back to its original sphere with no sign of She, and when Felix opened his eyes, he found that he was standing a mere few inches before the oldest rat he had ever beheld in his life.

"Your mother wished you to know that she is listening," Tiresias croaked. "That is why she sent her light."

"But where is she?" Felix challenged. "Why doesn't she appear before me now?"

"First, you must do something for us," Tiresias responded, lifting his frail gray snout off the ground with obvious effort, his long white whiskers hanging down to the sand. "Then she will be returned to you."

Now that his eyes had been given a minute to adjust to the faded light reflected by the moon, Felix could see that Tiresias was backed into the farthermost corner of the cave on a gradient somewhat higher than where he stood, up where the sand of the beach pressed against the underside of the dock. And while much of his body remained concealed from his vision in this fashion, Felix drew the immediate impression that he was no longer able to move his limbs without great effort, judging by how still he remained as he glanced down from his perch through large, blinded eyes clouded with a milky fog.

Once he had drawn his impressions of Tiresias and scanned the hostile throng of rats seething on either side of him, eager to pounce and defend its king, Felix picked up the thread of conversation by rejoining, "And what would you have me do?"

"Something very great," Tiresias rasped after a long pause, "as befits a reward as great as the return of one's own conscience. Only I warn you—it will be a very difficult thing for you to execute because it will require you to act against the very grain of your nature."

The rats surrounding Felix were pressing in so close now that he could feel the warm breath of their nostrils against his skin. He tried not to let the panic show in his voice as he countered, "And what do you suppose my nature is?"

"Why…" Tiresias sniffed at the fatuity of the question. "That of a killer, is it not? Are you not Felix the Red, Greatest Hunter of Them All? Or has your legend been misrepresented to me?"

"I'm the Red," Felix snapped defensively, shoving back one of the encroaching rats with his snout, "but I'm more than just a killer."

"So you say," Tiresias responded in a level whisper, "although being a killer is the only part of your nature that you understand because you know not who you are, not where you come from, nor how you arrived at this moment in time, nor the great forces at play that have shaped you into the creature you have become. You know nothing. You are lost in your own history."

Something about what Tiresias said awakened a vague notion Felix had kept stored at the back of his mind all these years, a shapeless suspicion he had carried with him since he was a young hob, that there were forces operating all around him, determining his fate. And how was it that this shriveled old rat, his sworn enemy, should know more about who he was than he did himself? Was it true that he was lost in his own history?

There were so many questions he suddenly wanted to ask the aged creature, but he was too afraid of appearing vulnerable and needy in such a charged atmosphere. So instead he continued with his own defense by saying, "If I'm nothing more than a killer, then why have I rescued one of your own this very night from the cross and brought him back to you? He's waiting now, just above our heads. Is this what a killer would do?"

Tiresias's milky eyes widened somewhat as he took in the news. Then he turned and gave a slight nod to the two rats standing guard on either side of him, who immediately raced down the slope toward the entrance of the cave in order to retrieve their rescued brethren. Felix could sense a warmer tone in the old rat's voice when his words next entered into his mind.

"Perhaps your mother was right about you after all when she argued that you were that rarest of all creatures, a hunter with the capacity for mercy."

"But how is it She speaks to you and not to me?"

"It is not to me she speaks but to the dam you murdered at the humans' elegant gathering, the one who died with her pups still inside of her. She was my mate, the Dam, and those were to be my offspring, the last I was likely to see walk upon this earth before I left it. But the Greatest Hunter of Them All put an end to all that now, didn't he?"

"I wasn't aware she was your mate," Felix muttered, hearing the shame creep into his voice.

"Of course, you were not." Tiresias sighed, closing his eyes from the effort of transmitting his thoughts, even as those thoughts grew more forceful inside Felix's head. "Why would you have even considered such a thing, that a creature as vile as she could be tied to another by cords of affection? Your job was to hunt her down and to kill her, and any larger consideration would only have made your task more difficult, would it not? It was not what you were trained to do, after all, to think about the full dimension of the life you were taking. Perhaps it would have caused you to hesitate for an instant had you known that she herself was brought there that night against her will by human hands, and such hesitation could be fatal to the hunter. Your duty to the humans was to act unthinkingly, and act you did. Still, actions have consequences, and it is those consequences that have brought you here before me this evening."

"Then tell me what I must do to make amends for my actions," Felix demanded, taking a step toward the old rat as the multitudes surrounding him surged forward to prevent him from reaching their king. "Is it food you want? I can bring you Man's food from the place where I stay. There are boxes and boxes of it piled high."

"We do not desire their food." Tiresias sighed, his voice fading.

"Then what?" Felix pleaded, desperate not to lose the connection he had established with Tiresias as he strained against the angry throng. "Tell me what it is!"

Tiresias slowly opened his eyes and fixed his blind gaze on Felix for a long moment before responding. When the words finally came, they were tinged with such ageless sorrow that they summoned forth a deep, nameless sadness that had haunted Felix ever since his days back on the Breeder's farm, a sadness he had done his best to suppress but could no longer find the strength to deny with Tiresias's words echoing in his head.

"We wish no more to feed off the crumbs of Man's table nor to skulk amidst the streets of his dirty cities for our survival, cities poisoned with hatred and violence against us. Since time began, we dreamed of living in peace alongside the humans, to keep within the narrow margins they allowed, only to have our efforts at peaceful coexistence met with death and destruction. So no more of it. It is that same dream that is killing us. Now there is only one thing left to desire. Help us attain it, and you will have once more the voice of She inside of you, to guide you along your path. She herself has agreed to the terms from the afterworld, believing you are capable of delivering to us this one last thing. Do so, and she will be yours once more."

"And what is this one last thing you seek?" Felix asked, although, in truth, he already suspected what the answer might be.

*****

Some time later, he found himself standing on top of the dock once more, gazing back at the lights of Wellington. Already the sun was beginning to color the eastern sky, and he knew that it wouldn't be long before the human inhabitants who dwelled therein would begin to stir and get on with the business of their day. Even now, the boy might be rising from his slumber, and he knew that he should be racing back at this very moment if he hoped to keep him from discovering that he was ever gone. Nevertheless, a heavy weariness had settled upon him since he had emerged from the rats' lair, and he could not as of yet bring himself to move.

Instead he stretched out onto the dock to rest for a moment, gathering his strength before the mad dash back to the warehouse. Painted across the boards in front of him was a thick trail of blood, which was all that remained of the rat he had gnawed down from the cross after his comrades had dragged him back to the safety of the cave. Had he survived or not? Perhaps Felix would never know.

Below him, he could feel Tiresias deep in thought, just as he himself was. No doubt they were thinking about the same thing, about the challenge that had been made to him and about whether or not he would be able to meet it. Yet She believed in him, and if She believed, then surely he must believe too.

But how would he do it? How would he find a way to speak to his human handler when they shared no common language, when there was no line of communication between them? The boy's participation was essential, though, if Felix was ever to succeed in winning his mother back to him; this much he knew instinctually. Just as he knew what the old rat would say when he pressed him earlier to name the one thing that would be required of him to deliver before She could be ransomed.

"A boat."

CHAPTER 14

Tiresias's words continued to echo in Felix's mind later that morning while he streaked about the cargo hold of a Portuguese steamer, chasing stowaway rats around enormous casks of wine and over tall stacks of canvas bags filled with cork. Could it be true—as the old rat claimed it was in a long recitation to persuade him to their cause—that Man had discovered a means to win dominion over all his rivals, which was by pitting each creature on the planet against the other? Was the natural enmity he felt toward the species he hunted down and destroyed not natural at all, as he had always assumed, but something he had been tricked into believing without question by his human overlords? And even now, this instant, as he was closing in on a young pup, preparing to pounce, was it instinct alone that was guiding him or was there an unseen hand behind the things he always took to be inborn, a matter of blood knowledge?

To believe what he had been told by Tiresias, Felix would have to reconsider nearly everything he once thought was true about himself in the world. Until their meeting beneath the dock, he had always taken great pride in being recognized by the other ferrets in the business as the Greatest Hunter of Them All. But if it was true that he was only being used as an instrument to do mankind's bidding, then what did such a title really mean in the end? Was it merely that he had allowed himself to be duped by empty prizes while unwittingly enhancing the power that the humans held over them all?

"Consider the victory you won through the Great Cleansing," Tiresias had said, challenging him, well into his audience with the blind seer. "A single rabbit might sustain an entire business of ferrets for days—weeks, perhaps. But were the humans satisfied after one rabbit life was taken? Or was it that they would not be satisfied, could not be satisfied, until every rabbit in the field had been slaughtered and set ablaze? Ask yourself. Why was all that further killing necessary? And whose needs did it serve? Did it serve the ferrets' needs? Or Man's?"

While he was replaying the moment over in his head, Felix was unwittingly slowing his speed, no longer advancing upon the young pup, shrinking the gap between them, but rather falling into a medium stride behind him. How could he concentrate on the hunt when all these thoughts were still fresh in his mind? He had only just made it back to the warehouse in time to slip back into the cage undetected before they were carried across the street and released into the hold to perform the day's ferreting. And the combination of sleeplessness plus the fire Tiresias had set off in his conscience made it nearly impossible for him to return to business as usual so soon after they had talked.

Tiresias spoke most eloquently through the night about the persecution of his own kind, the rats, and how they had suffered most at the hands of Man because they had nothing to offer him and so were made easy targets for extermination. His words, however, did not lack in sympathy for others charged to due Man's bidding since he saw all creatures as somehow caught up in the same web of human desire, each made a victim of the mankind's unquenchable thirst for complete domination, even ferrets like himself.

"Brother set against brother," the old rat had intoned, "stretching back to the dawn of time. What is history if not the story of mankind's subjugation of all the creatures of the earth to his will? *Ever has it been so.*"

The same words he had heard whispered from the mind of the first doe he had ever chased up onto the fence—the Queen, who had hung there looking down on him the day of his first hunt until the Breeder had come along to snap her neck—were now issuing forth from the mind of this verminous creature hidden in the earth halfway around the world. Was this somehow proof that the things

Tiresias was saying were to be believed? And if so, had Felix been little more than a pawn in this bloody history from the start?

But surely there must have been a time *before*, when he stood outside the cycle of murder and retribution. Back in his native homeland, for instance, back in the barn, he had never once thought to question the Breeder's motives toward him and the other ferrets but had always assumed that they were guided by a sense of genuine care and, to the extent such a feeling was possible between human and mustelid, love. Yet wasn't it he who had taught them to hunt in the first place, to become killers? And wasn't it the Breeder who had thought to ship them off to this new land where they might continue their campaign of slaughter in his name, only now on a much grander scale? Was it then the Breeder, in the end, who was most responsible for taking She away from him, for disposing of her when she was no longer capable of serving his needs?

When he considered his life in this light, there was no time *before*, no time when he had been free from the story of mankind's tyranny. There was only time itself. All of it.

"Ever has it been so."

Without fully recognizing what he was doing, Felix found that he was now subtly steering his quarry away from the farther reaches of the hold, where he might be more easily cornered; instead he was driving him back toward the stairs that led to the upper deck of the ship, the way the herd dog Victoria used to steer the sheep from behind back on the farm. He remembered Tiresias saying that most of the rats hiding below the dock along with him, those waiting for their deliverance, had themselves escaped in this same fashion, scrambling up onto the decks of the ships they had arrived on and leaping out into the water before swimming to shore.

Suddenly, he no longer wished to be the Greatest Hunter of Them All. Suddenly, he no longer wished to trap this young rat beneath him or to taste his blood in his mouth. Suddenly, he wished only for him to be free.

It was freedom, after all, that Tiresias was proposing as ransom for the release of She, freedom from the whole sorry spectacle of endless, all-consuming suffering. And having played his part in that spectacle for far too long, Felix found he wanted no more of circles upon circles either. He wanted to break free of Man's history as well and start anew, just as the rats wished to do.

"A boat," the old rat had explained, "to take us away from all this pain and suffering. Let Man have all that he believes is rightfully his to have. We only wish now for a place to call our own, where we might live and be free of him at last. Speak to your human and make it so—it is clear he favors you—for we cannot speak for ourselves."

Felix could almost taste the freedom he suddenly longed to possess as the young pup arrived at last at the foot of the metal stairs that led up and out of the hold. No sooner had he begun to leap up the steps, however, when something dark and powerful streaked past Felix on the right, knocking him sideways. Looking up from the floor of the ship, he saw Castor overtake the fleeing rat at the top of the steps, just before he made it onto deck, and pin him down with his vicelike jaws. Lifting him thus by the throat, the fearsome young hob turned and shook the pup violently between his teeth, all the while clamping down, until the creature's pharynx collapsed beneath the pressure and his eyes rolled back in his head. Then as Castor loosened his grip, the dead rat slipped from his opened mouth, and bounded back down the metal stairs, its body rolling lifelessly to a halt before Felix.

"I know what you're doing," Castor challenged him, panting heavily from the chase while looking down at Felix from the high step. "But why?"

And in that moment, Felix could think of nothing to say as he stared back into the frightened face of the young hob whose hero he once had been.

*****

Who can fully measure the effect that a single act of violence can have on the minds of the young? Since Felix had not been present at the time of the trauma but was still being nursed back to life in Tama's shack, he was not there to witness the moment when Murdough had crushed Riker's skull beneath his boot in an instant

244

of blind fury. Castor had seen it all with his own eyes, though, and the memory of that isolated act of cruelty had lodged itself at the very center of his thoughts ever since, torturing his dreams and haunting him in his waking hours.

Before the incident of savagery in the barn, Castor assumed he understood the nature of the bargain that his kind, the ferrets, had struck with their human overlords—hunt for them well and they would provide all the food and shelter the ferrets required. Now, however, he saw that the terms of that arrangement could reverse themselves without warning, that the humans might suddenly turn their displeasure against even those creatures that served them faithfully and unleash their pent-up rage upon them indiscriminately and without mercy. And the knowledge of this—that he stood, as it were, ever on shaky ground in Man's eyes—unnerved him and made him even more determined to please the humans so that they would never have cause to turn against him, like they had on his friend. Pleasing them naturally meant killing for them, and so he drove himself to become the best killer in the business, desperate to learn from the example of his betters, so that the boot would never find occasion to come down upon him.

And now those who would teach him to become the best were turning against him and placing him once more at risk of sudden annihilation. Why? Why would Felix have rescued him from his muddy grave on the day of the Great Cleansing, only to expose him now to the murderous retributions that would surely be in store for him if the humans were to discover that the ferrets were allowing their prey to escape from the ships and cutting them down from the cross?

Though he knew he owed the older ferret a debt of gratitude for what he had done for him, he also understood that he could not allow that gratitude to blind him to the need for his own self-preservation. And so after what he had witnessed of Felix both the previous night and that morning aboard the ship, Castor resolved that the only discerning light to consider him by from this point forward was as his sworn enemy.

Unaware that he had been observed the night before, Felix could not comprehend how Castor had come so quickly to intuit his change of heart toward the rats. He only knew—based on the way the young hob continued to glare at him from the opposite side of the cage as they rumbled along in the back of the wagon—that he had somehow apprehended his intentions and was resolved to do his utmost to prevent him from executing his plan. He did his best now to listen in on his thoughts as they were driven back out to Thackery's farm, to determine if he knew already just exactly what that plan might be ("A boat"), but Castor anticipated these efforts to intercept his thinking and remained conspicuously noncommunicative toward both him and Scruffer for the whole trip.

For his part, Scruffer was completely baffled by the air of simmering hostility that had suddenly developed between the two hunters. Until the previous day, Castor's attitude toward Felix had been almost painfully worshipful. But now, clearly something had changed, but try as he might to elicit some explanation for the change from either one of them, he was repeatedly rebuffed by both. Felix resolved to let the mystery be until later on that evening when he might revisit it once more in careful consultation with Kara.

*****

The ferrets were not the only creatures at an impasse that morning as the wagon made its slow progress across the sea of grass, back toward Thackery's estate. Amaia had been there to greet them at the dock once they disembarked from the ship with their first catch of the day. She had been sent on foot by Miss Hollis to retrieve them, but her sudden, unexpected appearance had nearly caused Amos to lose his grip on the burlap sack and drop the rat corpses within it into the water. He stood there frozen, unable to move his feet, and he watched as a slow, satisfied grin broke out across her face upon seeing demonstrated the absolute power she continued to enjoy over him. Immediately thereafter, however, he felt a second pair of eyes trained upon him, and when he turned, he saw Tama staring back at him from the bottom of the gangplank, the ferrets draped across his arms, imploring him to remember the unspoken agreement they had come to the previous night while sitting at the foot of the cross.

The three rode together in the wagon a short while later, each straining beneath a cloud of misgiving that caused them to retreat into an awkward silence. Wedged between them on the seat up front while her father drove the horses, Amaia, for instance, could not understand why Amos would be so visibly moved at the initial sight of her, as he so plainly was, only to distance himself now that their bodies were pressed tightly together. He stared off at the undulating waves of grass without uttering a sound. Absorbing the sting of his withdrawal, she gradually determined to withdraw herself behind the familiar mask of her steely reserve and to subtly withdraw her leg from his, denying the rush of emotion she had felt when she had first beheld him standing there at the top of the gangplank.

For his part, Amos could not understand how she could not natively sense just how much he longed to speak to her, to hold her in his arms, and to cover her with kisses. He had not realized until he saw her standing there on the pier just how much their time apart had increased his appetite for her company. Now, like a man in the desert who stumbles upon an oasis, he wanted only to drink in every part of her being and to never let her go again. And yet he had made a bargain with her father to not infect her mind as her mother's mind had been infected, and he was honor bound to abide by the terms of their agreement or risk losing the affection of his dear friend a second time.

With all her powers of insight, how could she not feel the waves of longing emanating from him and break through the misunderstanding by simply laying a hand upon his knee? Instead he could feel her leg inching away from his, and the crushing feeling of abandonment it sparked in him made him want to throw himself beneath the heavy wheels of the cart and to know the sweet oblivion that Murdough had attained for himself via similar means.

Only Tama was fully aware of the reasons why the two beside him suffered so—she for her pride and he for his honor. Only Tama could explain to them how they had arrived at such a place of stalemate and release them from the pain they were experiencing, but instead he chose to keep his counsel and hold his tongue as he shook the reigns in his hands and gently guided the horses toward their destination. Had not his own people suffered for a hundred years beneath the white man's boot and far more gravely than two young lovers ever could? To grow old was to suffer, he reasoned to himself, and the pain he was causing them to endure struck him as being the small price all were asked to pay for the purchase of greater wisdom.

And as the main house on Thackery's farm rose up out the ground and came into view, freshly painted since the night of the banquet, it was Tama alone in the wagon—taking into account both its human and mustelid passengers—who was not otherwise overcome by a powerful sense of foreboding at the sight of its glistening turrets piercing the sky.

Instead he whispered softly underneath his breath, "Wākāinga," the Māori word for home.

*****

"See, the Conqu'ring Hero comes!"

Amos could not recall ever seeing his old master this excited, as he turned in his seat to allow Amaia to brush past and leap down from the wagon first. Thackery looked years younger than he had the last time they spoke, on the morning after the shareholders' debacle. He clapped his hands enthusiastically as he descended the front steps of the house two at a time to greet them, his sallow cheeks now rosy with reanimated vigor. Had Ponce de León's rejuvenating fountain been discovered buried somewhere deep on his grazing lands while they had been away?

Ever the master, Thackery continued to shout out orders in his youthful guise as he made his way around the front of the wagon to where Amos sat frozen in his seat, still smarting at the hurt he felt for Amaia's hurried departure. It was as though she could not wait to be free of him fast enough, and he watched as she hurried to join Miss Hollis at the top of the steps, never once turning to look back to where he was.

"Unload these wonderful creatures back into the barn, would you, Tama?" Thackery fairly sang of the ferrets as he pronounced the command, fighting the urge to skip as he made it to the far side of the cart. "Then put this wagon away and help Miss Hollis with the staff in the house. We are having a guest tonight, we are. And a very, very important guest at that."

Thackery now stood on the ground beneath Amos, offering his hand in assistance, but the young man continued to watch as Amaia cast her eyes downward and followed Hollis into the shadows of the house. Noticing the trance he had fallen into and recognizing its cause, Tama purposely allowed the rear gate of the wagon to slip from his hands and drop open noisily after sliding the bolt in an effort to wake him from his reverie.

Amos jumped at the sound, then turned and looked down at Thackery, who continued to wait for him to accept his offer of help. "I'm sorry, Master Thackery," Amos said, clearing his throat while taking hold of his hand, "I'm still a little tired from the trip."

"Well, make yourself *un*tired, young man," Thackery insisted, merrily clapping Amos on the back once he had jumped down from the wagon. "Your efforts at the seaport with your little ferret friends have practically made you a legend throughout the colony, and tonight's the night for you to take your much deserved bow."

Transporting the cage of ferrets to the barn as instructed, Tama could not resist the final urge to look back over his shoulder, wondering where all this animated praise was leading. He had known his old master for far too long not to be suspicious of his motives, and never was he more suspicious than when he was doling out praise. Seeing Thackery drape his arm across Amos's shoulder in a fatherly fashion as he steered him back toward the house only confirmed his suspicions that something was amiss as he moved into the musky odor of the barn.

"That cross was a stroke of genius, if I do say so myself," Thackery self-congratulated, arriving at the foot of the steps but continuing to hold Amos to his side. "Everyone's been talking about it, the sheer number of devils you've managed to put up on the thing. I can't tell you the number of times I've heard the story: one hundred, two hundred…a thousand…ten thousand! Why, I'd say that in one fell swoop, that cross alone has done more to put people's fears to rest and to restore power back to its rightful place—which is squarely with me—than anything else we could've devised. So well done, young lad! We did it! Well done!"

Amos could hardly absorb the meaning of his master's words, so unfamiliar was he to being held this long in the old man's embrace. As though sensing at this point that he was missing the central idea, Thackery gripped his young charge by the shoulders and maneuvered him to face him. Then, lowering his voice and speaking in a slower, more deliberate fashion, the old master bent forward slightly to look Amos directly in the eyes.

"What I'm saying is that that parcel of land we talked about is practically yours for the taking." He smiled, raising his eyebrows as though to indicate his greater meaning. "There's just one last person we need to convince."

*****

Amos had placed the washtub just outside the entrance to the barn, the better to be seen carrying out the instructions he had been given should Hollis or Thackery look out through the windows of the house to check up on him. Having already washed and scrubbed clean Scruffer and Castor, he was attempting now to do likewise with his Little Red, gently lathering his aggravated skin with soap and a warm cloth; only Felix was restless in his current predicament and desperately fought to break free of the boy's grip. His efforts had proved to be in vain thus far, as all his squirming and clawing had only made Amos tighten his grip around his midsection while suspending him above the surface of the water.

"What's gotten into you, Little Red?" Amos muttered as Felix's nails scrapped at his knuckles and his body thrashed back and forth in his hand. "You want to look presentable for tonight's guest, don't you?"

How could he make this ignorant human understand that he had no time for a bath at that moment, that he was urgently needed back in the barn to finish a conversation that had surprised him to the core and overturned everything he thought he understood about the world up until that point? It was a conversation that had begun the moment Tama had released the three hunters from their cage and stood to exit. Kara had been the first among the barn ferrets to awaken to their return and had leaped from the top of their sleep pile, racing across the stall to greet them. Naturally, the one she went to first was her own flesh and blood, her son, brushing her nose to his and nuzzling the side of his neck with her snout. And then, overcome with an uncontained joy that they had been brought back safely to the business, she turned to Felix and telegraphed the thought she would almost immediately regret letting slip free.

"I thought I'd never see you again."

Had she greeted Scruffer in some manner before allowing the sentiment to flow out the way it had, the moment might have passed without much notice. If she had only whispered some kind words of welcome or nuzzled him the way she had Castor, he might not have felt so slighted, so betrayed by her obvious affection for his rival in all things. If she had only remembered in some small, insignificant way that it was him and not Felix who had stood by her after her violation aboard the ship, who had raised the hob she had brought forth as his own and who asked for nothing more in return than that she might some day grow to love him for his constancy and steady devotion.

But she had not.

And now that the moment had occurred, she was powerless to take it back, to somehow do it over again in a way that might make it less painful to him. Instead she tried to recover from the blunder by coming up with something to say that might somehow mitigate or erase the powerful gaffe she had made. But when she tried to whisper some such endearment to him, the thoughts came out all muddled and confused. Until, at last, she looked into his sad eyes and said the only honest thing she could think to say.

"I'm sorry."

For the truth was that she had never stopped loving Felix, not since that morning a long, long time ago when they had frolicked together in the snow, off in some faraway land. Seeing him frolic in the wool on the day of the banquet had only served to rekindle feelings that, in truth, she had always known had never completely gone away, that were still there buried deep down inside her. And she was not surprised, not truly surprised, when, every night since they had been sent away to hunt at the seaport, before closing her eyes and falling asleep, she had found herself longing to see his peculiar red face again in a way she had not longed to see Scruffer's pristine white mask.

Despite everything that had happened, it was Felix, in the end, that she loved the most. The heart is a fathomless mystery, be it human or ferret.

The silence that followed Kara's "I'm sorry" widened with every passing second, threatening to engulf them all, until Castor exercised the age-old prerogative of youth everywhere, regardless of species, which is to break the silence.

"What is it you're sorry for?" he asked, scanning the stricken faces of the three grown ferrets standing before him, none of whom could manage to meet his gaze directly. So he pressed on, "Why do you greet the red one so tenderly with my father standing so close by? Who is this Felix to you, anyway? To me? What aren't you telling me?"

Scruffer stepped forward to quiet his son's growing frustration at their collective silence.

"Now, Castor…"

"I'm not asking you, Father! I'm asking my mother! Who is he to me?!"

Felix scoured his brain for some answer he could give to satisfy the inquisitor, but his mind continually drew a blank. After all, who *was* the young hob to him, anyway? He had never once asked himself the question previously without already having the most convenient response readily at hand—that he was not *his*. And yet, now that Castor was standing there before him, demanding to know the most basic truths about who he was and how he had come into the world, that response hardly seemed to suffice; it seemed heartless, cruel. And so, as a result, he could think of nothing to say since he was only now asking himself the question honestly for the first time.

For Kara, the day she had always dreaded might come was finally here. And yet, for all her precautions, endlessly rehearsing the things she might say when it did, she found herself inexplicably struck dumb at the very moment she had braced for since her Castor was born. Instead she looked to Felix for help, help that would not be forthcoming, before lowering her eyes in shame.

"You knew we came from the same place by the mark on our ears," Scruffer offered wanly.

"But that's not it," Castor fired back, darting his eyes back and forth between Felix and Kara. "There's something else, something you're not telling me. What is it? What is it you're not telling me?!"

Then, suddenly, Amos arrived like a god to lift Castor and Scruffer out of the scene and carry them off to their bath. With Castor's voice still ringing in his ears—"What are you not telling me?!"—Felix attempted to move toward Kara, only to be pulled up short when she lifted her head and fixed him with a savage gaze.

"I was carrying your kit inside me before the Smeller of Blood came to take us away," she snarled, her hatred for herself boiling over to him. "Know that—should you ever choose to answer him."

Then she turned and moved off to the farthest reaches of the stall, burying herself deep at the bottom of the sleeping pile of ferrets in order to avoid any further communication with him. And Felix remained just as he was at the time of her revelation, too stunned to move, until Amos returned a second time with the other ferrets and carried him off for his cleaning.

It took a while for the shock of what she told him to wear off, and by the time that it did, Felix was already covered in soapy bubbles. And though he struggled for some time to break free, it was of no use; he would miss what was transpiring back in the barn between the two grown ferrets and their angry son. Or was it *his* son? Could Castor truly be his? How could he ever know for sure?

His sudden urgent need to discover the answers to these momentous questions only served to complicate the conundrum that had plagued him since his meeting with the rat king the night before—namely, how to transmit Tiresias's demand for a boat to a creature who did not speak as they did. The boy communicated through sound, not telepathy, and in a vocabulary that was entirely foreign to them. How could they ever arrive at a common definition for "boat" when their languages were so far apart? And if he could not communicate the meaning for "boat" to Amos, then how could he ever hope to communicate the fact that he was needed that very instant back in the barn, to take part in a discussion that might very well determine the outcome of the story for all of them?

Feeling the combined weight of both dilemmas pressing down upon him now, Felix gradually abandoned his attempts to break free of Amos's grip and submitted passively to the bath. With so many challenges stacked up on top of him, he would use the moment to ponder and catch his breath, sensing that he would not get many more like it in the future. And so he closed his eyes as the warm water ran down the length of his body and went aimlessly searching for She in his mind, not truly expecting to find her there until Tiresias released her from her interim prison.

What he encountered during his interior wandering, however, caused him as much surprise as if he had. For rising up out of the dark landscape of his imagination were the familiar red spheroids that, in the past, had announced her presence to him, appearing everywhere he turned. Only now, instead of She's dark mask materializing out of the heart of the red blossoms, there was another face revealed at the center of the crimson orbs, and it was Castor's. And he heard his own voice echoing in the void around him, questioning, as he looked into the eyes of his new polestar.

"Could it be? A son?"

*****

Had Felix been present in the barn, as he had wished, he would have been there to witness Kara fearlessly revealing to Castor each and every secret she had kept from him all those months on the farm, out of concern. The floodgates now opened; she was determined not to hold back or to leave anything unsaid despite whatever pain it might cause him, for fear of losing her child's trust forever. And so she told him everything, while Scruffer stood helplessly close by, powerless to stop the torrent of her truth. She told him of her love for Felix, first begun back on the Breeder's farm, far across the sea from where they were now; of her first litter of kits born dead one winter morning and how their deaths had caused her to retreat from the world; of how she found the will to live again once she had discovered that she had become pregnant for a second time; and finally, of their dark passage in the ship's hold and the horrible deed that had been done to her there.

To all this, Castor listened quietly without moving a muscle, absorbing each shock as though he were made of iron or steel, some impenetrable substance that could not be shattered despite the force of the heavy blows raining down upon him. All the while she was speaking, though, there was one question and one question only that came rising up out of the depths of his mind, a question that insisted itself above all others until at last, when she had finally completed her detailed account, it was the only question he could bring himself to ask.

"But is he my father?"

"The only thing I know for sure is that I am your mother." Kara sighed, the great unburdening having sapped the last of her strength. "And that will have to be enough."

But it was not enough for Castor, not enough by far.

Perhaps if his fears of sudden annihilation had not already been stoked by Felix's suspicious behavior toward the rats recently, he would have been more content to simply let the mystery be and to somehow move toward a point of acceptance over time. But Kara's revelations, coming as they did on top of everything that he had seen of Felix's behavior since the previous night, filled him with a primitive desire to avenge himself and those he loved against the evil red devil who had hurt them in the past and would no doubt hurt them again in the future if he was left to go unchecked.

While Castor struggled against this powerful instinct for revenge in a catatonic stupor (it was Felix, after all, who had rescued him from a muddy grave, was it not?), Kara had already given up trying to reach him in his stony silence and cried herself to sleep at the foot of the sleeping pyramid of ferrets. The young hob was watching her breathe in sleep from the far side of the stall, but his thoughts were so clouded by images of Felix being made to suffer the consequences of his villainy that he hardly saw her at all. Nor did he notice Scruffer when he left her side at some point and stealthily tiptoed across the hay to where he lay coiled up in his own black coat.

Felix had not been present for Kara's revelations, nor was he present to witness the moment his old friend Scruffer—good, loyal Scruffer, who was tired of never getting what he thought he deserved—stood above Castor and closed his eyes before whispering a thought into the hob's mind. Amos had already taken him into the house in advance of the arrival of that night's important dinner guest. Had he been there, he might have been able to intercept the thought before it penetrated the younger ferret's conscience and turn it back on its author. He might have even been able to make a case for himself that would have won the hob's heart to him once more, as it had been won after the Great Cleansing.

But he was not there to intercept or cajole, as it was, and the thought entered Castor's brain like a spike and immediately took root there, serving as a final inducement to push him over the edge, one last challenge he could not refuse.

"What does your instinct tell you to do?"

*****

The dining hall echoed with the sound of the men's laughter as they watched Felix greedily devour the small pile of rabbit meat that had been left for him on a plate at the center of the table. The meat had been braised only moments before in a light wine sauce, as per Master Thackery's instructions, and it was sweeter than anything he had ever tasted before, intoxicating his senses as he abandoned himself to its seductive richness. It was a meal designed to celebrate his accomplishments at the seaport while amusing the other guests at the table, and it had precisely the effect it was intended to have, even if Miss Hollis was forced to throw away her favorite frying pan in protest after it had been prepared.

Three human figures sat about the long table and cheered him on as he consumed his hero's feast. Amos sat in the chair closest to him at the center of the table in the silver-buttoned coat meant to make him look like a gentleman, still not having recovered from the surprise he felt when Master Thackery had ordered him to place his Little Red on top of the elegant white tablecloth so that they could all watch him eat. It had been startling enough to him when earlier he was told to bring the ferret with him to the dinner, given how things had turned out the last time he had been present in the dining hall. But this? This seemed downright decadent even to him who loved the ferret so and he looked nervously to the men sitting at either end of the table, wondering just how long their newfound goodwill toward the mustelid guest would hold out.

"That's right!" Thackery exhorted in a booming voice from the head of the table as Felix made it to the bottom of the pile and was licking the fine porcelain plate clean. "Get every drop, my fine ferret friend! You deserve it!"

As Felix dropped onto his side beside the empty plate, too full to move, and laid his head down on the fine cloth for a moment to rest from his exertions, Thackery took up his wineglass and proposed a toast to the satiated victor.

"A toast!" he bellowed. "To the red demon who has saved us not once but twice from the scourges of pestilence!"

"Here, here!" Mr. Rothchester seconded from the other end of the table, raising his glass and bringing it to his drooping lips.

Thackery hesitated to drink for a moment, overcome by a familiar wave of disgust as he watched this walrus-faced fop consume the entire contents of his glass in a single gulp. Then he remembered why he had asked Rothchester here as his honored guest in the first place and fought back his repugnance as he raised his own glass to his lips and sipped.

Amaia, who had been moving inconspicuously about the table as she had been trained to do, serving the men through the various courses of the meal, stepped from the shadows and moved to refill Amos's glass once the toast had been rendered. Seeing her beside him suddenly, he placed his hand over the mouth of the glass to signal that he wanted no more, and he turned his eyes to hers in an effort to catch her attention. Amaia merely stepped away without acknowledging his attempt in any way and moved to Mr. Rothchester, who made no such similar attempt to prevent her from refilling his glass.

"It's good port, Thackery," Rothchester belched, reaching for the glass as Amaia stepped back into the shadows. "French?"

"In fact, it's local," Thackery responded with practiced nonchalance, setting down his glass, "from Waitangi. I know how much you favor our native products."

"Here, here," Rothchester applauded, banging on the table with his free hand while lowering the glass from his wine-stained lips.

"You were right, Rothchester." Thackery grimaced, struggling to sound sincere. "It really is quite good."

The wine tasted like gall and was practically undrinkable, but Thackery was determined to do whatever was necessary to win himself back into the good graces of his chief critic in the company, who had been fomenting a campaign to run another candidate for his position as chief trading officer ever since the disastrous events of the shareholders' banquet. Thus, he was capitalizing on their success in exterminating the rat population of Wellington by having the filthy creature responsible for the success feted at the center of the table like a lord, all the better to appeal to the infantile tastes of his grotesque adversary. And if he had to drink a gallon of nativist swill to demonstrate that he was no longer the effete sybarite Rothchester had painted him out to be, then so be it. Once he had won reelection, he would have Hollis use what was left of the wine to kill off the weeds in the garden.

Nearly everything about the scene, in fact, had been engineered to reflect a more basic commoner's touch than the one that had been on display the night of the fire. The drapes on the window, even the tablecloth they dined upon, were hand sewn from the wool sheared off his own flock. The main course had been lamb, naturally, garnished by an assortment of locally sourced root vegetables. And, most prominently, the glass and ormolu chandelier he had once been so proud of had been replaced since Rothchester's errant pistol shot by one fashioned out of a dozen hurricane lamps fixed to a simple wagon wheel, which had been manufactured entirely in Nelson and shipped over from South Island.

All was a calculated attempt at populism that filled him with an added quotient of self-loathing at night when he sat alone in his study, listening to the ticking of the clock on the mantel. But if it was humility the shareholders needed to see in order to reelect him to his position, then Thackery was prepared to give them humility by the bushels. And Rothchester was the perfectly chosen town crier to spread the news of his recent turn toward humility.

Rothchester's blurry gaze fell upon Felix at the center of the table as Amaia stepped from the shadows once more to fill his glass. "It's hard to imagine that a creature so ugly could be so capable at what he does."

"Never judge a book by its cover, old friend," Thackery responded with barely concealed irony as Amos reached out to stroke Felix's side. "You yourself said how impressed you were to see the number of kills he was capable of putting up on that cross."

"Yes," Rothchester conceded, his gaze now shifting to the delicate hand that poured his wine, "that was really quite something. You really put me in my place with that cross."

"I was merely responding to the concerns of one of my shareholders," Thackery protested, shifting uncomfortably in his seat at the unexpected turn in the conversation.

"That's a load of shite, and you know it," Rothchester mumbled, looking up into the stoic face of his server as though seeing her for the first time. "You did it to put me in my place, and you succeeded. So bravo. Well done."

Amos involuntarily leaped to his feet when he saw Rothchester lean sideways and place his stained lips against Amaia's delicate wrist in a drunken attempt to kiss her. Startled by the suddenness of the gesture, Amaia released the decanter she had been pouring from and reflexively withdrew her hand. The glass carafe shattered as it struck the tabletop, causing a violent crash that jolted Felix upright from his torpor to a fighting stance.

"Bloody hell!" Rothchester bellowed as he rose from his chair, his lap dripping with spilled wine. Then he lurched at the servant girl and raised his hand as if to strike her before Amos threw himself between them and shoved him roughly back into his seat.

In the aftermath of the altercation, all was stunned silence, as each person in the room took a moment to absorb all that had taken place in such a short space of time. Meanwhile, a large pool of red wine was spreading itself out across the surface of the table, its tendrils reaching ever closer to Felix, who remained battle ready at the center while watching the stain advance toward him. At long last, Rothchester turned his attention away from the glowering boy looming above him, still standing between him and the servant girl, and fixed his eyes, bulging with offense, down the length of the table at Thackery, who slowly rose to his feet.

"Did you see that?" he hissed with rhetorical indignation.

"I did," Thackery acknowledged, sounding somewhat lost as he placed his napkin gently down on top of the table. In an instant, he had watched as a month's worth of careful planning had come crashing down around him and, as of yet, could not conceive of an alternative path forward. Instead he focused his attention on the hideous red creature back-pedaling toward him across the white cloth, retreating from the advancing spill. What had inspired him to allow such a monstrosity to sit upon his table and eat food off his fine china? And more out of anger with himself than with the ferret, he raised his right arm to its full height and violently swept Felix from his sight with the back of his hand.

The blow sent Felix sailing across the room until he crashed into the new curtains hanging beside the window and tumbled to the ground. Amos gasped and was on the move the moment the blow was struck, allowing Rothchester to get to his feet once more as he raced to help the dazed ferret. By the time he gathered the shuttering Little Red up in his hands and stood to look back at the scene unfolding at the table, Rothchester was already moving toward Amaia with a seething expression on his face, seemingly prepared to make a second attempt at striking her.

That was when Miss Hollis appeared suddenly from the direction of the kitchen, the hem of her skirts hissing faster than usual as she moved with lightning speed toward the table as though nothing unusual were taking place, as though she were coming in on a normal dinner party that had simply arrived at the desert course. She went right to work folding the cloth to keep any more wine from spilling off onto the carpet, hardly lifting her eyes as she went about her job cleaning off the table.

"Silly girl," she sighed. "Always dropping things."

The previous hostilities had come to an immediate halt at this point as all eyes fixed themselves on the officious head of the household going about her business, barely lifting her eyes to notice the strange tableaux she came in upon. Already she had stopped the spill from doing any more damage and was beginning to pick up the larger pieces of glass from around Rothchester's plate when she spoke next.

"Go to your room, girl," she commanded in a steely tone, hardly bothering to look up from the shards in her hand. "I will be with you shortly."

"Yes, Miss Hollis," Amaia whispered tearfully, quickly shuffling out of the room.

"And you, boy, kindly take that wretched beast away with you and wait for me in Master's study until I have the opportunity to come speak with you. Am I understood?"

"Yes, Miss Hollis," Amos faltered, though his feet remained frozen to the ground as Felix blinked and opened his eyes.

Sensing his hesitation, Hollis stopped her expert cleaning for a second and shifted her eyes to him. "Go."

Snapped from his trance by her hawkish glare, Amos pressed Felix to his chest and made a wide circle around Rothchester before fleeing the room. Hollis then sighed with irritation and continued to circle about the table, gathering up the plates and silverware while the men of wealth conducted their heated exchange from opposite ends as though she were not there at all, a figment with no ability to register what was being said.

"This is the second time I've come into this house, only to have my dignity besmirched," Rothchester fumed, reaching for a napkin to dry his pants with.

"The girl was merely startled by the gesture," Thackery defended. "She meant no offense."

"And what about the boy?" Rothchester snarled while swiping at his crotch. "Are you in the habit of allowing the help to assault your dinner guests?!"

"Miss Hollis will deal with the boy directly, as I'm sure she intends."

"Not good enough!" Rothchester howled, throwing down the napkin. "Dealing with him is not good enough! I have my honor to think about—honor that on two separate occasions has been trampled upon in the most outrageous fashion here beneath your roof!"

"Well, what would you have me do?" Thackery sniffed, momentarily incapable of concealing his full contempt for the childish fop pitching a tantrum in his wine-soaked jodhpurs. "Whip him for defending hers?"

"I see you mocking me, you bastard," Rothchester countered after taking a moment to register the sneer on his opponent's face. "And I promise you this—whatever this evening's trumped-up entertainment was meant to accomplish, your tenure as chief trading officer for the New Zealand Company is effectively ended as of this night."

"Now see here, old friend," Thackery hastened to interject, instantly regretting the slip in his performance.

"Don't 'old friend' me, you arrogant charlatan! I see the way you look at me, the way you look at all of us! With your highborn ways and your fancy Parisian attitudes! You think you're better than the rest of us put together, like we're a bunch of ignorant sheep in your flock! Well, I tell you what this ignorant sheep is going to do. I'm going to go home tonight and draft a letter to every other shareholder on the island, calling for an immediate vote of no confidence!"

"On what grounds?!" Thackery fired back, his temper now stirred to the point where it could not be held back. "You said yourself how impressed they were at the number of rats they saw on the cross!"

"True," Rothchester admitted and then flattened his tone while fixing Thackery with a steady gaze that suddenly made him appear formidable, even menacing to him for the first time. "But how do you think their attitudes might change if I took a few men down with me to the port tomorrow and started ripping up boards? Do you really think we wouldn't find more rats hiding there beneath the dock, a hundred times more than you could ever put up on that cross?"

Thackery sank slowly down into his chair, conceding defeat, as Hollis gathered the last of the used table items in a pile before her.

"That's the problem with leading by fear," she heard Rothchester add by way of twisting the knife, "there's always something more to be afraid of."

"What do you want?" she heard her master ask abjectly as she lifted the stack of dirty dishes in her arms and circled behind his chair to exit the dining hall.

"I want the girl," she heard Mr. Rothchester answer.

His words halted her in her tracks as she hurried across the room. It was but a momentary hitch in her step, the slightest hesitation, and she hoped that neither man had taken any notice of it as she continued on into the kitchen to retrieve their cigars and brandy.

*****

Everyone on North Island knew of Rothchester's affection for pretty young girls, particularly those of the variety he selected to work for him on his household staff. The scandals that had resulted from his predisposition to underage beauty were so numerous and so well documented that it hardly qualified as a scandal anymore when a new one erupted but more as a personal tic shared by many great men of the age, one meant to be borne and suffered silently by those who worked below them. Who among us, after all, could say they were without sin? "Let he who is without cast the first stone."

Many scullery maids had been dismissed from his employment under cover of darkness, sent off to live in Australia or some place farther beyond, once her belly had begun to show the evidence of Mr. Rothchester's continued helplessness to combat his unfortunate affliction. Always these sudden departures were greeted with a silent shake of the head and a *tsk*-ing acknowledgment of the flawed design by which the world was made to operate. And always Mrs.

Rothchester elected to remain willfully blind to the indiscretions occurring beneath her roof, constantly complaining to anyone who would listen about how hard it was to hold on to good help these days.

But Miss Hollis had been present that morning when Tama first arrived at Thackery's farm, searching for work. She had been out in the garden, choosing vegetables for that evening's dinner, when he came around to the back of the house, having received no answer at the front door. She had gasped at first to see the war-like aborigine loitering there at the end of her row of carrots, and her initial instinct was to run and call for help. But then she beheld the hand of the child pressed against his broad chest, a tiny brown fist reaching up from the sling around his neck, and a second instinct, more powerful than the first, immediately took over and had guided her ever since.

Bernadette Hollis had known from an early age that she was essentially unlovable. Since adolescence, there was thought to be about her an off-putting kind of intensity that discouraged the other children from wanting to get to know her better, girls and boys alike. She struck them as being overly willful, of having too high an opinion of herself to laugh or play along with the rest of them, though she was unaware of anything she was consciously doing to make them think these things of her.

She was not thought to be, at least at the start, an unattractive young woman, and there had been a handful of suitors at the dawn of her maidenhood who had even sought to win her heart, as hidden as it seemed. But always there was this wall between herself and the world, this invisible barrier that none could seem to penetrate, until at last she had persuaded her good and decent parents to buy her passage to the new colony, where she might hire herself out in service and spare them the anguish of seeing their daughter descend into spinsterhood.

No man had ever asked Bernadette Hollis for her hand in marriage; none had even dared to kiss her on the lips. But just because she was unloved did not mean she did not know *how* to love or what the word *love* meant. It meant precisely what it did the moment her eyes looked upon Amaia's tiny fist poking out of the sling around

Tama's neck, and she would be damned if she was going to allow the child she had loved since that first morning—with harsh words and discipline, true, but this was the only language she had for expressing her love in a world that had never shown her any—become just another sacrifice to Rothchester's sanctioned lechery. That was not the kind of love she believed in, and she was determined now to do whatever was necessary to stop it.

Who could have ever guessed at the depths of emotion hidden deep within the stony heart of Bernadette Hollis?

*****

The blow had looked worse than it actually was, seeing as how it had catapulted him through the air across half the length of the dining hall. The drapes had done their part to absorb the impact once his body struck against the wall, though, and the fall to earth thereafter was really not so high that he could not otherwise have brushed the whole matter off physically within minutes after it had occurred. Nevertheless, Felix remained trembling nervously in Amos's lap nearly half an hour later as the boy sat waiting for Miss Hollis to arrive in the study, still shaken by the emotional violence of all that had taken place.

"There, there, Little Red," Amos softly shushed, resting his warm palm on top of Felix's twitching flank as he stretched out on his side. "Everything's going to be all right. I'll make sure of it."

At that moment, with the clock on the mantelpiece counting off each fateful second as it had since the first morning he had stood before Thackery in this very same room, Amos would not have been able to say whether his consoling words were meant more for the ferret in his lap or for himself. He only knew that there had to be some way he could ingratiate himself back into his master's good graces after the stupendous failure of the dinner, and he was determined to find it at any cost. Otherwise, there would be no hope of his ever securing the land he had come to New Zealand in search of in the first place or of rescuing his mother from her impoverished existence back in England.

Just as he was picturing her as she was the last time he saw her—sitting in her rocking chair in the squalid room of her boarding house, pleading with him not to forget her—he heard whispered voices coming from just outside the door of the study and rose to investigate further. In doing so, he hoisted Felix up onto his left shoulder so that he might free up his right hand to turn the doorknob. Felix quickly adjusted to his new position and closed his eyes, his nerves continuing to fire just below the surface of his skin.

As Amos slowly cracked open the door, he saw Hollis and Tama engaged in a heated dialogue several feet down the hall from the study while struggling to keep their voices low. He had never seen the two of them alone together in such close confines, let alone having such a vehement exchange, and the sight of it shocked him with its unexpected intimacy. Once aware that they were being observed, Hollis broke off their conversation and turned to Amos, who was staring at them from the doorway.

"Do what you must," she continued after a long pause, turning to look back once more into the wounded eyes of the Māori who towered above her so that he might absorb the full implications of what she was suggesting. "And then go prepare the wagon."

Tama closed his eyes and nodded in recognition of her meaning. With his lower lip visibly trembling, it appeared for a moment as though he might give over to tears or lay his mighty head upon her shoulder for comfort. But the moment quickly passed, and when he opened up his eyelids once more, his gaze was filled with focused purpose as he shot a look of ferocious determination in Amos's direction before stomping off down the hall.

"So then should we add spying to your list of offenses?" Hollis suddenly asked, turning and moving toward him as Tama disappeared around the corner at the end of the hall.

"I beg your pardon, Miss Hollis," Amos stammered, stepping back to open the door wider and allowing the housekeeper's skirts to glide past into the room. "I thought I heard voices."

"As indeed you did," she responded in her coiled fashion, moving to stand beside Thackery's polished desk before turning to face him. "You may close the door now."

Amos did as she instructed reluctantly, fearing to be alone with the frightening woman in such a tight space, before summoning the courage to move to the center of the room while shifting Felix to his right shoulder. The transition caused Felix to open his eyes slightly as he settled into his new position, where he beheld the round face of the ticking clock above the fireplace, casting back his reflection in the glass. Its steady rhythmic ticking seemed to lure him down into deep unconsciousness, and he could feel his eyelids growing heavier as his reflection grew blurrier and more indistinct with the powerful pull of sleep.

"I just want to say…" Amos began in his defense, but Hollis quickly shot up a hand to silence him.

"I am sure you will agree," she began, lowering her hand before continuing, "that your employment here is no longer tenable."

"But, Miss Hollis…"

"Not only have you deeply offended Master Thackery's esteemed guest this evening," she said, glowering at him, raising her voice, "but as head of household, I am well aware of your past indiscretions, although circumstances at the time prevented me from acting upon that knowledge. Did you think I did not know about your unauthorized and completely inappropriate nightly visits to the private quarters of my servant girl? Well?"

Amos opened his mouth to defend himself, but the words caught in his throat; he had not expected the conversation to veer off in this direction. Now each tick of the clock seemed to toll forth the imminent demise of all his plans.

Felix, too, heard the tolling sound echoing in his ear as he allowed the ticking to carry him off into sleep. He could even see the constituent parts of the clock swirl against the dark field of his unconscious now as the time piece drifted up and away from the other items on the mantelpiece, dissolving into a tiny cyclone of dials and wheels and hands…

Suddenly, Felix found himself fighting his way back up from the depths of sleep and crashing through the surface of consciousness. And when he arrived there, he jolted awake and saw in an instant what had summoned him back the moment he opened his eyes—the miniature model of a ship resting just to the right of the ticking clock on the mantelpiece. He immediately began to squirm against the boy with all his strength, desperate to show him what he could not tell, but Amos responded to his efforts to break free by holding him even tighter to his chest, equally desperate to not give further offense to Miss Hollis.

"The only reason I said nothing about it before," she resumed once he had made it clear he had no words with which to answer her, "was because you clearly enjoyed Master Thackery's favor at the time and I did not wish to disappoint him by telling him the whole truth. But seeing as how all that is changed now, I see no reason to continue to maintain my silence."

Felix was now biting at Amos and scratching at him with his sharp claws, drawing tiny drops of blood on the side of his neck, but still the boy would not release him, still hoping to maintain some kind of decorum in the face of his inquisitor. Instead he peeled the thrashing ferret away from his body and held him at arm's length as he struggled to talk above the deep hissing noise emanating from the animal's chest.

"I was trying to teach her..." he began as Felix thrashed and hissed all the more loudly.

"Oh, do let that horrible creature go, would you?" Hollis hissed in kind. "You look like a positive fool, and it's impossible to speak with you like this."

As soon as Amos set him down on the chair in front of Thackery's desk, Felix threw himself down to the floor and then raced across the carpet and immediately began to scale the tall bookcase to the right of the fireplace, using his powerful legs to propel him from one shelf to the next. Meanwhile, Hollis had produced a cloth napkin from the pocket of her dress and was holding it out for Amos to take, moved despite herself by the scratches on his neck.

"You were saying?" she prodded as he took the offered napkin from her.

"I was trying to teach her to speak English," he said with injured pride while dabbing at the blood with the napkin. "Nothing else transpired between us."

"Be that as it may," Hollis responded, doing her best to conceal the deep well of affection she felt for the boy at the moment, "I hardly believe it fell within the scope of your influence to decide what to teach her and what not to. You were hired to tend to the animals in the field, not to be a maidservant's English tutor. Though clearly you have forgotten what your proper duties are, which is why I see no other course of action but to dismiss you now."

By the time she had arrived at Amos's sacking, Felix had made it to the top of the bookcase and was already estimating the distance between it and the mantelpiece displaying the miniature ship. The two were nearly equal in height, but there was roughly a two-foot gap between them. He could easily bridge the distance, he calculated, but only with a running start, and so he scurried to the opposite end of the bookcase and turned to prepare himself for his mad leap.

Amos distantly registered the sound of Felix's sharp claws against the wood surface as he raced across the top of the bookcase, but he was still absorbing the words Hollis had just uttered to him, words that had the effect of crumbling the ground beneath his feet. He could not even bring himself to look away long enough to watch as Felix soared through the air from one summit to the next; so complete was the power she held over him.

"Isn't there something...?" he heard himself begin to plead as Felix touched down lightly on the mantel side of the breach and slid to a quick stop.

"I am truly sorry," Hollis interrupted, simultaneously taking note of the ferret's odd behaviors over his shoulder, "but I can see no other alternative after tonight's activities."

Felix wedged himself between the wall and the miniature ship and began to push against the latter with his hind legs. The model was heavier than it first appeared, but eventually, it gave way and began to slide toward the edge of the mantel as a result of his exertions.

"You don't understand," Amos's voice quivered as the tears began to sting his eyes and he twisted the handkerchief in his hands. "I need this job. I'll do anything. I'll..."

And Felix continued to push...

"It's my mother, you see..."

And the ship continued to inch toward the edge…

"I need this job so I can bring her here. Master Thackery said if I worked hard enough, he'd give me my own piece of land, and then she'd be saved…"

Closer…

"Please, Miss Hollis…"

Closer…

"Please!"

Finally, the ship tumbled from the mantel and clattered to the floor behind him. Amos spun around on his heels, thinking that it might be someone crashing through the door to rescue him—Master Thackery, perhaps, bursting in at the last minute to say that it was all a giant misunderstanding, that all would be forgiven—but when he saw that it was no one there, just a silly old boat lying on its side on the carpet, he hung his head and allowed the tears to silently roll from his eyes.

Felix rested himself on the mantel and stared down at his human. "Does he understand what it is I'm trying to tell him?" he whispered to himself. "And why does the water flow down his face?"

It was a good thing that Amos's back was turned to her when he began to cry. Otherwise, Hollis might have dropped the charade entirely and taken him into her arms, as she wanted so desperately to do now. But there were things more important that she needed to accomplish than simply consoling a young boy—things that would require her to remain hidden a while longer behind the unsmiling, unfeeling mask she had been cursed to wear since birth, that the world had always mistook to be her one true face—and she swallowed the lump at the back of her throat while continuing with the performance, all the while regretting what she had to do next.

"I'm not sure if you are aware," she began slowly, speaking to his back, "but part of my duties as head of household is to open all of Master Thackery's correspondences each morning so that he might more easily read through them later on in the day at his convenience. One particular letter that arrived over a month ago—the morning of the banquet, to be precise—just so happened to catch my attention, and I notice that it's still here on top of the master's desk, though no action has as yet been taken on it."

Amos slowly turned back to face her after wiping the tears from his cheeks, unsure exactly of what she was insinuating.

At the same time, Felix rose to his feet, calling to him futilely: "Don't! Don't look away!"

"And while it's surely not my place to disclose the contents of Master Thackery's private correspondences," she went on, lowering her gaze to a pile of papers at the front of his desk, "I believe this one item might be of some small interest, given that it pertains especially to you."

Hollis stepped away from the desk, allowing him the room to approach and to find out for himself what she was referring to should he so choose. But was it a test of his loyalty? One last opportunity to prove that he could be trusted to stay? Or was she being sincere in the moment? He had no way of reading her.

Then the boy was moving away from the ship that he had toppled, and Felix's heart sank in his chest. What was he to do now? Leap from the mantel and sink his teeth into the back of his neck like he was a giant rabbit? Drag him back by the scruff so that he might see the truth that had been deposited at his feet?

Amos stood beside the desk now and looked down at the open letter on top of the pile. It was written in a familiar hand, and after hesitating a moment longer, he took it up and began to read. It began:

Dearest Father,

It is with a heavy heart that I inform you that the boy Amos's mother passed away sometime last week…

And then he collapsed into her arms and sobbed into her chest as Hollis held him firmly up and proceeded as though nothing unusual were taking place.

"It goes on to say she died peacefully in her sleep," she consoled while doing her utmost to keep any sign of emotion from breaking through, "no doubt proud of the fact that she had a son as remarkable as you."

Felix made a second running leap from the mantel back to the bookcase, moving closer to the scene he was witnessing while wondering what more he could do to make the boy understand his meaning.

"It's about a boat, you silly human!" he cried, the thought echoing in his head. "A boat!"

"He was never going to bring her to me or give me that land," Amos wept, "was he?"

"I have lived too long to pretend to know why men do what they do or what their motives are." She sighed, squeezing him ever so slightly in her embrace before pushing him away and taking the handkerchief from his hand. "I only know that, in this instance," she continued, "it hardly matters anymore."

Amos closed his eyes and straightened himself, allowing her to wipe away his tears with the blood-spotted cloth as Felix made his final running leap from the bookcase to the desk. The thud he made when his body touched down so near to them caused both the humans to startle as they turned to watch him slide across the polished surface before coming to a stop beside the letter that Amos had let slip from his hands. He was looking up into Amos's face now so imploringly that the boy could not help but let off from his grieving for a moment to wonder at what he was asking of him.

Hollis, meanwhile, turned her attention away from the creature's unsettling red eyes to where the model ship lay on the carpet at the center of the room, its upper masts snapped in two by the fall. Seeing how the damaged item might serve her final purpose, she moved silently to the ship while the boy was communing with his unearthly pet.

"Seeing as how it was the both of you who were involved in undermining my authority," she said, allowing her skirts to billow about her as she bent at the knees to pick up the broken vessel, "I only think it's fair that I dismiss the girl as well."

Listening to the sound of her words while staring into Felix's fiery eyes proved to be a potent combination. For in an instant, Amos was able to grasp what it was the old woman had been trying to tell him the whole time and its dire implications.

"It's Amaia," he suddenly realized, turning to face her. "Something's wrong, isn't it?"

"I think you should take your ferret friend's advice," she answered, holding the model in her hand as she straightened. "I think you should find yourselves a boat and get as far away from this place as you can. Tama should be waiting with Amaia even now in the wagon out front to take you both to the seaport. I took the liberty of lending him some of my savings so that you might have something to trade with, but you must go now without delay."

There was not time enough in a lifetime, let alone the moment, to calculate the many ways he had misjudged this inscrutable woman since he arrived at this place. Instead Amos immediately snatched Felix off the desktop and slipped him inside his coat as he hurried to Hollis at the center of the room and drew her to him in a final embrace, gently squeezing the ferret and the boat between them.

"I won't forget you," he said, placing his chin upon her shoulder. "Thank you for everything you've done."

"My poor boy," Hollis responded after taking a moment to absorb the shock of his emotional display, "I have no idea what you are talking about."

Amos sniffed and lifted his chin from her shoulder, smiling at her one last time. And then he was gone in a flash, bolting out of the study and racing toward the new life he would make elsewhere. And the old woman was left alone at the center of the room, looking down at the broken vessel she was holding in her hands.

*****

Amos crept on cat's feet out onto the front porch and carefully pulled the door closed behind him so as to not make any extraneous noise, only to discover when he turned and looked down from the top of the steps that the world outside the great house had already descended into chaos. Sheep were wandering aimlessly off in every conceivable direction while the shepherd dog, Victoria, bounded obliviously back and forth, chasing fireflies in the nighttime sky. The entire business of ferrets, too, had been removed from their stall in the barn and left out in the open without supervision so that they jerked and reeled together in the dirt now, performing their crazed weasel war dance beneath the stars. Felix peeked out of an opening in the boy's coat at the mayhem that had been unleashed while they were inside.

Once he had recovered from the shock at what was unfolding at his feet, Amos became aware of a dark silhouette hovering at the corner of his eye, and he turned to see Amaia. She was sitting with her back to him in the front seat of the wagon, which was parked at the edge of the light spill coming through the windows of the manor, and she was wrapped in her evening cape, as though prepared to make a long journey. At the same time, Felix recognized Kara's familiar silhouette at the bottom of the steps and struggled to lift himself from the coat as Amos began to descend. So that by the time he reached the final step, the boy was sufficiently irritated enough by his squirming to reach into the coat and lift him out himself.

"Say goodbye to your friends, Little Red," Amos said, setting Felix down beside her, "but make it quick." And then he hurried off to the wagon and to Amaia, who practically threw herself down into his arms as he came up beside her.

"What's happened?" Felix began tentatively, trying to gain Kara's attention.

"The one with the painted mask came and drove us all out," she explained without turning to face him, still taking in the riot of animal activity on display.

"I'm going now," he whispered after a long moment of silence. "I convinced my human to get us a boat."

"I'm happy for you," she said, lowering her head from the chaotic scene.

"Come with us," he implored.

"Us?" she sniffed.

"With me," he corrected. "Come with *me*."

"If it were only that simple," she sighed, closing her eyes.

"But it is that simple," he pleaded. "I love you, and you love me. What more is there to it than that?"

"Nothing's changed," she sniffed, opening her eyes and turning her beautiful mask to face him. "You're still the same arrogant hunter who approached me that first morning."

"But why is it arrogant to want to be together if we love each other?" he argued, searching her eyes with his own.

"Because too much has happened to ever allow it to be that simple," she answered, causing him to lower his own head now in recognition of the truth. "I have a son in great pain who needs me. I have a responsibility to him and to Scruffer, who stood by me when you couldn't."

"I'm sorry for that."

"I know you are, love, but it doesn't change the fact that I'm beholden to others now. We had our chance, but we let it slip away. And if I went with you, I'd only be doing to them the same thing you did to me. And I could never forgive myself for that."

He felt her nuzzle him softly with her snout and looked up into her sad face, little realizing that they were being watched the whole time by a pair of pitch-black eyes lurking in the darkness just outside the barn.

"I want our love to remain as pure as it was that day in the snow," she whispered. "But I will carry your memory in my heart forever, Felix, my love. Always."

Castor seethed in the darkness as he watched his mother rub her snout softly against the one who had betrayed them all. Scruffer, who had been lingering in the shadows, moved up behind him and took the opportunity to repeat what he had whispered earlier in the evening.

"What does your instinct tell you to do?"

Meanwhile, when Amos beheld the manner with which Tama came storming around the corner from the back of the house, marching with fierce determination, he immediately released Amaia from his embrace and hurried to reclaim Felix from the bottom of the steps, seizing him suddenly by the scruff of the neck and lifting him up and away from Kara's gentle farewell. Felix barely had a moment to open his eyes and look down upon her one last time before he was being heaved into the back of the wagon and its rear gate was being slammed shut, closing her off from his sight forever.

"Why did you release the animals?" Amos inquired, pulling himself up onto one side of the seat up front as Tama did likewise on the other, with Amaia once more positioned between them.

"To make confusion," Tama answered in a flat tone, taking hold of the reins. "It will take some time to gather them up. By then, we will be gone."

Then he whipped the horses with the reins, and the wagon began to roll off into the darkness, moving away from the glow of the manor. When Amos looked back over his shoulder to check that Felix was still behind them in the bed of the wagon, he glimpsed a solitary figure standing at the top of the steps, watching them disappear into the sea of grass.

It was Miss Hollis.

His own vision blocked on all sides by the surrounding walls of the cart, Felix curled himself into a ball at the front of the wagon and rested his head on top of his paws. He had rarely felt so conflicted in his life. On the one side, he had somehow succeeded in communicating the idea of a boat to the boy, which meant that if Tiresias were a creature of his word as he suspected him to be, he would be seeing his mother soon. She would be coming back to him again, and they would be free to start their lives anew. On the other side, he had been forced to give up Kara in order to make this new life possible, a sacrifice he had not anticipated would be necessary and filled his heart now with an unspeakable sadness.

Why did the price for such great joy need to be so much sorrow? And why did the hope for a brighter future require him to sacrifice everything that was beautiful about his past?

These were the questions that troubled his mind as he closed his eyes and attempted to surrender to sleep. Little did he realize that there was a second of his kind clinging to the axletree directly below him at that very moment, a stowaway hidden beneath the bed of the wagon, whose coat was blacker than the blackness that surrounded it, and that it would be this stowaway who would demonstrate to him in the clearest manner possible that the line between the past and the future is never as clearly drawn as we think.

*****

Perhaps if he had been more desirous of Rothchester's company, Thackery would not have sat for as long as he had in the parlor, would not have let so much time slip past without thinking to look in on his irate dinner guest. As it was, he let the long minutes drift by without moving to take any action, sipping his brandy instead while leaning back into the soft pillows of the comfortable settee.

Rothchester had retired to the washroom to see about the stain on his pants immediately after making his unexpected demand to have the girl transferred to his farm, and Thackery needed the time alone to consider the request from every possible angle without having to look into the man's stupid face and explain his decision. Surely, if he let her go, then he would have to let Tama go as well. He had observed the way they were when they were together and knew their bond was not of the usual father-daughter variety, the kind that would allow a father to send his daughter away without upset, the way he himself had done. The Māori had been an exceptional aide-de-camp since the day of his arrival, but there was no denying his hot-tempered nature or the recognition that he would become impossible to manage the moment the cord between he and his progeny was severed.

Rothchester's victory over him would thusly be complete. Not only would he be acquiring an excellent house girl, one that Miss Hollis had grown to rely upon over the years for all things, but he would also be taking from him a perfectly satisfactory manservant. Damn the man to hell, he thought, for imposing such a high cost on his allegiance. And yet surely he would be ruined if he did not concede, for Rothchester clearly intended to carry through with his plan to strip him of his office if he did not relent.

"Damn the man to hell," he said, sighing audibly, giving voice to the thoughts inside his head as he tossed back the last of the brandy left in his glass.

It was then that he heard the sound of the wagon wheels turning out front and thought that perhaps he was too late, that Rothchester had changed his mind about the compensation package and was already hurrying away from the house to begin exacting his revenge. When he threw open the front door, however, there was no wagon in sight, only Hollis standing there at the top of the steps, looking off in the direction of the grasslands.

"Where's Mr. Rothchester?" he asked, his tongue heavy with the brandy.

"Why, Master Thackery," his head of household answered, turning slowly to smile at him, "I thought he was with you."

Thackery stepped tentatively out onto the porch, feeling as though the ground was somehow shifting beneath his feet, and he came up beside his trusted housekeeper. That was when he first beheld the riot of animals celebrating their freedom from the barn and recognized at last that something was terribly wrong.

As per her master's orders, Hollis instructed the remaining staff to conduct a thorough search of the entire residence for any sign of their missing guest. Almost an hour was devoted to this fruitless charade before she stood before him in the study—where Thackery sat anxiously behind his desk, listening to the terrible tolling of the clock—to report that the only evidence they had uncovered was the fact that Rothchester's horse and carriage were still tied up to a post at the back of the house. It was only then, while staring up into her inscrutable face, that it suddenly dawned on him that he had not seen his trusted manservant in nearly all that time—nor his daughter, for that matter, nor the troublesome lad from England and his hideous pet.

It was Thackery himself who first discovered the gruesome gift left for him at the center of the table when he first threw open the door to Tama's shack. A second later, he was down on his hands and knees, heaving himself to pained exhaustion in the tall grass outside as the two aborigines who had accompanied him from the house with their torches, each dressed in his livery, pressed together and peered through the open doorway into the shack, which was lit up by a dozen candles at that moment, as though they had been expected.

In the Māori culture, the ritual of shrinking and preserving human heads was known in the native tongue as *mokomokai*. It had long been practiced by the indigenous tribes of New Zealand for two very distinct reasons before the British arrived to ban the practice altogether in 1831.

The first explanation for the practice was to maintain a spiritual connection between the living and their departed ancestors by fashioning a totemic reminder of the deceased's existence out of their earthly remains. This process would require those left behind to remove the eyes and brains from the skull once the head had been detached from the body and then boiling it in a pot to shrink its size before smoking it over an open fire to dry. Lastly, the head would be treated with shark oil to keep it from rotting before the hair, separated at the start, could be reattached.

The practice of mokomokai had been outlawed before Tama was ever born, but it was for this first reason that he had carried the heads around with him in a burlap sack on the day they arrived at Thackery's farm. They had been gifted to him by his own father, and he had hung them from the ceiling of his humble quarters to serve as a constant reminder to both himself and Amaia that they were the descendants of a proud and noble people despite everything their colonizers wished for them to believe about themselves.

Tama had not had the time that evening to gather up the heads before fleeing, and so he had been forced to leave them behind in the shack, where their candlelit faces gazed down from the ceiling at the bloody scene below in silent judgment. Nor had he had the opportunity to adequately preserve the head of Rothchester after separating it from its shoulders with a rusty scythe he had found in the barn, for the process of shrinking a head might take several days to perform properly and circumstances did not allow him such a luxury. And so the head was left there full-size and bloodied at the center of the table, its mouth open wide in surprise, causing it to seem somewhat incongruous vis-à-vis the heads looking down from above but nevertheless amply demonstrating the second purpose for the ritual of mokomokai: to rejoice in the death of one's enemy.

CHAPTER 15

A swarm of long-tailed bats was circling in the sky above the cross, snatching mosquitoes out of the air, as Tama reined back the horses and drew the wagon to a halt. Any gull that might have been tempted to alight on the crossbeam that night and feast upon a rat carcass had been chased away by the presence of the swarm, leaving the night unusually silent and still as the three human passengers disembarked and crept toward the entrance to the warehouse. And it was largely on account of the preternatural quiet hovering over the scene that the heavy doors to the storage facility sounded doubly clangorous when the Māori slid them apart, creating just enough space to allow the three to slip inside.

It was the sound of the doors being wedged apart that had awakened the customs inspector from a dream he had been having, one in which a whole army of bare-breasted native women danced around a fire for his pleasure as he sat upon a makeshift wooden throne, drinking rum out of a silver chalice. Weston opened his eyes and lay unmoving on the floor for a moment as the memory of the exotic fantasia gave way to the drab ceiling beams of his office. These repeating dreams he had of Sodom and Gomorrah never failed to puzzle him when he came back to consciousness, given that he was a happily married man with a wife and child sleeping peacefully even now in the house that he had carved out of the wilderness and built for them with his own two hands.

Where did it come from, he wondered, this unholy desire for wild abandon? Perhaps he was no better than a savage himself, he considered, rising to a sitting position on the floor beside his desk. Perhaps they were all nothing more than savages.

He took hold of the edge of the desk and pulled himself to his feet in order to investigate the sound that had propelled him from dreams to such a sad conclusion.

Weston had been given word earlier in the day of a late arriving steamer from the Orient and had made the decision, as he was sometimes forced to do, to remain in port rather than to trek all the way back from his house outside town once the ship put in. The hours of a customs inspector were never regular, given the unreliable nature of the sea, and the floor of his office proved firm enough to support his aching back should he ever choose to sneak in a nap. Oftentimes, on nights such as these, he would stay up late drinking and carousing with the roughnecks who worked the docks, gratifying his secret longing for hedonistic excess.

But tomorrow was a Sunday. He would be expected in church, sitting beside his loved ones in their family pew, giving thanks to God for sparing the young one's life, and he could not afford to appear worse for wear beneath the watchful eyes of the Lord and his Mrs. Weston. So he had begged off the usual invitations when they started pouring in that evening and instead chose to stay soberly locked up inside the customs house and catch up on his sleep until he had been disturbed from his less-than-pious rest by the screeching of the sliding doors.

It seemed ironic to him, therefore, that the first person he saw when he peered out of the window of the customs house was the native Tama moving stealthily along the waterfront, his unmistakable silhouette etched against the shimmering backdrop of the moonlit waves—ironic in that it was Tama who had given him cause to be grateful to a higher power at all. It was Tama who had once rescued his daughter's life with his dark potions. What could he be doing out at such a late hour, hurrying along the dock to the farthest reaches of the port? And who were the two other silhouetted figures dashing after him, whose shadows seemed dwarfed in comparison to his?

These were the questions Weston asked himself as he tugged on his hat and pulled open the door to investigate. What he could not see from his vantage point was that there was a fourth silhouette racing along with the others, one too small to register from a window across the street. And that it was this fourth unseen silhouette that was out in front of all the rest, leading them on to a place that he alone knew existed, one he had discovered to be in existence only the night before.

"Where is he taking us?" Amaia whispered from the rear of the procession, peering around the figures in front of her as they hurried along the dock.

"He seems to know something we do not," Tama whispered back over his shoulder, doing his best not to lose sight of Felix as he scampered ahead across the wooden boards.

"He's the best hunter we've got," Amos added from his place between the two. "If Little Red senses something, then I say we should follow him." He was happy for the opportunity to defend the tracking prowess of his prized ferret, not only because the words he said were true but also because it was he, Amos, who had lost his hold on Felix as they were exiting the warehouse, obligating them to pursue him now.

They had returned to the warehouse for the last few remaining items they had left behind—their bedrolls, some discarded clothes, a flask of Jamaican rum—but the whole while they were grabbing up their things, Felix squirmed desperately in Amaia's arms, struggling to break free. And no sooner had she handed him back to Amos at the door, glad to be rid of him, than the crazed mustelid wriggled out of his grip and fell heavily to the ground. Quickly righting himself, he lost no time in dashing across the dirt road toward the water, forcing them to give chase.

Felix did not break stride until he had reached the place where he was standing directly above the rats' lair once more. This had been his plan all along, to lead them first to the rats before securing a boat, even though he had not fully thought out what it was he would do after they had arrived. He knew that humans were instinctively afraid of rats, that it was this fear that had driven them to unleash his kind upon them and to slaughter them in the first place. How would he persuade them now to crawl with him below and to look into the faces of their sworn enemy, gathered there together by the hundreds? And how would they react once they took in such a sight as that?

Once he considered the likely answers to these questions, Felix began to lose hope in the wisdom of his plan as the humans' footfalls slowed to a halt in front of him. It was his own selfishness that had caused him to miscalculate so badly, he suddenly realized. If he had not been so anxious to get to Tiresias and to have She restored to his inner sight, then maybe they would have already solved the dilemma of the boat, thus allowing him the option of somehow boarding the rats by stealth. But now, without a boat, there seemed little to be gained in exposing the rats' hideaway to the humans, and he hung his head in shame, feeling as though he had failed them all.

And so it was with great surprise that he registered the tone of their voices coming from above since they did not seem to be consistent with the sounds humans usually made when they were either mad or disappointed. Rather, the notes drifting down to him resonated with a kind of satisfaction, and he lifted his head toward them, trying to reconcile the unexpected timbre to the expressions on their faces.

"He is very wise, this one." Tama smiled, his eyes fixed on a point farther along the waterfront.

"Well done, Little Red," Amos concurred, seemingly focused on the same point.

Felix spun around to take in the source of their satisfaction. Little more than fifty yards farther along, just before it ceased entirely, the dock made a sudden ninety-degree turn and jutted out into the water, culminating in a last wooden pier. And there, tied to the wharf with thick anchor ropes, was a twenty-five-foot-long mail steamer.

It was the same mail steamer that operated between North and South Islands, transporting letters and packages across the strait from Nelson to Wellington and back again. It was operated by a zealous young man named Gompers, Horace Gompers, who had traveled out from Boston to become a missionary and help bring the true word of Christ to the local heathen. In between his studies, he faithfully executed the mail run twice a week, religiously donating the small salary he received for doing so to the building of the missions at Auckland.

Both Amos and Tama were familiar with seeing Gompers around the seaport since he had tried to convert the both of them to his missionary cause on separate occasions, staring at them unblinkingly through rheumy eyes while rattling on about salvation and the life hereafter. Anyone who worked the port for any length of time was familiar with Gompers since he had tried at some point to convert each and every one of them. And if there was one thing they all knew about him, apart from his incessant need to proselytize, it was his absolute refusal to operate the mail steamer on the Lord's Day.

He was no doubt resting at that very minute in the Rothchester's comfortable guest room after completing a run, expecting to wake the following morning as usual and to squire Mrs. Rothchester to Sunday mass, as had become his custom in recent months. Mrs. Rothchester had taken a shine to the young missionary since the first time he had arrived upon her doorstep to deliver a stack of envelopes to her husband. To her, he seemed like a delicate princeling cast off into this barbaric wilderness, with his fine, angular features and pale skin. And once she was made aware of his devout nature, she was thrilled to offer him Saturday night lodgings in return for escorting her to Sunday morning services, particularly now that Mr. Rothchester had all but given up the practice himself.

Oh, what a different Sunday morning he would awaken to come the dawn, Tama thought, but how good it was, too, that Gompers would be there to assure Mrs. Rothchester of his God's divine plan once the details of Mr. Rothchester's incapacitated state were delivered to her. It pleased him to know that she would have somebody there to counsel her in her grief regardless of whatever opinions he might have held about her husband and the righteousness of his vengeance.

What pleased him equally as much was the knowledge that Gompers would not be coming back to the steamer anytime soon, that the boat was essentially theirs for the taking, and he stepped over the ferret in his path with a feeling of genuine confidence that he could operate and steer a ship of its size so long as he had the boy onboard to assist him. Amos and Amaia took hold of each other's hand and exchanged a brief smile at the new life they were about to begin together before likewise stepping over Felix and following Tama to where the boat was moored.

Perhaps the reason he had not seen it himself was because the steamer had not been tied up to the pier the night before. Or perhaps his haste to see She again had all but blinded him to what was right there in front of him. The only thing that Felix knew for sure was that the humans seemed happy with the boat he had inadvertently procured for them.

Now to the rats.

Felix dived down to the sandy ribbon of beach and quickly scurried into the cave beneath the dock, knowing that he did not have much time. Once the humans took note of his absence, they would come looking for him. And unless he had figured out a way to board the rats by then, he did not see a way that they would be allowed to pass. As soon as he reentered the dark catacomb, he felt the surging presence of the rats closing in on all sides, and he shut his eyes tight in order to block them out and to somehow locate Tiresias on the blurred field of his inner vision.

"I've found you a boat," he called to the billowing cloud of red vapor that appeared after a moment against the gray smear of his mind's eye, "but you must come right away. We haven't much time."

Tiresias's blind countenance bloomed from the center of the gathering mist, smiling benevolently down upon him. "You've done well, brave ferret. But what of the humans we will need to guide the vessel?"

"They're already onboard," Felix fired back, "but we have to go now."

"Very well," Tiresias responded, speaking now to the horde of rats assembled around them in the darkness, "you have heard the news of our liberation. Follow the one who has delivered us and do exactly as he commands."

Felix reversed himself out onto the sand just ahead of the restless tide of fugitive rats that, like a geyser of champagne bursting from a bottle once it has been uncorked, poured forth out of the mouth of the cave in a jubilant cascade of release. Backing himself up to the water's edge, he realized he needed to corral the rush of their enthusiasm right away or risk being overwhelmed by their numbers and drowned in the shallows beneath their stampede.

"Turn and go that way!" he shouted, hoping that the volume of his thought waves might rise above the wall of their audible squeaks and squeals, as he pointed his snout in the direction of the steamer. At the very last instant, just as it was set to collide with him, the raging river of rats turned and headed off in the direction he had indicated. As it did so, it narrowed itself into a single organized column, the rats falling into single file, each behind the other, as they herded across the sand toward the pier ahead.

The very last detainee to emerge from the cave once the initial flood had passed was Tiresias. As he nosed himself uncertainly out of the darkness and into the moonlight, Felix had the initial impression that he was not seeing a rat at all but rather the phantom remains of what used to be one. Fully exposed to view, the King of Rats seemed infinitely smaller, infinitely frailer than he had when he had occupied the complete scope of the ferret's mind. And after taking a moment to adjust his expectations, Felix raced across the sand to support him just as the feeble old rodent began to stumble sideways from his efforts to walk.

Resting his full weight into Felix's side, he seemed little more than skin and bones as he lowered his head and sighed. "Not so imposing now, am I?"

"You're still their leader," Felix comforted.

"How far is it?" Tiresias asked, lifting his head and turning his blind gaze toward the boat.

"Not far," Felix answered. "I'll help."

Just as he was starting to move, however, Felix suddenly heard the heavy tread of another human approaching rapidly from the direction of the warehouse and froze in his tracks as the footsteps came to a stop directly above them.

"Is that you, Tama?"

Tama's spine grew rigid at the sound of Weston's familiar voice. He had been moving to untie the first of the two anchor ropes, after assisting the younger ones aboard with their possessions, when the call rang out to him. He hesitated for a moment before acknowledging the other man, buying Amos and Amaia just enough time to drop to the deck and hide from view.

"It is me," Tama called back, turning to face Weston's dark outline once they were out of sight.

"What are you doing there with Gompers's boat?"

"Nothing...nothing," Tama stuttered, stepping away from the boat and moving down the pier. "Only thinking."

"Well, who else y'got there with you?" Weston continued.

"No one." Tama chuckled, moving down the dock toward him. "There is no one."

Weston instinctively took a step back as Tama's imposing silhouette closed the distance between them. Felix and Tiresias remained still as statues on the sand below as the two men squared off on the dock above them, each trying to interpret the substance of what the humans were saying.

Meanwhile, the first of the liberated rats had made it across the sand and, after hopping up onto the pier, was tiptoeing along the anchor rope like a tightrope walker. He in turn was followed by the next rat in the chain. And so on it went until there was an unbroken line of rats scuttling nose to tail along the rope, each climbing upward toward the brass railing of the ship.

"I could swear I saw other people with you," Weston pressed, his voice heavy with suspicion.

"It is only me, my friend." Tama smiled, coming to a halt before him. "Only me and the night air."

"Well, what's got you so restless tonight?" Weston stammered while attempting to peer around the intimidating Māori looming in front of him.

"My mind, it wanders sometimes." Tama grinned, clapping a hand on Weston's shoulder. "You know this feeling?"

"Yeah." Weston shrugged after recovering from the jolt of Tama's heavy touch. "I guess I do."

"Of course, you know," cried Tama, shaking him by the shoulder in a gesture of warm kinship. "And this is why we must drink."

"I… I shouldn't," the helpless customs inspector began as Tama used his superior strength to turn him around on his heels and drape his arm across his back.

"Nonsense," Tama protested, shushing him.

"Tomorrow's Sunday," Weston persisted even as he allowed himself to be steered back toward town. "I really sh—"

"One drink." Tama laughed. "What kind of god would deny a man the right to one small drink?"

"He'd have to be a pretty stingy god at that," Weston conceded after a few steps, giving into the familiar tug of pleasure.

"Yes," Tama cheered, shoving him along even faster.

"I guess one drink couldn't hurt." Weston chuckled, having abandoned all of his former suspicions.

"This is what I am saying," boomed Tama's voice as the two men clomped happily back along the dock, the bonds of their friendship restored.

And then the rats began to stream over the railing of the mail steamer. And then Amaia let out a sharp, unmistakable cry that pierced the night as the endless procession of rats breached the side of the boat and began to rain down upon her and Amos where they lay hidden on the deck. And then all their hopes for making a clean escape began to go terribly awry.

Felix jumped at the sound of the cry and scurried down to the water's edge to investigate its source, abandoning Tiresias outside the mouth of the cave. He looked directly down the shoreline at the boat; it seemed undisturbed at first to his naked eye, devoid of any movement. But when he closed his eyes to scan it more clearly with his inner sight, he perceived an endless procession of tiny dots streaming along the ropes that held it in place, like ants clamoring up the side of a hill, and he knew in an instant that the rats had somehow caused the disturbance.

Before he could think of what to do next, an angry voice insinuated itself into his mind, wiping away all other thoughts.

"Traitor."

Sensing it emanating from close behind, Felix snapped open his eyes as he whirled around in place. And there he saw a large dark spot moving steadily toward him across the sand, stalking him beneath the moonlight. It only took him a second to recognize what it was.

"Castor?"

On the dock above, Weston had already pulled himself free of his friend's false embrace and was staring back through the dark to where the cry had originated. Now he slowly turned his face back from Gompers's boat to the Māori's guilty expression and knew in that moment that he had been deceived. But as soon as he tried to flee down the dock to sound the alarm, Tama tackled him to the boards and the two men took to grappling ferociously.

Amos and Amaia, meanwhile, had dragged themselves to the bow and were watching in horrified amazement as the wave of rats continued to pour over the side unabated, clinging to one another for comfort. At the same time, out on the sand, Castor had moved to within inches of Felix and was standing before him with his back arched and with every muscle of his body coiled to spring as though he could attack at any moment.

"How could you do it?" he asked, turning to take in Tiresias and then looking back at Felix. "Turn against your own kind for *them*?"

"It's not as easy as that," Felix began tentatively, sensing the young hob's overwhelming confusion and pitying him for it.

"It is that easy!" Castor cried out of the depths of that confusion. "We're your kind! Why would you turn your back on your own kind!"

From above, Weston's voice rang out in the air as he struggled to rend himself free of Tama's powerful hold.

"Sabotage!" he cried, breathless with the effort at escape. "Come quick! Sabotage!"

Castor began to move in a wide arc around Felix, ignoring the chaos going on above. "You're turning your back on us, on me, just as you turned your back on my mother."

Felix felt the sting of the charge and knew that it was fruitless to try and defend himself against it. He had done something indefensible, and this now was the price he had to pay—to be looked upon by one who might very well be his own blood and to be found a villain, a coward, a creature beneath contempt.

Castor was entitled to his anger. Felix had been, and perhaps still was, all these things and more. If there was only some way he could make him see that what he was doing that night was a small attempt on his part to try and make it better.

Cries of "Sabotage!" continued to ring out, eventually reaching back to port and disturbing a handful of wharfies from their sleep. They rose to their feet groggily on the decks of the ships where they lay out under the stars and scratched themselves while looking off in the direction of the shouts.

"Nothing to say?" Castor sneered, coming to a halt between Felix and Tiresias and blocking the old rat from his view. "No words to defend yourself?"

"Come with us."

Felix was as surprised by the suggestion as the young hob was. He had not even thought of what he was going to say before he telegraphed the words; they were the first and most unguarded words that had occurred to him to transmit. But now that they were out, he realized how desperately he wanted Castor to accept the invitation and repeated it a second time to underscore the point, refining it for clarity.

"Come with *me*," he pleaded. "Give me time to make it better. Allow me to become the father you deserve."

"Father?!" Castor cried. Then he suddenly raced at Felix, backing him into the water as he continued to glare at close range, their noses practically touching. "I already have a father," he snarled, the water dripping from his mask. "He's a good and decent father who stood by my mother when cowards like you turned their backs on her."

"I know...," Felix whispered, feeling the cold grip of the water up around his legs.

"I should be ashamed to have a father like you."

For an instant, it seemed as though the words might have back-fired on him, that they might have caused Castor more pain to transmit than they did for Felix to hear. And for the briefest moment, it seemed as though his anger might have spent itself, that it had been overtaken by other emotions, that he was softening somewhat, that he could be reached.

At the same moment, Tama was experiencing a similar change of heart. Having finally managed to gain advantage over the customs inspector by straddling his chest and pining him to the dock, he hesitated now with his hands around his throat, suddenly reluctant to apply the necessary pressure it would require to silence him for good. That was because, just as he was beginning to squeeze his fingers tight and close off the man's air, a memory of Weston's daughter opening her eyes and smiling up at him the morning that the fever broke suddenly flashed across his mind, and he could not bring himself to do it. Even as he heard the footfalls of the roughnecks thundering toward him, he knew that he was lost.

Hearing the same footfalls approaching, Amos stood slowly at the bow of the ship as the last of the rats leaped down from the railing of the boat and followed the others down below deck into the hold. He saw a half dozen longshoremen advancing on Tama with lighted torches as the proud native lifted himself off the customs inspector and rose to his feet.

Below them, Felix had decided to risk exploiting Castor's moment of indecision by insinuating a final request into the narrow space his temporary wavering had opened up in his mind.

"Forgive me."

Castor shrunk from the request as though repelled. Then, after recovering his purpose, he summoned back the full strength of his fortifying rage as he spun around and charged across the sand toward Tiresias, the roar of his battle cry exploding in Felix's head.

"No more forgiveness!"

The wharfies overtook Tama at the same moment Felix managed to overtake Castor and drive him to the ground before he could do any harm to Tiresias. And the two struggles unfolded simultaneously, one above and one below, during which it was impossible to distinguish which was the more bloodthirsty creature, man or mustelid. As Tama fought off the savage mob, using whatever weapons he had at his disposal—fists, feet, teeth—so, too, did Castor fight to throw off the demon ferret who had sunk his teeth into the back of his neck by employing every trick he had ever learned in combat with other creatures, rolling and bucking wildly across the sand while slashing with his paws and snapping at him with his sharp teeth.

Every attempt he made to dismount him, however, only caused Felix to hold on tighter and to sink his teeth even deeper into the back of his neck. And while his efforts caused the elder ferret significant injuries—his sharp claws, in particular, opening up deep gashes on his side—he began to grow weary from all his exertions as Felix stubbornly refused to yield. Until at last his legs gave out underneath him, and he collapsed to the ground at the shoreline, just as Tama's own legs were buckling beneath the weight of the men's combined blows as they rained down upon him.

Amaia rose from her hiding position just in time to see her beloved father drop heavily down onto his knees and opened her mouth to let out a second cry, before Amos could think to take her in his arms and turn her away from the bloody spectacle. She wept silently into his chest instead as the men with torches parted on the dock and allowed the customs inspector to pass through and address the defeated native directly. As he stood before him, looking down, Weston was still trying to catch his breath after the recent struggle, and his hands and face were covered by a network of scrapes and bruises.

"I treated you like you were one of us," he panted, a shock of tousled hair falling across his injured face.

"You treated me like I was a fool," Tama said, staring down at the tips of Weston's boots as the blood rolled down his chin from his mouth, "like my only purpose was to amuse you."

"But I welcomed you into my home," Weston said, chortling, looking around at the other men incredulously.

"Only to serve you," Tama said, sighing, spitting a mouthful of blood off the side of the dock, "never as a friend." Then he slowly began to bend forward at the waist as though prepared to prostrate himself before the customs inspector, stretching his hands down to the ground in front of him. "Never as a friend."

Observing the confusion caused by the gesture as the men shuffled back, not fully sure what was happening or why, Amos suddenly realized that it was not meant for them at all, that it was intended to act as a signal to him. He gently pushed Amaia away and immediately began to untie the bowline at his side, signaling for her to do likewise with the anchor rope at the stern.

Meanwhile, Castor had lain still long enough beneath Felix's body to convince him that the sustained pressure from the bite had finally caused the hob to slip into unconsciousness without doing any more damage, just as the older ferret had hoped it would. Slowly releasing his hold, he stood for a moment longer above the insensate hob, poised to pick up their battle where it ended should he stir, before appeasing himself on that score and racing back to Tiresias.

"Lean into my side, and follow me," he whispered.

"But you're hurt," the old rat whispered back with genuine concern while pressing into his side.

"It makes no difference," Felix hissed impatiently, shouldering Tiresias's fragile weight as he guided him across the sand toward the boat. "We have to go."

Having untied the rope, Amos dived through the cabin door and raced to check the boiler at the center of the boat, praying that there was still water left over from Gompers's last crossing to stoke the furnace quickly. At the same moment, Tama had come to rest on all fours before the befuddled mob, his palms pressed flat against the dock. Felix, simultaneously, was hauling Tiresias up off the beach by the scruff of his neck, having made it across the sand to the pier.

"What are you doing?" Weston asked, looking down at the suppliant before him.

"I am surrendering to you," Tama answered, his arms trembling with the effort to hold up his own weight.

Having discovered enough residual water left in the boiler, Amos fired up the furnace as Amaia appeared in the cabin door to let him know that they were completely untethered. The boat, in fact, was already drifting away from the pier by the time Felix got Tiresias back onto his feet after lifting him to safety.

"I don't want your surrender." Weston sneered down at the kneeling Māori. "Get up."

Suddenly, in booming round tones that surprised them all, Tama began to recite a kind of incantation as he touched his forehead to the ground again and again. "In the name of the stars and the moon, I say surrender! In the name of the wind and the trees, I say surrender!"

Amos left Amaia to stoke the furnace as he dived back through the cabin door and shimmied up the ladder to the pilot house at the top, taking hold of the wheel. He was in far too much of a hurry to notice Felix and Tiresias making their way across the pier toward the boat, which was quickly moving out of range.

"In the name of all the creatures of the earth, I say surrender!" Tama continued, his voice growing even louder than it had been at the start.

"Make this savage stand up," Weston growled, stepping back in disgust as the wharfies grabbed hold of Tama and dragged him to his feet.

"In the name of all my ancestors, I say"—Tama looked back over his shoulder to the boat as the first cloud of smog belched from the top of the mail steamer's smoke stack—"*go!*"

Felix clamped down on the old rat with his teeth one last time and used his powerful neck muscles to heave him over the railing as several of the longshoremen, sensing they had been had, thundered down the dock in a desperate attempt to call them back. But the boat had already begun to be powered by its own steam, with smoke clouds puffing at regular intervals from the tall stack, as Amos spun the wheel in the pilot house and steered toward the entry of the port.

Felix tensed every muscle in his body and was just about to make his own desperate leap for the railing when he was struck unexpectedly from behind and rocketed forward into the widening gap, plummeting into the dark water. At first, he was unaware of what had hit him; so lost was he in the murky deep. But as he righted himself and fought to make his way back up to the surface, he felt a set of powerful teeth close around his tail, and he knew in an instant that Castor had somehow managed to recover himself.

He was trying now to drag him back down into the depths, to drown him, and Felix frantically kicked at him with his hind legs, trying to get him to release his hold, as his lungs began to burn for lack of oxygen. He was aware that the blood each was drawing from the other was circling around them, warming the cold water, as he scratched and clawed and struggled to escape the hob's murderous grip.

Had Amaia, in her haste, not allowed the anchor rope at the stern of the boat to drop off into the water once she had finished untying it, Felix would no doubt have been overwhelmed by Castor's superior strength and eventually sent to a watery grave. As it was, however, he was able to break through to the surface with his front paw and blindly seize hold of the rope as it slid past. And the tug of the engine, as it began to drag him along by his tether, provided just the right amount of extra jolt he needed to yank his tail free of Castor's sharp teeth.

Having managed to free himself at last after all his exertions, Felix was content to glide along like that for a while at the end of his rope, an inconsequential speck of jetsam, trailing behind in the wake of an anonymous steamer. But as the boat cleared the mouth of the port and set out into open waters, he summoned the final reserves of strength he had left in him to begin the long, arduous process of pulling himself along the rope to safety.

As for Castor, he was left with no other choice but to paddle his way back to shore and to heave his aching body, torn and covered with scars, back up and onto dry land. And for a long while, he stood there at the end of the pier and watched as the boat grew smaller on the horizon line until it disappeared entirely with the dawn, turning over in his mind the many things he could or should have done in order to have prevented them from escaping. So consumed was he by these thoughts, he hardly took notice of the sun as it rose into the sky or of Thackery, who had arrived at the seaport with the dawn and was now standing directly behind him on the pier, looking out to sea.

At last, Castor sensed the presence of the powerful human casting a shadow over him and turned to search his master's face above for any sign that he understood what had occurred. He wanted him to know how hard he had tried to capture the fugitives, stealing himself at the bottom of the wagon, his epic battle with the Red on the beach, even continuing their fight into deep water. He wanted to somehow tell him what a good and loyal hunter he had been, how he had risked everything to please him. He wanted him to know that he should be spared.

But when the human finally took his eyes off the empty horizon to glare down at him, there was no indication of any such understanding written upon his master's face. And as he lifted his boot to crush the ferret beneath it, assuming that the Black had been nothing more than a co-conspirator in the plot against him, Castor had a brief moment to reflect upon the bitter irony of his situation—that all his efforts at avoiding the same fate as Riker had only brought him to the exact same end—before Thackery's heel crashed down on his skull and shattered him into oblivion.

CHAPTER 16

Although the pilot house was crowded with stacks of old maps by which to navigate, Amos had decided to cut the engine just before midmorning as soon as they were out of sight of dry land and to allow the boat to simply drift for a while before setting their next course. It was unlikely they were being pursued, he knew, since the colony as of yet lacked a proper naval force to chase down criminals on the high seas. Retribution would only be there to greet them once they made landfall, assuming they chose the wrong port of entry. And given the heavy weight of sadness that hovered over the steamer at that moment, Amos did not feel that either he or Amaia was in a clear enough state of mind to puzzle out the right one.

Once the initial euphoria at their successful escape had worn off, Amaia took up her position on the railing at the stern of the boat and would not stop looking back across the water toward Wellington and her noble father, whom they had left behind, leaving Amos both to steer the boat and stoke the engine until he had made the decision to stop. She had withdrawn completely from him behind her impenetrable mask, and any attempts he made at consoling her were brushed off in no uncertain terms. She wished only to be left alone in her sorrow, and he disciplined himself to respect her need for solitude even while he himself was longing to be consoled by her embrace.

Had he not lost a parent, too, that night, his poor, lonely mother dying alone in her poorhouse, with no one there to comfort her in her final hours? Of course, Amaia was still unaware of his loss; there had not been time enough to tell her as of yet, and he felt like too much of a villain to add to her sorrows with his own. But why was she not able to somehow read his mind the way lesser animals seemed to be able to intuit these kinds of things between them and recognize that he was hurting, too, and that he needed her to be with him?

His spirits had been given a boost, naturally, when Little Red had suddenly appeared miraculously on top of the railing, having clamored up the anchor rope just shortly after they had left the port. Looking half-drowned and covered in wounds, Amos could not recall a time when he had been more grateful to see the ill-favored beast or when his alarming appearance had ever struck him as being so beautiful. But the ferret was bone weary from all he had been through to get there and fell into a trance-like sleep before he even had a chance to fully dry, abandoning Amos once more to his solitary sadness.

And so they each remained imprisoned in the quietude of their separate sorrows, the silence between them broken every now and again only by the squealing and scratching noises coming from the army of rats hidden below deck. And morning gave way to noon, with the sun burning down hot upon them. And they continued to drift.

Tiresias found Felix curled up in a ball at the bow of the ship, basking in the sun's hot rays. He had nosed his way tentatively up the steps from below after ensuring that all the rats were present and accounted for, careful not to arouse the alarm of any of the humans hovering above. What he could not have realized in his blinded state was that Amos, who had been sitting on the starboard railing, had been aware of him the moment he had inched out from the hold and had watched dispassionately as he scurried along the deck to the front of the boat before turning back to thoughts of his mother.

"She wishes to speak with you," Tiresias whispered into Felix's sleeping mind after nearly stumbling over him where he lay on the deck of the boat.

Felix's eyes snapped open automatically, and he rolled over onto his feet to face the oracular rodent. "My mother? Is it She who wishes to speak with me?"

"None other." Tiresias chuckled. "Is that not what you wanted?"

Felix could hardly believe that in the struggle to locate a boat and lead them to freedom, he had almost forgotten what it was the rats had promised to give him in return, why he had agreed to help in the first place. Now at the thought that the moment had finally arrived, that he was about to see her again, his heart began to race quickly in his chest, and he felt a wave of light-headedness come over him.

"Do not be afraid, son," Tiresias whispered, sounding gentler toward him than he ever had before. "She is very proud of what you have done. She has already told me so."

"Then…yes," Felix stammered, summoning his courage. "Take me to her. I wish to talk to her as well."

"Then come closer," Tiresias told him, "and lower your head to me."

Felix did as he was instructed, dipping his snout to the floor of the boat, as Tiresias nosed his way to the base of his neck. "You have faithfully executed your end of the bargain," he continued, rising up onto his back legs. "Kindly accept the humble thanks of my kind." And then he drove down with violent force, sinking his dagger-like teeth into Felix's neck at the exact spot where he had been bitten once before by Tiresias's mate, the Dam.

The pain was excruciating, like nothing he had ever known before. It was the kind of pain that tore his nerves apart and set his blood on fire. It felt as though the sun itself had dropped out of the sky and was forcing its way through the narrow corridors of his body, burning him out from within. And while he tried his best to hold his ground and bear it, the agony grew to such a crescendo that his mind eventually exploded into a thousand shards of light that swirled up into the center of the sun.

Tiresias was no longer there with him when Felix tumbled back to earth and opened his eyes. The pain that had shattered him into a thousand pieces a moment earlier had subsided in an instant, and he lifted himself up off the deck to see where the old rat had gone. Searching the length of the boat, however, he could find no trace of the blind rodent anywhere, nor could he locate either of the two humans who had been sitting out on the deck when he first came aboard. Scanning below, he discovered to his surprise that the hold was entirely empty, too; there was not a single rat in sight.

Felix was completely alone on the boat.

The sky was covered over in red as he made his way back up to the bow of the ship and climbed the anchor rope to stand up on the railing and look out over the water. The ocean, too, was tinted in red, reflecting back the rays of light cast down upon it by the bloody sun that burned overhead. All was quiet, a quiet so encompassing it seemed to absorb the very sound of the wind, and a profound stillness held sway over everything.

Then a shimmering pool of white light appeared beneath the waves off the starboard bow, capturing Felix's attention. The light grew in size and strength as it rose up to the surface of the ocean before coming into view. When at last She appeared before him, she was standing on top of the water at the center of the circle of white.

"Mother!" Felix cried, fighting the urge to throw himself off and swim to her even as his claws fought to maintain their hold on the railing.

"My sweet Felix," she said, chuckling at his evident enthusiasm, the sound of her laughter wrapping itself around him like a warm embrace.

"I did it, Mother," he boasted. "I freed the rats!"

"I know you did."

"And Tiresias says that you're proud!"

"More proud than I have ever been, sweet Felix."

"But why did you do it?" he asked, his mood suddenly darkening. "Why did you let them keep us apart?"

"It was a bargain I was required to make," She answered, her tone becoming grave as she began to move slowly across the surface of the water toward him, "to prove to them that you had a conscience after the death of the rat with her kits locked up inside. These are the terms of the place where now I dwell—that a creature with no conscience forfeits the solace of a voice to guide him to it."

"Is that what you are then? My guide?"

"That's what the test was meant to discover—whether I'd done my job well enough in the past for you to do the right thing on your own in the present. And you did, just as I knew you would."

"But what if I had failed?" he gasped, allowing himself to grow panicked at the thought. "What if I had decided that the cost was too high? Then I would've never seen you again."

"But you would've never failed," She whispered, lingering just a short distance from the boat, "because you are good. And who would know that better than I? The only reason you killed was because you were taught to believe that killing was your purpose."

"To do Man's bidding," Felix echoed, reflecting back on an earlier conversation. "Tiresias explained it all to me."

"But now that you've shown you're capable of more than killing," She said, beaming, rising up into the air to hover before him, "your conscience has been demonstrated and your guide has been returned. And I will not ever leave you again."

"Never?" Felix pressed for assurance, closing his eyes and leaning out to touch his nose to hers.

"Never," She confirmed, touching her nose to his. "But there's a price to pay for having a guide always with you?"

"Tell me the price, I'll pay it."

"The price is that there's always one more thing it'll ask you to do," She whispered, "just as I have one more thing to ask of you now."

Felix withdrew from the touch and opened his eyes. "And what's that?"

"You must go back for the others."

"The girl's father?"

"And your son as well."

For the first time in his life, Felix could feel himself growing angry with She as he began to pace back and forth along the railing. "That *son*," he snarled, "nearly tried to kill me while I was busy proving my conscience to you and the others. Then he tried to drown me in the ocean for a final reward. What do I owe such a son to risk my life again on his behalf?"

"It's not a matter of owing."

"Then what is it?!" he cried, glaring at her floating visage. "I'm not even sure he's mine! For all I know, his blood belongs to another! And yet for this *son*, you'd have me risk death a second time—after we've only just been reunited?! What kind of mother would ask such a thing?!"

She allowed his angry words to echo out across the water, but she withheld any response, allowing the silence that moved in afterward to speak for her as she met his challenging gaze. Then she watched as another thought suddenly occurred to him, one that visibly softened his features.

"You know, don't you?" he gasped, the shock of recognition forcing him to sit down on the railing. "From that place where you dwell, you can see these things. You know whether he's mine or not. You know."

"I do."

"Then tell me," he begged, "tell me so that I can know what's the right thing to do!"

"If you need to know the answer in order to do what's right," She answered, "then you wouldn't be worthy of the conscience you've been given."

"But he tried to kill me!" he shouted desperately.

"And do you believe that you're the only one ever taught to believe that killing was his purpose?" She asked, quieting any further protest. "He's a creature in need, and he's confused, just as you were. What difference should it make if he's not of your blood? Are you any less my son because *our* blood is not the same?"

"But I already did what they asked," he whimpered as She began to drift from him across the water. "I already proved myself."

"You proved yourself to them," she whispered back across the waves as she receded, taking the light with her. "Now prove yourself to me. And remember—even in the midst of the hunt, there is room for mercy."

She was but a distant star on the horizon now as Felix lowered his head and gave into the profound weariness that had suddenly settled upon him like a heavy blanket. "Yes," he repeated, closing his eyes, "even in the midst of the hunt, there is room for…"

Then he was falling back off the side of the boat, though the fall itself seemed to take a hundred years to accomplish, as he spun end over end through the red sky. And then he was jolted back to consciousness, finding himself face down once more on the deck of the boat. He pushed himself up onto his feet and turned to see Tiresias standing close by, scanning his face with his milky gaze. Before he could communicate what the vision was like or telegraph to him the words that She had said, Tiresias spoke as though he were already aware of the awful challenge she had laid before them.

"It is not true what they say, you know," the old rat whispered, "that rats will run from battle, that we are terrible fighters. We just have not yet found anything worth fighting for—until now."

Felix nodded, absorbing the rat's meaning. Then he turned and left the old rat standing alone in the bow as he moved shakily to the stern of the craft. There, stopping at the center of the deck, he waited for the young woman and the young man to each turn away from their separate contemplations and to locate him standing between them, which they did simultaneously. And in the moment when all three pairs of eyes met, they accomplished something that Felix had previously thought to be impossible—interspecies telepathy.

*****

The only constable on North Island had been summoned away the previous night and, by noon, had still not arrived back from Wanganui, where he had been called to put down a minor rebellion. A handful of Māori had taken it upon themselves to light a fire in a farmer's distant field in order to give thanks and praise to one of their heathen gods. The farmer had discovered the savages dancing around the flames, caught up in their diabolical ritual, and had immediately sent for the peace officer, who was normally stationed in Wellington, to ride out and put down the unlawful assembly. All over the island, it seemed, the natives were becoming restless.

Given it would be a few more hours before the constable could be expected to return, Tama was being held back in the warehouse, his hands and feet now tied to the cot where he had previously slept. The cuts and bruises he had received from the previous night's beating had been left unattended, though the blood had coagulated in the open wounds on the dome of his head. His right eye was swollen shut entirely, and the cheekbone beneath the left, horribly purple and misshapen, gave every indication of being broken.

Despite the extent of his injuries or because of them, Tama could barely keep from nodding off to sleep, his chin repeatedly falling to his chest. Whenever it did so, one of the wharfies standing guard over him would reach out and strike him across the face, mustering him back to consciousness. Castor's equally broken body lay still at his feet, although no similar effort was being expended to keep him awake. It was better that he remained insensible to the events going on around him so that he could not put up a struggle when the time came to nail him to the cross.

"Keep your eyes open," a familiar voice directed as the latest clout caused Tama's head to jerk violently to the side. And when he forced his one good eye to open and searched the shadows behind his captors, he saw his old master move through the line of men to stand before him. "I want you to see what it is you've brought upon yourself."

Once he had recovered from the shock of discovering Rothchester's dismembered head enough to stand upright, Thackery had ordered one of the natives to hurry on foot to the shareholder's estate and to report the news of his death to his widow. The other he ordered to round up all the animals that had been released from the barn, which proved to be a difficult and time-consuming task to execute in the dark. Then, arriving at the port in Rothchester's abandoned carriage just in time to see the others escape aboard the mail steamer, he intended to visit the full weight of his wrath down upon the two who had been left behind, starting by stomping the Black into his current stupor.

"You can take the savage out of the primitive," he said, grabbing hold of Tama's chin and forcing him to look up at him, "but you can't take the primitive out of the savage."

"You were going to sell her to him," Tama gurgled, the blood thick in his throat.

"And as her owner," Thackery hissed, "that would have been my right."

"No man should have such a right," Tama whispered, allowing his eyelid to slide shut as his head grew heavy in his master's hand.

Thackery released the chin in disgust as Tama's head dropped once more to his chest. Looking down at his hand, he saw the native's sweat and blood blended together at the center of his palm and withdrew a cloth handkerchief from his inside pocket to quickly wipe away the repugnant mix.

"We'll see what right I have once the constable gets here," he continued, swabbing desperately at his hand, "but I promise I'll live to see you hung by the neck before this is all over, so help me God."

Thackery signaled for one of the longshoremen to continue with Tama's beating in the meantime, and the man rolled up his sleeve to happily oblige. But before he could land the blow, a strange chattering sound began to fill the air. Half squeak and half hiss, the chattering rose in volume like a great wall of sound until it filled the warehouse, bouncing off the walls and causing the men to wheel around in panicked circles, searching for whence it came.

Weston, who had been standing somewhat off to the side, imagining himself too civilized a man to participate in the interrogation, was the first to locate the source of the noise; more accurately, he was the first to locate one small part of its source. Lifting his face to the high ceiling of the warehouse, his eyes fell upon a grizzled old rat, Tiresias, perched at the very apex of the highest tower of boxes behind them. He was leaning over the edge of the highest crate, glaring down at the men with demonic white eyes while brandishing his razor-sharp teeth, his jaws vibrating in rapid motion to produce the chatter. Scanning the tops of all the other towers, he could see that each one of them had a rat roosting at its peak as well, one of which was also vibrating its jaws to contribute to the chorus of chatter that swallowed up the empty space.

Before he could let out a warning, the rats leaped from their high perches, raining down on the men below as a second wave of rats charged through the maze of boxes from the front door and swarmed across the ground beneath their feet. Then all was pandemonium as the scene descended into utter chaos, with the longshoremen thrashing about in agony, each struggling to tear a rat off the top of his head, while even more rats crawled inside their pants and sank their teeth into their legs. One wharfie, previously charged with holding up a lantern to dispel the gloom at the back of the warehouse, allowed the oil lamp to slip from his fingers as he grabbed and swatted at the army of rats streaming over him from above and below.

As soon as the lantern shattered on the ground, the widening pool of oil that spilled forth carried the fire to nearly every part of the warehouse like quicksilver. Feeding on the dry wooden boxes that lay in every direction, the conflagration had an endless supply of fuel to feast upon as it gathered into columns that shot up into the air like pillars of flame. The heat of the blaze quickly became unbearable as thick clouds of black smoke choked off the oxygen, driving the men out into the sunlight while still under attack from the rats.

Even as the men were fleeing the warehouse for their lives, Amos dived back through a wall of flame in the opposite direction, the lower half of his face covered by a wet towel he had tied around his neck to keep from choking on the fumes. He immediately raced to the cot and began to cut away at the ropes that held Tama in place, using a scaling knife he had found in the pilot house of the boat. As he worked to free his friend from bondage, Felix, who had followed him into the burning building, located Castor where he lay on the ground and positioned himself above him. Sinking his teeth once more into the scruff of his neck, Felix began to drag the heavy ferret across the ground, summoning the last of his strength to pull him from the fire…

*****

First published in 1863, *The New Zealand Herald* had been in existence for little over two decades and was mostly devoted to recycling stories of news items that occurred back in England, doing its best to copy the house style of the still much more widely read *Daily Telegraph* in every conceivable way. Nevertheless, it was not unheard of for its editors to dispatch one of their correspondents from time to time to cover some item of regional interest. And as fate would have it, there was a reporter from the *Herald* present in Wellington on the morning of the fire. He had been sent to investigate reports of a giant crucifix that been put up by the townspeople to suppress the insidious rat infestation. Ironically, what he witnessed that morning proved so much more spectacular than the story he had been sent to cover that he wound up leaving out any mention of the cross in the final copy of the report that appeared on the cover of the newspaper a week later.

This is what he wrote instead:

Fire Consumes Port at Wellington; Rats to Blame
by Archibald Keaton-Welles

In the most brazen animal attack ever witnessed in the Colony, an army of pestilential rats stormed the Port at Wellington, Thursday last, causing widespread damage and panic among the population. Eschewing the cover of darkness, the insolent vermin executed their assault in broad daylight, destroying most of the commercial enterprises along the waterfront and forcing the evacuation of all residential properties within a three-block radius of the seaport.

The incident began sometime after noon with the mysterious arrival of a tramp steamer christened the *Manumission*. Shortly after the pirated vessel put into port, the rats began storming forth from its belly by the hundreds, charging out onto the main loading dock in a vast, thundering herd. In an instant, a day that had begun like any other was thrown into complete and utter turmoil as the ordinarily stouthearted strongmen who work along the docks were sent fleeing for their lives like frightened little schoolgirls out in front of the vile horde. Some could even be seen leaping into the water below to avoid coming into contact with the fatal bite of the disease-carrying pests.

No battalion of hominid warriors in the vast history of military engagement has ever advanced with such frightening speed and precision as the rat soldiers did on that day. In a single lockstep phalanx, they surged across the main road without ever once breaking formation and quickly penetrated Wellington's largest storage facility, one operated through the local customs house.

The impression they gave to this reporter—who happened to be present to witness the event—was that the rats were somehow performing under orders, that the storage facility had been targeted even before they made landing, and that they were operating under the directives of a superior officer in order to be able to take it with such military precision. Perhaps that superior officer was a recent émigré from England named Amos Martins, who many at the scene would later identify from having worked with him along the docks. Martins was employed by the New Zealand Company to rid incoming vessels of unwanted vermin, utilizing a trained team of hunter ferrets to roust out the stowaways from their hiding places below deck. Multiple sources report that it was Martins who leapt from the deck of the *Manumission* at the same time the rats were pouring forth and Martins, too, who was seen leading the charge from the rear, although he had tied a square of fabric across his face to prevent easy identification. To these eyewitnesses, the fact that a weasel-like creature was seen charging alongside him only gave further support to the notion that the masked figure was, in fact, Martins.

What would lead a seemingly normal young man to turn his back on his own kind and to side instead with the rodents in this anarchic mission remains a mystery. All that this known for sure is that the warehouse into which the rats charged, followed by the masked bandit and his mustelid sidekick, was entirely engulfed in flames within minutes of them entering it, although the exact cause of the blaze continues to remain under investigation.

This reporter watched with his own eyes as the towering pillar of fire from the warehouse spread like a hungry jungle cat, leaping from rooftop to rooftop, devouring everything in its path, until there was hardly a freestanding structure along the waterfront that had not fallen within the circumference of its voracious maw. Arriving late to the scene, Constable Cornelius Talbot quickly organized a group of citizen volunteers to fight the conflagration after he ordered the evacuation of local residences. The volunteers fought bravely for hours, racing back and forth to the shoreline to hurl buckets of seawater onto the flames. So invested were they in the effort to save their town that they hardly took any notice of the rats when they made their retreat from the burning building en masse or of their masked general, who seemed to have rescued a second man from the blaze and was supporting him beneath the arms as they made their way back down along the dock.

Shortly before nightfall, the last of the fire was extinguished but not before most of the buildings along the waterfront had collapsed in upon themselves and crumbled to their foundations, rendering the port of Wellington little more than a smoldering ash heap as darkness descended. By then, the *Manumission* was long gone.

Constable Talbot chose to remain sanguine about the devastation wrought upon his town by the invasive rodents.

"We are fortunate that the fire did not spread to the surrounding community and that no one was bitten by a rat."

While it is true that no citizen of Wellington claimed to have been directly attacked by a rat, I can report that many of their fears regarding secondhand contagion—which had already been high—were now so pronounced that they were openly contemplating abandoning the Colony altogether and returning to their native lands. Meanwhile, the full financial impact of the damages caused by the fire has yet to be determined, leaving worldwide markets anxious as reports of possible trade interruptions spread throughout the globe, causing stock prices in the New Zealand Company to plummet precipitously overnight.

Given all the uncertainty unleashed upon the population by the rat invasion and subsequent fire, some Wellingtonians have even been tempted to interpret the active hand of God working behind the day's events. One Horace Gompers, a missionary-in-training out of Boston whose own boat, the *Manumission*, was pirated and used in the attack (Gompers was able to provide an alibi and was quickly cleared of all charges), saw in the smoking ruins of the seaport proof of the Creator's displeasure at the ways of Man and an apocalyptic warning of His imminent return.

"For the LORD will execute judgment by fire," he said, quoting Isaiah 66:15 while standing amidst the devastation, "those slain by the LORD will be many."

Postscript: Since this news item was first reported, the body of wealthy landowner Waldo Rothchester was discovered horribly mutilated by law officials at a location not too far away from the scene of the fire. And while officials would go no further to disclose the details of the murder, they have not ruled out a connection between Rothchester's death and the individual or individuals involved in the assault on the seaport. It is for that reason that officials ask our readers to remain on the lookout for the missing boat and to consider said individual(s) armed and dangerous. As of the publication of this edition of the *Herald*, there has been no reported sightings of the *Manumission*, and all those on board—human and otherwise—remain at large.

*****

Fire can be a great distraction. Who among us has not at some point felt themselves drawn so deeply into the center of an open flame that its hold upon us becomes almost hypnotic, blocking out all other stimulus? So inextricably are we bound to our first and most primitive discovery—that Man can make fire and control it to his will—that the fascination it inspires in us remains nearly undiminished across eons of time, luring us back to our most primitive roots.

It was fire, after all, that had caused Archibald Keaton-Welles to forget all about the wooden cross he had been sent to investigate, so distracted was he by its devastating power. And it was fire, too, that had kept the townspeople of Wellington from taking any action against Amos and Tama as they fled back to the boat or of noticing

Felix at all as he fought to heave Castor up onto the dock after dragging his lifeless body across the dirt road.

The only one present who took any notice of this final happening was Thackery, who alone was able to resist the lure of the fire—once he had coughed out the last of its smoke from his lungs—and spot the evil creature, the one who had brought such havoc down upon him ever since the day of his arrival, now struggling to escape without punishment. And as the ever-widening flames consumed everything he had managed to bring forth out of this godforsaken wilderness, the chief trading officer of the New Zealand Company alone began to make his way deliberately in the opposite direction of the blaze, crossing toward the water in a calm, steady gait so as not to attract any unwanted attention from the distracted townspeople.

Before Felix could detect the danger advancing toward them, the wind shifted direction off the water and forced a thick cloud of smoke back toward the shoreline from the top of the burning warehouse. The dense smoke curled around him like a dark fog, shutting off Thackery from his sight, as the weary ferret finally managed to pull Castor's heavy frame up onto the wooden dock before collapsing onto his side and releasing him. Somewhere behind him in the fog, he could still make out the sound of the boat's engine idling; they were waiting for him to appear so that they could flee. But he was so tired, so very tired from all that had happened, all that he had been through, and he needed just a moment now to catch his breath despite the acrid air before he rose up to complete the final leg of his journey...

And then Castor was hovering above, staring down at him with a confused expression on his face. Had he given into fatigue and fallen asleep? How much time had gone by?

"Why did you do it?" the young hob asked in bewilderment. "Why did you come back after everything I'd done?"

Felix could see that Castor's whole body was trembling as he waited for a response, but he had no way of knowing whether the involuntary shaking was caused by the emotions he was feeling or by the injuries he had suffered. He only knew that he had never felt as close to him as he did at that moment and never happier to share with him what he was about to whisper into the deepest recesses of his mind since it was the only thing he found to be to be true in the end, the only survival, the only meaning.

"Because even in the midst of the hunt, there is room for…"

Suddenly, the wind shifted a second time, pulling back the curtain of smoke to reveal Thackery towering above them, his face distorted in a mask of pure hatred. In a single reflexive motion, Felix kicked Castor clear with his hind legs as he rolled over onto his side, saving them both from the old man's initial lunge as he shot out his hand to take hold of them.

"To the boat!" Felix cried, racing to where they were waiting at the end of the pier. Even as he closed the distance between them, he could tell that they had spotted Thackery, too, and had already begun to cast off the anchor lines to avoid capture by their former master. The boards below his feet shook with Thackery's thundering footfalls as he pursued them, but Felix was confidant, given the human's advanced years, that they would be able to stay out in front and make it onboard before the boat pushed off.

When he turned aside, however, he saw that Castor was falling behind, slowing his stride the closer they got to the end of the pier. It appeared he still had not fully recovered from the force of Thackery's crushing blow and that the sudden imperative to run had started to make him feel dizzy once the initial burst of adrenaline had worn off. Felix could see that Castor was starting to veer off course, that his feet were becoming entangled in each other, and he knew that if he did not do something to intervene, Thackery would soon overtake him.

He was close enough now that he could make out every detail of the boy's face as he called to him from the deck of the boat, his arms wrapped around the final post in a desperate attempt to physically keep the vessel from drifting from the pier. He was a good one, this human. He needed to remember that, that such a thing was possible—to be both good and human. They had managed to communicate in the end, after all, to find a common language, and if such a thing was possible with this particular human, then maybe it was possible with others. Either way, he would miss him, this boy who had followed him across the sea to save his life.

Turning from the boy, Felix raced back to where Castor had collapsed, arriving just in time to sink his teeth into the soft skin around Thackery's wrist joint before he could seize the young ferret up by his black coat. The old man gave out a wounded howl and spun about in a reel of pain, struggling to shake Felix loose as he unwittingly spun farther away from the disoriented Castor. All his screaming and turning in circles only made Felix more determined to hold on tight, and he clamped down even harder until his incisors met beneath the surface of the skin and his upper canines scraped against the brittle bone close at hand.

As the two remained locked in to their heated battle, Amaia took the opportunity to spring from the boat and run to where Castor lay, scooping him up in her arms. When she saw the angry mob of dockhands hurrying down the pier in Thackery's direction to offer their assistance, though, most of whom had only just pulled themselves from the water, she knew that they had run out of time, that Little Red was lost. And as she jumped back onto the boat with the men circling around their comrade left behind, Amos was forced to accept the same sad conclusion as he let go of the post and allowed the engine to pull the boat clear of the dock, tears beginning to sting at his eyes.

Now there were many hands grasping at Felix from all sides, pulling him in every conceivable direction, but he fought to hold on as long as possible, to provide the boat with as much time as he could to clear the harbor. Finally, however, Thackery's papery skin tore free from the bone beneath all the pressure, exposing a deep gash that spurted blood up into the blue sky and out onto the shirtfronts of the surrounding wharfies as the rotten flesh slipped from between his teeth. Having thus lost his purchase, Felix next felt himself being hoisted aloft into the air and paraded roughly back to shore by the mob as the old man's agonized screams faded out behind them.

For a time, the world reeled about his head in a mad jumble of sun and sea and sky. Then he felt something hard and unyielding press up against his back; it was as though the humans had decided to pin him down against a solid wooden floor. Once his senses had had a chance to settle, however, he realized that he was not looking upward into the sky but out onto the harbor. And it was then that he recognized that the wood against his back was not from the floor at all; that they were holding him back against the giant cross they had erected outside the warehouse.

Every inch of the building was consumed in flames at this point while the leading edge of the fire had spread itself out along the rooftops to the customs house. The citizen volunteers battling the blaze had followed along with it, leaving what was lost to be lost, while they fought to keep the fire from advancing any farther into their town. It was for this reason that no one took any notice of the small band of men loitering behind outside the warehouse, not even the keen-eyed Archibald Keaton-Welles, who was in the midst of his breathless reporting on the conflagration.

Not a one noticed as the circle of men gathered around the foot of the cross parted itself down the middle to allow Thackery to move closer. He had found a piece of sail cloth to tie around his wound, but the blood was already seeping through the makeshift tourniquet, staining his injured wrist. Despite the hemorrhaging tear, he was holding a heavy mallet in his bleeding hand, a mallet similar to the ones they had used on the day of the Great Cleansing. In his opposite hand, he held a long metal spike, the kind used by the men along the dock to pry open the lids of shipping crates.

Felix turned to the side and stared into the grinning face of the man on top of the ladder, holding him back at the center of the cross. Dangling from the crossbeam on either side of him were the ravaged carcasses of the vanquished rats that had gone before him, their skeletal bodies twisting in the wall of heat cast off by the burning building behind them. They were seeking to humiliate him, to execute him in the company of creatures thought even less clean than his own kind, failing to recognize that, in matters of purity, Felix had lost the ability to draw easy distinctions between species a long time ago.

He still had some strength left in him, he thought. He could scratch at the fingers of the grinning man, try to get him to open up his hand and release him, fight until the last breath. But as he looked back out onto the harbor again and saw the boat slip into open waters, he knew that there was little sense in putting off the end now that his mission had been accomplished.

Besides, he knew that She would be waiting for him on the other side once this final bit of business was resolved. One final stroke of the hammer, and then he would be released forever to go to her. And with this idea to console him, he abandoned any plans for resistance and surrendered to the inevitable.

He thought one last time of the Breeder and of how happy he had been in that other life before this one; of the painted native they had rescued that day and how he had once nursed him back to health in a room filled with shrunken heads; of the boy with whom, against all odds, he had achieved an impossible communion with; and of Castor, the son whose good opinion he had finally won, whether he had authentically been a son of his or not. Lastly, he thought of Kara, whose love he had never truly deserved until now—Kara, who taught him that the greater part of love was sometimes expressed in sacrifice to it. He would take the memory of them all with him to that other place and never stop loving them until time itself, in all its measures, ceased to exist and the universe ran out.

Felix was wrenched back from these reveries as the grinning man slid his hand up around his throat, suspending him by the neck, and Thackery lifted the spike into the air, pressing its sharp end against his vulnerable pink underbelly. He was seized suddenly by a last-minute wave of panic at the thought of the pain he was about to endure and began to thrash about on the cross, setting the rat skeletons to rattle and dance all about him as he struggled against the sharp pressure pushing into his stomach.

Then a voice sounded inside his head, summoning him back to stillness. "Close your eyes, my sweet," he heard She whisper from afar. He did as she instructed, allowing his limbs to go limp once more, as Thackery steadied his feet beneath him and drew back the mallet.

It was there to greet him the second he closed his eyes to the world, the reddest star. It was glowing off in the distance, beckoning him to follow, just as it had always done in the past, leading him on to victory. Now that he had the star back to guide him once more, his fears evaporated, and he knew that he would win this fight. Of course he would win. He was Felix the Red, the Greatest Hunter of Them All.

With this thought to comfort him, he hardly felt the spike at all as it pierced through his body and drove him hurtling through space toward the very heart of the star.

EPILOGUE

The Beach

Our story ends where it began, with a ship sailing into harbor.

Centuries have passed, however, since that first ship arrived to steal Pollux the Polecat away from his native land, the first of his bloodline to be pressed into the service of Man. The sputtering *Manumission* could hardly incite the same kind of awe that that original craft had stirred in the hearts of the wild beasts who gazed out upon it through the veil of their jungle curtain and wondered at its winged magnificence. And the harbor into which it sailed the morning after the fire was a far cry from the shores of Mother Africa, although the humble mail steamer was no less being watched at that moment than its majestic predecessor had been as it steered into the shallows of the uncharted new land.

To the indigenous ones monitoring the steamship's approach from the safety of the tree line, the island was commonly called Takapourewa, although it had been rechristened Stephens Island on Western maps after the explorer Captain Cook had made its discovery in the late 1700s. Located at the northernmost tip of the Marlborough Sounds off the South Island of New Zealand, the tiny island remained largely untouched by European influence in 1885, the year Tama guided the *Manumission* to its shores, navigating from memory of when he had visited there as a small child with his tribe. It seemed as safe a place as any for them to hide out and escape colonial rule now that they were wanted fugitives. How could he have known that within five years of their arrival, the British government would descend upon it in force for the purposes of installing a lighthouse, thus destroying the indigenous culture on the island and devastating the Māori population once more?

We make our plans, chart our course, and hope for the best, but none of us can truly predict what the future holds. Ever has it been so.

Tama had positioned himself in the bow of the boat so that his would be the first face they saw from the forest, his fellow Māori. Hopefully, recognizing him as one of their own, they would be welcomed to stay there by the local tribe, whose eyes he could feel upon him as he stripped off his shirt and offered his whole body for their inspection. Amos peered out through the glass window of the pilot house, waiting for the signal to cut the engine, as Amaia stood at the ready to drop anchor off the stern. Tiresias was perched on the railing to Tama's right, leaning his pointed snout out over the water to take in the unfamiliar scents coming back off the island. Castor allowed the sea breeze to ruffle his black coat from the opposite railing, flanking him on the left.

Tama was starting to see flashes of the harbor's bottom appear through the crystal blue shallows of the water, and he gave the signal for the younger ones to halt the boat's forward advance. Without a dock to tie up to, they had come as close to the island as it was safe to do on steam power alone. And with no lifeboats in which to row them ashore, he knew that he would have to swim the remaining distance and sighed heavily as he kicked off his boots and prepared to take the plunge.

It was not the idea of the swim that filled him with apprehension as he unbuckled his belt and stepped out of his pants. Like most Māori, Tama was an excellent swimmer, having grown up around the ocean all his life. The distance between the anchored *Manumission* and the shoreline of the island was hardly anything at all; he would be climbing out of the surf and onto the beach in no time. What he was anxious about was the encounter that would follow shortly thereafter, wherein he would have to convince a related but no less unfamiliar tribe of aborigines to permit them to live there among them while also allowing them to release upon their island several hundred rats that they had brought along with them on their boat.

This would not be an easy conversation, he knew, as he climbed up onto the railing in his undergarments and looked down at the curious creatures perched at that moment on either side of him. How could he explain why it was necessary to give sanctuary to such abhorrent creatures when he himself was unsure exactly why he felt the need to make the case on their behalf? He only knew instinctually that the rats and this last remaining ferret had somehow played a part in his own rescue and that he was bound by honor to somehow do the same for them now.

He would figure it out during the swim, he told himself. He would locate the right words to say as he paddled his way across the remaining distance of the harbor. He had encountered greater challenges in the past, after all, and he would meet this one as he met the ones before it. And with this belief in the ultimate success of his mission, Tama lifted his powerful arms up over his head and dived off the bow of the boat.

Amaia watched her father's silhouette arc across the sky. Then she turned her attention to Amos, who was just stepping out of the pilot house as Tama was making his introductory strokes in the direction of Takapourewa. Amos faltered in his steps when he became aware that she was regarding him, and for a brief while, the two did little more than stand perfectly still in silent acknowledgment of the lasting bond between them. Whatever would come next, they knew that they would face it together, that they no longer had any choice but to trust in the power of the union they had forged.

The night before, as Tama navigated beneath the stars, Amos had made his way to the back of the boat and sat upon the railing at the stern while Amaia kept her father company in the pilot house. His heart was still heavy at the loss of his courageous Little Red, but he no longer had tears left to signify that loss. Instead he listened as father and daughter conducted a conversation in their native tongue over the sound of the engine and wished that he could know what it was they were saying. But there would be time enough to learn a new language, he thought to himself. He had cast his lot with these good people, and for better or for worse, there was no turning back.

Next, he slipped his hand inside his coat pocket and came up with the note his father had left for him and the tooth that had been gnawing at his side since the day he had first set sail for the colony. Dropping them both off into the dark wake of the boat, he watched as they disappeared into the churn. Then he lifted his eyes back to the receding lights of North Island and the friend he had left behind.

"I'm sorry, Father," he said, "but I no longer wish to subdue the earth. I wish to free it."

Castor was looking out over the water, admiring the native's powerful strokes, when his mother's voice came to him on the breeze and drifted inside his head.

"There you are, my son," Kara whispered. "I've been searching everywhere for you."

"I thought you'd left me," Castor responded, lowering his head to search the sandy bottom of the harbor.

"I would never leave you, Castor," she reassured him. "It just took some time for me to find you, what with all the change unfolding."

Then she went on to recount all the events that had taken place since Thackery had returned from the battle at the seaport; how the master had spent the better part of the night storming throughout the great house and smashing all his worldly possessions, judging from the sounds of destruction that reached her where she stood in the shadow of the barn; how the men who had accompanied him back to the farm had carried off a human corpse draped in canvas on a heavy board, the blood seeping through the fabric like roses; and how, as morning dawned along the horizon, the old woman who served the master had exited from the house in her cape and bonnet, clutching an oversized travel case in her hand. The old woman lingered for a moment at the top of the steps, setting down the case to tie the strings of her cape beneath her chin. As she did so, Kara, who had avoided recapture earlier by retreating to the tall grass, crept out of her hiding place and moved to stand beneath her at the bottom of the steps.

"That's when she spoke," Kara continued, "and although I couldn't make out the meaning of what she was saying, I was sure she was speaking to me."

"You've ruined him," Hollis accused, scowling down at the masked ferret at her feet, "you and your kind. It won't go easy for the lot of you—trust me. I suggest you clear off now if you know what's good for you, just as I am."

Her cape fastened, Hollis took up her suitcase and hurried down the steps, the hem of her cape brushing against Kara's snout as she turned and began walking away from the house. She had only made it several steps along the rutted path, however, before that troublesome pest that lived inside her conscience began to scratch at the walls of its cage, and she could bring herself to go no farther. By the time she had turned back to address the horrid ferret once more, a second ferret with a coat of pure white had moved out from the grass to stand alongside the other, silently beseeching her with his eyes as much as the first.

"Curse you," Hollis said, sighing, her shoulders slumping in defeat. "Curse you both to hell."

"Then we were riding in her case," Kara went on, "Scruffer and I, hidden among her clothes. We're hidden there now, although to where we're headed I couldn't say. I only know that I trust her, this woman, and that I believe all will be well."

They were destined for South Island. Hollis had secreted away just enough money to buy herself a one-way passage aboard the noonday ferry, though what she would do once she arrived was still a mystery to her. She was an ugly old woman alone in the world with little more to her name than a suitcase full of ferrets. But she would make her way. She would find another situation, and she would survive, just as she always had. She was Bernadette Hollis, and she was alive. And life was not finished with her yet.

"My father was wrong," Castor admitted at the end of her recitation. "I shouldn't have allowed my instincts alone to guide me. They cost Felix his life, and Felix was good."

Castor closed his eyes in anguish, recalling in his mind's eye the scene back on the dock. How wrong he had been to put his faith in humans over trust in his own kind and how wrong he had been to have ever counted Felix as his enemy—Felix, who, in the end, had saved his life twice.

"Scruffer knows he was wrong," Kara consoled, reaching down into the depths of his anguish, "and he'll search you out in his own time to say as much once he's found the proper words to do so. Until then, I'll watch over him and do my best to forgive. He deserves at least that much from me. But there's one last thing I must show you about your father while the memory of it is still fresh in my mind. Open your eyes, my love."

Castor did as he was told, slowly opening his eyes. And when he did, he saw the floor of the harbor shimmering back at him like a mirage, reflecting back the images she was now sending. At first, he was unsure of what he was looking at; the pictures were obscured and confused. A muddy road pitted with puddles of brown water, the passing feet of humans scurrying to and fro, all shrouded in a thick cloud of smoke—what could it all mean? But as he listened to her explain, it eventually was made clear to him.

"There's a hole worn in the side of the case we're hidden in," she began, "and I was able to look out through it while we were boarding our ship."

That was it. He was seeing the port of Wellington once more on the morning after the destruction as the humans woke to the task of having to repair and rebuild, only he was seeing it now as Kara had seen it with her own eyes, telescoped through the tiny opening in the side of the suitcase. And he startled in complete recognition when the wooden boards of the dock began to roll beneath the vision since he was seeing once again the same pier he had only just been rescued from the day before after fleeing for his life.

"At first, there didn't seem to be much to see," Kara continued, "but as we moved farther from the town, I was able to take more of it in."

By this point in the narration, Hollis was nearly halfway down the pier. And just as his mother was describing, he, too, was able to take in more of the smoldering landscape left behind, the waterfront buildings largely left in ruins, through the narrow aperture she was peering out of.

And that was when he saw it.

"And that was when I saw it," Kara whispered, her voice echoing his simultaneous recognition.

It is a strange circumstance of our existence that the hair on our bodies continues to grow even after we are gone. This odd fact, however much based in truth as it might be, would seem to have very little application to a ferret born, as Felix was, without the ability to grow any hair of any kind. But the spike that Thackery had used to nail him to the cross had pierced directly through the heart of the tumor that had weighed upon his adrenal gland since birth, releasing its power over him. And all throughout the night, as his body hung there with the rats, the coat that had eluded him his whole life grew out at a furious pace as though to make up for all the time it had remained hidden within, stillborn inside.

It grew as the sun went down and the townspeople were forced to abandon their efforts and seek out shelter elsewhere. It grew as the earth below him continued to send up steaming tendrils of smoke into the nighttime sky. It grew as the stars appeared in the firmament above to shine down and bear heavenly witness to the miraculous transformation underway. And it grew as the first light appeared out of the east, announcing the start of a brand new day.

The transformation was all but complete when Kara, through the small tear in the suitcase, was able to look out through the oculus and behold Felix's lifeless body suspended in the air, the cross standing out brilliantly against the fallen nothingness of the town behind it. Castor was seeing him there, too, seemingly at the same time that Kara was, before Hollis stepped onto the deck of the boat and the vision was lost.

And Felix's coat was as black as his own.

"Your father will be with you shortly" were the final words Kara whispered before she drifted from him. Castor lifted his gaze to the shoreline and saw Tama's dark silhouette emerge out of the waves and walk up onto the sands of the island just as the mighty dam of fear that he had built up inside finally gave way.

"...there is room for *mercy*," he whispered, recognizing the final thought that his one true father, Felix, had been trying to express to him before they were separated on the dock. But then he could manage no further words as a powerful flood of emotions was unleashed inside him and swept throughout his whole body, overwhelming his heart.

*****

At the same time that Tama was crossing the sand to encounter his distant kinsmen, Felix, too, was walking up onto a beach. No ship had brought him there, however. In truth, he was not completely sure of how he had arrived. He only remembered that there had been a sharp sting of pain, and then it was as though he had been rocketing forward through space for all eternity, forever toward the distant star. And when he awoke, he found himself standing upon this unfamiliar shore, restored to his true state of hairless nakedness, in a place where the color of one's coat made very little difference in the end.

The sun in the sky burned differently here than elsewhere—its light less equivocal, more iridescent—and the water lapping at his feet as he surveyed the landscape had a warmth to it that he had never experienced before. Across the powdery sand, he got the sense that there were others recording his arrival, watching him from behind the dense curtain of jungle tree line. Caught between ocean and land, Felix hesitated for a brief while, uncertain as to whether it was safe to proceed any farther into this strange new territory.

As though sensing his hesitation, a figure emerged from the shadows of the jungle and stepped out onto the beach. As the figure drew closer to him, moving cautiously across the white sand, Felix had the distinct impression that they had somehow met before, he and the one sent out to greet him. There was something familiar and not about the creature as he stood before him now.

"Welcome home, brother," the polecat said to him, his voice warm and inviting inside Felix's mind. It was Pollux the First, son of Zeus, and he was there to welcome his kinsman back to the place where their stories had both begun.

"Welcome home, brother!" the gray parrot Dakari screeched overhead as the mustelids below nuzzled their heads together in shared recognition. "Welcome home!"

Then a second figure moved out from the jungle behind them, and Felix suddenly found himself racing toward her with all his strength, leaving Pollux behind at the shoreline. And while the sand beneath his feet made it difficult to find his footing and the air burned hot in his lungs, he knew that he would not give up until he had crossed the beach that divided them, even if it took him a hundred years to get there.

He knew that he would never stop running until he had bridged the space between them and fallen once more into the loving embrace of She.

ABOUT THE AUTHOR

Stefan Francis Kelleher is a proud public school teacher who has taught literature to high school learners in the classroom for over twenty years. He is the author of two previous books for young adults: *Hagitha* and *The True Confessions of Prince Willie*. He currently lives in New York City with his husband and his daughter.

CPSIA information can be obtained
at www.ICGtesting.com
Printed in the USA
FSHW011524160621
82415FS